THE POWER OF SHADOWS

ABBY GEIGERMAN

For Win.

TENEBRIS
ARTANGE

Myllanor
Alynthia
Presa
Braiwyth
Aleving

CHAPTER

1

Shouts rang out from the soldiers running down the hall. I snuggled in my armchair and flipped the page.

"Are you sure you should be here?" my brother asked, looking up from his sketchbook.

"There's nowhere I'd rather be," I said, smiling for his benefit. By my estimate, I had five more minutes; the West library was known by few. Its door blended into the intricate carved walls, only identifiable to those who knew to look.

I kicked off the cursed shoes my mother had picked and tucked my feet under my legs. The clock ticked above the fireplace, unnerving him with each minute.

"Are you sure? We both know Mother—"

"Calix," I interrupted. He shifted with unease, but I refused to waste our precious time discussing her. "What are you working on?"

"Nothing," he said quickly. He ducked his head and went

suspiciously still.

"Your pencil has been moving quite fast to be drawing nothing." After a moment of silence, I set my book down and stood. Calix slammed his sketchbook shut.

"You wouldn't want to see them." He clutched the book to his chest.

"Hand it over," I said, extending a hand in front of him. "We both know I don't have forever." He hesitated for a moment longer, but guilt won out.

I opened it to the page bookmarked with a green ribbon, finding sketches of a rose blooming. The next page a wolf bit it from the stem as if our older brother Bastian had willed it to. My chest tightened, but I didn't want to give Bastian more space in our lives than he already demanded.

Calix picked at his nail beds, stealing glances up no less than every three seconds.

"They're beautiful." I flipped to a different section, hoping to find something untouched by Bastian, and stopped at a hyper-realistic sketch of a Summer enchanter Calix's age. He glowed. Even in just black and white Calix made him look vibrant.

"Who's this?" I asked. Calix suddenly took interest in a loose thread on the armchair.

"It's no one." He reached for the notebook, and I pulled it out of his reach, a smile spreading on my face.

"Doesn't look like no one." Steps pounded in the hall, but we both decided to ignore them.

"No, really, he's just someone in our training class." Calix reached again, but I held it just past his hand.

"That's an awfully detailed picture you drew of a supposed no one."

"Estyn."

"Calix." We stared at each other for a few moments, and I hoped the silence would pressure him into elaborating, but all of a sudden I felt the book lift from my hands and looked back to see the houseplant with the book in its grasp.

"I see training is going well then." I smiled, a reaction that only Calix and occasionally Calliope could elicit. "I'll stop pushing, but if you want to talk about it I'm always here."

Before he could respond, the door swung open, slamming against the adjacent bookshelf. Calix and I braced for the worst, but once I saw the familiar brown waves and blue apron I relaxed. Even if she looked ready to kill me.

"Oh good, Calliope. Come look at the drawings Calix did," I said.

"What in the gods' names are you doing?" she whisper-yelled, storming over to snatch the sketchbook from the plant. "And you," she said turning to Calix, "You were supposed to be at training twenty minutes ago." Calix grabbed his book and scrambled to the door, flashing me one last sympathetic smile before running to the courtyard.

Calix didn't hate practicing magic; just the other day he grew all sorts of flowers and vines in my room, tangling them through my headboard and around my balcony doors. He even had them brush my hair for me as I'd rolled out of bed, barely needing to focus on the vine manhandling my hairbrush. I didn't have the heart to tell him I couldn't brush my curls, so I had just borne my mother's searing glares as I walked into that day's high tea sporting a beehive.

No, Calix was a talented enchanter who genuinely enjoyed practicing his craft. It was Bastian's fault he hated training.

Bastian wasn't the only cause of the near-toxic competitive culture in the training groups—our enchanters had to become the skilled somehow—but he didn't make it easy for

Calix either.

Whereas Calix and the Spring enchanters' gift was manipulating flora, Bastian and the Fall enchanters' gift was commanding fauna. Spring enchanters channeled magic into the earth, helping nature bloom, while Fall enchanters inspired hunger in animals to bend them to their will.

Bastian was a natural. From a young age, he practiced on small rodents, leaving them on my doorstep like some twisted gift. Then, when Calix was born, Bastian seemed to thrive on destroying what Calix created. Calix loved to spend his time alone in the gardens or the forest, playing with the small creatures. Bastian would command them to turn on Calix, nipping at his fingers or running away entirely. If he was in a particularly twisted mood, he'd kill them outright. Bastian said Calix was soft, that he needed to grow up. I always thought it was a poor excuse for being an ass.

"Estyn, what is this?" Calliope said, snapping me back to reality.

"I know, I know."

"I thought you were going to lay low? Get along with your mother?"

"I don't know what happened. It's just this morning my mother was being, well, you know, and then there was a moment when my ladies in waiting all left and I was just standing there, staring at myself, and I just couldn't. I couldn't Calliope." I felt tears tearing from the corners of my eyes, but I didn't let them affect the rest of my face. I wished I had a better explanation for her.

"We only have one week," she said. "There's no way we can pull this off if your mother thinks she has to keep a close eye on you." She crossed her arms, so I stared at the carpet below my bare feet, the silence infinitely heavier with the imminent threat of my mother barging in.

I lifted my gaze to the frayed hem of Calliope's apron. I could be the princess my mother wanted for one more week.

"Calliope, I need to—"

A voice echoed down the hall, commanding without yelling, equal parts cold and searing. The only voice that could silence grown men capable of crafting floating ice swords and spiraling fire whips.

Calliope grabbed my sleeve, barely giving me enough time to grab my heels before she dragged me out into the hall. The entire corridor was several degrees colder, and I fought the urge to nestle into Calliope's side for warmth.

"I found her, your highness," Calliope said, ducking her head into a low bow as she approached the Queen. Other kitchen servants and maids stopped their frantic searching as they watched my entrance, eyes darting between my mother and me. If Calix was twelve minutes late, then I was twelve minutes late to being thirty minutes early; in other words, unforgivable.

Calliope faded into the background as I felt the pressure of my mother's full attention. Her Winter enchanting ice blue eyes scanned my face, likely evaluating whether the excessive rouge was enough to hide my 'lifeless complexion.' Every set of eyes in the hallway snapped to us with insatiable curiosity. She raised a hand to my face, painfully slow, and I pressed my hand to my skirts to stop from shuddering.

Her long, white nails grazed my cheek before catching a stray curl and tucking it behind my ear. I felt the ghost of her touch long after she pulled away.

"Back to work," my mother said. The corridor emptied in moments, staff scattering through doors and around corners until it was just me, my mother, and one of my handmaids.

They stood half-hidden behind a column, supporting the same silver tray that had followed me my entire life.

Between one breath and the next, my mother transformed. Subtle shifts that most would miss were painfully obvious to me: the tired slump of her shoulders, the slight twist of concern between her brows, the sadness edging her gaze.

"You missed your medicine this morning," she said, beckoning the tray over.

I swallowed hard, feeling the guilt sink from my throat to my chest to my stomach, settling beside the single bite of scone I'd managed to eat. The tray held a powder vial and a single cup of tea, and voices murmured in my head as if begging me to take it.

I should've taken it earlier. It was ridiculous of me to resent it; it's not like the medicine caused my illness. But no matter what mother said, that it treated something far worse than the headaches, that she thanked the gods there was a treatment for my affliction, I couldn't be grateful. It was just another reminder of my defectiveness.

I just—I wished I could be like the rest of my family. Or, if not magical, then at least *normal.*

When I didn't reach for the cup, the air cooled, my mother's concern as palpable as my discontent.

"I know you're nervous about today, but it's an exciting time. You have an opportunity to strengthen our kingdom, just like your brothers," she said.

"This is *not* like what they do," I said under my breath. They train to fight for the liberation of other kingdoms, to help the less fortunate, to go out into the world and *make* something of themselves. I'm not even supposed to think about the war.

I felt a phantom touch, as if Calliope was here reminding

me to calm down. Just one more week. My mother opened her mouth, ready to spit words colder than her magic, but I grabbed the vial before she could.

"I'm sorry. I'm just nervous, like you said." I popped off the cap, the motion seared into muscle memory by now, but paused for a moment as I leaned over the tray. I didn't recognize the reflection staring back at me. My wild black curls were tamed at the base of my neck in a simple knot, the perfect complement to my carefully curated smile. After years of the same primping, I thought it would've stopped feeling like a costume by now. Maybe it never would.

I dumped the medicine over the surface, disrupting the image.

Two stirs and I threw it back, swallowing in one gulp. The thrum of murmuring voices quieted. My head still hurt, but the cool effect of the medicine spread from my chest to each fingertip, wrapping me in its healing weight.

"We need to go," she said, turning on her heel and wrapping me in an invisible leash of cool air.

We arrived at the towering ballroom doors just as the bell tower chimed out six tolls for the hour.

"Since we did not arrive *before* the guests, as we should have, we must make an entrance. Shoulders down. Chest out. Smile smaller—you're to look pleased, not unhinged—and be quiet as I address the crowd." She brushed nonexistent lint off my bodice and inspected my appearance one final time before motioning to the guards by the doors.

Any lingering compassion, however she expressed it, disappeared as she assumed the mask of the Queen. The doors swept open before us, revealing the cavernous ballroom below, but I didn't turn from her. I just watched as she lifted her chin, folded her hands together, and floated out to the banister.

The crowd fell silent as we emerged, watching me more than my mother, even as she greeted them. The ballroom was lined with rows of chairs on the sides, all filled with eager nobility, surrounding a stage fitted with supplies for the contestants in each corner: tubes of chemicals stuck into a pile of sand for the Summer enchanters, a pot of greenery for the Spring enchanters, a tub of water for the Winter enchanters, and cages of birds, snakes, and other small animals for the Fall enchanters. One of the crows opened its beak, beady eyes looking directly into mine, and squawked at me. I instantly found Bastian on the dais.

He was sprawled out in a chair beside the main throne, a glass of wine tipped haphazardly in his hand, with two of his pet wolves slumbering by his feet. As our eyes met, a disappointed scowl twisted his already unpleasant features. The bird kept squawking, loud and obnoxious, until our mother turned her icy gaze on him, rebuking him without dimming her smile. Bastian silenced the cursed thing.

"We gather here today for a momentous occasion: the Veirden qualifying demonstrations for Princess Estyn Lamoret." She paused for a moment, the room deafeningly quiet before applause broke out. "Tonight, we will see great displays of power from the best enchanters in Tenebris, the best in the world." Although she continued her speech, full of inspiring anecdotes about Bastian and Calix and the strength and generosity of our kingdom, I stopped listening.

My gaze trailed to the ceiling, where the gods' calendar was carved, spreading across the length of the room. The concave circle below today's date was filled with ice, exactly one week from the Winter Solstice. At the far end of the ceiling, the Winter goddess encircled her solstice, draped in jewels of ice to thank her for the gifts she gave children born on her holy day.

Despite her grandeur, my attention drifted to the center. Night and Day, the parents of the seasonal gods and inspiration for my favorite novels, lounged in the rotunda directly above the stage. They bestowed us with the seasonal gods—well not *all* of us, since those of us born on unremarkable days didn't get—

"And look!" My mother exclaimed, breaking through my distracted thoughts and directing our attention to the windows. White blanketed the courtyard outside as snow pelted its stones. "Even the gods are blessing the occasion. Let us begin!" This time there was no pause before the applause split the room, a raucous accompaniment to our descent.

I followed her down the steps, across the stage, and finally to our seats beside Bastian. The main throne was glaringly empty.

"Why isn't father here?" I whispered to mother as we sat.

"You think he would bother himself with something as minor as your Veirden when there's a war going on? Do you really think you're that special?" Bastian said. I spun towards him to argue, exactly as he wanted, but stopped when I saw Calliope over his shoulder.

She carried a tray of hors d'oeuvres comically big for her slight frame, navigating through the rows with ease. As if she felt my attention, she turned and caught my gaze. *One week*, I thought I heard her voice say in my head, muffled but distinct among the thrum.

"No, of course not," I told Bastian. He narrowed his eyes

at my overly polite response, but deemed me unworthy of further attention. I didn't know why I bothered to ask in the first place. I couldn't remember the last time I interacted with the King, let alone have him support me. He was Bastian and Calix's father; I was just his progeny.

A courtier, dressed in ceremonial winter robes stepped onto the stage, drawing all attention to him.

"Lord Hathens, born on the Spring Solstice, and Sir Olyn, born on the Winter Solstice," he announced. Two men, both of sturdy builds, stepped onto the stage. They were of similar statures, but held themselves differently. Both had the striking eyes of their respective gods—bright green for Hathens, and glacier blue for Olyn—but whereas Hathen's accompanied a lazy grin, as if he had already won, Olyn's were hungry. They were calculating, already assessing.

"This should be quick. Olyn is from the countryside. Hathens will make quick work of him," Bastian said. I'd seen Hathens fight; he'd trained with Bastian since they were young. As tempted as I was to root for the underdog, I knew there was little chance for him. I just prayed it would end swiftly.

The presiding courtier stepped to the side and struck a bell, beginning the match.

Hathens was still looking at the crowd, raising his arms in encouragement, when Olyn stepped forward. He barely paid attention as Olyn advanced, still reveling in the crowd's shouted support, even as Olyn struck.

For a moment, I doubted my blind confidence in Hathens.

But the next second Olyn was flipped on his back, vines wrapped around his ankles, twisting his legs around one another on the floor. The crowd went wild, setting down their drinks to jump up and scream Hathen's name like it was their victory to share.

Hathens stepped into the center, over Olyn's struggling form on the ground, to embolden the audience. His arms were raised and his back was turned and no one seemed to notice Olyn's dark smile but me.

Through all the celebration, barely anyone noticed liquid lifting from their glasses, streaming to the stage in arcs of slowly freezing doom.

I followed the trail of my wine as it froze, sharpening into a knife and severing the vines restraining Olyn.

A few people began to take note, and word spread like wildfire, turning shouts of joy into hushed speculation. Hathens turned around to find Olyn standing behind him. As if waiting for that exact moment, all the champagne came down in meteoric arcs that froze into bars around Hathens. Vines shot out for Olyn, desperately reaching for purchase, but ice daggers cut them down whenever they neared.

A vortex of ice and vines surrounded Olyn as he approached the bars. Vines grasped at the bars, trying to shatter them, but they held strong.

Green and off-white ice glass swarmed them, preventing anyone from catching more than a glance of either contestant. Because I could barely see, because no one could, we were entirely unprepared for when the cage shattered.

Ice shards rained down.

And through the storm of shredded leaves and splintered champagne, we got a clear view of Olyn's fist colliding with Hathens' jaw.

No one said anything for a prolonged moment. Hathen's heavy breathing was the only sound echoing throughout the hall, a physical reminder countering people's disbelief.

"Next," the Queen announced, cleaving the tension with

her tone. The crowd began murmuring again, and in minutes their champagne glasses were refilled and court gossip had forgotten the upset entirely.

"A surprising result, but a Winter enchanter will never be a real contender," Bastian said to our mother, not even bothering to lower his voice.

"Yes, but maybe news of his victory will appease our people," mother said, her voice only carrying between our seats. I couldn't stop watching Hathens, wiping blood on his sweat-slicked forearm, ambling out the glass doors into the snowy courtyard. A healer followed after, calling after him to stop, but his pride kept him walking until he was out of sight.

He was strong. At times, stronger than Bastian. Definitely stronger than Calix. And now he looked…defeated.

"Mother, do the enchanters really have to demonstrate their magic on one another? We can see their skills just as well without violence," I said.

"What's the point of magic if not for violence?" Bastian's voice was so calm, so casual that I doubted he saw any issue at all with what he'd said. There was no way he really believed that. At least I hoped not. Especially when the prize of this brutality was my hand.

"Lord Ramos is next—pay special attention to him, Estyn," Bastian said with an uncharacteristically friendly tone. The crowd seemed to agree as they stilled for Lord Ramos' entrance.

If I'd thought Lord Hathens was large, he was nothing compared to Lord Ramos. Even flanked by two jaguars, he looked like the most fearsome predator of the trio.

"I like his confidence," mother whispered to Bastian. I couldn't disagree more.

The jaguars sat by the steps, not allowed to enter the ring.

I didn't listen to the announcement of his opponent. The garbled voices seemed to scream in my head, drowning out any other thoughts or sounds. I'd seen Lord Ramos; he was a close friend of Bastian's. But I'd never *seen* him. Not like this. Not when he was favored to be my husband.

Whether or not I would be here to honor it.

I saw the courtier ring the bell more than I heard it. And then I saw Lord Ramos pick the snakes, somehow manipulating them to release themselves from their cages and slither to his side. His opponent was dwarfed in comparison, and no amount of fire could make him seem competitive. Fire whips unfurled to his sides, and he dipped them in chemicals until they burned bright green and purple. It was beautiful, it was foreboding, but more than anything, it was tragic. Because the snakes still pressed on.

This fight, I knew, would not be long.

I closed my eyes, unwilling to watch the bloodshed, waiting for it to be over, when the main doors burst open.

General Turrek, commander of our army, stood on the platform above flanked by four guards. He wasted no time descending the stairs and crossing to Bastian, ignoring the frozen crowd and fight as he marched forward.

"The King requests your presence," he said. Bastian straightened in his seat, sobering in a matter of seconds.

"Did we secure Myllanor?" Bastian asked. The name sounded familiar, but I couldn't be sure. All I knew was it was in Alynthia. General Turrek shook his head.

"The white castle stands," he said. The vein in Bastian's neck bulged as he stood, working over his frustration as he rolled up his sleeves.

"Maybe he'll listen to me now," Bastian half muttered under his breath. He grabbed his wine glass, two fingers spanning the rim, and tossed the rest back before handing it to the closest server.

The server didn't take it. Bastian's wolves rose behind him.

No—not server. He stood in line with General Turrek's guards, wearing the same burgundy uniform, standing with the same erect posture. Only his eyes marked him as different.

Brown. Not the mesmerizing hazel of fall enchanters—unremarkable brown. How had a non-enchanter become a royal guard? We had more than enough, and there was little a commoner could do that an enchanter couldn't. I would know.

Calliope hurried over to take Bastian's glass, taking the edge off the storm brewing in his gaze.

"This is our newest recruit, Your Highness." General Turrek gestured to the guard I didn't recognize. I leaned forward, not wanting to miss a word about the mysterious guard, but General Turrek didn't elaborate. Bastian still stood on a step above the guard in some ridiculous power pissing contest, staring him down and waiting for his respect. I counted the seconds in my head, my fear for the guard growing with each second.

He lowered his gaze on the fourth. Bowed on the fifth.

Longer than I would've lasted.

Bastian's wolves huffed and he stalked toward the doors, not saying a word to mother or me as he exited.

"Restart the match," the Queen announced. Had it always been this hot in the ballroom? I don't know why I thought we'd end early with Bastian gone. My leg bounced furiously, but I held it down with my hand before my mother could admonish me.

"Your glass, Your Highness?" Calliope nodded toward my

empty glass, standing half behind my chair. *Soon*, I heard her voice say in my head. Soon. I twisted in my chair to hand her the glass with my opposite hand, obscuring us from prying court eyes.

Our hands brushed as we both gripped the stem, her thin fingers just barely stroking my wrist. A wave of calm flooded my chest. My leg stopped bouncing. I turned back to my mother, confident I could hold my smile as I met her disapproving squint.

"Sit up straight. And no more wine. You look sloppy," she whispered. Her scowl wasn't for me. She was just upset Bastian had been stolen away. She hated feeling less important. She was taking it all out on me.

So I nodded and sat taller, able to reason through her criticism because all my attention narrowed on my left hand, clenched below my skirts.

And the note folded inside.

CHAPTER

2

I let the shadows wash over me, stepping on the quietest floorboards in the darkest alcoves until I reached the kitchen. It was too late for the dishwashers to be lingering and too early for the bakers to have started; in other words, Calliope and my window of opportunity.

In the months we'd been meeting down here, I'd grown more comfortable, no longer constantly looking over my shoulder in fear of discovery. Now I loved the kitchen at this hour. The pots and pans hanging from the wire grid, reflecting the soft rays of moonlight filtering in through the open windows. The cold breeze drafting in, washing away the smells of the previous day. The pantries of ingredients that I was forbidden to touch during the day.

Best of all, I loved the line of mugs hanging from the bottom shelf. When I was younger, my mother used to take Bastian, Calix and me down here when we couldn't sleep and warm us mugs of spiced chocolate.

"Chocolate," she'd say, "is magic. It makes everything better." I believed her. It tasted like magic; how could it not be? But then Bastian and Calix started training *real* magic, and I was left behind with my medicine and the spiced chocolate to wash it down.

I was gathering spices in the pantry when I heard Calliope ease the door open.

"Estyn?" she called, so quiet I almost missed it.

"Over here," I said as I walked out with an armful of spice jars.

"Shhh," Calliope said, running over to catch the nutmeg dangling precariously from the nook of my arm. "You're going to get us caught."

"Sorry," I whispered. Her scowl melted away at the perk of my smile and the mischievous gleam in my eyes.

"We're just so close," she said, still half-whispering.

"I know, I know." I walked over to the pot of milk on the stove and started sprinkling spices in. We both watched as I dropped a few squares of chocolate in and started stirring, the brown swirling through the pot in an almost mesmerizing pattern.

"How have you been feeling?" Calliope asked, as she always did, even though she knew the answer.

"Same as always. Headaches are bad, I'm tired all the time and I still don't know why." For the first time, I was tempted to mention the voices, the constant hum that only disappeared at night. But I didn't. I was already crazy enough.

"Maybe we'll find a better healer in Braiwyth." She sounded so hopeful, I almost wanted to believe her. But I didn't want a better healer. I wanted to *be* better.

"Maybe," I said, because I needed her to believe for the

both of us. "You know, I was thinking… maybe I should start only taking half my dose and saving the rest to last until we find another healer."

"Do you know if a lower dose will work?"

"Better to try here than when we're on the run."

The silence felt even quieter now with the hypotheticals playing in my mind, but the spiced chocolate nearly boiling over yanked me from my anxious thoughts. I turned off the burner and grabbed two mugs—the two Calix had brought me from one of his diplomatic trips with my father—and poured the steaming liquid into them.

"There is something else we have to consider though," she said as I brought the pot to the sink. "I've heard rumors that Alynthia might be advancing soon." I stopped scrubbing, stopped thinking, stopped everything. There was no way they were coming here. Not again—they couldn't, right? Suddenly the kitchen melted away and I was back in my room, the warning bells ringing through my skull, drowning out my screams and fists as I pounded on the door.

I ran to the window and watched Alynthia dock a fleet of ships at Artange's harbor, flooding the city with soldiers. Calix had been training in the garden, and I found him, refusing to look away until he was led inside. But he wasn't.

The instructor had led the classes of children—children—to the battlefront. I screamed, hoping my voice would carry across the gardens, over the bells, but it was no use. Calix disappeared into the city where Alynthian soldiers were slaughtering our people.

I ran back to the door, banging on it for hours, screaming until my throat was raw, hoping someone would let me out. I needed to go save Calix. I was his older sister, and all I could do was cry and scream and wait for them to get me too.

"Estyn?" Calliope's voice broke through my thoughts.

"Sorry," I said, shaking my head as if I could shed the memory.

"I don't think it will impact us, but we should make sure we have weapons, just in case."

"Can we talk about something else?" I knew it made me a coward to avoid the topic, but I just couldn't think about that right now. Especially when I was leaving Calix behind, when I wouldn't be here to protect him if Alynthia attacked again.

"Okay," she said, soft and cautious. I must've had every bit of emotion written on my face. "Are you excited for the next qualifying round?"

"Yeah right." I barely made it through today, let alone two more. Maybe I could if Bastian left early again, but if he was there, making snide remarks and judging every second of the event, I doubted I'd be able to keep quiet. Wait—"Do you know anything about that new non-enchanter guard?"

"The one Bastian had a pissing contest with? He's some new hotshot from a training camp out in the country. First commoner to ever be appointed to the royal guard. People say he's one of the best fighters Tenebris has ever seen."

"We'll need to learn his patrol routes," I said. I knew most of the guards' routes, at least the ones nearing our path to the castle wall. I scrubbed furiously at the pot, running through the list of things we still needed to nail down this week, but froze at a sound from the hall. A rhythm of soft footsteps sounded, growing louder by the second.

In a moment Calliope was gone, the pot was hung and I was left sitting with my mug, sipping my spiced chocolate in peace.

My hand shook slightly as I raised the mug to my lips. I

hoped I looked calmer than I felt.

"Princess?" The voice was low, gravely, and not at all familiar. I set the mug down, perhaps a bit forcefully, and a bit of spiced chocolate splashed over the rim. "Do you need any help with that?" Bastian's favorite guard, the one we'd just been talking about, stood in the doorway. He looked pointedly at the small puddle on the counter.

"Oh, it's okay, I got it," I said, standing and rushing over to the towels to avoid looking at him. I'd seen him before at the qualifiers, but whether it was what Calliope had said or the late hour, it was entirely different now. Overwhelming.

My back was turned to him as I pulled out a small cloth, but I could feel him standing there, still watching.

When I turned back around it was like his presence hit me all over again. I ducked away to wipe down the counter, avoiding his gaze.

I hadn't noticed before, but a long scar stretched from his left ear to his forehead, cutting through his thick brows. It was fitting, in a strange way. His whole face felt strong and rugged and not at all like the manicured style of most the guards I knew.

"Do you know how late it is?" Something about the way he said it, either the way his phrase turned up at the end or the serious set to his brows made me feel like I was in trouble. I was not in trouble, and he certainly was in no place to talk down to me like that.

"Oh gods, I had no idea." I looked out the window to the half moon shining directly through the curtains. "Well, would you look at that. Crazy how time works."

Shit. I stopped cleaning, pressed my hand down into the cloth, wishing I could push through the counter and disappear into the floor. Where had that come from? There was no way for him to know I was doing anything wrong, but on the off chance he had heard something and were to report it… what was I thinking?

When I finally gathered the courage to look back up at him, he wasn't angry. In fact, if I didn't know any better, I'd think that was a smile.

"Shocking." He stepped closer—closer meaning one step into the kitchen—but it took the edge off my anxiety. At least he wasn't running off to tell on me. "What are you using to polish the counter?"

I choked out a laugh. Was he trying to make a joke? The words certainly sounded like it, but his tone was so flat I swore he could've been delivering orders.

"I was drinking spiced chocolate. My mother always used to make it for us when we couldn't sleep," I said.

"Smells delicious." His lip tilted up at the corner, so slight I might've imagined it. "If only there was any left."

"I didn't spill the *entire* thing," I said.

"Remains to be seen."

"And to think, for a second I considered offering you a sip." What was he doing down here anyway? Didn't he have something better to do? Like his job?

"Wouldn't have mattered anyway," he said, leaning back against the door jamb, "I'm on duty."

"It's not alcoholic?"

"It's unprofessional."

"Oh, because you've been the picture of professionalism." I took a sip from my still very full mug, peering up at him over the rim.

"You're right. My apologies," he said, ducking his head in deference.

"No—um, it's okay." I spoke as reflexively as if a healer

had tapped my knee. Whatever this dynamic was, I didn't want to lose it so soon. "You don't need to do that kind of thing with me."

"What kind of thing?" He looked back up and quirked a single brow. All of his expressions were so subtle that if he shifted slightly, the moonlight might not be enough to make them out.

"Like the stuff with my brother. I'm sorry about that, by the way." I remembered the second of defiance I'd seen in the ballroom and wondered just how much he had to swallow to advance as much as he had.

"No need to apologize." Something about the way he said it, so resigned and accepting of Bastian's stupid power plays, made me want to push more.

"No, Bastian can be a real prick." It was only because his face tilted toward the window just so that I caught the twitch at the corner of his mouth. "You deserve some spiced chocolate just for having to deal with him." I closed the distance between us just enough that I could extend the mug. The space around him felt taut, as if I crossed a boundary that put me within striking distance.

"Do I now?" He took a step forward. He was close enough for me to feel the body heat radiating off of him, and I may have even leaned in a little—but only because it was so damn drafty in here.

"Only one sip though. I'm already missing some because *someone* startled me." I extended the mug.

"My sincerest apologies." Two of his fingers overlapped with mine as he wrapped his hand around the base. They were so warm despite the chill. For a brief moment, I considered asking him to wrap my entire hand in his, just to warm it up.

Where did that come from?

I pulled my hand away and stepped back until the backs of my thighs touched the counter. He raised the mug to his lips and I glanced over to the window again, his gaze suddenly too heavy to handle.

"Pretty good." He lowered the mug and looked down at it as if he hadn't just tasted a culinary masterpiece.

"*Pretty* good? You mean incredible? Life changing. Magic in liquid form." I wanted to go take the mug from him because he clearly didn't deserve it, but something kept me planted a safe distance away.

"Don't think that's how magic works, and even if it was, I've gotten by fine without it so far."

"Cynic."

"If you say so." He walked over and set the mug down beside me, and all my attention narrowed to the spot where his arm brushed mine. *It's because I'm still not sure whether he overhead Calliope and me*, I told myself. I needed to be on guard around him.

"I need to get back to my patrol. Do you need an escort back to your room?"

"I think I can find my way," I said. A small part of me hoped he'd insist, but my brain reminded me he was a guard and I still shouldn't be out at night. He probably just didn't know yet because he was new, but soon enough he'd be just like everyone else. He'd see me for who I'm supposed to be.

"Thanks for the cocoa, Princess." I never really liked being called princess, but for some reason, the way he said it—almost like an inside joke—made me want to hear it again.

"Anytime." I forced myself to turn away from him, to walk through the steps of cleaning my mug like it could distract me from his presence.

I still felt every second he lingered.

24

CHAPTER

3

I never thought I was particularly picky with my mornings, but having my blankets tossed back and curtains ripped open to sunlight streaming in my face was not my favorite.

"It's lunchtime," my mother said flatly, which was not a good sign. "Do you want to tell me why your ladies in waiting told me that you haven't risen before noon in *weeks?*"

Because I had been disturbed after not nearly enough sleep and was still rubbing crust from my eyes, it took me a moment to respond. Which was apparently the wrong answer.

"Estyn, your Veirden is only a week away. You mean to tell me that while I've been slaving away for your future, you've been sleeping half the day away?" She busied herself running a bath and tossing a dress onto my face as she deplored my lazy, gluttonous habits. No matter that my illness made me constantly fatigued; no, I needed to push through and focus on the important things, like what flowers to hang from the banisters and which tulle best suited my coloring.

I sat up and pushed the half-read book off my chest.

"I'm sorry, Mother. It's just—I think I'm getting worse. I don't think the medication is working anymore." Even from my spot on the bed I could see her jerk upright and tense up. Talking about my sickness always did this to her; she'd rather pretend I was well than face the reality of my condition.

"We just need to up the dose. I'll talk to the healer later today," she said before going quiet as she finished pouring rose salts into the water. She could be painfully critical and cold, but she cared. And she looked so tired.

My gut twisted with guilt. I *did* think I was getting worse, but what I really needed was more medication so that I could save some. I swung my legs over the bed and pattered over to where she stood bent over the tub, swirling the water to dissolve the salts.

I gave her a light side-hug, and she softened in my arms, albeit awkwardly.

"I'm sorry, mother," I whispered against her chest. She paused, and for a moment I thought she'd say something sweet, like she loved me or everything would be okay.

"Lunch is in half an hour," she said before disentangling herself from my embrace and exiting as clamorously as she'd entered.

My brothers had already started eating when I arrived. I sat in my usual chair beside Calix, hoping no one noticed my skittishness.

"How is training progressing?" Mother asked Bastian.

"It is going very well for me, though I noticed Calix hasn't been giving much effort lately." Bastian leaned back in his chair, staring pointedly at Calix. Calix picked at his food.

"Is this true, Calix?" Mother asked, genuinely concerned, but I knew better.

"No, mother, I have been learning a lot. It is simply hard to compare to Bastian." If I had said that, I would not be able to resist lacing it with sarcasm, but Calix sounded earnest.

"You know how important it is to continue working hard and training your skills."

"Yes, mother." Calix looked like he would rather be anywhere else.

"You'll have plenty of opportunities when you shadow the generals patrolling the city this week. Maybe they'll help you toughen up." He nodded and stared at his food.

"Very well, then. How was your proposal received, Bastian?" Mother asked, and Bastian stiffened.

"General Turrek agreed with me; however, Father decided against it," he seethed, gripping his fork so tightly I thought he'd bend it.

"What proposal?" I asked.

"You wouldn't understand," he spat, stabbing a potato as he finished.

"Your brother had such an innovative idea for how to finally infiltrate Alynthia," mother said. I didn't know Bastian had graduated to war strategy; last I checked he was still training and shadowing father, nothing more. I supposed I hadn't cared to ask. Bastian glared at her, but she ignored him, instead changing the subject.

"Well, I must be going. Calix, be safe in the city tonight. And Estyn, don't forget to go to your etiquette lesson this afternoon, and try to pay attention for once." It took great restraint to not make a snide remark, but I managed a simple goodbye. Bastian followed shortly, not offering much beyond a nod before exiting.

Once they were gone, Calix relaxed in his chair, but he kept stealing glances at me.

"Estyn?" Calix asked, voice apprehensive.

"Yes?"

"Have you ever been in love?" Of all the things he could've said, I was not expecting that.

"Honestly?" He nodded. "No. I don't think I'll ever get to be," I tried to stay lighthearted, but my words were tinged with sadness.

He looked down at his plate and pushed the food around for a few moments.

"I'm sorry to hear that." For a moment, his tenderness made me want to believe that love could triumph. If not for myself, then for him. "How about you? Anyone of interest?" I said, remembering the Summer enchanter from his drawings.

"I've been reading a lot lately," he offered, clearly disinterested in talking about his love life, but he smiled a little. My heart warmed, but it was bittersweet. If he had ties here… we'd figure it out.

"Aren't you supposed to be training?"

"Who says I can't do both?"

I rolled my eyes, knowing very well that Calix would rather read or draw than train any day. I knew it was selfish, but part of me had to know. I had to ask. I glanced around, but we were alone save for the two guards outside the door.

"What if you didn't have to train anymore?" I asked, watching his reaction for any sign I shouldn't ask him to leave.

"What do you mean? Of course I have to train," he said, pushing his potatoes into a heart shape instead of eating them.

"I mean, what if you didn't have to be a prince anymore?" He finally looked up at me, expression thoughtful and cautiously hopeful.

"I don't think father would ever let that happen," he said after careful consideration, spearing a potato and wrecking his carefully arranged plate. "I have to go."

I considered stopping him, but I'd find another time to ask. "Have fun. I love you," I said as he opened the door.

"Love you too, Es," he said, giving me a smile that had to be one of the best in the world. I couldn't leave without that smile.

I looked at the vial of medicine beside my tea. I was alone now, but not for long. Calliope said she'd distract anyone from coming to grab the dishes, but she couldn't buy me more than a few minutes.

I pulled a small leather pouch from where I'd tucked it into the bodice of my gown. I picked up the vial, like always, but I didn't pour it into the tea. I poured half into the pouch and cinched it quickly, blowing a few particles in the air in my haste to tuck it away.

Then I put the rest into my drink and gulped it down, praying to the gods the dose would be enough for me to make it through the day.

CHAPTER

4

I should lay down. No doubt it would be easier to sleep that way than sitting in the half-crouched position on the middle of my bed. But every time I considered it, my muscles refused to move.

Thank the gods I hadn't had to think much today. I didn't think halving the dose would make a big difference. And, to be fair, the headaches were far less severe.

But the voices were far more aggressive.

Especially during the practice run-through for the ball, where we walked through my entrance and the logistics. There were so many people and so many voices and so many times I wanted to run as fast and far as my feet would take me.

Half was not ideal. But half was better than none, which is what I would have if I didn't save some.

When the moonlight shone through my drapes, reminding

me just how long I'd sat in bed floating hypotheticals that had no place in my mind, I decided to make myself useful. I padded out onto the balcony, wrapping my robe around me as the winter air bit into my skin.

I looked down to the ground below. I was only on the second floor. I scanned the wall, trying to find a pattern of cracks I hadn't used before.

I went back inside and quickly changed into the leggings and tunic that Calliope had gotten me. I walked to the railing, looking around for guards. My window was surrounded by a copse of trees which obscured me well enough. I fit my hand into one of the cracks over the balcony, and then found another hold off the side. I lifted my leg over the banister until it found purchase on a stone that jutted out slightly from the wall. I lowered myself carefully, finding the next crack that I had identified. Even though I'd made this climb many times—if three counted as many—I didn't dare look down.

My forearms ached with the effort of holding myself against the wall, but if I let go, then I would probably break a bone, which, besides being painful, would be difficult to explain.

I finally allowed myself to look down, afraid that I'd be barely lower than when I first began, but the ground stared up at me, mere inches below my feet. I simply stepped down.

My heart pounded, adrenaline rushing. I looked out to the castle wall and considered whether I should just go into the city. I already made it this far; I could leave, forget my duties, and be free. But then, as if on cue, I remembered my medication. I couldn't leave yet.

A twig cracked somewhere nearby, terrifying me enough to slip into the shadows. I looked around, made sure no one was there, and then scampered back up to my balcony. Adrenaline fueled my climb, but once I reached the top my muscles reminded me how much harder it was to go up than down. I nearly collapsed, my legs turning to jelly beneath me. My brow glistened with sweat, and I hurt almost all over, but I smiled. *Maybe one day*, I told myself.

"Princess?" The voice that I'd tried to push out of my mind rumbled from below my balcony. *Shit.* He'd definitely seen me. Even if he hadn't, there was no way I could sneak inside. I sat up and pressed my face between the banisters to see the hotshot guard from the kitchen standing below, just as I remembered him.

"Uh, yes, hello," I called down, hoping my voice didn't sound as out of breath as it felt.

"Is everything okay up there?" he called, just loud enough so only I could hear.

"Yes," I said, pressing a hand to my chest to still my racing heart.

"Do you need any help?" he asked, surprisingly gentle given his overall dark and stormy demeanor.

"No, really, I was just..." as I scrambled to brainstorm a plausible excuse, he interrupted me.

"Can I come up so we don't wake the whole wing with our shouting?" He wanted to come up here? With me? On my personal balcony? I tried to imagine his large frame beside me, just mere steps from my bed, but my brain short-circuited.

"Good idea," I shouted, once again breathless.

He scaled the wall in seconds, not giving me nearly enough time to run inside, bathe, change into my most flattering gown, and return to my spot as if nothing happened. No, I was stuck in my sweat-soaked tunic and messed hair, only able to let it loose around my shoulders before he crested the banister.

"I told you I was okay." I tried to calm my breathing, but it was still shallow and faster than normal. His face stayed serious, giving me a once-over, which was completely innocuous but felt charged.

"Just doing my job," he said, meeting my eyes in a heated gaze that made me want to keep him here, if only to find out more about him. But he turned to leave, bracing his hands on the rail once again.

"You know, you never told me your name."

"You never asked." He glanced back, the strong profile of his jaw illuminated in moonlight.

"When was I supposed to? Before or after you called me clumsy?"

"Was I wrong?" He looked pointedly at the wall and then back to me before leaning against the railing. So he *had* seen me.

"I was not going to fall off the wall." He crossed his arms over his chest, and the moon decided to shine its light directly on the shift of his arm muscles, highlighting the strong silhouette of his shoulders. "If you're such an expert, then show me."

"I don't have to prove anything to you," he said. He rushed to correct himself, but I interrupted before he could ruin the moment.

"No, I mean…teach me. Please." He assumed the same calculating eyes I'd seen a million times on Bastian, but instead of cold, they were hesitant. Wary. I cleared my throat. "I uh," I started. "I have pretty bad nightmares. The last time Alynthia attacked, they locked me in here while my younger brother was out there, fighting. I had no way of getting to him. I just…I need a way out."

"It's safer inside." His words warned, but his shoulders relaxed.

"I know. It'll just make me feel better." I clenched the bottom of my tunic in my fists, wrinkling the fabric in anticipation of his answer.

I felt every second of his interrogation training as his gaze bore into me, reading my every thought. Well, maybe not *every* one.

"Okay," he said, relieving and anxiety-inducing at the same time. My muscles barked at me, wondering why I felt like making a fool of myself in front of this guard for the third time since meeting him.

I walked towards where he stood by banister, waiting for his direction, but he just observed me as I moved. "Now?" I asked, perhaps a bit impertinent, but it made him chuckle. The sound was somehow better than the normal cadence of his voice; it sang to me and begged me to draw it out again. I wish I knew how.

"Watch me," he offered, hoisting himself over the rail and deftly swinging onto the wall. As I watched him find the perfect cracks without even looking, making it to the ground as if it were a ladder and not a several hundred year old castle wall, I was hit with the overwhelming sensation that I wanted to know more about him.

I peered over the rail to where he stood looking up at me, arms crossed over his chest. "You know, while impressive, that wasn't very helpful," I said.

"Get on the wall, smart-ass." Even though it was silly, even though he was calling me names, his comment sent a flutter through my already sore core.

"Your hands are too far from your feet. Move them down

to the crack by your hip." By my hip? I'd fall off. There was no way in hell—well, would you look at that. I didn't fall.

He instructed my next few moves and I got used to making riskier choices, descending faster than I ever had before. My muscles screamed in the contorted climbing positions he put me in, but I forced myself to push through, not wanting to show him just how out of shape I was.

"Not bad," I heard him say. No—I *imagined* him say, his voice in my head. Black edged my vision and my head showed me what it would feel like to smack it against the stone. My grip slipped, but I was close enough to the ground that it may have looked purposeful.

"Are you okay?" he asked as I jumped the final gap to the soft grass below. I dug the toe of my boot into the dirt and the pain receded, but a wisp of darkness danced in the corner of my eye. I blinked, but it stayed. In fact, it looked like it was on the ground. Like it was nearing.

And it brushed my foot, its touch warm and comforting.

"Estyn?" he asked. I jumped, reminded of his presence, and when I looked back down the wisp was gone. If it had ever been there in the first place.

"Oh, yeah, I'm fine," I said with a smile. It wasn't one of my best, but it would've been sufficient for my mother, or any of the court members. He didn't look so convinced.

Maybe if I took the full dose every other day, then this wouldn't be so...

"Ryker."

"Hm?"

"My name," he said.

"Oh," I said, resorting to monosyllabic speech.

"Will you be okay getting back up?" We both looked up to the balcony, and it looked so much higher now. My head was quieting, but I still needed a little more time. My gaze drifted to the stars above, as it always seemed to, and they winked back in recognition.

"Do you know the story of Nyx and Hyperion?" I asked him. Ryker looked up then, as if he was looking at the central constellation for the first time.

"No."

"Well, that bright one up there represents Nyx, the Goddess of Darkness. And right next to her is Hyperion, the God of Light. In the beginning, there was just Nyx. Other stars appeared, but they were all sucked into Nyx's orbit, absorbed into her light.

"Until, one day, Hyperion came into the sky. Like all the stars before him, he was pulled towards Nyx. However; unlike the rest, Nyx was also pulled to him. They fell in love, an explosive kind of infatuation, until they crashed into one another. The stardust around them is the result of their connection.

"After that, stars began to pop into the sky once again, but they were not pulled into Nyx's orbit because Hyperion's own pull balanced Nyx's. They had four children, the gods and goddesses of the seasons, and the rest is history."

I realized that I may have rambled on for a bit long and looked over expecting to see Ryker yawning, but he watched me intently. I didn't notice when he had stopped looking at the sky and turned to me. I held his gaze, terrified that he'd tell me it was stupid, but he smiled. It was slight, like all his expressions, but it was one of the best smiles I'd ever seen.

"I have to get back to my rounds." He didn't move, though, waiting to make sure I was alright. My head felt quiet again, and the balcony didn't look so high anymore.

"Okay," I said. I walked over to the wall, fitting my fingers into a nook just above my shoulder. I looked back to where he was walking back to the path.

"Ryker," I called out after him. He paused to look over his shoulder. "Thank you." He nodded in acknowledgment, but as he turned back, light shifted over his face, revealing the slightest hint at a dimple.

I made it up the wall twice as fast as I had before.

"Estyn, darling, pinky up," my mother said, hiding her disappointment behind a tight smile.

"Apologies, mother." It was not my first choice of response—not even in the top ten—but we were five days away now. I had enough apologies to last that long.

The other ladies of the court chattered mindlessly around us, pushing their finger sandwiches around on their plates. Every so often one of their voices drifted in my mind, quiet and distant, as if being spoken underwater, saying things they didn't. I clenched my teeth and fought through it. Half was better than none.

The unasked questions about my Veirden loomed over my head, making me feel far too hot for the cold winter day. Even though we were seated inside the grand ballroom, the wall of glass doors were thrown open to the courtyard, allowing us to view the training cohorts from a comfortable distance. Enchanters were rarely allowed to use their magic for trivial purposes, but my mother's comfort was always deemed worthy.

That was probably why I was so warm; the summer enchanters heating the air were doing their job too well. I shook off my overcoat and tried to distract myself from the impending gossip about my future. I focused on details, observing the room like it could ground me from the ever-present swarm of sound in my brain.

The Winter cohort stood closer to the fountain, bare-chested despite the freezing temperatures, manipulating and cooling the water. They barely broke a sweat, their magic seemingly strengthened by the imminent Winter Solstice. They lifted water into the air, freezing it into daggers and swords, fighting without hands.

The Summer enchanters stood off to the side in a sandpit, also underdressed for the weather, warmed by the magic in their veins. They mixed chemicals and set off small bombs, the impact directed and controlled by their magic. Bastian always claimed that the solar enchanters were inherently weaker than the earth enchanters, but I never saw why. Their ability to control temperature seemed just as powerful as the earth enchanters' abilities with nature.

As I lost myself in the colorful fire dancing around the sandpit, I felt a heated gaze wash over me. My eyes darted from enchanter to enchanter, flitting from trainers to trainees to guards until—there, by the hedges. Ryker.

I offered a slight smile, but he stared on, unaffected.

"Estyn," my mother's voice broke through my thoughts, her tone stern. "Frida just asked you a question. Ignoring her is incredibly rude."

"My apologies," I said, head bowed. "What is it you asked?"

"Are you looking forward to your Veirden? It must be a great honor to have it on the Winter Solstice."

"Yes," I said, intending to stop there until I saw my mother's expectant stare. "I am excited to formally meet all of the suitors."

"Is there any suitor in particular you favor?" *Gods no.* I

barely hid a grimace, attempting to transform it into a placating smile instead.

"I am trying to stay unbiased during the qualifiers." Frida seemed dissatisfied with this answer, obviously hoping for some inside news. She and everyone else. It's not like I had much choice; in a few days, I'd be sold off to the most powerful enchanter.

Not that I'd be here to honor it, I thought.

"You do think that all the most eligible enchanters will still be here, right? I've heard they may be sent to Alynthia," one of my old classmates asked my mother. Her chair angled away from me to account for her nine-months pregnant belly, hiding the striking green eyes she was so damn proud of. It was better this way. In a few days, if her child was born on the Winter Solstice, her normally irritating haughtiness would become unbearable. As we'd been taught, every little girl dreamt of bearing an enchanter.

Just another way I was defective.

"Serafina," my mother reprimanded, sharp enough that even I flinched. "Ladies should not speculate about such things. And even so, the rumors are entirely unfounded—we just had a great victory. Our troops are nearing Myllanor."

Myllanor? I racked my brain, trying to remember why that was significant. Mother always said I shouldn't worry myself with politics, but I wished I knew enough to not be lost at times like these.

"Myllanor? Does that mean they will take the white castle soon?" Frida asked, more tactful than Serafina from years of court gossip. My mother didn't answer, but the slight tilt to her lips said enough.

"Anyways, I ordered the most beautiful floral arrangements to line the courtyard," she said, launching into another tale that I'd heard several times already. My gaze drifted back to where the new guard had been, but a Spring enchanter had replaced him. Where did he go? It wasn't time for a shift change yet.

I gathered my napkin from my lap, dabbed the corners of my mouth, and set it beside my plate before silently excusing myself. My steps echoed in the ballroom as I walked across the seemingly endless floor to the door, hoping they were all too engrossed in conversation to pay close attention. Not that it mattered; I was just going to the bathroom. My exit had nothing to do with Ryker. Absolutely nothing.

I had to go to the restrooms closer to the guard's quarters because they were… cleaner. As I walked, I kept glancing around the corridor like a lunatic, but the halls were empty save for a few courtiers and maids.

I entered the washroom, rinsed my hands, all the while planning my tactful banter that would have him playing into my plan. Calliope would be so proud. I'd regale her with the tale of how I charmed him with my dazzling personality, finding a way to defend ourselves once we left.

Well, maybe not proud. She'd probably say I should focus on our planning and not risk anything that might draw too much attention to ourselves. And she'd be right.

A few minutes later, I exited the washroom, resolved to forget about Ryker entirely until a deep voice greeted me from beside the door.

"Princess," Ryker said. I jumped, completely ruining the smooth encounter I'd planned.

"Shit, you scared me." I held a hand to my chest and watched as his eyes darted down to where I was still catching my breath. We were alone in the corridor, but he still elected for a sardonic raised brow instead of commenting. "I know,

I know, it's my own fault. I need to be more aware."

"For your own safety." He held himself with the stiff posture I'd first seen at the qualifiers. Soldier Ryker. Now was my chance.

"Wouldn't matter much though if I couldn't defend myself." I shrugged and looked down at my skirts, resisting the urge to clench the fabric in my hand. He tilted his head slightly.

Soldier Ryker wasn't nearly as fun.

"They didn't train me like my brothers. Said I didn't need to know how to fight." I tried to look as pitiful as possible, hoping Ryker would take the bait.

"You shouldn't need to." He spoke in a lower register than last night, his voice rumbling with command. I scoffed.

"It would just be nice to know basic self defense," I said. "Since I'm so clumsy." He looked down at me, his face a perfect mask of calm, but his eyes danced with stifled repartee.

"Ryker," a general shouted from down the corridor. I turned and walked as fast as looked natural, my heart beating so fast he could probably hear it from the other end. I wasn't doing anything wrong. I could talk to guards. But for some reason Ryker felt like he belonged to stolen moments; the less he mixed with my life, the better.

As I turned the corner, I realized I'd never gotten an answer. One way or another, I needed a way to defend myself. If Ryker said no, I could convince Calix to help me, but that would come with far too many questions, and worse yet, emotions I wouldn't be able to explain.

I crumpled my skirts in my fists and ran the rest of the way, working off my nervous energy before returning to the prying eyes of the court ladies.

I nearly tripped over the endless tulle draped over my dresser as I reached behind it. My mother had hung my ball gown on one of the vines over my dresser so that every morning I would wake to a sea of blue fabric. The four remaining mornings, that was.

This was likely the last time Calliope and I would meet before the ball. I wish I could report I got Ryker to agree to teach me to fight, but we would be okay without it. I'd just ask Calix to show me a few moves tomorrow. It would be enough. It *had* to be enough.

This was just disaster planning, anyway. My mother said it herself. The chances Alynthia attacked were slim to none. We were winning.

Calliope and I would be fine on our own.

I dressed and avoided the billowing skirts on my path to the door, yawning as I crossed the room. I was barely sleeping now that mother woke me with the sun.

At least it was quiet. I was managing with only half the regular dose, but my head was louder than ever. The voices were clearer than before, demanding my attention nearly more than my mother.

I felt fabric brush my ankle and looked down to find not blue, but black. Not fabric. I shook my head, but it came back, tugging at my foot, as if pulling me back to bed.

I guess the medicine had been doing more than I'd thought.

I kept walking forward, but the shadow held on, nearly tripping me.

"Go away," I said. Another joined it, winding through my fingers as if it were holding my hand. A *shadow* holding my *hand.* "This isn't real."

The shadow squeezed, or at least I imagined it did. This wasn't happening. I got headaches, not hallucinations. I really needed more sleep. And maybe a full dose.

I squeezed my eyes shut, willing the world to be normal when I opened them. *I'm not crazy.* I pictured Calliope's face, let it reassure me that I could make it through this.

When I opened them, I was alone. No shadows. Acknowledging how silly it was as I did so, I knelt on the floor to check under the bed. Nothing there either.

I really had imagined it.

A curse froze behind my lips as a sound came from the balcony. A footstep, just outside the doors. Thank the gods I had drawn the curtains.

I threw on a robe and jumped back into bed, just before a knock sounded on the door.

"Estyn?" Ryker whispered from the balcony.

My heartbeat hammered in my ears, but I tried to calm it as I donned a drowsy expression. I threw back the covers and ambled over to the doors, trying to time it as if I'd been sleeping. I peeked my head through the drapes.

Ryker paced in front of the doors, his nervous steps eerily similar to a march. I blinked a few times and took my time undoing the locks.

"Hm?" I rubbed my eyes, though they were perfectly clear.

"You want to be able to defend yourself?" he asked. I nodded. "I only have half an hour."

"Give me one minute," I said, and closed the door.

Shit.

Calliope was expecting me. I could tell him to go away, but would he come back again? It seemed like a time-sensitive offer.

Our plans were mostly in place. Calliope and I could meet tomorrow night.

I tossed the robe over the green behemoth and paused to make it seem like I'd just gotten dressed. I eased out onto the balcony, blinking as my eyes adjusted to the moonlight. I saw a shadow slither in the corner of my vision, as if twirling around the banister behind Ryker, but I shook my head. No. I couldn't have any distractions tonight. Especially not from my imagination.

"Where do we start?"

CHAPTER

5

"I'm sorry." I was wrong. Calliope could not meet the next night. Or the next. Or the next. So it wasn't until the night before the ball that we found ourselves back in the kitchen, rushing to pin down all the details. I shifted on the kitchen stool, burying my hands in between my thighs to still them.

Calliope shook her head and I felt her disappointment like a punch to the chest. Or maybe it was just the lingering bruise from the actual punch I'd taken just above my sternum.

Ryker had made a habit of coming to my balcony every night, at the same time, to train. I could still barely throw a punch, but I was steadier on my feet. And I felt more confident, which was invaluable. I just needed to convince Calliope of that.

"Ryker had just showed up—"

"The hotshot?" Calliope interrupted.

"Yeah, him, he came to my balcony because I asked him to train me—"

"To what?"

"Well, if Alynthia comes, then we need to be prepared—"

"We would've been prepared. Why did you get him involved?"

"I know how to fight better now, I can help if anything happens to us." Calliope sighed and dragged a hand down her face, sounding more like an exasperated older sister than my best friend. I know I shouldn't have missed our meeting, but what did she expect me to do? I likely would've missed the guard change anyway after he delayed me.

"I'm sorry I missed our meeting."

"That's why you think I'm mad?"

"Isn't it?"

"Estyn. We're *leaving.* Now is not the time to make new friends who might question where you are and why. Do you not see that?"

"I do, but I just—I thought it would help. I thought you'd be proud."

"We don't have time for this," she said. In seconds, her face shifted from anger to pity. Somehow, the pity was worse. "How have your headaches been?"

I considered telling her about the voices. About the shadows that kept appearing. That some part of me thought—hoped—that they were real. But she was right; we didn't have much time.

"Fine. I think I have enough medicine to last until we find a healer."

"That's great." Her smile made the lie worth every word. I already knew I was a burden. I didn't need to weigh her down any more.

The next hour passed quickly as we discussed the minutia of tomorrow. We needed to time everything just right, for every guard to be in the exact spots for us to avoid attention.

Less than twenty-four hours and we'd be on a boat sailing far, far away from here.

"I'll see you tomorrow?" she asked. The next time we'd talk, it would be as we were running toward the docks, dressed as strangers. I nodded. I'd been looking forward to this for so long, I never expected to feel so…sad.

This was the last time I'd sit in the kitchen at night. We hadn't even made spiced chocolate—when was the last time I used my favorite mug? I didn't savor it enough. I hadn't known it would be the last time.

Calliope wrapped me in a tight hug, squeezing all the anxious thoughts away.

"We're finally going to be free, Es." Her breath was warm against my neck, and I nodded as a single tear fell onto her shoulder. This was what I wanted.

I knew I should go straight back to my room. I needed all the sleep I could get before tomorrow, but I couldn't stop thinking about Ryker.

Calliope was right that I shouldn't have gotten involved. But I did. And I couldn't shake the thought that I needed to thank him.

I knew his route now, thanks to Calliope, so it wouldn't be hard to find him. I could just say a quick thank you and be on my way.

This wasn't a *terrible* idea.

Instead of walking toward the stairwell, I took a right, toward my father's office. Bastian and Calix were often called in for strategy meetings or to shadow him, but I was only allowed in on the rare occasions that my father felt he needed to punish me. I tried to make those few and far between.

Too much trouble, my father's voice said in my head. I froze, looking at the ostentatious oak door to his office and wondering why my mind decided now was the time to play his voice.

"How much does she know?" my father asked, this time muffled behind the door. Shit.

I pressed myself against the nearest column, hoping no one heard me approach. It was the middle of the night. Why was he awake? I looked to the stairwell, suddenly aware of how long the hall was. If he came out, there would be nothing stopping him from seeing me.

"She's unaware." I'd recognize that voice anywhere: just the person I'd hoped to find.

All the air sucked out of the room as realization dawned on me.

Ryker was never my friend. He was my father's spy.

I felt a whisper of a sensation brushing at my toes. When I looked down, the shadowy fog from before lapped at my ankles, as if asking for permission to hide me.

"Good, good. I know my wife thinks she is worth the risk, but I'm not so sure," the king said, then paused for a moment. "What do you think?"

"Maybe if she wasn't so difficult—" Bastian's voice was unmistakable.

"I was asking Sir Ryker," the King said.

"I think it is hard to determine the right decision, Your Highness." My stomach dropped. What decision?

"Very good. I think you are ready for more responsibility."

I heard footsteps approaching from down the hall and jumped, running as quietly as I could towards the stairwell. I didn't have time to make it to my door before the figure turned into the hall, so I ducked into the closest room.

I slumped back against the door, heart still pounding.

Betrayal stung in my chest, and I struggled to steady my breathing. Was Ryker reporting on me this entire time? Was that why he befriended me? To spy on me?

Had I told him anything that would ruin our plans?

My chest ached and I couldn't move. All I could do was sit, stew, and curse myself for being so stupid.

I looked up and realized I had never been in this room before. It looked like a normal sitting chamber, walls lined with books. There was a hearth and a few chairs gathered around it.

My mind felt cloudy, anxious thoughts taunting me without becoming concrete. Through it all, I heard the familiar buzz of unintelligible voices.

I never heard that when I was alone.

Please don't let it be him. I didn't recognize the voice, and it didn't seem like anyone was around but—

"Estyn," Bastian said as he swung the door open, far more serious than his casual derision. "What are you doing?"

I looked at him, frozen in place, trying to come up with a valid excuse.

"I couldn't sleep." He stared at me as if he could see through to my bones, making my skin crawl. I wanted nothing more than to run back to my room, but he was blocking the door. Hours passed; or maybe it was minutes, but standing under his gaze made judging time impossible.

"Well you're not going to sleep here," he said, an obvious dismissal. I scampered out of the room and back to my bed, jumping in it as if I were a child pretending to sleep and my mother was coming at any moment. My heart pounded in my ears and my mind swam with everything I'd heard.

I didn't sleep a wink.

All my muscles hurt. I could barely hide my wince as the tailor asked me to hold out my arms, making last-minute adjustments to my dress. Ryker's training was finally catching up to me, and every muscle twinge felt like another knife sliding in with fresh betrayal.

My mother stood beside the mirror with her arms crossed, evaluating every detail.

"Can you tuck it in any more at the waist?" she asked, and the tailor nodded.

"We can try, Your Highness," she said, though I didn't know how. I could barely breathe as it was.

"That will be all," My mother dismissed her, leaving us alone.

I stepped down from the platform clumsily, legs still stiff. I wanted to get out of my dress and soak in a tub for the rest of the day, but there was no time. I only had mere hours until the ball began; and only a few more until I left forever.

I walked over to where my day clothes lay folded on a chair, wincing as I leaned down to pick them up.

"Estyn?" My mother asked, voice unusually soft. "I know I've been stressed these past few weeks, but it's just because of how important tomorrow is, to you and to our family." She brushed the hair off my neck and held my shoulders, looking at me with such warmth all I wanted to do was break out in tears and lean into her arms. I wanted her to brush my hair and tell me that it would all be okay, that everything that happened in the last few days would go away. I knew better, and yet I still wanted it.

"Mother?"

"Yes?"

"I'm scared," I admitted, my voice impossibly small.

"Of what?" she asked, letting my hair loose around my shoulders. There was too much I couldn't tell her, no matter how much I wanted to just melt into her arms and let her take care of me. I wish I could tell her goodbye. That I loved her. That I was sorry, and that it wasn't her fault.

She was doing the best she could. But her best wasn't enough for me.

"Tonight, am I…I mean, after the ball," I started, stumbling over my words until she interrupted me.

"Oh, Estyn, don't worry. Bearing your husband an enchanter is the greatest way to honor the gods." I nodded, even though I already knew this. My whole life I had been told just that; my purpose was to bestow Tenebris and our bloodline with more strong enchanters.

It was my duty, and I was running from it. I was scared of what the gods would think, whether they'd consider me a coward, but either way I couldn't stay here.

"I know, I know," I said.

"Was that all that worried you?" she asked, tugging me down to sit next to her. As I settled, she brushed a curl behind my ear with a touch so gentle I couldn't reconcile the woman before me with the cold queen everyone knew. I couldn't tell her I was leaving, but there was one thing I needed clarity on. One person I would be glad to never see again.

"Can I ask," I started, and her face twisted in concern, "I know I shouldn't, but I was wondering—"

"Spit it out, dear."

"Has father ever assigned guards to spy on me?"

"Oh, Estyn," she said, tilting her head like I sounded crazy. "I thought the medicine had stopped making you imagine things."

"What? It's not the illness, I promise—"

"The healers said you might become paranoid. If guards follow, it's only for your safety. We can talk about raising your dose tomorrow." She tried to pull me back into a hug, but I resisted.

"Mother, I feel fine. I'm not imagining things."

"It's okay, we'll get you more medicine, and everything will be fine," she said, seeming to miss my last comment entirely. This time I didn't resist when she pulled me in, running her hand up and down my back and whispering how everything would be okay. "Today is important. The gods are watching over us. Everything will be okay."

I couldn't tell whether she was saying it to me or herself, but it didn't matter. The gods never cared about me anyway.

Calix sat by the hearth in the interior library with a book in hand. He was in his element, and the houseplants in the room grew a little faster because of it.

I wished I could leave him undisturbed, but I only had a few minutes before mother would come retrieve me to dress for the evening.

Calix glanced up and smiled at me before returning to his chapter. I spotted a book beside him, a love story about Nyx and Hyperion he'd laid out for me. Just that small gesture squeezed my heart far more than felt possible.

I walked over to the chair beside him, curled up and

opened my book. I wanted to read it, but there was no way I could focus now.

"You know, you don't have to be here with me right now. I know you're busy," he said, glancing up above his pages. I could've cried right then and there, but he didn't need to know that.

"There's nowhere else I'd rather be," I said. I needed to memorize him here, like this. Curled up in a position no one else would find comfortable, happier than I could make him out in the world.

"I'm sorry I won't be there tonight," he said.

"It's alright, even I'd rather be out in the city with General Turrek," I said. His eyebrows rose so high I couldn't see them under the messed hair covering his forehead. "It's true. He may be scary, but at least you won't have mother and Bastian breathing down your neck."

"Agree to disagree." He turned back to his book, once again drifting off into a fictional world. I opened my book but barely read a word, just stealing glances up at my brother and trying not to cry.

"Estyn?" he asked.

"Yes?"

"I have a question, but I don't know how to ask it." Calix often posed bizarre questions, usually without context, so this had to be serious. Had he found out about my escape? Was he going to ask to eat breakfast together tomorrow? I didn't think I could hold it together if he did.

"Ask away," I said, looking back down at my book.

"Are you okay?" His green eyes swam with concern, bearing his emotion for me to see and feel for him, just like always. I tried to memorize them, from the wave of dark green marring his left iris to the curl of his lashes that made him look years younger than he was; I memorized the quirk of his lip, the nick in his nose from when one of Bastian's wolves had pounced on him as a kid, the way his right ear stuck out a little more than the other. I wanted to remember him just like this, remember us like this.

I wasn't okay. I wasn't sure if I ever would be, but I had to try.

"Of course, why would you ask that?"

"Just wondering," he simply said, though I could tell he didn't believe me.

"Are *you* okay?" I asked, needing to know for my own sanity's sake. I doubted he'd answer as seriously as I meant it, but I needed the reassurance nevertheless.

"Yeah, of course," he said.

"How about happy? Are you happy?" I asked.

"Yes, I'm happy." He smiled at me, and I wanted to memorize that look. *I can't wait for you to meet Walcott,* his voice said in my mind, and tears threatened my eyes. So that was the Summer enchanter's name: Walcott. I wanted to tell him I'd love to meet him, that I was sorry I never would, but it wasn't worth tainting the short time we had left together.

"Okay, good," I said, in place of everything else I wanted to say. He turned back to his book, his way of ending the conversation. I lingered, looking at him while he read for a minute. At first his expression was troubled, but it soothed as soon as he got back into the steady rhythm of reading.

Mother would be expecting me now. We only had four hours until the ball began, after all, barely enough time to paint a single nail. So despite every beat of my heart begging me not to, I got up. I looked at him one last time, at the mop of black hair I'd recognize better than my own, and I didn't even think about how if I was just imagining things, I wouldn't have known Walcott's name.

CHAPTER

6

The two doors to the ballroom's grand staircase towered ominously over me. My ladies in waiting fussed over my hair, tucking tiny flowers into the folds of the plait. They had tinted my cheeks with rouge and highlighted the freckles dusting my nose and cheeks. I had one of the family's tiaras wrapped into my hair, a small gold piece set with blue topaz to match my dress.

The gown was my favorite one I'd worn yet; it had flowers embroidered over the top layer of fabric, winding up the bodice and into the thin straps. It was more revealing than what I'd been allowed to wear in the past, but that was expected given that tonight I was to be paraded around. Festivities had started an hour ago, but I was not allowed to join until my mother announced me, which she'd do whenever maximized the drama.

"It's time." She fluffed my skirt in the back as she prepared me for my, or rather her, entrance.

The Queen stepped out onto the landing, commanding the attention of the room. The music stalled, and all eyes snapped to where she stood.

"Thank you all for coming this evening, to not only honor the gods, but to celebrate my daughters' Veirden." She paused for effect and the crowd applauded in response.

"Good luck to all of the suitors. I could not be more excited to welcome a new member to the royal family this Winter Solstice." More applause ensued. In looking out at the crowd, I had the unfortunate displeasure of catching Lord Ramos' gaze. I looked away as quickly as I could, but not fast enough to miss his wink. I felt his gaze searing into my skin like a brand. She kept talking, but I tuned it out, staring intently at a single flower on my dress. Maybe I should just run away now.

I was sinking into a daydream of bursting through the courtyard doors and sprinting as far as my feet would take me when something brushed my ankle under my skirts. I shook my foot to dispel it. This was the worst possible time for my mind to play tricks on me.

"Please welcome Princess Estyn Lamoret of Tenebris." On cue, as we had practiced several times before, I stepped onto the top balcony of the ballroom. The crowd erupted in applause as I descended the stairs, chin high and posture erect. I saw something flicker in my mother's eyes— approval, perhaps? Maybe it was just surprise that I wasn't messing it up. As I reached the handrail beside my mother, the crowd quieted and waited.

The nobles looked dazzling as ever. Female enchanters wore unbelievable dresses; gowns woven of living, shifting vines, bodices constructed of colored ice reminiscent of stained glass, trains burning with heatless purple fire that brushed against others without consequence. My gown was beautiful, but it felt pale in comparison.

I froze for a moment, my eye catching on a man leaning against a column in the back, running a hand through hair so blond it almost looked white. The corner of his mouth lifted in an amused smirk as our eyes met, and I must have been mistaken, but I thought I saw him wink. I broke his gaze, looked at the crowd, and realized I had held the silence for too long.

"Let the festivities begin!" I announced, forgetting my speech entirely. Music and chatter erupted from the silence and couples made their way to the dance floor. My mother leaned in to say something, and I don't know why, but I let myself hope it would be complimentary.

"What happened to your speech? And next time, hold the silence longer. And don't fidget. You looked weak."

I simply nodded, taking her criticism. I couldn't risk fighting her on anything tonight.

As I walked into the crowd, thoughts bombarded me. My head spun, and I struggled to find my own train of thought in the mess. I wanted to collapse, to cover my ears and scream to drown them out, but I couldn't.

It felt like trying to dam a river with sticks. A few words rose above the rest, nearly intelligible. Trying to make them out felt like holding water in my cupped palms, draining right before I got anywhere.

A comforting hand rested on the small of my back and my skin electrified at the contact.

Estyn, I heard in my mind, clear and enunciated above the thrum. The voice felt comforting, but it wasn't one I knew.

I blinked my eyes open, suddenly realizing they'd been

closed. The blond man stood in front of me, one hand wrapped around my back in a gesture much too familiar for strangers. I stepped back, looking around to see if anyone had seen us. Now, more than ever, was the time for propriety.

"Relax, princess," he said, his warm baritone washing over me.

"Who are you?" I asked, perhaps too abruptly. Everything about him was throwing me off.

"We'll get to know one another soon enough," he said with a smile that spelled trouble, raising his glass to me. I opened my mouth to speak, but he had already disappeared into the crowd.

All the people I saw seemed to be enjoying the party, most in varying degrees of inebriation. Young women glided across the dance floor, twirling at their partners' direction. Groups crowded by the food, gushing over the rare delicacies only seen at solstice balls. Calliope was nowhere to be found, busy preparing for our escape.

My gaze caught on Ryker standing in front of one of the columns. He smiled at me, but I just glared back. He had the gall to look confused.

The bastard.

I needed to move on anyway—I'd already gotten what I needed from him. My only regret was that he'd never know I discovered his betrayal; that he'd go on thinking I was blissfully ignorant. I hated giving him that satisfaction.

"Good evening, Princess," Olyn said with a small bow, drawing my attention back to the party around me. He was almost unrecognizable from the scrappy enchanter I'd seen in the ring. A dark navy suit hugged his frame, which looked far more imposing now that he wasn't beside another hulking figure.

"Good evening to you as well." I curtsied and bowed my head slightly, looking up at him through my lashes. Like all enchanters, he was beautiful. His eyes flared blue, a display of his Winter enchanting power.

"My name is Olyn. It is an honor to meet you."

"The honor is mine, Olyn."

"May I have this dance?" His outstretched hand trembled slightly with nerves, but he also had an air of confidence about him. On anyone else, it might border on irritating, but I found it endearing.

Bastian and my mother hated that he'd made it past the qualifying rounds. Naturally, it would be endlessly satisfying to give him the first dance.

"It would be my pleasure." I placed my hand in his and let him lead me to the dance floor.

He placed his hand tastefully at my waist and lifted our hands to shoulder level. The music began, a classic waltz that allowed for casual conversation.

"So, Princess, how are you enjoying the ball?"

"It's been wonderful so far. And you?"

"I've never been a huge fan of large crowds, but I do so enjoy the berry tartlets. Makes it all worth it." He smiled wide, breaking the traditional restrained expressions reserved for court affairs.

"I have to agree, I've never been a fan of schmoozing." If only my mother heard me. She would be appalled. He laughed openly, his joy contagious, and I smiled despite myself.

"Look at the buffet, there's a world-class schmoozer," he teased. I tried to peek over his shoulder, but he was too tall.

"I can't see, you'll have to spin me around." He spun me

so gracefully that I felt weightless, until I saw who he referred to. Bastian reclined against a table, charming a group of young women encircling him.

Olyn's brows furrowed in concern. "Is something wrong?" He asked. I quietly cursed how transparent my emotions were, then schooled my face into a pleasant smile.

"It's nothing," I deflected. "You're right, he is quite the charmer."

"Are you two close?" I studied his expression, looking for a hint of ulterior motive, but he seemed genuine.

"Not particularly. He's awfully busy shadowing the King." *Not to mention the fact he's an ass.* I looked over to where the circle of women were swooning over Bastian, laughing at a sorry excuse for a joke. He leaned in to the closest woman and whispered something in her ear before leading her away from the crowd. Poor girl. I almost forgot Olyn spinning me around the dance floor until he spoke again.

"You don't approve?" It was asked as a question, but it was more of a statement. Olyn was observant.

"I'm not in a place to approve or condemn any of his actions."

"That doesn't mean you don't have an opinion." I liked Olyn; most people wouldn't dare be so blunt. I smiled, but it didn't reach my eyes.

"I suppose you're right." Something about him made me want to continue, to divulge my true thoughts on the matter, but I stopped just in time. The music faded out and Olyn released me, bowing slightly.

"It was truly a pleasure meeting you, Estyn."

"Till we meet again." He melted into the crowd, lost among the masses. It wasn't until he was out of sight that I realized he hadn't used my title.

Four enchanters descended around me, eager for a dance. None of them were unbearable, but none remarkable either. I couldn't stop thinking about the blond man I'd seen. Who was he? What had he meant? He must be from another city, potentially a suitor's brother.

Though his eyes were not an enchanting color, they were mesmerizing; a sky blue with a gold ring around the pupil. I'd never seen anything like them. I found myself scanning the faces in the crowd, trying to find his. Every time I drifted towards Ryker, I averted my gaze. I couldn't think about his betrayal tonight.

I thanked my current partner and waved off the rest, finally getting the reprieve I needed. I grabbed a glass of wine off the nearest tray and drifted to the windows. Revelers wandered in the courtyard, illuminated by torches lining the shrubs. The ballroom was bright, almost suffocating in light, but the courtyard looked rife with mischief and fun.

Of course that's where I'd rather be.

I looked around, trying to find the blond man I had spotted earlier, but to no avail. I did recognize one man in the crowd: Walcott, Calix's Summer enchanter. Intrigued, I wandered to where he stood on the perimeter, quietly observing the festivities. The next dance began and couples floated around the room in sync, their shadows stretching over the cobblestones outside.

"You don't want to dance?" I asked.

"It's not that I don't want to; I just don't think there's any woman willing to be tripped across the floor tonight." He smiled and I instantly felt warmer. Calix had captured him perfectly. Even without knowing him, we stood in comfortable silence.

All enchanters were beautiful, but he was quietly so. Burnt

orange flecks edged his iris, speckling the Summer enchanter orange. Tight dark curls framed his face, slightly disheveled, which was all the more endearing. A few burn scars peeked out from his collar, marring his otherwise flawless dark skin. His injuries must have been considerable to cause scars, given that he had magic to help him heal.

I debated asking about Calix, tooling over the wording so much it sounded strange in my own head. All of my ideas, like "take care of him for me" or "please make him happy," sounded strange and ominous. If Calix had wanted me to know, he would've told me. So I settled into the comfortable silence for the rest of the song, hoping that would be message enough.

At the end of the song, Walcott turned to me and smiled. "It was lovely to finally meet you, Princess," he said with a bow before drifting back inside.

I walked towards the fountain, head turning to each person that looked reminiscent of the mystery man.

"Looking for someone?" I heard a soft, playful voice whisper behind me. I spun around to face the blond man I'd been looking for.

"No," I insisted, ignoring my heart beating out of my chest. I couldn't decide whether the adrenaline was from fear or excitement, but either way he set me on edge.

"How's your evening?" he asked, eyes lazily examining me, making me feel more seen than I had all night.

"It's been lovely," I lied, realizing how much of my attention had been occupied searching for him. Now that he was in front of me, I forgot why I wanted to find him in the first place.

"You look awfully bored for someone having a 'lovely' night," he quipped, making me drop my carefully curated smile.

"I'm tired, not bored," I protested. Who was he to think he knew me?

"Your face says otherwise. I'm willing to bet you'd get into some good trouble if given the chance." He smirked, eyes dark and taunting as he sipped his wine.

I opened my mouth to tell him exactly what I thought of him, but was stopped short as Bastian sauntered up, hair tousled from what I assumed was his dalliance in the bathroom.

"Dearest sister, are you trying to make a fool of our family?" I turned back to look at my nameless companion for help, but he was gone. I sighed.

"No, but if I embarrass you that's a bonus."

"The entire purpose of tonight is for you to choose a suitor, and yet you have yet to dance with anyone of importance—is this another act of rebellion?"

"I hardly think you're entitled to determine who is and isn't important," I said, which was apparently a poor choice given the clenching of Bastian's jaw. His hand shot out to grasp my wrist, gripping so tight that I winced and tried to pull away.

"You'll never please a husband with a mouth like that," he said, lowering his voice so that only I could hear. "I told several suitable partners that you're interested, so behave yourself for the next few dances." He threw my wrist down, and the cool night air washed over my skin, easing the pain of his hold.

"I always do." I flashed a saccharine smile I was sure would earn me another strike, just to find one of the aforementioned partners standing behind me.

"Pardon me, Prince Bastian, but I was hoping to ask the

Princess for a dance."

"She would love that," drawled Bastian, practically throwing me into his arms.

For the next hour I was passed from partner to partner, making mindless small-talk. I was just thanking the gods that I'd been able to avoid Lord Ramos.

Once I finally had a break between songs, I grabbed a plate of food and began walking toward the head table. I wove between noble enchanters, all several spirits in and sloppy as they danced and drank. When I finally emerged, shocked I was able to keep all my food on the plate and off my dress, I stopped short. Lord Ramos sat across from the King, in Calix's chair beside mine.

I only had a few moments before my mother turned and noticed me, but I didn't move fast enough. Lord Ramos saw me.

He excused himself and began making his way over. I needed to get out and my brain was foggy from the wine and Ryker was near, so I did something stupid. I walked over to Ryker, feeling warm and loose and ready to give him a piece of my mind.

"Do you want to get out of here?" he asked, stopping me in my tracks.

"We need to talk," I said.

"I agree," he said placatingly, taking my hand and leading me to the courtyard.

He held onto my hand as we exited the ballroom, not letting go even as we crossed the courtyard and entered the maze. We kept walking until the music became a distant hum.

"You lied." I said before I could think better of it, sounding more hurt than angry. He spun around, puzzling over what I meant. He still assumed I was blissfully unaware.

"I trusted you." I ripped my hand away and put a few feet of space between us.

"You can still trust me," he said, stepping forward. I stepped back.

"I thought—I thought we were friends." I hated the tears brimming in my eyes, I hated how he looked so sympathetic, and most of all I hated how I didn't hate him.

"We are friends. Please Estyn, just let me explain—"

"Why is now any different? You've been lying to me for weeks, and all of a sudden you want to explain?"

"I didn't know you were mad at me."

"I'm not mad. I'd be mad if I cared, but I don't." I turned around to leave, but he caught my arm.

"What are you talking about?" If I were more optimistic, more gullible, then I might have believed him. But I knew better. He was every bit the scheming military man Calliope said he was, and now he was digging, finding out what I knew so he'd know the perfect thing to say.

"You know—" I started, but I felt someone watching us. I spun around to find two men approaching.

There was the blond man, and accompanying him was one of my suitors—Olyn.

"Shit," Ryker muttered under his breath.

I glanced back at Ryker, silently asking him to turn them away, but he didn't look at me. He watched them, observing their body language and reading their intentions before they opened their mouths.

"Princess," the blond man purred, kissing the back of my hand.

"And you are?" I asked in my second attempt to get his name tonight.

Azden. His voice echoed in my head before he could

answer aloud. The name was familiar, but I was sure we hadn't met before.

"Zave," he supplied out loud, lying effortlessly, before turning to Ryker. "And your name?"

"Ryker."

"Could I get a moment with the Princess, Ryker?" Azden asked with a charming smile.

There was no way Ryker would say yes. For one, I was the Princess, and even though he was not *my* guard, he was still sworn to protect me. Two, we did not know these people, and were something to happen, there would be no one to hear my screams.

"Of course," Ryker said.

I looked at him, eyes pleading to take me with him, to give me an excuse, but he just slipped away without further comment.

I watched Ryker disappear into the hedges, leaving me to the whims of two strangers.

"So, Princess, can you tell me about these voices you've been hearing?" Azden drawled.

I blanched, backing up until my legs hit the brush. Shadows swirled around my feet, wrapping them in warm depths, fiercer than the previous strokes. They purred to me, asking to do more, to swallow me whole.

"I don't know what you're talking about," I said, but my voice wavered. They had me pinned. Olyn just stood with his arms crossed, a few feet behind Azden, who was idly twirling a ring around his finger. They both looked at my feet, where the shadows I'd been imagining were twirling up my calves.

"So she has shadows too," Azden said to Olyn, ignoring me entirely. They lurched higher in response.

"Tell me, what am I thinking?" Azden coaxed. I searched

frantically from him to Olyn, looking for an out, for anything. How did they know about the voices? I didn't even know. *No one* knew.

Besides, it wasn't like I could control it. The voices were my own imagination, only bad now that I didn't have my medication.

"I can't," I said, this time with more conviction.

"Interesting," he mused, studying me with such intensity I swore he could see through my dress. I cowered against the bush, wishing Calix were here to wrap the branches around me and swallow me into safety.

Brambles scratched at my back, a cold reminder of reality. Judging by the way Azden was studying me, I doubted the scratches would matter in a minute.

"We're not going to hurt you," Azden said, seeming to pick up on my thoughts.

"Somehow I don't believe you," I seethed, glowering at him. I hoped I looked fierce, but my hands shook in fear.

"We're here to help you," he said, face softening as he stepped forward, reaching a hand towards mine—or to the shadows twirling around it.

"I don't want your help," I spat. I didn't have many options and I'd have even fewer if I waited much longer, so I noted the small gap between Olyn and the nearest hedge and tensed my muscles and—

A bell echoed across the gardens.

One bell, then another, a steady succession of ominous tolls. Azden and Olyn glanced at one another, then to the wall.

The ceaseless ringing could only mean one thing.

Alynthia was here.

CHAPTER

7

I froze, my mind spinning in an endless pendulum of the past and present. First I was trapped in my bedroom, banging on the door, then back in the garden, trapped with two strangers.

Deep breath, I heard a voice think, swinging me back to the present. Azden's voice.

I reached for the dagger that I had sheathed to my thigh and ripped my skirt off to reveal the leggings I wore underneath. Azden and Olyn jerked back to me, faces wide with surprise.

I took the opening, spun out and sprinted for the wall. Only once I reached the first turn did I dare a glance back, but they had disappeared.

Calix was in the city shadowing a general. I was going to find him.

The bells were deafening, drowning out the sounds of

hundreds of gentry pouring into the safety of the castle's walls. I was swimming upstream, fighting against the hoard of nobility fleeing to the castle.

I finally broke from the mob into the empty copse of trees lining the wall. The enchanters had already been dispatched into the city, leaving only gentry and guards inside the castle walls.

I found the closest door, throwing it open and racing up the stairs until I stood among the archers at the top of the wall. No one saw me since I came from inside, their attention fully trained on the Alynthian soldiers swarming the city. I snuck forward until I could peek over the edge.

It was a bloodbath. Bodies lined the streets. The arrows raining down from the castle did not discriminate against Alynthian or Tenebren, striking anyone in range. The majority of the Alynthians' force were still several blocks from the castle, but they were covering ground quickly. Screams rang out from every direction as innocent citizens were pierced by the Alynthians' swords. My stomach threatened to empty over the wall, but I swallowed my own revulsion as I scanned the streets for Calix.

I finally spotted him in the main square, surrounded by a group of Alynthians. He had four enchanters beside him, but they were fighting a losing battle. Another Alynthian unit that outnumbered them ten to one was heading straight for them.

I didn't pause to think. I took the steps in twos until my feet pounded cobblestones after the stairs, moving as fast as I could without tripping over the bodies that were strewn on the street. I only stopped to grab the sword of a fallen soldier, the cleanest one I could find. It was still dripping in blood. I'd never been allowed to wield one before, but it couldn't be that different from my dagger…I hoped.

The blade was clumsy in my grip as I ran down the street. I passed an Alynthian who swung at me, but I jumped out of the way, accidentally catching his leg with my blade. Blood spurted out of his thigh, but I continued pounding my feet to the pavement, looking down alleyways to check if Calix had moved.

Two more blocks. I was moving so fast that the buildings blurred beside me.

A body slammed into me, almost knocking me to the ground. I stared into the face of an Alynthian soldier. She called behind her, "It's a *lady*."

Five more soldiers followed behind, emerging from an adjoining alley and backing me into the wall behind. My mind raced, looking for any escape. I was surrounded. A windowsill hung to my left, but there was no way I could jump to reach it without getting stabbed. There was no one around to see my death, no one to even try and protect me. They didn't recognize that I was the Princess. I didn't think they would; no one would dare to think that I was out of the castle, fighting amongst the civilians. This was it. I was going to die.

Thoughts ascended above my panic, clear as my own.

Curse Tenebris. Curse Alynthia. Curse it all.

Oh gods, I don't want to do this.

I faltered, hearing fear that mirrored my own. They closed in around me, swords pointing at my chest.

"Any last words?" The woman who caught me asked. I wouldn't stand a chance in a fight. I turned the sword over in my grip, coming up with a stupid and dangerous plan, but the only one that gave me any shot.

I'm sorry. I thought, directed at the girl closest to the wall.

My sword flew towards her, clumsy and with the blade pointing away, but enough of a distraction for her to jump back. My muscles moved on instinct, latching onto a crack in the stones. I climbed, forgetting every tip and trick and simply scampering up each foot with adrenaline fueling every lift.

Only a few stones separated me from the nearest balcony, so I reached up with one arm, grabbed onto the rail, and hoisted myself up. A dagger flew by my head, embedding itself in the wall next to me.

Curses rang out as I opened the door. I risked looking down for a moment to see the girl unharmed, looking almost relieved.

Inside, the apartment appeared to be empty. I hoped that the tenants had found good hiding spots; I didn't want to think about the alternative. I ignored the family portraits as I ran down the hall, opened the door, and burst into the stairwell.

As the shouts grew louder with my descent, I realized I'd never be able to fight my way through several blocks of chaos. I looked up the stairs spiraling towards the flat roof.

I took them two at a time until I emerged onto the flat pebbled roof underneath the eerie moonlight. The stench of blood and sweat choked my senses. I had no time to waste.

I ran across the roof, crossing to the next building and the next, grateful that the city planning left no gaps between the buildings. Down below, Alynthian soldiers ran in the same direction as me. Were they going to Calix as well? If they were, I had no chance. I still had to try.

Because the roofs were clear, I outpaced the herd of soldiers below, but it didn't matter. There were no Alynthian soldiers left. They had all turned, running back to the docks.

Leaving devastation in their wake.

The square was littered with bodies. The cobblestones were all stained red, and I spotted many of Calix's personal guards. I found the stairs and ran, the walls blurring as I nearly slipped down the flights.

When I emerged back into the night, I almost tripped. A body had been flung against the wall, legs splayed out awkwardly. I made my way towards the ships, stepping on the small patches of exposed ground until I crested the hill and got a clear view of the harbor.

Despite the masses of people, the frenzy of soldiers boarding and fending off our enchanters, I spotted Calix. He was slung over the shoulder of a soldier twice his size, knocked unconscious with his hands bound and mouth gagged. I stifled a sob, my knees crashing to the pavement, barely registering the reverberation through my bones.

My legs begged me to run to him, army of soldiers or not, but I couldn't. Our enchanters hadn't even stood a chance. Despite all our focus on training, on developing the best army in the world, we were losing.

I just watched from a distance as he was carried across the dock, up a ramp and onto the enemy's ship. I felt shadows swallowing my legs, begging to be let loose, to wreak havoc on them. *No*, I thought. *Not yet.*

Through my cloud of pain and fear was something stronger: anger. They would pay. I was going to save Calix, and they would be sorry they ever came.

I stayed glued to the cobblestones until the last ship sailed into the distance. The air felt heavier, burdened with loss and carnage, but I refused to look. I just kept my gaze on the horizon, on the sea that carried the best thing this world had to offer far, far away from me.

I ignored the wetness on my hand as I planted it on the cobblestones and got my feet under me once again. One more breath gave me the strength to tear my gaze from the ghost of Calix's presence.

Bodies slumped against the buildings, blood was splattered on shattered storefronts. A few heads peeked out from behind furniture, hazarding a glance into the street. When they realized it was empty, they stepped out, taking in the horror before them.

I didn't stay long. I dragged myself back through the city, back to the wall. I don't know how, but no one spared me a glance as I crossed the top, descending the stairs to deafeningly quiet castle grounds. I walked to the wall below my bedroom. I forced myself to climb, to break the glass and reach in to unlock my door. I glanced at myself in the mirror, at the blood splattered across my cheek and on my ripped dress. The flowers in my hair had been crushed. I laughed, a dry, joyless sound, as I ripped them out.

They'd be looking for me. I knew that. But they would have checked my room by now, so I had a little time.

I grabbed my sack Calliope and I had packed. I needed to figure out a way to find her, to tell her what happened, the change of plans. But I didn't know where she was. I hoped she was safe in the castle, but even then, there was little chance she'd be able to escape unnoticed, and it was even less likely I'd be able to go in and get her.

I clenched the pack strap like it could bring her to me, but it couldn't. Either she'd be at the docks like we planned or she wouldn't. There was nothing I could do at this point.

I ran a washcloth over my skin, roughly cleaning up before changing into pants and a simple tunic. I ripped out the pins still in my hair, letting them clatter to the floor, and wove it into a simple plait. I moved, but it felt like someone else. My mind was elsewhere.

What would they do with him? Bargain with him? What would our parents do *for* him? What happened to someone when they were caught in the middle of a war?

I looked back at the room I'd grown up in, ensuring I wasn't leaving anything important. Turns out I didn't care about any of it at the end of the day.

The cool night air washed over me once again, redolent of the cherry trees outside my balcony. How was that fair when the city streets hung heavy with the stench of the attack?

I was swinging my leg over the banister when I heard the door open.

"Estyn?" A voice called, warm and rough and terrifying.

I scrambled over the rail, clutching the stones as I climbed down. I prayed he wouldn't come out to the balcony, but there was no way he would miss the smashed glass.

Ryker's head appeared over the rail, spotting me halfway to the ground.

"What are you doing? You need to get back inside," he ordered, sounding panicked and concerned and entirely unlike Ryker. I couldn't risk stalling any longer, so I jumped the last stretch to the ground, crashing down onto my hands and knees. I dared one glance up as I stood, finding Ryker shaking his head before swinging himself off of the balcony.

I sprinted towards the wall, going as fast as my legs would take me. It wasn't fast enough. There was no way I'd outpace him.

I kept running, even after I heard his footfall pound behind me, nearing with each step. The trees grew thicker and I wove through them, hoping I'd throw him off. I was veering to the right when my arm jerked back, caught by

Ryker's hand. I twisted out of his grip, a maneuver he taught me, before swinging my leg around to his knees.

He grabbed my ankle with deadly accuracy, yanking it towards him. I stumbled forward, crashing into his chest. He grabbed my wrists, holding them against my back and pulling me close until my front was flush with his. I felt his hot breath on my forehead as he glared down at me.

"There are a lot of people looking for you," he said. I wriggled to free myself but only managed to make Ryker tighten his hold.

"Then you should tell them I'll be fine. I have to go." I jerked my knee up, ready to catch him where it hurt, but he thrust his thigh between mine to stop me.

"And where do you think you're going?" He pressed his lips into a thin line, the stupid stoic expression of all the guards here. I hated him. I wanted to kill him for holding me back, for risking my chance at saving Calix.

"They took Calix," I said. At least my voice didn't betray my fear. Ryker eased his grip slightly, but not enough for me to escape.

"Oh," he said, face softening. "I'm sorry." I didn't want his pity.

"Don't act like you care," I spat, digging my nails into the palms of his hands. It felt good to hurt. I wanted him to hurt as much as I did. "Now let go of me."

I was prepared to twist away, maybe even bite him, but he let go. I was so shocked it took me a second to move.

"I'm coming with you," he said, leading the way to the wall.

"Like hell you are," I shouted at his back. I grabbed his arm, spinning him around to face me. "I don't need one of my father's spies following me. Go home, Ryker."

"I can't let you go alone," he said, his eyes offering no room for argument. I noted he didn't deny my accusation.

"I don't want you to come."

"Well then I guess we're at an impasse." Ryker crossed his arms, and stood with the full intimidating guard effect. It wouldn't work. I held his gaze with as much anger and hatred as I felt, hoping he'd just give up, but if my animosity affected him, he didn't show it.

"You're not coming," I declared, stomping off toward the wall. I tried to ignore the crunch of leaves as he followed. I wished I could slam the wall door shut behind me, lock him out, but I couldn't. I still needed to get into the city undetected, which was even more of a gamble with Ryker in tow.

I peeked around the threshold, spotting three sentinels huddled nearby. If I timed it right, I could sprint across when they weren't looking.

Ryker shouldered past me, opening the door with no caution. So this was it. Tricked, again.

The guards spun to him, lifting their swords until they saw his uniform.

"Sir," they said, lowering their heads. I pulled my hood tight over my face, hiding behind his back.

"Get back to work," Ryker barked. He sounded like a natural. How could I have ever thought he was anything but a soldier? We descended into the city without any further questioning.

"I would have been fine," I muttered. His scoff echoed off the damp stone stairs as we exited into the city.

The buildings closest to the wall had already been sprayed clean in the hour since the attack, debris swept from the walkways, bodies removed to soften the gory reality for the rich.

We walked in silence for a few blocks. As we got further from the castle, the cleanup was sloppier. Blood still stained the cobblestones, and storefronts had shattered glass and broken doors. I wondered how many of them didn't have an owner to return and fix them. My heart sank with the thought of how many people died, both those trying to protect our cities and the innocent bystanders.

"Why are you mad at me?" Ryker asked, cutting through the heavy silence.

"I'm not," I whispered, not caring whether he could hear or not.

"Convincing."

"It's true—you behaved just like the soldier I knew you were. I was the idiot who wanted to believe better." I walked a little faster, always keeping just enough distance to prevent conversation. Ryker didn't speak again.

We neared the docks and I ducked into an alley, pulling Ryker to me. I peered around to where the ships were tied up. Only a few people were on duty, which was good for us. We were getting to the parts of the plan that I didn't have quite as many details on.

"Okay, do you see that ship?" I pointed to a large merchant ship flying the Braiwyth crest, Alynthia's neighboring kingdom. He nodded. "We're getting on it. Got it?"

"How do you plan on sneaking past the guards?"

"We're going to be the cargo." Ryker looked at me like I was crazy. "It'll be easy enough. We just need to find a partially empty crate. They've already filled them and are just going to load them onto the ship tomorrow."

His mouth formed a line as he nodded slowly. "So… we're

going to die."

"Don't be ridiculous. We're not going to die. Calliope and I planned this."

"Calliope?" he asked, and I realized he didn't even know about my best friend. He didn't deserve to know.

I dashed out towards the crates, ducking behind one. A guard stood in front of the crates, looking out to the main street, but I was hidden in the shadows of the towers. I pulled my dagger from its sheath and pried the first lid off. It was full. I pressed the lid back into place and moved to the next one.

I checked a few more until I found one that was nearly empty. I glanced back to wave Ryker on, but he wasn't waiting in the alley.

He was walking in the middle of the street, straight for the ship. I cursed under my breath, shoved my dagger back into my boot, and grabbed a cap to tuck my braid into. It wasn't a great disguise, but I had to hope the night was dark enough to hide my face. Ryker was walking slowly enough that I caught up with a quick jog.

What the fuck? I thought at him, hoping it was laced with as much anger as I felt. He looked at me, a little shocked, but brushed it off, maintaining his purposeful gait as we approached.

Had he heard that? There was no way.

As we edged closer and closer to the ship, my mind spun, trying to come up with a backup plan. They could see us coming; we needed a good excuse, and fast.

"Gentlemen. What are you doing out this late?" one of the sailors asked.

Ryker answered before I got the chance to.

"Captain Lydan requested we secure his cargo before

loading commences tomorrow." The guards looked at one another. We were doomed. My stomach flipped over itself. How embarrassing would it be to fail before I even left Tenebris? Stupid Ryker. It was all his fault.

"Very well." They nodded to us, and stepped aside to let us board. I walked behind Ryker, looking to the ground so that my face was as covered as possible.

I blindly followed Ryker deeper and deeper into the ship. He checked several doors, closing each one.

"What are we looking for?" I whispered, barely audible over the water lapping at the hull.

"A false closet."

"How do you know there's going to be one?"

"They're on every ship. How else do you think people leave Tenebris?"

"No one wants to leave Tenebris," I said reflexively. Well, no one except Calliope and me.

"You don't really believe that, do you?"

"Well, I don't know, I mean…" I drifted off as Ryker finally opened a door to what looked like a cleaning closet. He pressed the back wall and it gave, opening to a small chamber behind. It was barely big enough for one to fit comfortably, let alone both of us, but it's not like we had any other choice.

Ryker gestured for me to climb in, and I stepped over the mops and squatted behind the false back. Ryker climbed in after me, shutting the closet door after himself.

"Scoot up," he said. I inched forward a little, my back no longer resting against the wall. Ryker eased down behind me, wrapping his legs around mine. I tried to put space between us, but we were cramped against the wall, bending our legs to fit in the width of the closet. He replaced the false back, blocking off the small flicker of light that had come in under the closet door. It was pitch black, forcing me to focus on my other senses, like how Ryker's chest felt as it rose and fell against my back. I sat up straighter.

"How did you know about all of this?" I whispered. The ship was still nearly empty, but it felt wrong to speak at a normal volume in the dark.

"It's pretty well-known that Lydan's real main export is of a more… illicit nature, so it wouldn't be unexpected for him to have people come and go during the night." What did he mean by well-known? I didn't know anyone in the castle that knew of that. Then again, I didn't know much about what people in the castle did or didn't know.

"Why are you doing this?" I asked, so quietly it could barely be heard over the crash of the waves. If he was doing his job, he would have stopped me before we got this far. *That's what he does*, I reminded myself. His job. *He's probably doing it right now*, I thought. *He'll go tell my father all about this as soon as we're done.*

"I promised I'd help you." It was so quiet that I could have misheard him. I didn't have the energy to keep questioning his motivations, so I didn't respond. I just leaned forward, bracing my head in my hands and loathing every place the small confines of this room forced us to touch. My mind flashed images of Calix's limp figure slung over a shoulder, of blood in the streets, of my last conversation with Calliope, but soon enough exhaustion pulled me into a fitful, restless sleep.

And just before I faded into unconsciousness, I heard Ryker's voice in my head whispering words that changed nothing. *I'm sorry, Estyn.*

CHAPTER

8

I jerked awake soaked in sweat, my throat as raw as if I had been choking. Ryker stirred behind me, gently tugging me back with the arm he had wrapped around my waist.

"What is it?" he whispered.

"Just a bad dream. Nothing to worry about." I held tight onto his arms around me, grounding myself. Calix would be okay. He was alive. He had to be alive.

My mind buzzed with a background hum of voices, gruff and crass and undoubtedly belonging to sailors. I reached for my bag to find my medication, but as I rooted around, all I grasped was fabric.

"No, no, no no no." I scrambled, nearly dumping it out, but Ryker tightened his arm and shushed me. He squeezed my wrist once, as if asking what was wrong. I couldn't tell him. He'd take me back.

Like a cruel joke, I remembered my stocked medicine

tucked into the back of a drawer in stark detail. All the way back in Artange.

"I'm fine," I choked out. It didn't convince either of us. My heart beat through my back and into his chest, and Ryker just held tight.

I didn't know what would happen if I stopped taking it. Half the dose and I was already imagining shadows and hearing voices, but taking none at all?

I might die.

Boards creaked just outside the closet and we both held our breath as the closet door opened. Seconds stretched into minutes as a sailor rooted around for a mop, finally finding it and closing the door once again.

We couldn't risk talking anymore.

I didn't sleep again. I couldn't do anything but sit up, frozen in fear. Luckily the journey was short, only lasting the better part of a day. I got lost in my thoughts, zoning out to the lull of the ship rocking and the quiet rhythm of Ryker's breathing.

What was he thinking? What we were doing now amounted to treason, and we both knew how my father handled that. Stowing away the princess, smuggling her across the sea. No matter that it was my idea, if he was discovered and tried for his crimes, he would be spared no mercy.

My skin tingled every place it pressed against his, begging me to run, to get far away from this person whose motives were muddled and loyalties were not to me.

Maybe he wanted to be the one to save Calix. If he rescued Calix before the army, he would be lauded for his bravery. He would earn medals of valor, possibly even a court position.

That must be it. I'm inconsequential, just as I was before. I'm the means to an end.

But if that was true, why did he let me come along? A bartering tactic? How would I fit into his plot?

I won't, I promised myself. I wouldn't be a pawn. I'd use Ryker just as he used me, then leave when I was sure I could rescue Calix myself.

If I could get to him before my illness got me. Calliope had said we could find a healer, but now…

Was Calliope on this ship? I wished I'd had a way to warn her of the shipping containers, that they may be dangerous. Who knew if she even made it that far.

Goddess Nyx, please watch over Calliope, I prayed. Maybe she'd make it and we'd meet in the harbor. If I thought about it anymore, I knew I'd cry, so I forced myself to stop. Like that ever worked.

I had no way of knowing how much time passed. Ryker eventually awoke, and we sat in heavy silence. He stroked idle circles on my arm. I bristled but stayed silent.

I heard voices from outside, close to our level. I was nearly dying of boredom, but I was scared to leave. Was the rest of the world as bad as I had been taught? I doubted that, but maybe there was some truth to their stories.

I looked back at Ryker and made out the curves of his face. How long had he been staring at me? There was no way he could see anything.

Steps shuffled outside the closet, heading towards the exit. People passed for at least an hour, carrying crates off the ship. I wished I could see something, anything.

We waited until what must have been the middle of the night. The sounds outside had long since quieted, but I was hesitant to move. Ryker tapped my arm, nudging me to get up. He jimmied the fake wall loose and cracked open the door. He looked back, signaling that it was okay to leave. He walked into the hall and I followed closely. Were we going to just walk off?

"What's the plan now?" I asked.

"I should be asking you that."

"You're the expert," I said, admittedly a bit bitterly.

"I got us on the ship. It's your turn."

"Such great team spirit," I said sarcastically, then thrust out an arm in front of him. "Stop here." A few voices buzzed in my mind, but it was only a quiet hum. Were there still people around? That never happened when I was alone. I stopped, trying to formulate a plan. "Turn around."

"Why?" he asked, clearly not following my plan. That was only fair, as I left out approximately all of the details.

"Just trust me." He looked skeptical, but turned around. I grabbed my pack and quickly changed into the plain dress Calliope had given me. I wished I had a better idea, one that would leave the dress and my dignity intact, but I didn't. So I began paring down the fabric with my dagger, cutting the neckline lower and slicing a long slit over my right leg. I loosened my hair from its braid and let it hang around my shoulders.

"Okay, we can go," I said. Even in the dim light, I could see his eyes widen.

Stunning, Ryker's voice said in my head, the word drifting over to me above the rest. I wished I could turn it off. I wished the blond man hadn't made me wonder if the words were real.

"You need to stumble out as if you are drunk, and I am just one of the ladies brought for entertainment," I said.

"Yes, Princess," he said, eyes gleaming in delight. He

grabbed my pack and slung it over his shoulder, then grabbed onto my arm, stumbling as we walked. We walked down the ramp, and as expected there were guards waiting outside.

"My apologies, but it appears we lost track of time." I looked up at them with half-lidded eyes and a disarming smile.

Ryker fell forward and I pulled him back up with my arm. "I better find a hotel for this one." I laughed easily and winked, hoping they wouldn't notice anything amiss.

The guards nodded and the one closest bid us goodnight with a smile for me. We stumbled out into the night, wandering up towards the brilliant lights of the city. Even though it was late, the streets glittered with music and nightlife. I supposed this was what a city looked like when it wasn't at war.

I hadn't spent much time outside the castle in Tenebris, but from what I could tell this city was far better maintained than Artange. I'm not sure what I expected, but it wasn't the towering stone buildings that loomed before me.

Ryker leaned on me the entire way up the hill, holding on even after we were out of sight of the guards.

"You can let go now," I snapped, jerking my arm away.

"Apologies," he said, ducking his head in an almost shy gesture. It might have been endearing if he wasn't a backstabbing prick. I sped ahead, walking as fast as I could to civilization.

The street quickly transformed from a modest harbor into a delightful town. Buildings rose several stories into the air, not nearly as towering as those in Artange, but far more approachable. Nearly every facade seemed to be draped with greenery. Whether it be ivy crawling up the facades or flowers spilling from balconies, the entire area was touched by flora. Calix would love it.

I followed the music to a wide street lined with taverns and shops where people spilled out into the street, chatting, drinking, dancing. It was nothing like the solemn castle affairs; people laughed and moved with no rhyme or reason. They looked free.

There were several inns on every cross street, but they were all full. We walked until my feet tired, but I was grateful to stretch my legs after being crammed on the ship.

Ryker nodded to the left and I was so thankful to see a vacancy sign that I nearly spoke to him. Luckily I stopped myself before I could.

It was a small, cozy getaway nestled between shops on a quiet side street. The inside was decorated with dark mahogany furniture and tapestries covering every inch of wall, making the entire lobby feel like a warm hug. I stifled a yawn, wishing I could just curl up in one of the lobby chairs and fall asleep.

"I got it," Ryker said, walking ahead to the desk attendant. I followed a step behind.

"Good evening, sir," the woman greeted Ryker.

"Do you have a room?" Ryker leaned on the table, almost batting his lashes at the woman. She softened under his gaze. I gagged.

"Are you together?" she asked, looking between us.

"No," I answered before Ryker could interject, stepping aside.

"Okay, one room it is." She leaned over, pushing her cleavage out and practically throwing herself at him now that she knew he was available. I resisted rolling my eyes, instead looking out to the street. A few people strolled, some stumbling back to their rooms from the main strip, some just sneaking away from the bright lights for a moment alone.

Ryker finished at the desk and stepped aside with his key.

"May I also have a room?" I asked, hoping I sounded like I'd done this before.

"I'm sorry, but that was our last room," she said, not sounding sorry at all. Apparently the warm giggly voice was only reserved for Ryker.

I glared at Ryker but he just raised a single broken brow.

"I'm going somewhere else," I told him.

"Don't be ridiculous. None of the places we passed had any rooms." Ryker tugged on my arm and I jerked away. The woman at the desk was pretending to shuffle around papers as she watched our exchange.

"Fine," I said, my need for sleep outweighing my sense of propriety. I yanked the keys out of Ryker's hand and dragged myself up the stairs.

The room was quaint, with a single bed, a bathroom, and a small balcony. Ryker dropped my bag on the side table and sat on the edge of the bed, unlacing his boots. I merely stood frozen in the doorway. He looked so natural, completely at ease with sharing a bed with a woman. For all I knew he did this all the time.

I leaned down to pull off my boots, thankful for something to do with my hands. Why was I so nervous? I needed to get some sleep.

I edged closer to the bed and he lifted his shirt over his head, flinging it to his bag. His muscles rippled as he lowered his arms, revealing a long scar that extended from his collarbone down to his belly button. I tore my gaze away, but not before he noticed me staring.

"Are you going to get in bed?" he asked.

"Are you going to put on a shirt?" I countered, not moving from the threshold.

"My apologies, I didn't have time to pack a set of sleeping clothes when we fled from Tenebris," he deadpanned.

"We didn't flee."

"Close enough," he said, walking to the bathroom. His shoulders flexed as he opened the door, more defined than I thought muscles could be. My face burned, both embarrassed and infuriated. Who was he to complain after forcing himself onto *my* rescue mission? He didn't have to come. In fact, I'd explicitly asked him not to.

Shadows nipped at my legs, asking for permission to go to him. They swirled towards the bathroom, acting without my permission, finding the source of my anger.

"Stop it," I told them under my breath. They dissipated, but not before lingering, as if protesting. I stomped over to the bathroom to find Ryker splashing water on his face.

"If I recall correctly, I didn't ask you to come." I should've stopped there, but my anger had been brewing for so long I couldn't keep it in. "In fact, I didn't ask for any of this. I didn't need you to saunter into my life, throw off all my plans and force me to trust you. Was that always part of the plan? Get closer to me so you could feed information to my father? Get that promotion you've always been after? Huh?" Ryker lifted his face, bracing himself with both hands on the side of the wash basin.

"Well, congrats. You got it. You can go home now." I would have thrown him out myself if I could, but I settled for crossing my arms and demanding answers.

"It's not what you think," he said quietly. He looked remorseful, but he didn't deny my accusations.

"Then what is it like, Ryker?" I asked, wishing he had a better answer for me, a plausible explanation that I'd just failed to imagine. He turned around, finally looking me in the eye.

After a long, awkward pause, I assumed he wasn't going to respond. I turned to go to bed, to tell him it was fine, to pack my emotions away, to finally stop caring, but he grabbed my waist and spun me around, mere inches from his parted lips.

He still didn't say anything. He just looked down at me, conflicted. My head hurt, I was exhausted, and I was tired of arguing. I wanted to give in; to find comfort in his embrace. But it didn't change the fact that I didn't know this man, I didn't know if Calliope was dead or alive, and the only thing I *did* know was that Calix was in danger.

So I pushed him away and stormed out the door, slamming it behind me.

It was colder in Braiwyth. I wrapped my arms around my legs, hoping to save some warmth from escaping. I was balanced precariously on a roof's edge, perched with a perfect view of the docks. They wouldn't open the crates until morning, but they had already been unloaded and stacked by the ship. I didn't know what I was expecting; even if I watched all the crates all night, it wouldn't change whether Calliope had made it or not. If she had, she had probably already crawled out and was somewhere in the city. If she hadn't... well, I couldn't think about that right now.

Had she waited for me? She was a better friend than I; maybe she was still in Artange, searching for me.

I hadn't had time to get her, but I could have left a note, or at least tried, but then if someone found it—there was no good option.

Where is she? Ryker's voice thought in my mind. Was that really Ryker? The blond man had asked me to read his thoughts. Was I already doing it?

Either way, I didn't want to know what Ryker was thinking, and I definitely did not want him to find me.

A light breeze pushed me from behind, and I tilted forward slightly, leaning over to see the three-story drop. *I should really scoot back.*

But for some reason, sitting this close to the edge felt like the only thing keeping me from falling apart.

Something grasped my waist with a feather-light touch, pulling me back. I would have gasped if I hadn't looked down to see the now-familiar shadows tugging at me, asking me to back up. I didn't move, but they didn't let go either.

"Estyn?" Ryker called from the street, eerily similar to our first meeting.

I didn't say anything. I just sat and stared forward, refusing to tear my eyes from the crates.

"I'm coming up," he said, and in a few moments he was behind me, his presence filling the space and warming me without touch. I didn't turn around, but I felt him walk over, sit beside me, and dangle his legs over the edge.

We sat in silence for what felt like hours, yet in all that time the crates stayed still. No Calliope. I knew it was time to give up, but my body refused to move, glued to that spot like moving would be accepting defeat.

"It wasn't supposed to be like this," I whispered, my voice sounding as small and broken as I felt. Ryker looked over, watching the silent tears slide down my cheeks.

"Like what?" he asked.

"If I tell you, you'll just turn around and report to my

father," I said with dry laughter, rubbing my eyes. The shadows tightened their grip as if the slight movement would tip me over.

"Estyn," he said, "I don't know what you're thinking or what you think you heard, but I'm here now. I'm here for *you*." I finally looked over, and his damn face was so genuine and open I really wanted to believe him. And more than anything I didn't want to feel so alone. So I leaned into his warmth, laid my head on his shoulder, and I told him everything.

CHAPTER

9

I only had a moment of ignorant bliss before memories of Calix and Calliope flooded in. Did Calliope come out while I had been sleeping? If she had, there was no way I'd find her now. I turned over in bed, not yet ready to face the day, to find the other side empty.

The pillow next to me smelled like Ryker, but the blankets were carefully smoothed out on his side. Memories of last night flashed through my head.

Everything had taken on a dreamlike quality in the early morning light as we'd stumbled back to the inn. I collapsed on the bed immediately, half-asleep, but Ryker had nudged me over so he could pull back the blankets.

I snuggled beneath them, but he didn't do the same for himself. He'd laid on top, as close to the edge as possible, giving me nearly the entire bed.

And now he was nowhere to be found.

I quickly shed my dress and changed into pants and tunic before tucking the dagger into my boot. After shoving the dress into my pack, I swung it over my shoulder and went to open the door. I had told Ryker too much—no doubt he was gone to tell my father about the voices and shadows. He'd acted like I sounded sane, but I'm sure that changed in the light of day. They'd be coming for me soon.

But before I could turn the knob, it twisted in my grasp and the door swung open in front of me.

"Good morning," Ryker asked, holding two hot teas that had splashed a little onto his sleeves. I couldn't tell him my fears, so I just ignored his question and set my pack back down.

Ryker just shrugged and walked inside before setting the teas on the table. I jerked away as he passed. "Someone's a little skittish this morning."

"Well, we need to get Calix," I said. I started collecting my things, but Ryker put a hand out to stop me.

"I can promise you that Calix will be a lot better off if we take time to think this through instead of barging in and demanding they let him go," he said. I eyed him hesitantly, but he was right. I scrunched my nose in irritation. "You'd probably be dead if I hadn't come."

"You think too highly of yourself." I reached for the tea and sipped it eagerly, singeing my throat to distract myself.

Now that there was light outside, I could see the city much better. The buildings were more spread out than in Artange. Rather than dominating the landscape, they seemed to blend into it. Every house seemed to have a garden, something that would be impossible back home, and people roamed the streets, drifting in and out of stores. They looked happy. Or, at the very least, not dreary. I never realized how morose our capital was.

Almost every windowsill had flowers blooming and the streets seemed well cared for. There were barely any stones cracked or missing, and landscaping along the streets didn't seem to belong to any one house.

Most surprising, enchanters were amongst the people walking. Apparently they weren't all conscripted for the military. Magic was everywhere: from the raccoon sweeping a doorstep, to the flowers blooming outside a cafe, to the dining patrons shedding their coats despite the cold weather.

I turned back to Ryker, pressing my mouth in a disapproving line. "Okay, here's the plan: the border to Alynthia is currently closed, but I heard that there are some underground groups that are taking refugees and supplies across, and…"

"Calliope told you this?"

"I have many sources, and I will not…"

"So it was Calliope." I sighed. I shouldn't have told him about her. Hearing her name racked me with all kinds of guilt, but I remembered what Ryker had said last night: *one thing at a time.* Calix first, and then we'd find her.

"Fine. It was Calliope. Moving on, I think we should go to a tavern tonight and ask around to see if we can get the attention of one of these groups."

"Are you done?" He folded his arms.

"Yes. That's the plan." He was silent for a minute, studying my face as if I had the plan scrawled across it.

"Okay," he said, agreeing far quicker than I'd expected. I opened my mouth to question him, but he asked "Do you want to go for a walk?"

I debated saying no just to be contrarian, but I wanted to

get my bearings in the city and I couldn't stay here without getting flashbacks from last night.

"Fine."

Ryker offered the crook of his arm, raising his stupid broken brow. I shoved past it.

We walked into the street, no one giving us a second glance. It felt so ordinary, like Ryker could just be Ryker and I could just be me and we could be two people on a walk, uncomplicated and unbothered. But we weren't those people.

"So how do you like being a guard?" I asked, and he thought for a moment.

"I like feeling helpful."

"Any interesting missions?" I asked. I wanted him to tell me about what I had overheard him talking about with the King, to clarify that he wasn't reporting on me, but it was a stupid thought.

"I can't really talk about it, Estyn." The next few blocks passed with a taut silence.

We turned onto a busy street lined with shops, passing a window that sparkled in the midday sun. Silver and gold shone and stones reflected light onto the walls of the jeweler's shop in mesmerizing patterns.

"Do you want to go in?" Ryker asked, nodding to the door. I thought for a moment. I didn't bring enough money to buy anything, but the craftsmanship was so beautiful I couldn't help but be drawn inside. Ryker watched me admiring the merchandise and smiled, putting a hand on my lower back to lead me inside.

The shop was like a treasure trove with jewelry piled on shelves, draping and nearly spilling out of the shop. The owner sat behind the counter, engrossed in a book. A bell rang as we entered and she looked up. Her eyes were almost serpentine, matching the snakes winding themselves around her chair. A fall enchanter.

"Feel free to look around." As she turned back to her book I thought I saw her steal a glance at us. Ryker and I walked around the edge, and in the midst of the jewels my gaze drifted to an arm cuff of a black so deep it seemed to absorb the light around it. I'd never seen anything like it. Stars and the phases of the moon were carved into the face, revealing the silver underneath. It seemed to shift between reflecting light off the silver and shadowing it until it was barely visible.

"Isn't it pretty?" The voice came from just over my shoulder and I jumped a little, broken from my trance.

"It's beautiful."

"It's onyx and silver, and very old, very valuable." She emphasized each very, drawing out the word as if that would convince me. I felt bad wasting her time, but I couldn't seem to pull myself away. "Only 200 silver pieces, and it could be yours."

"Thank you, but I'm only looking for now." Even as I said it, something in me protested, almost begging me to buy it.

"Let me know if anything changes." She walked back to her perch behind the desk, but I felt guilty lingering. I turned to where Ryker sifted through a pile on the opposite wall, gesturing toward the door.

As we left, I spotted a bookstore across the street with beautiful ivy draping over the facade. I crossed the street in between passing carriages, opening the front door to discover a labyrinth of bookshelves and stacks. Books stuck out of every nook and cranny, spilling onto the floor in some places. I picked my way through to the front desk, not checking whether Ryker followed.

A stout old man sat behind the counter, flipping through the pages of a book nearly as large as he was. He didn't look up as I approached, just raised a single finger in acknowledgment. I waited as he finished his paragraph and looked up at me, adjusting the spectacles along his nose.

"Can you point me to your enchanting section?" I asked. He pointed a decrepit finger into the mass of stacks in an entirely unhelpful gesture.

"Aisle twenty-four," he said, his voice dry from disuse.

I weaved through several aisles, acquainting myself with the numbers and sections. They looked similar to the books in the castle library, albeit more varied in subject matter. I stumbled upon the history section and scanned titles of books about kingdoms I'd only heard of in passing before picking up a book on Tenebris.

Tyrannical, militant, isolationist. I slammed it shut, dust billowing in my face. We were always told that other kingdoms looked favorably upon us. We were supposed to be the gold standard. *We are the gold standard,* I reminded myself. Authors could have their opinions. I didn't stop again until I found aisle twenty-four, which was more of a staircase than an aisle. It was one of the largest sections, books piled on shelves two stories high.

I scanned the titles, finding a wide selection of books. At home, our enchanting section was focused on fighting tactics, military strategy, and a few domestic uses reserved for the castle. Here they had books on using enchanting to make art and all other sorts of nonessential uses, confirming what I'd seen outside. Magic ran wild in these streets with enchanters free to use their power how they pleased. How did the city not collapse? Were the gods not upset with the rampant misuse of their gifts?

I spotted a beautiful collection of thick gold-plated volumes. Brown, blue, green, and orange, as expected. I pulled the green volume out, tracing the gold engraved ivy on the cover. Calix would love it. My chest felt tight. Why was I out here while he was suffering? Why couldn't it have been me?

I slid the book back into place, spotting two slightly thinner volumes capping the set. They were black and white, likely complementary material or overarching subject matter. I turned away, but I felt a stray shadow tug at my sleeve. It twisted in the air, weaving towards the black book.

"You know, you have to actually pick one up to read it," Ryker said as he walked up. My shadows recoiled instantly.

"Let's go," I said, brushing past him as I headed for the door.

We said nothing as we walked down the street, making our way back to the inn. Shopping had provided a welcome distraction, but now that it was coming time to actually set the plan in motion, I questioned every decision I'd ever made. Who was I to think I could save Calix from the kingdom we'd been at war with for a decade? Whether or not I could, I had to try.

The tavern we'd chosen was dark, which helped to hide the thin layer of grime covering the walls and floors. People surrounded the tables, some playing cards, most drinking. Every table seemed to have a sticky veneer of spilled ale and liquor.

Ryker and I sat at a small table in the corner, canvassing our surroundings. The city felt smaller than it had this morning, almost suffocating now that I actually had to execute our plan. Ryker finished the last of his ale and set down his empty mug.

"Wait here. I'm going to go ask around."

"Why can't I come?" I asked. He stared at me as if the answer was obvious, but it clearly wasn't.

"Estyn, I think people may be more comfortable talking to me. Just sit tight," he said, before disappearing into the crowd.

Who was he to tell me to "sit tight" on *my* rescue mission? I wanted to get up just to spite him, but I had to at least finish my drink. As I observed people tossing back drinks and chatting with no regard for etiquette, I had the feeling he might be right. I had barely been outside of the castle, let alone in a bar like this.

At least he was here to help.

A few tables away, a group of women and one man chatted over drinks. A woman on the end of the bench seemed removed, both included and an outsider. She elected to sit back and watch instead of participate, her reactions muted compared to the rest. I observed her in stolen glances, noting her keen awareness of my attention.

Her hair was chopped in a short bob, a style that would have been looked down upon in Tenebris; and her arms were sleeved in tattoos. Her eyes were slanted slightly at the corners, kind of like Calliope's, but Calliope's were rounder and not nearly as intimidating. She had the same hard demeanor as the men at the card game, but it lacked their undercurrent of apprehension. I wanted to both draw nearer and run as far as I could.

I sat, sipping my drink for a few minutes, trying to listen to their conversation. They didn't speak of Alynthia or the war, just idle chatter.

After a few moments of staring at the woman, her eyes shot to me, both an invitation and a dare.

I glanced around to make sure Ryker wasn't watching. I'd be back before he even knew I was gone.

"What's your name?" she asked as I approached. Her head cocked to the side as she studied me, and for a moment I thought she recognized me. It was unlikely. The people in Tenebris barely knew what I looked like, let alone those in another kingdom.

"Serafina," I supplied.

"Serafina," she repeated, rolling the name over in her mouth as if she could taste the lie. "What are you doing in Presa, Serafina?" she asked, more investigative than curious.

"I am passing through on my way to Aleving." Although I'd never been, I knew basic facts about Braiwyth's capital, a trade epicenter, from when my brothers visited a few years ago. They had accompanied our father on a visit to Aleving to monitor trade relations, and when Calix came back, he had a small gift for me—a handcrafted tea set from a distant kingdom I'd never heard of. I'd begged him to tell me every detail he remembered, to describe the bustling markets, the smells of the spices, every part that was distinctly not Tenebris. He'd obliged, recounting the most mundane of his travel tales several times over, the details twisting and growing with each iteration.

"How big were the elephants?" I had asked.

"Three times my height. And they were draped in the finest fabrics, finer than your dress even," he said, running my sleeve through his fingers for effect. We fell into a steady rhythm for months, me asking about how different objects around the castle compared to what he'd seen, and him diving into a new story about the trip.

Who knows, maybe we'd get to see it together when all of this was over.

"Hm." She pondered for a minute, tapping her fingers on the wood, which I suddenly realized were sheathed in pointed metal sleeves about the size of her nails. Each one was intricately welded to look like serpents. I wondered if that was her weapon of choice.

"Why are you really here, Serafina?" she asked, and I froze. How did she know I wasn't telling the truth? Now was as good a time as any to practice my magic. I tried to focus on her thoughts, but I couldn't find it over the thrum of the patrons' murmuring voices.

"I'm trying to find passage into Alynthia," I said, lowering my voice. She raised her brows and lifted her chin in recognition, but all her expressions were restricted.

"Estyn," Ryker interrupted from behind me, his voice both protective and commanding. The woman's lips quirked into a smile that reached her eyes in the worst way.

Ryker held her gaze in silent conversation. I glanced between them, trying to read the interaction, but Ryker tore me away before I could.

"I told you to stay put," he said, holding me by the shoulders. He was angry, but I could hear the fear in his voice.

"I'm sorry," I said, and I was. Whoever she was, she had scared a royal guard, and I had just been chatting with her completely oblivious.

"I'm sorry, too," he said, and I thought he'd apologize for being so stern, but he just let go. "I didn't have very much luck."

"Oh," I said. I didn't know why I'd thought we'd make any progress tonight. I had been holding out hope that I could learn how to get into Alynthia, or at least more about the kingdom in general, but I didn't. The only thing I learned was how very little I knew.

"Let's go," Ryker said, wrapping my hand in his and leading me back into the street. And because I didn't know what else to do, I let him.

It was just the first night, it'll get better. I tried to cheer up, but thoughts never lied convincingly, especially not mine. I hung my head, brainstorming what I'd do better the next night and chastising myself for each mistake.

Ryker walked next to me, aware of my dejection but not addressing it. Now that we were away from the crowd, his thoughts rang clear in my head, so potent I didn't need to concentrate to make them out.

Is she sick? She doesn't look good. What should I say?

I looked up at him with a poorly faked smile, hoping to assuage some of his unease, but I didn't have enough energy to try harder than that.

Music drifted from a tavern we passed, a beautiful violin playing a love ballad.

"Hold on a minute," Ryker's voice cut through my thoughts, soft in contrast to my admonishing inner monologue. He reached for my hand and cradled it in his own, pulling me into the street.

"What..."

"Shhh," he said, drawing me in close. He wrapped an arm around my lower back, gentle, as if he feared that I'd break. "Pretend with me for a moment."

He lifted the hand that held mine and started swaying, leaning down to rest his head against my temple. At first I just stood in his arms, limp, unable to disentangle from my thoughts. I listened to the music, letting it wash over me, and I raised my other arm to rest on his, my fingers curled around his shoulder.

I leaned into his warmth and swayed, my anxiety melting with each measure. The moonlight filtered through the clouds in columns, one angled perfectly over us like our very own spotlight. Although my thoughts pulled me in a million directions, I let myself pretend. He was just a boy and I was just a girl, in a small perfect moment, dancing in the street.

CHAPTER

10

Ryker was gone again when I awoke, his side of the bed already cold. Sun streamed through the slit in the curtains, as bright as midday. How late had I slept? I drew the curtains and walked onto the balcony, the cool air shocking me awake.

The street bustled with merchants and workers lined outside of cafes, presumably grabbing lunch. Unfamiliar but delicious smells wafted to the balcony, making my stomach grumble. I went inside to change and found a now room-temperature bun and tea waiting for me.

I took a large bite out of the bun, almost spilling the mulled quail stuffing onto the floor. Even having cooled, it was delicious. After my stomach was appeased, I picked up the note tucked under the plate.

Estyn—

I'll be back soon. Please stay in the room. It's not safe for you to wander alone.

—R

I almost threw the bun down in protest, but it was too good to waste. Who was he to tell me to stay inside? He wasn't my guard. Besides, it's not like anyone would recognize me.

I wasn't just going to sit around all day, waiting for him to come back.

I finished the bun and took a long gulp of the tea, setting it down so forcefully it splashed onto the note. I threw on some clothes, not sure what I'd do, just knowing I had to leave. I yanked the door back. It didn't budge.

I pulled again, thinking it was some sick joke. Maybe the door was just sticky. It was an old room, it was possible.

Shadows slithered around my feet, brushing against my trousers, gathering with my frustration. They twisted up around my arms, to my hand that was uselessly pulling on the handle.

"Why are you so fucking useless?" I yelled at them. They recoiled slightly before growing larger, stoked by my anger. I turned and sank against the door, anger giving way to something far worse.

My shadows continued to swarm me, cloaking me in a darkness that felt as cold and empty as my helplessness. He trapped me. In a second, I was back to my youth, banging on my bedroom door for hours with no answer.

My head fell back against the door. Silent tears fell down my cheek, a phantom of the sobs I wailed before.

A shadow brushed one of the tears away, a gentle and kind

gesture from a dark and unpredictable magic.

What are you, I thought. I don't know what I was expecting. There was no answer. The longer I sat, the more my shadows shrank back into me, cooling with my emotions.

And to think, I was just starting to forgive him.

I was sitting on the balcony when Ryker returned. People roamed on the street below, filtering in and out of restaurants and taverns in varying degrees of folly. A couple walked below, hand in hand. The shorter woman looked up at her partner with unabashed love and the other planted a kiss on the top of her head before crossing the street.

Voices drowned in my head. One of my shadows peeked out as if to check on me. I didn't feel like dealing with them today.

I focused on a woman wearing a bright pink dress and tried to find her voice above the rest, filtering through thoughts like pages in a book. It was impossible. How was I supposed to find her thoughts when I didn't know what her voice sounded like, let alone what it sounded like muddled by dozens of others? I stared at her, almost willing her thoughts to reveal themselves, but she disappeared into another store.

I tried again on a few others without success. It was only when I opened myself to the entire street that I heard any words and only caught phrases, slipping out of their minds just as quickly as I slipped in. They were not happy with rising taxes, they thought some shoppers were suspicious, they wondered what was for dinner. Some thoughts were more interesting than others; sometimes it felt invasive, listening to their gripes and fears about relationships and families. I didn't know which person or where they came from.

"Estyn?" Ryker called, setting something down on the table. I didn't stir from my perch on the balcony, still watching the street below. Shadows stirred around my feet, purring *mother mother let us out.* I didn't so much as turn my head.

"Oh, you're out here," Ryker said, relieved, sliding the door shut behind him. Anger brewed inside, but it was a cold, silent fury. I didn't say anything, didn't look at him.

"You locked me in here," I said, quiet, composed.

"I'm sorry, but I had to be sure you didn't leave. You don't know how dangerous it is out there."

"I don't know?" I burst out, finally turning to him. "And whose fault is that? You didn't even try to tell me. To reason with me." My shadows spilled over onto the balcony floor, inching towards him with each word.

"It was safer this way." He backed away from the shadows swallowing his feet into their depths.

"Safer? Because you're so concerned with my *safety.* You're just a hotshot guard, doing the King's bidding. Isn't that right? Stupid little Estyn, she doesn't know anything." I was spitting with fury now, my shadows bigger than they'd ever been. Ryker backed up until his back was against the wall. He glanced to the street where a pedestrian had looked up, balking at the clouds of darkness billowing out around me.

"Can we please go inside to talk about this?" Ryker asked, voice trembling slightly. I shouldn't have enjoyed hearing it, but I did. I really did.

"We can go inside once you tell me what you were doing and vow to never lock me up again. This is *my* mission. I will not be left in the dark," I said, stepping to where Ryker was backed against the wall. He tried to lift a hand, but one of my shadows pinned it down. He looked at it in horror, and I smiled.

His thoughts were a stream of frenzied fear. I couldn't make out the words, but I could hear the emotion as he scrambled. I'd never scared someone before. It felt incredible.

"Estyn, I'll tell you everything, but you need to calm down, and we need to get inside. No one can see you like this." He spoke like a trained professional, calm under pressure. I realized he wasn't scared of me, but for me. It was just enough for me to falter, to look into the glass of the balcony doors and see what he saw.

Dark clouds swarmed my irises, almost blocking out all the serene gray blue I was so used to. My shadows twisted around me, pulsing and flowing with my emotions. *Maybe he's right,* I thought. I looked dangerous. *I am dangerous.* I didn't know how to control my magic. Hell, I didn't even know what my magic *was*.

Stop. I thought, trying to command my shadows. They didn't waver, still tightening around Ryker's wrist. *Let go,* I thought, more forcefully. They ignored me.

"Estyn, please," he pleaded, with a futile attempt to free his wrist.

"I'm trying," I snapped, my voice not entirely my own. *Stop,* I commanded again. My anger at Ryker still simmered, and so did the shadows. Ryker clawed at them with his free hand, but they slipped through his fingers like mist. How were they holding him there?

"Let go," I shouted, anger turning inwards. I'd felt useless all my life, but never like this. They finally relented, evaporating, a dark bruise the only evidence they'd been there.

I threw the door open, running into the bathroom. I'd seen magic all my life. It was unpredictable, unruly, but it had never been this dark. The shadows seemed to act on my worst impulses, impervious to reason.

Even as I leaned over the washbasin, sick with self-loathing, I felt fantastic. I'd never felt so powerful, magic pouring through me like adrenaline, pure, heady, too much.

I grasped at the counter, for a vial that wasn't there. Was this what the medicine protected me from? What was happening to me?

The next time I looked into the mirror, my eyes had returned to normal and shadows were nowhere to be found. Ryker was behind me, stroking comforting circles on my back.

"Get away from me," I rasped, throat still raw.

"No," he said, resolute and with a kindness I did not deserve.

I stayed keeled over the cold porcelain until I could be sure I had calmed down. Ryker stayed behind me until I finally stood, taking a deep breath to steady myself.

"Okay?" Ryker asked, and I tried to glare at him, but his face was so wrought with care and concern it just made me feel worse.

"I'm fine now," I said, sitting on the edge of the bed. "Why did you…?" I asked, which always seemed to be the question when it came to Ryker.

"Even if you don't want to believe it, I care about you," he said, rubbing his wrist subconsciously. *Oh gods,* I thought. *I did that.* His wrist was red and purple, bruised raw in parts.

"I'm so sorry," I said, tears pricking at my eyes. "I didn't mean," I choked on the words, my mind spiraling with self-hate, "It just—it wasn't on purpose."

"I know," he said, sitting down next to me, as close as he could get without touching.

"Please don't tell anyone," I whispered.

"I won't," he responded instantly. If I looked into his thoughts, I might be able to judge whether he was telling the truth, but I didn't want to use this magic that I didn't understand. I didn't know its demands, and I was terrified it would take too much from me.

"I got you something," he said after a few minutes of sitting with me. I looked up to meet his gaze and he took it as a sign to go retrieve the gift.

When he reappeared in the bathroom doorway, he pulled a small parcel from behind his back. My mouth dropped a little. There was no way.

"I noticed that you…" his voice seemed to drift off as my senses all narrowed on the present he was handing me. I unwrapped it, delicate with the paper, to find I was right. It was the arm cuff. I didn't even know that he had noticed that I liked it, let alone gone out and bought it. My eyes welled up with tears. I looked up at him, his face so hopeful that my heart melted.

"It's perfect." I looked back down to where it rested in my hands, running my fingers over the surface. I slid it on my arm, and it fit perfectly, resting a few inches above my elbow.

His expression turned wistful as he looked at where the cuff rested on my arm. "I wish I could be the man you deserve, Estyn." My chest felt like it cracked open. In a second I snapped into the body of Estyn from a few days ago, the girl who dreamt of Ryker saying something like that. I wanted to tell him he was wrong, to make him feel like he was enough.

But I didn't know if that was true. I deserved the truth, something he wouldn't offer. When I looked at him I was so overwhelmed with anger, at him for lying to me, spying on me to my father, treating me like a child, locking me up. But there was also something else. Something born of him standing by me, of not balking in the presence of the magic that threatened to consume me, of teaching me to defend myself.

Was it enough? Was that even the right question?

He stepped in, wrapping one arm around my back and tangling the other in my hair, pulling me in until our foreheads touched. He ran his thumb over the curve of my ear, whispering "You deserve so much more than I can give you, but that doesn't stop me from wanting you." My breath hitched, trapped in a place between anger and desire.

I wanted to hit him, I wanted to kiss him, I wanted to push him away, I wanted to pull him closer. What he said was not a promise of happiness or love. It was an admission, and I could not fool myself into believing it was anything more.

His mouth crashed into mine, unspoken words staining our lips, but he kissed me like he could take it all away. I met his pace, welcomed his body pressed against mine. I could hate him and want him. This meant nothing. He lifted me, and I wrapped my legs around his hips.

He kissed my neck, worshiping my body. I felt decadent, intoxicated with the feeling of every place our skin touched. He punctuated his kisses with teeth nipping at my skin, the sensation so heady I forgot everything else.

My body arched, ready with desire.

One dress strap slipped from my shoulder and Ryker's hand brushed the exposed skin as he trailed kisses to the base of my neck. My eyes fluttered shut, losing myself in the sensation, until cold air replaced his mouth and I felt his fingers pulling the strap back into place.

"Ryker?" I asked, breath still shallow, trying to read the emotions on his face as he stared at the floorboards. His fist clenched by his side, resisting reaching for me, or possibly just angry at himself. His gaze lifted for a moment, heavy and conflicted, but instead of explaining he looked toward the balcony door.

"I'm sorry," he said, before ducking out onto the balcony, leaving me feeling his absence in an entirely new way. I hated him more for it.

Ryker and I walked into the tavern in silence, and he split off to try and find information. If that was still the plan. He'd gone out all day, but at least he hadn't locked the door. I didn't mind. I didn't want to see him.

I sunk onto a barstool and searched the crowd for his face.

He was sitting with a woman, which I almost disregarded until she looked up. It was the woman with the snake nails, the same one he'd seemed to know. As her eyes locked on mine, she smirked at me. Did she remember me?

I listened to the conversations at nearby tables, not getting any closer to passage into Alynthia, but learning more about the war. According to the people of Braiwyth, Tenebris was participating in the war to try and take over Alynthia, which didn't make any sense. We were helping the people of Alynthia free themselves from a tyrant, not conquering them.

I looked back at Ryker's table to find the woman with the bob gone, replaced by a new one, who was now leading him to the door. My stomach clenched in jealousy, but it had no right to. He could do whatever he wanted. He didn't owe me anything.

I sighed, nearly slumping onto the counter. At this rate, I wouldn't make it into Alynthia, let alone to Calix. I started to think Ryker might have been right. Who was I to think that I could waltz in and hitch a ride to Alynthia? No one seemed particularly open to talking about Alynthia, let alone planning to go there.

"Are you okay, missus?" The bartender stood in front of me, shaking a drink.

"Do you have anything stronger?" I asked. Besides infrequent wine at dinner, this was the first time I had really indulged, and I was already feeling the buzz of my first drink. I wanted to be numb, just for a night. I wanted to stop thinking about Calix and my increasing awareness that this was an impossible rescue mission. I wanted to forget the complications with Ryker. I didn't want to go back to our room just to wait around, not knowing whether he'd come back. Most of all, I didn't want to be a Princess. I just wanted to be Estyn.

He gave me a crystal glass with a dark amber liquid. I sipped it and my face puckered, but it went down easier with each successive sip.

"Hello there." A dashing summer enchanter slid onto the stool next to me.

"Hello," I said, feeling surprisingly and pleasantly social.

"I couldn't help but come introduce myself," he said, and it could have been the drinks, but his voice sounded as smooth as I had wished the liquor would be. "I'm Lassrin. And you are?"

"I'm Es—Serafina." I caught myself just in time, feeling looser and looser as the alcohol set in.

An amused smile spread across his face. "Well it's nice to

meet you, Es-Serafina." I giggled a little, interrupted by my own hiccup. I had hoped that I would be a moody, mysterious drunk, but the more I felt the effects, the gigglier I got.

"It's nice to meet you too, Lassrin." I nodded to emphasize my point.

"Can I buy you a drink?"

"That would be lovely, thank," hiccup, "you." I hadn't realized mine was empty until the new one slid in front of me.

"So Lassrin, tell me about yourself," I said as I wrapped both my hands around my glass.

"Well, my line of work is awfully dangerous. Quite lucrative, though." He shrugged, polishing off his drink.

"Dangerous?" I asked.

"Well, I work by the border, so we get a lot of refugees from Alynthia, and we can't take them in. It's really messy business, it is." He gestured for another drink from the bartender and turned back to me, his gaze straying to my lips.

"Does anyone try to cross the border?" I asked, drawing his attention back to my eyes. I needed to sober up as quickly as I could, but each second felt slower and less stable than the last.

"Well, no one really wants to cross *into* Alynthia, of course, but there is one group who goes back and forth…" he lifted one brow and looked both ways as if to check that no one was there and then leaned in to whisper in my ear, "the Alynthian rebels." He was inches from my neck and my skin prickled where I felt his breath on my ear. Between the alcohol and the night I was having, it was sounding like a better and better idea to have fun with a stranger. Maybe I could be Serafina for a bit. He lingered by my neck and I turned to face him, our mouths so close that I could smell the alcohol on his breath. I leaned in—

"Fuck." I looked around, my vision lagging. Lassrin staggered a few feet back, gripping his nose and then looking down at his hands which were now covered in blood. A hand gripped my arm and I swung around, ready to twist free like Ryker taught me, but it was…Ryker. He was shaking his hand as if he'd just punched someone…oh my gods he had just punched Lassrin.

"Let's go," Ryker grumbled. I didn't say anything, wanting to get as far away as possible, backing up into the crowd gathering around us. "Estyn," Ryker called, but I had already turned and was running toward the door, smacking straight into the woman with the bob.

I stumbled, the bar spinning around me. How much of my third drink had I finished? Or was it the fourth? I tried to remember, but the memory was fuzzy.

"So, you want to know how to get into Alynthia, *Serafina?*" The woman asked, narrowing her eyes in a time-sensitive offer as I looked back to see Ryker searching the crowd for me.

"Yes," I said.

"Follow me." She turned, graceful in everything she did, moving through the crowd like mist.

"Wait," I said, tugging at her sleeve. *I shouldn't leave with someone I don't know,* my brain supplied helpfully. Thank the gods I was still somewhat sober. "What's your name?"

"Rahni," she said without turning around, giving me no time to second guess myself. *Rahni is such a nice name,* I thought, smiling to myself.

I'll be right back, I thought to Ryker. He saw me right as I slipped out the door, but he was too far to stop me from leaving.

Rahni moved quickly, walking so fast that I almost had to break into a jog to keep pace, but she barely looked like she was working at all.

We walked a few blocks before ducking into a side alley. I noted that it was a dead end and stayed close to the edge. I tried to think of what Ryker would do, plotting at least two escape routes before turning back to her. She leaned against the building, arms crossed in front of her, focused on examining her nails. Light, almost undetectable, footsteps approached.

"Who's that?" I asked, suddenly bracing myself. I reached for my dagger in my boot, but it wasn't there. I looked back up to see its hilt glinting from Rahni's belt. When had she taken it?

"Thanks Rahni," a man's voice said from behind, strangely familiar. "Sorry it took so long to get here." I turned to face him, just to get a cloth drenched in some repulsive chemical pressed to my mouth.

I'm sorry... I thought I heard him think, but it was so far away, too far away and I felt too far away, and then I felt nothing.

CHAPTER

11

My eyes drifted open slowly, crusted over with sleep. I lifted a hand to rub them, but it was yanked back to the wall by cold steel at my wrist. I blinked until my vision cleared to see bars in front of me. A guard was posted in front of my cell by the door, turned away. Where was Ryker? He had to know I was gone by now. I hoped he could figure out where I was, but I doubted he'd have much luck. Would he even try? *He must,* I thought. *I am the princess.*

I couldn't afford to wait for him.

Only one guard stood outside my cell. He nervously pulled at his sleeves, and when he glanced back at me, his face looked as young as mine. My head was clear besides the mumble of his voice. I only caught one phrase, but it was good enough.

Alert Azden.

Azden… *Oh shit,* I thought, realizing where I knew the

name. The blond man at the ball, the man who had cornered me and questioned my powers. This couldn't be good.

I tried to quell the panic rising in my chest, but I didn't have many convincing reassurances for myself. All I had was a cold stone floor, shackled wrists, and no hope of anyone coming to save me. What had I been thinking running away? I should've listened, should've heeded mother's warnings about the voices, about the world, about everything.

"Where am I?" I asked, my voice more even than I had expected it to come out. I clenched my fists, grasping onto his train of thought with everything I had.

I heard nothing.

The guard didn't respond, the only acknowledgment a slight shift to his eyes.

I hoped my nerves were just as concealed. My dwindling hope of rescue was looking less and less likely.

"Bring me to Azden," I said, which made the guard visibly panic. Even with his tunic being black, I could see sweat soaking his underarms as he scrambled for something to say. Maybe he'd take me himself and I could escape. He was likely trained in combat, but between Ryker's lessons and my rudimentary command of my magic, I might be able to get away.

The door handle jiggled, and the young guard relaxed as an older one entered.

"He requests her presence," she said, ignoring me entirely. The young guard unlocked the door, walking toward me hesitantly before unlocking my cuffs from the wall and pulling me to my feet.

As we walked through the halls, it quickly became apparent that we weren't in a castle. If we were in a normal dungeon, we would have emerged aboveground at some point, but the winding corridors only descended further into the earth. Torches lit the hall, causing our shadows to dance on the damp floor and ceiling.

We approached a large set of doors that were ornately carved and inset into the stone wall. The guards knocked a few times with no response. They shared a look, then knocked again.

"Come in," called a voice from inside. The doors opened to reveal one of the most beautiful men I'd ever seen, wearing a smirk that was just as grating as it had been the first time I'd met him.

The most beautiful? You're too kind. I heard in my head, a dark, raspy and slightly smug voice that I assumed belonged to him, even though I hadn't tried to listen to his thoughts. Had it just come to me? Even worse—did he say that out loud? Had *I* said that out loud? My cheeks blushed a furious red.

His white-blond hair was fiercely disheveled, looking as if the only comb it had seen was his hand. What had he been doing in Tenebris? Who *was* he? He leaned casually back in his chair, seated behind a large and rather ostentatious desk. The room itself was sparsely decorated beyond stacks of books piled on simple bookshelves lining the walls, two chairs facing his desk and a single lounge chair tucked into the corner. There were no windows or visible lit torches, but somehow the room was bright and airy.

Half of his lips quirked into a smile, forming a dimple in his cheek. It was not sweet, and it was not for me. It was for the shadows gathering at my feet. For what I was.

"We meet again," His voice was just as amused as it had been the first time we met, but his eyes were calculating now. I kept my mouth shut, not wanting to give him anything to work with, though my mind was burning with questions.

"Not so talkative anymore?" He exaggerated a pout, folding his hands and resting his chin on them. I raised my eyebrow, hoping my defiance would distract him from me studying the room.

My eyes caught on a map pinned to the wall in the back corner. I tried to make out the shapes of borders and pins, but the light reflected off of it in a way that obstructed the information. If only I could somehow block the light, I might be able to figure out where we were. I started tracing the light to its source, but the man spoke again before I could find it.

"Well, I have a few questions for you." He was no longer smiling, but his eyes were still glimmering with pleasure. He paused, hoping I would take the opportunity to speak, but I would not give him that satisfaction.

"What are you doing outside of Tenebris?" He asked. I stayed silent, willing my face to be expressionless. The amusement quickly drained from his face.

So she's a stubborn one.

I slipped into his mind for a moment, then slipped out just as quickly. I'd hoped to hear something more useful, but at least I knew I could get in.

The lines of his jaw were hard now, as each minute of my silence wore him. "Okay. Let's try a different one. When did you first realize you were a night enchanter?" This time, I could not hide my surprise. A night enchanter? Was there such a thing?

Yes, there is, he thought, again inside my head.

"You can hear my thoughts!" I accused. He smiled, clearly quite pleased with himself.

Potentially, he thought, again inside my head. Had I done this to Ryker? Spoken in his mind? It was different than when I listened to other peoples' thoughts. With that, I was going into their head, a different space—now he was in mine. It felt violating.

"I'll answer your questions if you stop doing that," I bit out, trying to wrangle my thoughts before he could get even more of an upper hand. I wished I had better control of my powers. Then I'd be able to hear his no-doubt cocky, narcissistic perspective. Probably better I didn't.

"Hey, I'm not narcissistic," he said, feigning hurt feelings.

"I said cocky *and* narcissistic."

"I know." He smiled again, a roguish, obnoxious expression that affected me far more than I'd care to admit. His smile turned down as he leaned forward, examining me. "So you haven't been trained?"

I weighed my words, wondering how much to reveal. "Not extensively," I said. Did he want to use me for my powers? Was he trying to take me out? Use me as a bargaining chip?

"Hmm," he said, looking at me with the eyes of an experienced negotiator. I tried to think like Bastian, to examine all the angles and strategies, but my brain hurt and I felt very out of my depths.

"I'm going to make you a deal," he said, as if he was doing me a great service by kidnapping me and deigning to give me his good graces. "I will train you, help you understand your magic and hone you into a great enchanter, if you agree to help us on a mission." He paused, and I waited for him to finish.

I waited for a few moments before blurting out, "That's it?"

"What do you mean?" he asked.

"Just so I have this right—you want to train me in magic to help whoever compromises 'us,' to complete an undisclosed and ambiguous 'mission?'" I said, slowly, enunciating every word.

"Yes," he said, without any elaboration. I laughed at the entire situation. He must be insane. Yes, that must be it.

"I'm not insane," he said aloud, and I stopped laughing instantly.

"You said you'd stop doing that."

"Technically, Freckles, I said nothing of the sort." He smiled again, but his nonchalance was hiding an undercurrent of desperation.

"Who are you?" I asked.

"I'll tell you once you agree," he said.

"What's the mission?" I tried.

"Again, agree and I'll say."

"Will I have to do something illegal? Steal? Kill?"

"As I've told you, you must agree first." *So yes,* I thought sourly.

"Will you let me go if I say no?" I asked, a silly, overly optimistic question from someone ill-versed in hostage situations.

"Yes," he said, and my eyes narrowed in suspicion.

"Let go as in set me free," I clarified.

"I know," he said again, his short responses unnervingly irritating. I could say no, go back to Braiwyth. If Ryker was still there, we could come up with a new plan to get Calix. But what plan? It's not like we were getting anywhere before.

If only I knew something about Azden, then maybe his team could help. I'd already lost gods knows how much time down here when I should've been looking for Calix. Maybe, just maybe, they could help me save him. I could add it to his ridiculous terms.

"Where are we?" I asked, and with the last dregs of my

energy, I focused on his thoughts.

I'll say we're still in Braiwyth. What interest would she have in Alynthia?

If we were in Alynthia, that meant... maybe this would work out after all.

"Did you hear that Prince Calix was kidnapped by the King of Alynthia?" I asked, and though I could not reason why, Azden flinched.

"Yes," he said, schooling his features into cautious indifference.

"Rescue him and I'll agree to your conditions," I said, mustering as much confidence and authority as I could fake. Azden narrowed his eyes, leaning back once again and crossing his arms over his chest. I could practically see the wheels turning in his head, weighing the costs and benefits. For all I knew, it could be easy for him. He could report to the King himself.

I don't, he snapped in my head, disgust dripping from his words. I grimaced at the reminder that I was not alone in my thoughts. How was I supposed to negotiate when he knew every move I'd make?

He needs you willing to help. Your magic is useless without your compliance, I thought, a reminder to both myself *and* Azden.

"I'll have to think about it." Azden played with his bottom lip, deep in thought. "Hemm and Corline, please take her back to her cell." Their hands closed around my arms, more timid now, turning me to the door. I glanced back to see Azden running a hand through his hair, pouring over the papers on his desk with a newfound determination.

The next few days blended together. Save for the few meals

I got, I didn't see another soul. I could hear a guard posted outside the door, but no one had been inside since I initially woke up here, and I suspected that they were being extra cautious since my meeting with Azden.

The silence was deafening. I had nothing to do but think, stressing over every last detail from my meeting. Should I have asked for more information? What was I agreeing to? If he changed his mind about freeing me and I needed to escape, it would be much more difficult now. But I couldn't escape—I needed them. It would be impossible for me to infiltrate the Alynthian government and rescue Calix alone, and no matter how little I knew about them, they were capable enough to consider helping me.

Shit, I thought. Should I have added saving Calliope to the terms of our agreement? I didn't even know how I'd begin. It was one thing to rescue someone when I knew their location, but another entirely to search for someone I still didn't know if we could find.

No, I'd have to get Calliope after.

I might be able to do it by myself. Especially after they trained me. *A Night enchanter.* Shadows swirled in response to the thought. If that was true, how had I never heard of it? There were four types of enchanters. Four seasons. No more.

But if that were true, then how would I explain the thoughts? The shadows?

The cuff around my arm felt cold against my skin. If there was an opportunity for me to learn how to control the shadows, to keep the people around me safe... I'd be stupid not to take it.

I hoped Ryker was okay. I imagined him alone in the city, searching the streets for me. He had no doubt gone back to

Tenebris by now, though I wasn't sure what he'd return to. What would he say? That he had helped the Princess leave on a death mission? That would be a quick recipe for execution. Maybe he'd find a plausible excuse, potentially say I was kidnapped, which *was* true, and that he'd followed to save me. Either way, I doubted he would be welcomed back, which made my heart hurt. No matter how I felt about Tenebris, it was his home. And in choosing me, that would never be the same for him.

I drifted in and out of sleep, but it was never restful. My worries followed me into my dreams, visions of Calix being tortured, of Calliope being discovered and punished for my escape, of Ryker hopelessly searching the streets in a city I was not in.

I tried to think through Azden's perspective, judging the chances that he'd just kill me. It would be easier, but I had to hope I was more valuable alive.

"Get up." The guard I now recognized as Corline stood in front of my cell, jarring me awake. She yanked me up by my arm, but I could feel the fear in her thoughts. She was overcompensating, trying to appear authoritative, but underneath she was scared of what I was.

Two more guards waited for us outside. The apprehensive one, Hemm, was nowhere to be seen, but I recognized the others: Rahni and Olyn. Rahni pulsed with a natural energy of danger, and my own magic pulsed in response, almost begging to be used. Olyn was less electric, but I did not dare mistake that for a lack of power. They were all tight-lipped as they led me down the halls, this time directing us to a different room.

Azden was inside, sitting at a round table, chatting with a man to his left. Both of them looked up, and as they did, I recognized his companion with a sinking feeling. It was Walcott—Calix's Walcott. What was he doing here? He was dressed differently, no longer in the decorative Summer enchanter uniform from Tenebris, but rather in a plain tunic and trousers with goggles slung around his neck. His eyes flared with my entrance, and the room heated slightly around me.

Corline pulled me to a chair closest to the door, attaching my chains to the back and tucking the key into her pocket before walking to her post.

Once I was secured, my escorts walked around to sit at the table, Olyn and Rahni to Azden's right, and Walcott to his left. I felt their eyes bore down on me, a mixture of hesitant curiosity, reluctant fear, and, in some cases, hatred. I noticed that Rahni seemed to have the most unbridled disdain for me, though I couldn't place why. She kept her thoughts tucked deep down, rarely letting them drift to the surface. I tried, but I couldn't pick up a single word.

"We've come to a decision," Azden said, addressing the room in a much more formal tone than I'd heard before.

"Who is 'we'?" I asked, interrupting him and looking around at the faces staring back at me.

Azden just glanced around to the people at the table.

"I'm Walcott," Walcott said with a short wave. Did he not want the others to know he knew me, or did he think I didn't know him? Either way I didn't want to risk the deal, so I offered him a small smile, looking to the others for them to follow suit, but they regarded me with cool indifference. I frowned, but Azden continued.

"We will work with you to rescue your brother *if* you agree to our terms. If at any point you break our agreement, we will not only leave him to the mercy of the King, but we will see to it that he never leaves. If you mention anything of our deal to anyone, we will kill him." His words were carefully measured. It felt like we were trying to calculate one another's moves, but predicting the progression of events was getting exponentially more complicated. Rahni rolled her eyes as Azden said it, and I could clearly see the divide in the room between those who supported the decision and those who didn't. Rahni and Olyn had been overruled.

My mind scrambled for alternatives, but I already knew there were none. I'd spent days combing over the details, cataloging just how bleak my options were. Now that they knew about Calix, I was at their mercy. But there was one more term I needed to add.

"One more thing," I said. "I need a healer." I tried to cross my arms, but they were yanked back to my chair. Azden's carefully curated indifference blinked into confusion, but it returned just as quickly.

"For?"

"Medicine." I didn't know how much to reveal about my illness. I hoped it wouldn't make them reconsider, but I couldn't ensure they went through with the rescue if I was dead.

"You don't need medicine, Freckles," Azden said.

"Yes, I do." Who was he to disagree with the healers who had cared for me my entire life? Who had kept me *alive*? I didn't need him to come in and incidentally kill me just because he couldn't see my ailment.

"Fine, we'll get you what you need." That would have to do.

I took a deep breath, trying to steady myself under their

scrutiny. "Then it's a deal."

Azden relaxed his shoulders slightly and Rahni clenched her jaw. "Can I be unchained now? I can't help you if my hands are tied." I asked, albeit a little facetiously.

Don't make me regret this. Azden's voice filled my head, and I shivered again. I would never have a chance, not when he had unfettered access to my thoughts.

Don't make me regret this, I shot at him, and he smiled, a dimple punctuating his amusement at my threat. I wanted to punch him.

Oh Freckles, this is going to be fun. I scowled at him, but it only made him smile wider.

Azden nodded to Corline, and she walked up to me, unlocking my handcuffs from the chair and then from my wrists.

"Don't mistake this for something it isn't," Rahni spoke softly, but her words held me captive. "I will not hesitate to kill you if I need to." She finished with an unnerving smile curling at the corners of her lips. Looking into her eyes, I feared it would take far less than I thought for her to feel my death was warranted. The others looked a little unsure, but none of them corrected her.

"So what's my mission?" I asked, rubbing my skin where the metal had chafed.

"You're going to kill the King of Alynthia," he said, stone-cold serious. If I'd been drinking water, I would have choked. I almost choked on air as I gulped.

"You're kidding, right?" I asked in disbelief, looking to the others for confirmation. They looked just as serious as Azden did. "I can't do that," I sputtered, both a comment on my ability and the sheer insanity of it. We'd been at war with Alynthia for over a decade, and they expected *me* to kill the

King? This was it. I was doomed. It wouldn't matter that I added the healer clause to our agreement when I died on this ridiculous quest.

Maybe that's what Azden had intended. I still didn't know who he was, who he worked for or what they wanted, but if they wanted the King of Alynthia dead it wasn't a far leap to think they'd want me dead too. The only question then was why they didn't just do it now.

"Go clean up and get changed, and then we'll discuss details." Azden dismissed me, turning to talk to Rahni. I paused for a moment, looking to the others for confirmation that I wasn't the only sane one here, but they all averted their gazes.

As I walked into the hall, unchained but flanked by three guards, I couldn't ignore the sinking feeling that I had lost.

CHAPTER

12

The room they led me to was simple, but far nicer than the holding cell. It had a bed, a dresser, and an attached bathing chamber. A change of clothes was set upon the dresser, a plain tunic and pants in the same style I'd seen Rahni wear. Although the accommodations were comfortable, I couldn't help but notice the door lock behind me as it slammed shut.

I drew a bath and eased into the water, rinsing off the grime and sweat from the past few days. I felt my magic come alive in my veins as shadows swirled around me like mist. I tried coaxing them into shapes, but they resisted, twirling in the steam in protest. If there was a secret to channeling magic, I did not know it. At least I had hope now. Even if it was purely for his own benefit, Azden would train me. I smiled a little at the thought. Me, an enchanter. If only Calix could see me now.

I reached out my hand into the mist, brushing against a surprisingly material shadow that seemed to purr under my touch. They danced around the tub, approaching and retreating, almost playing with me. I tried to direct one to where my towel hung on the door, but it ignored me.

I ran a comb through my hair, feeling thoroughly clean for the first time in days. The clothes were soft and hung well on my body, and, best of all, they smelt pleasantly woodsy. I slid my arm cuff back under the sleeve of the tunic, not wanting to share it with the world. No matter how conflicted I felt about Ryker, it comforted me to know he was out there somewhere.

I sat on the edge of the bed, facing the door, waiting for something to happen. I heard murmurs of the guards stationed outside my door and considered trying to speak in their thoughts, but didn't know where to begin.

I rapped on the door instead, calling out "Hello?"

"Yes?" The guard to the left answered.

"When will I be let out of here?" I didn't love being left to the whims of Azden and his crew, simply waiting until they graced me with their presence.

Neither guard responded, so I resorted to listening to their thoughts. The hall must have been fairly empty because my mind only buzzed with their consciousnesses, which made it easier to latch onto the train of thought.

Azden told us not to talk to her. When did he say he'd be back?

Great, so not even they knew when I'd get out.

Shadows were flying around the room when I heard the lock turn. I quickly retracted them to where I sat on the edge of the bed, facing the door. I heard quiet protests from the guards as Azden entered, alone, closing the door behind him.

"What do you want?" I infused my voice with as much

contempt as I felt for being locked up for the past few days. He didn't say anything for a prolonged moment, quietly studying me and likely trying to establish dominance. A small smile quirked at his lips when I thought that. I scowled, again acutely aware of how little privacy I had with him.

"I need to figure out how much you know," he said.

"Seems like you went light on torture devices for that," I retorted, which, to my chagrin, made him chuckle.

"Oh, if I wanted to torture you, I wouldn't need tools. But that's not what I meant."

"Oh?" I raised an eyebrow.

"Follow me." He turned, opened the door and started walking down the hall. I looked around reflexively to check if I was forgetting anything, just to remember that I had no belongings anymore.

Azden walked quickly, and I followed him as well as I could down a ridiculously circuitous series of turns. Either their base was a labyrinth or Azden was trying to disorient me, but either way I was thoroughly lost. I checked behind once, just to find that no guards followed us. Was Azden that powerful, or was he just not as important as I'd thought?

We finally turned into a large room carved from the stone. The walls were lined with weapons and training materials, surrounding a fighting ring elevated a few feet above the floor. Azden stopped just over the threshold, and I walked up to stand beside him, examining the room. The room must have been over twenty feet tall, the only natural light came from a small skylight receded into the ceiling, which was covered in a grid of iron bars.

"Are we not going to talk first?" I asked, suddenly nervous as he walked over to the corner with the weapons, ignoring the blades and simply taping his hands.

"We can multitask." He tossed a roll of tape my way, and I barely caught it against my chest. I looked around the room, expecting more guards, but we appeared to be alone. I followed his lead, taping my hands.

"You want to fight me?" I asked.

"I want to see what we're working with."

"I thought your offer was to train my magic," I said, pulling and readjusting the tape.

"My offer was to train you to complete the mission. You're going to need more than magic for that," he said, ducking up into the ring. I followed close behind, flexing my fingers and loosening the tape on my knuckles. We stood across from one another, Azden shifting into a ready position and me copying his stance. I raised my hands into a defensive position, blocking my face. Whenever I'd fought Ryker, he was careful to avoid my face. I didn't think I'd be given the same luxury here.

"So," I said, careful not to drop my focus on his movements, "Who do you work for?"

"How about you answer some of my questions first?" He countered. We circled one another, every muscle tense.

"How is that fair?"

"I need to know whether or not I can trust you with the answers." He shifted a step closer.

"And how do I know I can trust you?" I questioned, narrowing my eyes at him. I inched into the ring until I stood just outside striking range.

"You can't," he said, a smile lighting his eyes. Can't know or can't trust him?

Neither, he thought, and I paused for a second, still put off guard by hearing his voice in my head. He spotted the opening and swung, catching my side in a full force punch. I doubled over, clutching my stomach and completely forgetting to keep my guard up.

Get up, he thought, and I glowered at him between coughs. I rubbed my side and stood, raising my hands once again.

"What the hell was that?" I demanded, the effect lost to my wince at the sharp pain from speaking.

"If it hurts to speak, just talk to me in my mind," he said sardonically. I lunged forward, swinging straight for his face in blind rage, which he deflected easily. "Tsk, tsk. If I didn't know any better, I'd think you weren't trained at all." I scowled, returning to my spot just out of reach.

"I wasn't," I snapped.

"Now I know that's not true," he said, and for the millionth time since I met him, I cursed his magic.

You could do it too if you tried, he thought.

No, I can't, I thought, still planted firmly in my own mind.

Not with that attitude, he taunted, and I forced myself to take a deep breath despite the overwhelming urge to attack.

I swallowed the pain in my side and asked "where are we?"

"Like I said, answer my questions first."

"Fine."

"Why did you leave?" He advanced until I was within arm's reach. I backed up a step, teetering dangerously close to the edge.

"I told you, to find my brother."

"Surely there are other people looking for him," he said, and I paused, his words hauntingly similar to ones I'd heard before. Azden took my hesitance as a chance to strike and swung his fist around where I guarded my face. I ducked away, shifting on my feet so that I could shoot my fist up towards his jaw. He easily evaded, but his brows lifted in approval.

"I don't want him to be caught in this shitstorm of a war he has nothing to do with. And I can't just sit still while he is," I answered. Azden's eyes softened a little as if he empathized. I knew better.

"So you left your healers?" The softness was quickly replaced with a mocking brow.

"Don't look at me like that. I had a plan, it just..." My heart froze for a second, flashing back to the Calliope and the kitchen. I didn't want to linger on the thought, so instead I squatted and swung my leg at his ankle, catching it with my foot and almost throwing him off balance. I spun up as he stumbled back a step. He recovered almost instantly, back to neutral position, but the gold in his eyes flared in frustration. I looked to see if shadows appeared as they did when I got mad, but I didn't see any. Maybe I could learn to control mine too.

"And how's it been without the medicine?" His voice was unmistakably mocking now. The headaches had actually been better, not that I'd tell him that.

"Stop that." He had no right to question my entire life.

"What was it for again?" He darted around me and I spun to face him again.

"I'm sick." The words felt wrong. I'd *always* been sick. If I went too much longer, it would get worse, right?

But *what* would get worse? The shadows? The voices? The very things Azden claimed were Night enchanting?

"With?" He was provoking me, I knew that, but no amount of self-awareness could stop the tears from pricking my eyes. What he was suggesting, it was just too much. I started to drop my arms, ready to run out before he could see me fall apart, but in seconds I was pressed against him, wrapped in an incapacitating hold.

"You know what I think?" He lowered his voice, a gravely, earthy sound as he whispered into my ear. "You were never sick, Freckles. They wanted to control you, just like they want to control Alynthia. You're lucky you got out." He let go and I staggered away. My heart raced, acutely aware of just how dangerous this man was. He'd been playing with me. He let me go, and I scrambled away. My entire body still pulsed from the proximity. He smirked at me again, with the casual arrogance he seemed to always have.

I wiped at my eyes before I put my guard up again. He was wrong. He was bitter and biased and horribly wrong.

"Why were *you* in Tenebris?" I spat.

"I didn't know we were moving on to your questions now." He lazed against a post at the edge of the ring, and for some reason his casual posture was even more disconcerting than when he'd been on guard.

"You haven't given me anything." I wanted to hit him, but I knew I couldn't. I'd just hurt myself.

"You haven't tried very hard," he said, raising one brow as if daring me to prove him wrong. My shadows spilled around my feet, begging me to sic them on him.

"It's not like you're particularly forthcoming."

"You have another way to get information," he said, stepping forward to spar once again. I was growing more annoyed by the minute, from his incessant questioning to his unruffled posture. Even when he was braced to fight, he was at ease, just as comfortable as he was lounging at his desk.

"Okay. Your turn," he said, softer than before. I waited a moment, expecting a catch, but none came. *How dare you* waited on my lips, but I needed to control my emotions. I couldn't waste this opportunity.

"Who are you?"

"Azden," he said simply, and I rolled my eyes.

"You know that's not what I meant."

"It's what you asked."

"You don't have a last name?"

"No," he said, cryptic and entirely unhelpful. I advanced, watching for an opening, planning my next approach.

"Now that's just ridiculous."

"Ask a better question," he countered, stepping in until I was once again within striking distance.

"Who do you work for?"

"The Alynthian rebellion," he said, as if it were as mundane as what he had for breakfast. I threw a punch, but he easily evaded, first taunting me with a distracting wink and then slamming his fist into my jaw. Pain split through my mouth as my teeth bit down on my lip, but it wasn't hard enough to do any real damage.

I wiped my mouth and spit to the side, biting out "Why?"

"I have my reasons," he said, as evasive as ever.

"You don't like King Ruzu?"

"I was loyal to the Duramoux family." I didn't know much of the family that was ousted by Ruzu ten years before, just that they were rumored to be just as evil as King Ruzu was now. If I'd paid more attention in lessons, I may have retained more details, but I was never one for international politics.

"Where are they now?"

"Dead. Ruzu killed them all," he said flatly, throwing a left hook that I just barely managed to deflect. I should have known that. *Stupid, stupid,* I chided, once again feeling entirely unprepared for this repartee.

"If he's that bad, why are you hiding out here instead of allying with us? Tenebris is fighting to free *your* people after all." I said, swinging my leg around to connect with his side. He caught it just before contact, stopping the momentum and tugging me towards him. I barely managed to stop myself from falling on my face, swinging my arms to keep my balance. Azden didn't take the winning blow, instead lowering his fist and staring at me, utterly dumbfounded.

"You really think your people are helping us," he said, slowly, incredulous and horrified.

"We are," I insisted, tugging my leg to free it. He tightened his hold, the pressure turning slightly painful.

"I don't know what you've been taught, but I need you to know—your people may be fighting our tyrant, but it's not for *our* people. It's for yours."

"What does that even mean?" I asked.

"Your King wants Alynthia for himself," Azden said, throwing my leg down in disgust. He said it with such conviction that I was tempted to believe him, if he wasn't speaking sheer lunacy. So this is why they hadn't asked for our help; they were paranoid.

"My *father* wants what's best for both our people," I spat.

"Oh really? How's that working out for your people?" Images of Artange flashed before my eyes. Orphans starving in the streets, garbage rotting in dark alleys, the angry mob shouting at my family as we filed into our carriage. Azden's eyes flared gold with his anger, almost overtaking the blue entirely. I looked to see if his shadows reacted as mine did, but he had far better control over his magic. I clenched my teeth, unwilling to belie the doubt I felt.

He was wrong. Jaded, cynical, entirely uneducated and obtuse. "Are we done here?" I asked, ready to storm out. He scoffed, folding his arms in front of him.

"Are you blind or just willfully ignorant?"

"I'm leaving." I ducked out of the ring without looking back, ignoring Azden as he shouted at me to come back. Even if I was stuck in an impossible bargain, I didn't have to stand there and take that.

I walked into the hall, looked both ways, and took my best guess at which way would have food. We came from the right, so I turned left. I didn't look back.

After a few turns, I checked behind me to find no one following. Was this place just that inescapable? Or was I not a threat? If they were as paranoid as Azden seemed, I was surprised they didn't guard me *more*.

As I turned around the next corner, I collided with Olyn running at full speed.

"Shit," he said, stepping back and recognizing me, cursing again. "Where's Azden?" He asked, glancing around feverishly.

"He's still in the…"

"I have to go," he said, interrupting me and turning around to sprint the other way. As he ran, arms pumping beside him, I couldn't help but notice his hand dip to his side, patting his pocket as if to check for something.

I watched him round the next corner, shook my head and decided I'd think about it once I had food in my stomach.

I wound through the maze, eventually smelling food and following my nose to a dining hall. I heard Rahni's laughter echo in the hall, but as I stepped into the door, Rahni and Walcott froze with their forks midway to their mouths. I wanted to melt into the wall. A few shadows escaped around my feet, but I quickly pulled them back and found an empty table.

The dining hall was far smaller than any room in Castle Lamoret, but it was full of life. People chatted and laughed and the enchanters scattered amongst the tables practiced their magic casually.

Winter enchanters froze themselves ice cubes, Summer enchanters reheated lukewarm coffee for others. A few others were doing practice exercises to keep their skills sharp. A Spring enchantress wrapped a small sprout around a pencil, compelling it to write a letter for her. A Fall enchanter was leading a trail of ants to stack sugar cubes into a pyramid, then getting them to drop a cube into their tea.

The room was alive with magic, the air almost pulsing with all the enchanters in such close proximity. My own powers called to me like a siren, begging to be used, but even if I wanted to I wouldn't know how.

So he's let her out. Rahni's thoughts almost screamed at me as if she wanted me to listen to them. She and Walcott were stealing glances my way.

She looks upset. Walcott smiled at me, clearly trying to catch my attention and wave me over. I took a few deep breaths, hoping I'd look a bit more composed. I wasn't particularly inclined to go sit across from someone who actively hated me, but I needed to ask someone where to get food.

"Hello," I said simply, standing in front of their table. Rahni openly glared at me. Walcott's eyes lit up, and I was reminded of his comforting countenance from the ball.

"Please, sit," Walcott said, gesturing to the spot next to him. I lowered myself into the seat, feeling Rahni's eyes bore holes through me the entire time.

"So, Estyn, tell us about yourself." Whereas from anyone else it might sound friendly, Rahni made it seem like a threat.

I looked to Walcott, hoping for some sense of guidance, but he was busy cutting a green bean.

"What do you want to know?" I asked.

"What are you doing here?" Rahni's words were so carefully pronounced, I could tell she had resisted adding more colorful language.

"As you know, I need help saving my brother." I tried to sound strong, but even I couldn't help but shrink under her glare.

"Why. are. you. here?" She said it again, clearly not satisfied, this time through clenched teeth.

"I don't know what you're trying to get at." I furrowed my brow, and I could tell she thought my naïveté was a front. The boy I recognized as Hemm brought me a plate and silverware, quickly setting it in front of me before scurrying away as fast as he could. I didn't blame him.

"Well, I for one am starving." Walcott interrupted, trying to ease some of the tension, but Rahni was unfazed. She continued staring at me, as if she could uncover some hidden agenda. I turned to Walcott, eager to talk about anything else. I didn't know how to convince Rahni I was telling the truth. I suspected nothing I said would be sufficient.

"It looks delicious," I picked up my fork, taking a small bite. It was quite good, but nothing could compare to the fresh Spring enchanter-grown produce we had at the castle. "Who can I thank for the meal?" I asked, turning to Walcott. Rahni looked slightly surprised, but her face quickly returned to cold indifference.

"We have a few cooks, who are all amazing. I can take you to them if you'd like." He was more curious than Rahni, intrigued and pleasantly surprised by my request. I wondered how much Calix had told him of me, or if he'd spoken of me at all.

"I would love that," I said.

Gathering intel. We've welcomed a spy right into our home. Rahni's thoughts drifted into my mind, unintentional and unwelcome. She was even more paranoid than Azden.

I finished my meal in silence, though I could hear Rahni nearly screaming her thoughts at me. Her emotions were so potent that it was draining to try and block them out.

"Should we bring the plates to the kitchen?" I asked Walcott.

"Yes, let's go." He gave Rahni a pointed look, but I could tell she didn't give two shits if he disagreed with her. She wasn't going to change her opinion of me. I looked at the corner of the room, an old habit from when Calliope used to be there. I shivered slightly after realizing there was no one to tell about this. She wasn't here. I took a deep breath, then rose with Walcott and followed him to the kitchen.

The kitchen was a small room, clearly not designed to support this many people. Compared to the castle kitchen, it looked like a camping setup. There was a fire set by a Summer enchanter, designed not to emit smoke. There were tables for chopping on either side, and a metal box cooled by a Winter enchanter. Two women stood over a wash basin, scrubbing at dishes. I walked up, holding my dish in front of me, waiting for them to finish so I could scrub it. They waited for me to place it in the water, but after a few minutes of me standing silently, one of the women looked up.

"Can I help?" I asked, knowing how tiring dishwashing was for Calliope.

"Thank you for the offer, but no help is necessary. We're happy to take kitchen duty tonight." She smiled at me warmly, and I handed my dish to her outstretched hand.

"Well, let me know if there's anything I can do. I'm Estyn, by the way."

"I'm Lillya, and this is Sylryn. Hope to see you around."

They turned back to their sponges, scrubbing the dishes until they glistened. Walcott followed behind me, giving them his dish before joining me at the door.

"Kitchen duty rotates?" I asked with a mix of surprise and awe.

"Yeah, we rotate all chores. It's a team effort." Walcott said it as if it was ordinary, but I had never heard of such a thing.

"Do you know why the others don't... like me?" I sounded like a child, but I was dying to know. Walcott stiffened a little at the question, but he didn't brush it off.

"You'll have to ask them." That was the last thing I wanted to do. We walked back to the table, but Rahni had left.

Standing at the table in the empty dining room, I had the sinking realization that I had nothing to do. I also had no sense of what time it was. I hadn't seen a window since being down here, and in my cell I had drifted in and out of sleep so often that I lost track of the days.

"Do you know what time it is?" I turned to ask Walcott, but it seemed he had left to do something as well. I was alone.

The now constant hum of voices buzzed in my brain, but it wasn't enough to drown out my own thoughts. I didn't want to listen to them.

They sounded far too much like Azden.

CHAPTER

13

I couldn't remember the last time I'd been awake for breakfast. At least I guessed it was breakfast—without any windows it was difficult to tell when I'd woken up, but given that I barely slept it couldn't be that late in the day.

I wandered the halls for a good half hour trying to find the dining hall, and when I did, Walcott, Rahni, Olyn and Azden sat at the same table as before. I felt all the eyes in the room turn to me in the doorway, lingering a second too long but shorter than they had the previous night.

"Estyn," Walcott called to me from their table, waving me over. I saw Rahni kick him under the table a little too forcefully, but he hid the grimace well.

I walked over, not intending to sit. I had spotted an empty table where I could enjoy the book I'd found while exploring yesterday in silence rather than subject myself to another meal of Rahni's animosity.

"Good morning." I willed as much compassion into my voice as I could muster, directing it all at Rahni. She might not like me, but I didn't have to sink to her level.

"Please, join us." Azden gestured to the empty chair and Walcott pulled at my arm, tugging me into the seat beside him. Olyn gave me a quick smile, but it fell as soon as Rahni saw it. "We were just debating whether Walcott or Olyn would win in a fight sans-magic." Azden was leaning back in his chair, his eyes dancing with amusement, looking over the others with what could only be described as familial adoration. How long had they all known one another?

"What are you doing?" Rahni snapped at Azden. "Just because she's working with us doesn't mean we have to be friends."

Olyn looked at the table, but he clearly didn't disagree.

Walcott looked at Azden for direction, but I could tell he was embarrassed on my behalf.

"Our team has always worked this way." Azden said, meeting the intensity of Rahni's stare. My breath caught watching Azden defend me. I knew it wasn't for me, but rather the principal of the matter, but my heart reacted as if it were the former.

"Our *team* hasn't had one of *them* before." Rahni infused each word with hostility, shoving her chair back and storming away, food left half finished. She didn't even so much as look my way before slamming the door behind her.

"I should probably go after her." Olyn also avoided eye contact, but I could sense that he would always side with her.

Suddenly it was Azden, Walcott and me left at the table. Someone brought a plate of food, setting it down in front of me as we all sat in silence. Walcott tried to melt into his chair, slumping over what was left of his breakfast. I got a sense of deja-vu watching him push his food around his plate, remembering how Calix always looked sitting at our dining table, trying to hide from the inevitable bickering.

"Let's go, Estyn." Azden's voice was low and restrained, lacking his usual levity. It warned against asking too many questions, so I just nodded and shoveled a few more bites in before following him. I waved to Walcott on my way out, and he offered a tight-lipped smile before turning back to his sulking.

As we walked down the halls, I debated addressing what had just happened. Would that make it worse? She wasn't wrong; they didn't owe me anything. Especially not friendliness.

"What are we doing today?" I asked Azden's back as he walked a few steps ahead. We returned to the training room from the previous day, but he didn't tape his hands like before.

"You stormed off yesterday before I could test your magic," he snapped, though his anger wasn't entirely directed at me.

"So… what do you want me to do?" I hated how unsure I sounded, but I was supremely lost. Worse than that, I feared that after seeing what I could do he'd realize he made a mistake in trusting me and would go back to Rahni, telling her she was right and lock me up again.

"Read my mind," he said, crossing his arms and leaning against the wall.

"I—I," I protested, but he simply raised a brow. He seemed to be lost in thought, likely playing back the argument from breakfast. I focused on his thoughts, feeling my magic rush into my veins as I tried to make out the words.

Rahni will get over herself soon.

As soon as I latched on, the words drifted away, unintelligible once again. I looked up, but Azden's knowing look made me want to show him I could do more. I clenched my fists, trying to focus on the way the magic felt, on anything that would bring me back into his mind.

She's kind of cute when she concentrates so hard.

I snapped out of it, stepping back. That was enough. I decided to stow that away to dissect at a later time. Or never.

What did you learn? he thought in my mind. My gut clenched in embarrassment, at how much I'd struggled to hear so little. He'd probably laugh at me.

Just arrogant nonsense, I thought, which was true.

Surely that wasn't the most important thing you found. He quirked an eyebrow and crossed his arms. I just shrugged, turning to step up into the ring. He followed, leaning against one of the outer posts.

"What else do you know?" He asked, the conversation switching from thought to spoken word as if we'd been talking that way for years.

I walked to the middle of the ring, rubbing my palms together and unsuccessfully willing away my nerves. I felt his eyes trail me, patiently waiting for something to happen. Shadows pulsed with my nerves, and I let them.

I called to the shadows, coaxing them out of their slumber. They swirled around me in dark clouds, obscuring parts of me in darkness. I watched Azden blink, stepping towards me as if he couldn't see me.

"Can you wrap them around yourself?" he asked. Although they were wily and unpredictable, I tried my best. The room dimmed as I wrapped them around my face. I could see Azden perfectly well, but his eyes looked unfocused, as if he couldn't pinpoint me. They thinned, moving on their own accord as soon as I lost focus.

"Interesting," he mused, and I felt the weight of his full attention as he studied me.

"What?" Did I do it differently than he did? Did I do it wrong? I didn't even know what it was, let alone how I could be messing it up, but...

Calm down, you're doing fine, he said, interrupting my spiral. I glowered at him, but was secretly thankful for the interruption.

What's interesting? Isn't this the same as your magic? I asked.

Why would you think that?

I don't know of anyone else who can use telepathy.

Day enchanters can. It was my turn to look surprised. I should have known he was different; his eyes were a dead giveaway.

You're a day enchanter? The gold ring around his pupil spread into the blue of his iris as scraps of light wound around him, a fraction of the magic that I usually felt palpitating from him. My shadows twirled towards his light, mischievous as ever, and his light intensified and multiplied, almost too bright to look at. The beams of light snaked over to me, wrapping around my hands. They were almost playful, licking at my skin. Everywhere they touched me felt electrified with power.

They wrapped all around me and my magic thrummed in my veins. I felt stronger than I'd ever imagined. When Azden recalled the beams my body deflated, nearly crying out for him to bring them back.

"What was that?" I asked.

"My light. I assume your shadows function similarly." He was reasoning out loud, and I realized he was as in the dark about my capabilities as I was.

"How do you control them?"

"It's all about intention. You have to be clear about what you want them to do."

"Wow, I get it now. Thank the gods I have a teacher as great as you."

"We'll work on it, Freckles." He shook his head at my mocking tone, and I wished we were sparring again so I could hit him for the nickname.

You know you like it, his voice whispered, a caress to my thoughts. I shivered.

"Are thoughts the same?" I asked, eager to change the subject.

"Thoughts are different. My light is like a manifestation of my magic, one I have to communicate with. With thoughts, it's like using magic as a bridge, traveling into others' consciousnesses."

"I can never seem to hold on for that long. I just hear bits and fragments when I try, but most of the time it's just a steady pulse of jumbled words. It's exhausting."

"You're probably drifting, not fully planted in your own mind. What do you see when you close your eyes?" I wasn't sure where he was going with that, but I closed my eyes to oblige him. It was the same darkness as always, with little spots of light speckling the nothingness.

"It's just black," I said, frustrated and slightly dismayed.

"When you face me, there's nothing there?" I turned to him, eyes still closed, and clenched them tighter as if that would help. I saw a dot where I heard his voice. I assumed it was just a lamp, shining through my lid, but when I opened my eyes there was none to be found.

"I saw a light. Almost like a star," I said, hoping I didn't sound as crazy as I felt.

"Good. That's my consciousness. When you try to listen to my thoughts, focus on that light, ignoring everything else you see," he said, stepping closer. "Try again."

I nodded once, quickly, nervous to prove myself. I didn't have high hopes, but at least it was something. I closed my eyes once again, seeing the light he said was his mind. I peered further into the darkness, finding a few smaller stars dotting the sky behind him. *Those must be the guards posted outside*, I thought.

I scrunched my brow, turning my attention back to the light in front of me. I focused on it, ignoring everything else, imagining myself reaching for it.

My eyes snapped open, his voice filling my mind as clearly as my own.

You can do it, Estyn. Just focus. Are you here yet?

Yes, I thought, as if I was speaking to him aloud.

About time, he thought, flashing that stupid dimple.

Can you hear my thoughts when I do this? I asked. This felt different than what I'd done before. My body didn't entirely feel my own, my mind tangled with his.

Only the ones you want me to.

How do I stop the thoughts? I asked, letting myself believe for the first time that I could have peace and quiet.

It's just like this, except you focus on your own mind. Do you hear any other voices except mine now?

No, I answered, all too aware of the absence of background noise.

You just need to plant yourself in your own mind, rather in the nebulous middle. Picture your own light growing bright, outshining the others.

That's it? I asked.

Try it, he thought, and I let go, finding myself once again in the dark sky as I closed my eyes. If I focused, I could feel my magic, see the light on the edge of my vision, distinctly my own. I imagined the light wrapping around me, shutting out the ever-present hum of voices I heard from others.

He was right, I thought, my smile spreading from ear to ear.

"It's quiet," I breathed, still in shock, so grateful and relieved that I could've hugged him. My shadows paused in the air where they'd been twirling, as if awaiting my command.

Come to me, I beckoned, and they pooled at my feet instantaneously.

"I did it," I said, my excitement growing with each second of quiet. Azden looked at me in such wonder, but I barely acknowledged him. The magic that felt like a curse now hummed with potential, more potent than ever. The shadows still nipped at my feet, as if with a mind of their own, but the second I thought for them to move, they did.

"You did," he said, with a fleeting smile I hadn't seen before. It wasn't smug amusement, teasing or knowing. It was pure, and it only made me smile wider. I looked at my body, at my hands, searching for some physical representation of my newfound clarity, but everything was as before.

In all my years of taking powders, talking to healers, I never felt as healthy as I did now. Even if I learned nothing past this, I would be eternally grateful.

Maybe I didn't need a healer.

"This is just the beginning," Azden said, his classic smirk back in place.

"What?" I asked, still focused on twirling my shadows around my fingers, up my arm, marveling at how they moved at my request.

"You can do so much more," he said, and when I looked up at him, I realized that this wouldn't be enough anymore. Now that I had a taste of power, I wouldn't be able to stop until I knew what I could do with it.

"And I can help." Rahni sauntered in, all traces of this morning's altercation wiped from her face. Both Azden and I whipped our heads around to face her. She ducked into the ring, graceful as ever, as Azden stared at her intensely. I bristled at the uncomfortable silence before realizing he was probably talking to her in her mind. I'd have to get used to that. She shrugged and turned back to me.

"I'll help Estyn with her physical training," she said, her voice surprisingly not dripping with the sadistic pleasure I expected.

"Thank you." My voice was level, but not without effort. I wanted to recall my shadows and melt into them, but I knew it was important to take the olive branch. Maybe she had come to terms with the alliance.

"We'll start this afternoon." She was facing me, but her words were directed to Azden.

"Sounds good." She directed one last glare at Azden before walking away. We both watched her disappear into the hall.

Azden's face contorted in confusion, but he shook it off before turning back to me.

"Okay, let's do a few practice exercises to train your control."

I walked into the kitchen to find Lillya stirring a pot of vegetable soup.

"Hello!" I said cheerfully, walking up to her. She jumped a little, apparently lost in her own thoughts. "Sorry, I didn't mean to scare you. I just wanted to see if there's anything I can do to help?"

"Don't you need to eat?" she asked, glancing at the door to the dining room.

"I can graze while I cook," I said, but she looked skeptical. "I can do anything, just let me know what you need." I knew the basics, and more importantly, I was desperate to find an excuse to not sit through another miserable meal. I didn't want to have to decode Rahni, especially right before our one-on-one training that had been worrying me all morning. Thankfully, Lillya understood and nodded towards a chopping block and a stack of squash.

"We're prepping a stew for dinner and need to chop those vegetables."

"Thank you," I whispered and she smiled, turning back to the stove.

I settled onto the stool and got a sudden pang of heartache. I had been doing my best to push Calliope out of my mind, but I couldn't help but glance to my side and hope she was there. I silently prayed to the gods that she was okay, wherever she was. *Soon*, I thought. Soon I'd get Calix and we would find her together.

I made quick work of the squash, and Lillya looked back approvingly before bringing another bag of vegetables.

The chopping was meditative. For a moment I could zone out, free of my ever-present anxiety. I fell into a steady rhythm, losing track of time until people started filtering into the kitchen with dishes.

I noticed as Olyn put his bowl in the sink Lillya fished a chocolate from her pocket and covertly passed it to him. I almost smiled, but it fell as soon as Rahni sauntered in.

"Let's go, Princess." Rahni didn't even look back to check if I was following before pushing through the door as if it shouldn't have dared to be in her way.

I said a quick apology to Lillya for leaving my task unfinished before scampering after Rahni.

Rahni walked down the halls as if she owned the place. She looked relaxed, but again I had to jog to not lose her.

"Let's see what you can do," she said, circling me like a predator. When I had sparred with Azden, I knew he was testing me, but he had some restraint. I doubted Rahni would hold back. I calmed my breathing, trying to find an opening.

I saw her falter and took my shot, throwing a right hook. Mid strike I saw her eyes and knew I'd fallen for her trap. In a second I was slammed onto my back with the wind knocked out of me. I gasped, desperate for air as she leaned over me, her jet black hair falling in a halo around her face. "So, Princess, are you going to tell me why you're really here?"

"To train?" I breathed out, my chest stinging with each word. I propped myself up on my elbows, still trying to collect myself. Rahni rolled her eyes and crossed her arms. "I told you," I grumbled, "I need to rescue my brother. Nothing else." She squinted, studying me.

"Get up, let's do it again."

We didn't talk for the rest of the session. She was an incredible fighter, worlds better at hand-to-hand combat than even our best men. She was lithe and agile with an enviable command of her muscles. She showed me how to be light on my feet, constantly moving to evade hits. By the time we finished, every muscle ached and I barely stumbled out of the ring.

"See you tomorrow." Rahni walked out of the room as if she had just been taking a casual stroll, not beating the shit out of me. I doubled over, almost vomiting on my shoes. A few minutes after Rahni left, Walcott peaked his head in.

"How'd it go?" He tentatively walked towards me. I managed to stand up, sweat dripping off my brow as I glowered at him. "You're alive at least."

"Barely." I grabbed my ribcage in protest, my body complaining whenever I tried to talk.

"Do you need to go to the infirmary?" Probably, but I didn't want to give Rahni that satisfaction. I wasn't going anywhere until I had Calix. She couldn't scare me off.

"I'm alright. Just need some water." My voice was hoarse. Walcott handed me a glass, and I downed it in a few gulps, already feeling a little better.

"Maybe someone else should train you." He looked concerned. I would be too if I saw myself.

"No, it's fine. I'm good." He gave me a look that said he didn't fully believe me, but that he'd respect my wishes. "Can you help me find my way back to my room?" I asked, both for direction and support walking. I didn't want to be left alone in the labyrinth if I collapsed.

Walcott bit his lip as if he was figuring out how to say something.

"What is it?" I asked, my patience worn thin.

"Do you think Calix is okay?" he asked. I smiled a little even though it hurt my split lip.

"I hope so. He didn't talk much about his love life, but I could tell he really liked you," I said.

He looked at his feet with a sad smile, his pain rivaling my own. We both stared at the floor for a moment, settling into our own grief, comforted by the other's understanding.

"Why were you in Tenebris?" I asked after some time. I had been wondering for the past few days, but I was putting off asking. I didn't know what I'd do if I found out he'd lied to Calix. I wanted to keep their relationship pure in my thoughts, keep Walcott's motives uncomplicated, but I had to find out at some point.

"I was born there." His eyes went distant as if bad memories were resurfacing.

"Then how'd you get here?" I had to be careful with my words, but I was too curious not to ask.

"When I was fourteen I was sent on a mission overseas. I had been trained my entire life, but when I got there…I was still not prepared to do what they asked. I ran away and was hiding in the woods with no food and no plan when Azden found me. I never had a family, but he, Rahni and the others accepted me as one of their own.

"Eventually we decided I was ready to go back to Tenebris. I pretended that I had been taken as a prisoner of war, and I was eventually let back into training. Azden came back every so often to check on me, and recently he decided it wasn't safe anymore, so I'm back here." His voice was soft, and I absorbed his story, trying to digest all he'd said. Not only was he a spy, but a traitor? What did he expect me to say?

"Did Calix know?" I asked, coming out far more accusatory than I intended.

"No, but I wanted to tell him." His voice said that he didn't think he'd ever get the chance to.

"So you're a traitor," I said, slowly, trying to internalize the words as I said them.

"You don't know what it's like there."

"It doesn't change the fact that you're not only a deserter, but a spy." I said through clenched teeth, my shadows pulling me towards him, begging for action.

"What they're doing isn't right," he said, still as calm as ever. How could he do this? Betray his own kingdom, and for what? Because training was a bit too grueling? How else would we get the best army in the world?

"Who are you to judge that?" I accused, but Walcott simply crossed his arms, unruffled.

"The Tenebris you knew and the Tenebris the rest of the world experiences are two very different things."

"What does that even mean?" I clenched my fists, not sure what I would do but knowing I needed to defend my home, my people. That's what a princess would do.

"They say the rest of the world needs our help, but that's not true. Do you really think that other Kingdoms are out here struggling more than we are? Have you been in Artange? Do you think that's some ideal we should be imposing on people who don't want our help?" He asked, his voice steady and calm. I wanted to hit him all the more for it.

"What, like you know better?" I shot back.

"I don't know better, but they sure as hell don't," he snapped, finally breaking his cool demeanor.

"*They* are my family. Calix and I are part of the 'they' you so clearly despise. How can you stand here with me, disparaging our home and the crown *you* were supposed to serve, and still think you have the moral upper hand?"

"The crown I was supposed to serve?" He scoffed. "You mean the crown that kidnapped me as a child, forced me to go to battle in a war of their own making, while they sat back in their castle? That crown?"

"You don't know what you're talking about."

"One of us was trained from birth, beaten and burned when they didn't measure up, forced to use their magic to kill innocents," My eyes flicked down to the scars peeking out from under his collar, "and the other has lived their entire life paraded around in pretty dresses. So I'd be very careful about passing judgments about what I do and don't know." With that, he shouldered past me, stormed out into the hall, and left me to contend with all he'd said.

I thought back to my limited time in Artange. Compared to what I saw in Braiwyth, everyone had a heaviness that they seemed to carry with everything they did. Despite what the King claimed, they didn't seem to love or respect him. Maybe we weren't even what was best for our own people.

Mother said it was out of the kindness of our hearts that we took in enchanters, many of them orphans, offering them the honor of serving their Kingdom. I'd never wondered if they thought the same.

I couldn't sleep, my mind racing over what Walcott had said. Was the army really that bad? Had he told Calix the truth?

Worse yet, did Calix agree? And I would've left him there to suffer.

The more I replayed Walcott's words, the more I agreed with him. I couldn't imagine going through what he had. Had Ryker ever considered leaving? What did he think of the brutality at my Veirden and during training? Did he think it was justified?

What did it mean about me that I had?

I tossed and turned as the hour slipped closer to dawn, finally deciding that it was late enough to wander outside my quarters. I walked out into the hall, strolling along, looking into the doors I passed. The corridors were quiet but looked just as they did in the middle of the day. I longed for a window, for some touchstone to the outside world.

As I walked, I passed a door that looked familiar, but I couldn't quite remember what it was. I cracked it to find Azden's office—his empty office. I knew I shouldn't go in, I really shouldn't, but I did.

I ran a finger along the books piled along the perimeter, seeing titles on war strategy, but also a few novels. I reached a table that was almost all Nyx and Hyperion retellings, and couldn't help but smile at the thought that this tough rebel leader liked the same stories that I did.

I pulled one I hadn't read before, and curled up in the armchair nestled into a corner of the room. As I curled into the chair, I realized I should probably be taking this opportunity to search his desk and find out more about the assassination plot. Or maybe about the organization, or Azden himself, but I couldn't help thinking that it all sounded so tiring, and I was exhausted from trying to play politics.

"Estyn?" Azden's surprised voice jolted me awake, and I scrambled out of the chair, the book falling from where it had rested on my chest.

"Sorry. I uh,…" I said, fumbling over what to say. The truth sounded suspicious at best, but I couldn't come up with anything better. "I couldn't sleep. I didn't go through your stuff, I was just reading."

He stared at me a few moments, eyes narrowed in deep thought. My heart beat like I was in trouble. Was I?

He closed the door, walking over to his desk. I saw him give it a quick once-over, confirming that nothing had been moved, and then looked back up at me as if I was an enigma.

"I'll leave now, sorry again for intruding, it won't happen again." My words fell out of my mouth in a rush, and I clutched the book to my chest as I reached for the door handle.

"Estyn?" He called just as I turned to the door, and I whipped my head around. Well. This was it. He was going to reassign guards to my side, maybe even break the deal and put me back in my cell.

"Do you want to hear the plan?" he asked. What the? His voice was gentle, with not even a trace of anger. I nodded and walked back into the room, settling into the chair across from him. "Okay, so—"

"Why are you trusting me?" I interjected, which was probably a bad move on my side, but I couldn't seem to keep my mouth shut around him. If all that Walcott had said was true, then not only should he not trust me, but he should actively *dislike* me. He looked at me for a moment, seriously contemplating his answer.

"I like to believe the best in people." He was so earnest I wanted to prove him right.

"Okay, so the plan. Before anything else, we need to gather intelligence on the dictator. We need to know the ins and outs of his routine, from his guards' schedule to when he's asleep. When we get in there, we don't want any surprises." He was serious, but maintained his trademark casual confidence. I nodded, following every word.

"The castle is well-protected. Just like yours, there is an outer wall which we'll have to scale. The dictator's room is on the ground floor, facing the garden. Luckily, the forest offers both a good view and natural coverage. We won't have a Spring enchanter with us, but the natural brush has become overgrown enough in recent years.

"Now, you probably know this, but Ruzu is a powerful and dangerous enchanter. He used to be an advisor to the

King and took the throne by force, leaving no one alive in his wake. We must take every precaution. That means we'll train as much as we can, but ideally we run before we fight. Got it?"

I nodded again, my brain working to process everything he said. I tried to remember anything about Alynthian history from my classes, but came up short.

"Do you think…" I struggled to maintain my composure, but I needed for force the words out. "Do you think Calix is alive?"

Azden paused, pressing the pencil that he'd been mindlessly twirling to his bottom lip. "I think Calix is more useful to Ruzu alive. He's ruthless, but he wouldn't just kill Calix for his own pleasure." Even as Azden said it, his eyes flickered with a second of doubt. I hoped that he was right, but even if he wasn't I would fight until I saw it with my own eyes. I nodded slowly, pursing my lips and hoping my emotion wasn't as obvious as it felt.

"Azden?" I asked, shier now.

"Yes?"

"Why do you think we're trying to take Alynthia for ourselves?" It had been mulling in my head ever since he said it. I could see why he thought that; it was true my father could be called power-hungry, and it would explain the war efforts, but I still couldn't believe it.

"Even before this war, Tenebris had been in constant negotiations to try and annex Alynthia as part of their Kingdom. It's always been in the plans, just now is an opportune moment with the political unrest in our lands. We monitor Tenebris, as you know, and we've overheard many discussions that support that reasoning. Is it that difficult to believe?" His last question was not sarcastic, but patient and genuinely curious. I thought for a moment, but I knew what my gut said.

"So what's your role in this? You are trying to overthrow Ruzu, yet you waste resources monitoring us?" I asked. I didn't want to address his question; it was much easier to deflect with my own. Even when I had hated my mother and the King, I never thought them capable of such deception.

"First and foremost, I fight for Alynthia, for my people, whether that's from a throne or underground," he said. He was so sure of himself, so entirely confident in his purpose in life that I felt compelled to support him. No doubt that was why he was so successful.

"And you don't think we're good for your people?" I knew the answer, but I still wanted to hear it from him.

"No kingdom is perfect, but I've never seen any other rulers commit atrocities with such blind moral righteousness and then turn around and feel justified imposing that on others. So no, I do not think your kingdom is good for our people."

"Is that why the others don't like me?"

"Possibly."

"And what do you think?" I was curious to see if my newfound freedom was a hint at trust or a test for it. Azden paused for a moment, looking into my eyes as if they'd hold the truth. *No*, I realized. He was reading my thoughts. I would need to get used to that.

Do you think I'm a spy? I thought, knowing he would hear.

No. I could hear the hope and fear intertwine in his admission, and again I wanted to prove him right. He took a deep breath, looking back down at his desk and collecting his thoughts.

"Don't you think it's a little invasive to constantly read

others' thoughts?" I asked. He shrugged, but it was more deflection than nonchalance.

"I do what I have to do." He broke eye contact and I saw a wisp of light curl around his pinky as if comforting him. I couldn't imagine the pressure he put on himself.

I struggled to stifle a yawn, and my eyes drifted to the clock on the back wall. The sun would be rising any moment now in the real world above.

"I should be getting to bed." I had many questions that I still wanted to ask, but my mind was begging for sleep. Azden ran a hand through his hair, which I now recognized as one of his nervous tics. He yawned after me, but tried to swallow it, looking down at his papers regretfully.

"Do you have a lot of work left?" I asked, unsure of whether it was too casual too soon.

"I always do. Let me walk you back to your room." He walked around to where I sat, not offering a hand, but simply leading the way.

"Why thank you. To be honest I have no clue how to get back." I laughed nervously, but it developed into yet another yawn. A smile tugged at his lips, but he turned away quickly, walking down the halls with me following close behind.

CHAPTER

14

I continued to help and eat in the kitchen for every meal, though it was more for comfort than avoidance now. With the chore rotation, I got to know a lot of the people in the camp. The rebellion was much smaller than I expected; it seemed like there were just under a hundred living in the base. Maybe there were more in the network, but I got the impression that the organization was a lot scrappier than I'd originally thought.

There were a few enchanters, but most of them did not have magic. I got to know their stories, hearing about how they found the group and came to live here. Everyone had glowing reviews of Azden, speaking of his endless compassion and fearless leadership. I always smiled, resisting the urge to mention his sarcasm and arrogance. I'm sure it wouldn't get any better if he heard the way people talked about him. Or maybe that's what fueled it in the first place.

Many were refugees who had refused the draft into Ruzu's army. Others just felt strongly enough about the government that they'd risk their lives for change.

A few days in, Lillya told me that the movement used to be much larger. They'd had thousands, but failed during an attack on the castle. She didn't say much, and I didn't push it because I could tell how hard it was for her to share that much. It was amazing that spirits were so high considering. How did Azden think that we'd succeed when he failed with *thousands?* I almost asked him about it several times, but I always stopped short. He breathed life into every room he walked into, and it was almost painful to see him down.

I trained with Azden in the mornings, both of us exploring my skills. He had ideas for what I could do, going off of his own magic, but we were mostly making it up as we went. We soon discovered that we could talk to one another in our minds over much further distances than normal. Usually people would have to be within a block or so for him to communicate with them, but we could always hear one another. We'd be able to push the limits further if we were above ground, but I doubted any distance would change it. He was ever-present in my mind, his light not so much indicative of his proximity to me as much as just his existence.

I admired how adept he was at manipulating his magic. He seemed to coax it to his every whim, the light an extension of himself rather than an unruly companion. He suggested I try to use my shadows more often, comparing it to a muscle that I needed to flex.

So I started asking them to move things, carrying books and other small objects to me; which, besides being a good training tool, was rather convenient—when they didn't drop them, that is.

I once made the mistake of trying to make the shadows bring me hot tea, and Olyn passed just as it spilled all over my lap. He laughed himself silly, wiping tears from the corners of his eyes. He helped me clean up after, which was the least he could do after I provided such high-quality entertainment.

Olyn seemed to be warming to me, but he hid it around Rahni. She wasn't as hostile as before but not welcoming either. At least she respected me for putting up with her training.

Her methods were brutal but effective. I was getting better. *Much* better, and fast. Ryker had done a good job of showing me the basics, but it was nothing compared to Rahni's graceful technique. Through a combination of pain in muscles I didn't know existed and the acute fear of the aforementioned pain, I gained a new awareness of my body. All my muscles worked together in a symphony, bending to my will. I actually got some strikes in, which was an accomplishment in my book. Rahni didn't appreciate it, but I glimpsed something akin to pride in her eyes.

Walcott and I had fallen into a comfortable pattern of adjourning to his lab after dinner, him tinkering and me reading. He made all sorts of things, bombs for the rebellion, but also inventions I hadn't thought possible, heating metal and elements into devices I would never be able to conceive. I loved watching his mind work as he scrambled around, collecting and forgetting samples before jotting something down on a spare note that he'd promptly lose.

It was amazing he kept track of everything before he had me to keep him organized.

I knew I should apologize to him, but I never found the

right time. No matter how much he resented Tenebris, he still treated me with kindness. Maybe he knew how hard it would be for me to accept what he had to say. Maybe he'd brushed over it. Either way, I appreciated his company.

Every time I settled into the worn chair in the corner of his lab, my body groaned, acutely aware of every muscle and place I'd been slammed that day. For an hour or two, I could relax until my lids grew too heavy and I retired to my room. It was clear why Calix liked him so much. Walcott was an old soul, wise beyond his years and more patient than I'd ever be. I could imagine him fielding Calix's philosophical questions, falling into a lively debate about whatever it was that interested Calix that day. Every time my imagination drifted there, my heart grew heavy, wondering if they'd ever see one another again. For both Walcott and my sakes, I wished they would.

"You should eat with us tomorrow," Walcott said, looking up at me from where he stood over a vat of questionable chemicals. I looked up at him, contemplative, but trying to figure out how to politely decline. I enjoyed my quiet time in the kitchen, meeting different people as they cycled through kitchen duty. Plus, as much as I didn't want to admit it, I was scared.

"Um, I would love to, but…"

"I think Rahni's warming to you," he said, a plume of sordid smelling gas blowing into his face.

"*That's* her warming to me?" I asked, aghast. He laughed through his coughing fit.

"She's not the warmest person."

"You could say that again."

"But she's been through a lot. I think you guys would be friends if you got to know each other." He waved the smoke toward a vent in the stone ceiling, but we both coughed long after the last plumes disappeared.

"If you say so." I looked back at my book, flattered that he wanted me to be a part of the group, but not entirely convinced.

"So you'll come?" I looked up at him then and behind the thick goggles his eyes were so hopeful that I couldn't help but say yes.

I never thought I'd miss sunlight so much. I'd lost track of how long I was underground, time blending together without the rising and setting of the sun. Azden and I were training outside today, and he had been as opaque as usual when I'd asked questions, giving non-answers and forcing me to follow him blindly through the halls. He'd led me into a secret door off the hall that I hadn't seen before, pulling a sconce to reveal a damp, stone stairwell leading up into ominous darkness.

I stepped out of the cave that the base exited into, brushing away the moss curtain hanging over the entrance. After my eyes adjusted to the light, I found Azden standing a few feet ahead, looking into the distance. I walked up beside him, squinting between the trees to see what he did.

A white stone castle loomed just up the hill on a steep cliffside, its daunting exterior wall warning against intruders. Flags bearing the Alynthian crest flew high above the wall, which could only mean...

Welcome to Myllanor. Azden's voice interrupted my thoughts, and I spun to face him. He wore a bittersweet smile, still looking at the castle.

"We're in Alynthia's *capital?*" I asked, shocked and scared and more concerned than ever for Azden's sanity. "What are you thinking? They're going to kill us."

"They don't know we're here," he said calmly, not taking his eyes off of the cliffside.

"So you're just hiding in a complex tunnel system under the city *without them knowing?*"

"Yes," he said, and I just stared with my mouth open, not sure of what to say. Who built the tunnels? How? How could they make them without the rulers knowing? I was about to unleash my interrogation upon him when Azden said, "We're out here today to practice using your magic for tracking."

"Wait what? Tracking?"

"The stars you see when you close your eyes, do they get dimmer and brighter? Change location?" He finally turned towards me, crossing his arms and learning against the nearest tree. I closed my eyes briefly before nodding. "Well, you should be able to find where people are in the physical space based on that."

"You can do that?" I asked, and a lazy grin spread across his face.

"Of course I can, Freckles," he mused. If I wasn't so damn stir crazy, I would've marched right back into the base. Azden reached into his pocket, procuring a long black blindfold and running it between his fingers.

"Oh, no. Not happening," I said, backing away as Azden grinned, amused as always.

"I need to make sure you aren't cheating," he said, cocking his head to the side.

"Fine," I said through gritted teeth. I thrust a hand out for the blindfold, but he ignored it, walking forward until only inches separated us. He brushed the hair out of my eyes, his touch impossibly and infuriatingly gentle, before wrapping the blindfold over them and securing it in the back.

"I couldn't have you tying it too loose," he breathed, his hand lingering in my hair a moment before falling to his side.

I held my breath long after he stepped away.

"I want you to practice seeing me in your mind. Count to thirty, and when you're done, come find me."

"What about the trees?"

"You'll figure it out," he said, his voice growing more distant as he walked into the woods. I started counting, becoming more and more irritated with Azden. What kind of training was this? Maybe he was just leaving me here to die. Or maybe he'd struck a deal with Tenebris and they were coming to retrieve me now. I probably looked the fool for trusting him, standing in the middle of the woods, willingly blindfolded.

As much as I resented him, he was right. I watched as the light in my mind that I now recognized as his drift into the distance, roughly northwest from where I stood. Thirty was too long. The moment I hit twenty-five, I started walking towards him.

Even though I grumbled about Rahni's methods, I was more aware of my body than ever. I moved through the woods effortlessly, sidestepping trees and fallen branches, not needing to see to be agile.

Azden's light grew larger as I neared, and I smiled to myself at this new trick. I could already imagine all the uses, seeing people before they knew I could.

The salty sea air stuck to my skin as the trees cleared. I kept walking, Azden's light growing brighter and brighter in my mind. What if this was a trick? Could he be making me see things?

Even though the blindfold was tightly secured, I felt the

sunlight on my face as the tree cover broke. Waves crashed somewhere far below, growing louder with each step. How close was I to the edge?

The light was so bright, I could've sworn he was right in front of me. I stepped forward, reaching my hands out, but he wasn't there. I lifted a foot, about to take one more step when arms reached around my waist and yanked me back. I stumbled back into them, pressed far too close for comfort as I yanked my blindfold off.

The cliff's edge was a breath away from where we stood. If I'd stepped forward, I'd be tumbling down to the rocks below.

I whirled around to face Azden, shoving him back and screaming "You could've killed me!"

"I would've caught you," he said, but his normal nonchalance was strained.

"You're insane."

"But you did it. And it seems like your training with Rahni is helping too," he said, deplorably pleased with himself.

"We're done here," I said, still fuming, my shadows pulling me towards him, begging for action. I stomped back towards the cave, knowing that I'd relent if I didn't put distance between us.

"But how'd it feel?" he called out after me, keeping pace with a lazy gait as I moved my legs as fast as I could.

It felt...great. Empowering. It was one more step away from that helpless feeling that plagued my dreams. Every day I learned something I didn't even know was possible. I wanted to try it with more people, in the city, with moving targets. I wanted to keep challenging myself, getting better and better until...

Until I could protect myself and the people I loved.

Estyn, Azden's voice broke through my thoughts with a sense of urgency that made me pause. I looked around to see what spooked him, but the woods seemed empty save for a few small animals.

Be quiet, he thought, and before I could protest he grabbed my arm and pulled us behind a tree. We were too far from the cave. *Look,* he said, his heart racing against my shoulder.

I did, I bit back.

No—look, he thought, nodding down at my head silently. I obliged, closing my eyes to see Azden's light bright before me. Was this another part of his training? A sick joke? I was just about to tell him as such when I saw movement in the corner of my vision. Four dim stars neared, brighter by the second. When I opened my eyes, Azden was looking down at me with an intensity I hadn't seen before.

Okay Freckles, time for your next lesson. Hide us, he thought, his voice trying to stay calm, but betraying all the panic he felt.

I took a deep breath, trying to focus on my light as Azden had taught me. Clarity, intention. That's what I needed. I felt the magic humming in my veins, energized by my adrenaline. *Cover us,* I thought, and the shadows crawled up around us but stopped around my knees.

Cover us now, I repeated, this time more frantic. I kept flashing from my mind to the men quickly approaching to Azden's mind, trying to control the situation but only making the shadows weaker.

Please, I pleaded, to myself or the gods I didn't know, but the shadows shrank just further down.

Two strong hands cupped my face and my eyes snapped open to see Azden filling my vision.

Breathe, he said in my mind, his voice my anchor in the sea of darkness. *Don't worry about them. Focus on yourself.*

I did as he said, taking a deep breath of clean, salty air and focusing on my own light. *Cover us,* I tried again, but this time the command was clear amidst the quiet of my own thoughts.

The world grew dark as they swarmed around our heads, enclosing us in a pocket of night. I saw the bright forest around us, but no light breached our bubble.

Good job Freckles, he thought, slightly more collected than before. He even managed to smile down at me as I looked up, offering the small reassurance I was looking for. His hands had fallen from my face, but they were still wrapped around my shoulders, pulling me close to him.

I heard the men before I saw them, leaves crunching underfoot as they wandered through the trees. Who were they? Why was Azden so shaken?

Azden's arm was still wrapped around my midsection, pressing me against him. I itched to make a snarky remark but I didn't dare break my concentration. If only I could peek into their minds, then I could see who they were. Could I control my shadows and listen to thoughts at the same time? Whether I could or not, I wasn't about to try now.

My heart beat against my ribcage, so loud I was sure they heard, before it stopped entirely. One of the men was looking directly at us, close enough that I could see his face. He stopped and tilted his head ever so slightly in a gesture that made my heart squeeze.

That face, that broken eyebrow that quirked ever so slightly in my direction and sent my heart racing—

What was Ryker doing out here? Had he found out who took me and sent a search party? Who was he with? My shadows wavered ever so slightly, flickering with my indecision. I could reveal myself now, go to him and have this all be over with. We could find a different way to get Calix, together.

He looked so tired. His hair was matted with sweat around his face, and his usual well-trimmed stubble was growing into an unruly beard. Had he slept since I left? Azden must have felt my struggle because he tightened his arm, grounding me in reality.

I couldn't just leave. Who knew what Ryker would do? He could have brought Tenebris soldiers with him, in which case I'd be taken back home with no hope of escape. I couldn't abandon Calix.

Then, as if he hadn't stopped at all, he turned around and walked in the opposite direction.

Azden and I stood against the tree for a long time after, waiting until the lights had fully disappeared from our minds before I let my shadows dissipate. Even after they were gone, his hands lingered for a moment, almost reluctant to let go.

I didn't think he was in my mind; at least I hoped he didn't hear the wild pendulum swinging between telling him about Ryker and letting it go. Would it be worse if he knew that there were people searching for me? We'd have to be more careful. Would he reconsider our deal?

As I organized my reasoning, I knew there was a train of thought I'd blocked off, one I would *not* consider, but even without acknowledging it I had a feeling that was the deciding factor.

Azden didn't need to know about Ryker.

I walked to the threshold of the dining room in record time. I longed for when I didn't know the halls, just so I could waste a little time on a few wrong turns. Azden had barely said a word as we trekked back inside, as lost in thought as I was. Ryker could be above me now, hopelessly searching a city in enemy territory.

Seeing him had thrown me off; I had just started getting used to my routine down here, and now I felt torn between the world above and my life in the tunnels. I missed him, but it was getting duller every day. The fuller my days became, the fewer opportunities I found to think about him, which was for the best. Ryker and I were nothing. Except that wasn't true at the end, was it? *No.* Nothing.

I cursed my past self for telling Walcott I'd go to dinner. The last thing I wanted to do right now was face Rahni and force myself somewhere I didn't belong.

A few people looked up when I entered, but they turned back to their tables, familiar with me by now. I spotted Azden and the others at their regular table. Walcott and Azden beckoned me over, and even Olyn smiled. Rahni didn't move, but she didn't show any signs of outward protest.

I slid into the empty seat, and to my surprise, the conversation continued on uninterrupted. They joked with the familiarity of old friends, adding some much-needed levity to my last week of intense training.

I observed, quietly absorbing their joy until Olyn said my name. He recalled the tea story, unable to make it through without laughing. Rahni didn't even glare at him. In response, I called to my shadows, compelling them to bring my tea to my mouth to sip.

"You're welcome," Azden teased, his smug lips taunting me.

"You can't take all the credit." I directed a shadow over to him, lightly slapping him on the shoulder.

"All I'm saying is that you couldn't do that when you got here." He lifted his hands in protest and a beam of light nudged my shadow away.

I set the tea back down, retracting my shadows. Even though he was annoying, I couldn't help but smile. Azden was a force of nature, that's for sure.

"Well magic isn't the only thing she's learned," Walcott said, nodding to Rahni.

"I suppose," she said, pressing her lips into a line, but I saw a smile tugging at the corners. Her eyes lit up a little, the restrained expression a big win when it came to Rahni. "At least she doesn't move like a freshly birthed fawn anymore."

Everyone's jaws dropped.

"What is everyone looking at?" Rahni snapped.

Azden was the first to break into a chuckle, and before we knew it the whole table devolved into laughter.

"I hate to break up the party, but since we have everyone here, we should talk about the plan for tomorrow." Smiles fell as a serious silence fell over the table. I set down my fork, no longer hungry. "We move in three days. Our mission is to get in and get out without being seen. We'll break into two teams: Rahni, Olyn, and Walcott, you'll be observing the guards' patterns. Estyn and I will watch Ruzu himself, see when he's vulnerable and whether there's anything we can use against him. We're not taking anyone else—we can't risk it. Don't talk to anyone, and if you're seen, get out as quickly and quietly as possible. Sound good?"

I raised my hand slightly, and everyone turned to me. "What about Calix? Are we going to try and find out where they're keeping him?"

Azden paused and thought for a moment, but Walcott cut in before he could say anything.

"Maybe you guys could check for him on your way back."

Azden worried his bottom lip, calculating the best way to do it. "Yes, that should work. We'll reach out and see if we can hear his thoughts in the dungeon."

Rahni pursed her lips and looked down, but didn't say anything. At least Walcott was looking out for me.

After I finished my romance novel, I picked up a history book from the library for my nightly reading with Walcott. Everything I read confirmed what Azden said. Compared to our textbooks, these painted Tenebris as an isolationist kingdom, claiming that we didn't often entertain ambassadors or trade agreements and that all relations were conquering. It was so jarring I often found myself reading it like fiction.

Sometimes I would ask Walcott questions as he worked, trying to corroborate the story with someone who had been in both places; but instead of giving me hope, he seconded most of what was written.

They had always recruited enchanters saying it was a noble profession, but it was seeming more and more like they were just groomed to feed the King's greed. Did Calix know? He had far more freedom than I; surely he'd discovered some of this. I knew Calliope wasn't happy. What about Ryker? Did he know what other kingdoms thought of us?

His haggard eyes flashed in my mind and I wished I hadn't thought of him. If only there was a way to tell him I was okay, but…I couldn't. Not without compromising our plans.

I reached for my arm, to feel the comforting cuff he had gifted me, but it wasn't there. Come to think of it, I hadn't worn it the past few days. I guess I had been too sore to reach for it.

I turned back to the page I was on, following the words with my finger. The text was dense, and often hard to get through, but I read fervently.

"As the seasonal enchanters are born at the height of the gods' rule on seasonal solstices, day enchanters are born at the height of Hyperion's rule during the solar eclipses. Historically, childbirth on these days is nearly always fatal for both the mother and the child. There is only record of three children surviving, the most recent being the late Prince Azden Duramoux,"

I stopped, my eyes caught on the last three words. I reread it a few times to make sure I'd understood correctly.

"Prince Azden? Heir to the throne?" I nearly shouted, making Walcott jerk up from his work soldering with a fire rope.

"Gods Estyn, you don't have to be so loud. What are you talking about?"

"Azden is the *prince?*"

"Why else would he be trying to take back the throne?"

"I don't know," I stammered, frustrated that I hadn't connected the dots before. He just didn't seem like a prince. I suppose Calix was also a prince, but I always imagined Bastian when I thought of heirs. Azden was nothing like Bastian.

You're the prince? I thought at Azden.

How'd you find out?

In a book because you conveniently forgot to tell me.

Does it change anything?

It—I mean you, I stuttered, thinking through the implications. He was a prince. A prince everyone presumed dead, leading the rebellion. *I suppose not.* I conceded.

Then what does it matter?

I don't know. I really didn't. Why did I care anyway? I was just here to get Calix and get out.

Want to come help me with something? He asked playfully. I worried my lower lip, considering.

Depends. I'm in the middle of something.

I'll make it worth your time. I could almost imagine the glimmer in his eyes that would accompany his promise.

Fine. Your office? I attempted to sound put out, but I couldn't help how little thoughts hid.

See you soon. It could have been my imagination, but his voice almost sounded suggestive. Definitely my imagination.

I half-walked half-jogged down the corridors to his office, then stopped a few feet away. What was I doing? This was a bad idea. I should just go to bed. Then again, I'd lived by shoulds long enough.

"Estyn." Azden perked up as I walked in, offering me a brilliant smile with his dimples on full display. My heart warmed in response.

"What'd you need help with?" I asked, this time able to make myself sound imposed upon.

"I've been reading everything we have on Night enchanting, which admittedly is not a lot, but I had an idea." Oh. So he actually did want help with something. "The other day, when your shadows touched me, my magic felt stronger than it ever had. I don't know how it would work, but I was thinking that maybe our powers somehow work off of one another." He was talking quickly, excited about his new theory. I raised a brow, doubtful and not wanting to disappoint him by proving him wrong.

"We can try." My voice was unsure, but he blazed past it.

"Okay, great. Now I'm not really sure what will happen, but envelop me in your shadows and tell me what you feel."

"Okay." I obliged, directing my shadows to him. They quickly enveloped him in darkness, and I saw his eyes flare in response. I closed my eyes and connected to my magic, trying to see if it felt any different. It didn't. I opened my eyes to see Azden a few inches from my face. Subconsciously, my shadows had pulled him to me while I was focused on my magic. I quickly retracted them, bringing him back into the light.

He looked at me, waiting for my report on what happened, but I was distracted by his smell, an overwhelming woodsy scent with a hint of citrus. It took all my restraint to not lean in closer and sniff him. It would have been extremely inappropriate, so thank the gods I didn't. He didn't step away, so I had to tilt my head up a little to look him in the eyes. They lit up with excitement. I didn't want to kill his hope, but I supposed it was all in the name of science.

"Did you feel anything?" he asked.

"Nothing out of the ordinary," I said, and he ran a hand through his hair, deep in thought.

"Try again. I could've sworn—just try again," he said, looking so convinced that I wanted him to be right.

I stepped back and beckoned my shadows once again, enveloping us both in the cloud of darkness. My magic still felt the same, but this time I also stepped into his mind. I felt Azden's thoughts, his magic, felt his power and mine at once. I opened my eyes to see he had called one of his light beams inside the cloud, casting shadows on his face that exaggerated the wonder painting his features.

Estyn, he thought my name reverently, calling out to me through my haze of magic, *you did it.* I blinked a few times, looking at the beam dancing between us.

I did what? I asked, although I felt different. It was more than being in his mind, I felt his power pulse with mine.

I don't know how, but my magic feels stronger, he thought, and I could feel his excitement, see it in his eyes as the gold burned bright, flared out to the edge of his iris.

A creak sounded from the door opening, and I snapped to attention, retracting all the shadows back into me in a whoosh. I stumbled back against the desk, dazed from the sudden exertion.

"Is now a good time?" Olyn asked, peeking his head through the door.

"Yeah, come on in." Azden walked to his desk chair and sat down, leaving me standing next to him awkwardly, unsure whether I should leave or not. Shadows lapped at my feet, begging for permission to hide me in darkness. Olyn looked from me to the door pointedly.

"Estyn, have a seat." Azden said, gesturing to the other chair opposite his desk.

"What's going on?" Azden asked Olyn, who shifted uncomfortably.

"One of our informants discovered that Tenebris has sent a legion of troops to the Braiwyth border, near where we found Estyn." Olyn looked at me with directed suspicion, as if it were too much of a coincidence to be chance. Again, I wanted to shrink into my shadows. I had nothing to do with it, but I couldn't hide the hope that they might rescue Calix.

"We'll monitor the situation, but I don't see any reason for concern yet." Azden reasoned with the seasoned logic of a born leader. I waited, but he didn't mention the people we'd seen earlier. He must've known they were from Tenebris; he likely knew more than me, having been able to listen to their thoughts as they searched around us. Why wouldn't he tell Olyn? Would he now? Had he already?

"Well I'm going to get some sleep," I interjected, not wanting to rehash the day's events and eager to leave the tension of the room. It was probably best if they had time to discuss without me present.

As soon as I got out of earshot, I took in as much air as my lungs could hold. Were they going to save Calix? Or were they coming for *me*? My chest felt tight as I suddenly realized I didn't want them to be here for me. Or for Calix for that matter. I wanted to be the one to take him, save him and bring him back to Walcott and me. I wouldn't—couldn't— go back to my life from before.

My breath quickened and I sank to the floor against the wall, exhausted from channeling Azden's magic and emotionally exhausted from coming to terms with the fact that I no longer had a home. Calliope and Calix were my home, and they were both gone. I wanted to cry, but I didn't feel like I could get enough air to even breathe, let alone sob. I hung my head between my knees, trying to regain control of my breath.

"Estyn?" The voice was so hesitant I almost didn't recognize Rahni as she walked up. "Are you okay?" I struggled to nod, and then I tried to stand. I leaned against the wall but managed to stay upright as she stared at me from a few feet away. Silent tears slipped down my face, and my shadows brushed them off in a tender caress. I'm sure I looked like a mess, albeit a magical mess.

"What's wrong?" I could tell she was uncomfortable with the role of consoler. I had never seen Rahni look out of place, but right now as she tried to comfort me, she looked as if she didn't know what to do with herself.

I couldn't form words for a good minute, but she stood by me as my breath evened out enough to say, "I'm fine, don't worry about it."

"Well," she started, "let me know if you need anything." And then she proceeded to wrap me in the most awkward hug I had ever received. It was uncomfortable, quick, and barely reminiscent of a hug, but it was nice. At the very least it helped me to stop crying.

"Thank you," I whispered, and she nodded and turned away to walk back to her room.

I gathered myself enough to go back to my room, eyes still raw and blurry, walking until I was only a few turns from the safe haven of my bed and a deep, restorative sleep.

You can't keep using her. I whipped around, suddenly wide awake. That was a voice I never expected to hear down here. Could I hear sounds from the surface? Unlikely. I must have been more tired than I thought, and exceedingly homesick to think I could hear Ryker's voice in the depths of enemy territory.

CHAPTER

15

I went through the motions, never fully present. Breakfast was just as lively as usual; everyone seemed to be in high spirits despite having a non-zero chance of dying tonight. My mind played through all the possible scenarios, not sparing any gory detail, until I felt a nudge at my arm from Walcott.

"You okay?" He lowered his voice so the others couldn't hear.

"Just nervous," I whispered, trying to collect myself. I wanted to be as strong as the others, unflappable in the face of danger, but what if I forgot everything? What if my magic simply dried up? It was irrational, I knew, but I couldn't help but worry about every dire possibility.

Azden stole a few glances at me throughout the meal, furrowing his brows every time. I'm sure he was listening to my thoughts, but I didn't care. Let him hear all the ways tonight could go wrong. Maybe then he'd take something seriously.

Now that's not fair. I didn't even jump in my chair; I was used to his interjections by now. *I take most things seriously. I've just found no use in wallowing in dread.* It could have sounded bitter, but it wasn't. He was offering a slightly firm reminder that my anxiety wasn't helpful. It did help; not that I would ever tell him. It would just inflate his already annoying ego.

Don't you think this is a little intrusive? I asked.

But it helped. He looked at me with a smirk. That damn smirk. I rolled my eyes and started listening to the conversation for the first time that morning.

"All I'm saying is that I think Rahni should get a puppy. It would be a huge upgrade from all the snakes," Walcott said.

"Snakes?" I asked before I could stop myself.

A fiendish grin spread on Rahni's face as she looked up at me.

"Can I see them?" I wasn't sure I meant it even as I asked.

"You will tonight," Olyn promised. I should've been afraid, but it only assuaged my fears. Looking around the table, not only were we all enchanters, but trained fighters. Not to mention we had both a day *and* a night enchanter.

"Calm down, Princess. It'll be fine," Rahni said. I took a few deep breaths and focused on trying to stomach some of my food.

Everyone was busy after breakfast, so I wandered the halls aimlessly. I was going to be let out, back into the real world. I had lost track of the days down here. I ran my hand along the wall, feeling the cool stone beneath my fingertips. I remembered when I used to get lost trying to find my room. *Who are we kidding, I still get lost.* The winding corridors were never-ending.

Not for the first time, I wondered how they came to be. I

doubted Azden and his friends were able to construct all the rooms by themselves. Though Lillya *had* said that the rebellion used to be bigger. And yet Azden expected us to be okay now?

I took a few more deep breaths. No use in working myself up over it. Or as Azden put it not-so-lightly, no use wallowing in my dread.

I went back to my room in hopes that I could make the day pass faster with sleep, but as soon as I entered, I saw a full set of black fighting leathers set on my bed.

It looked like something Rahni would feel at home in, not me. I rubbed the leather between my fingers, feeling the thick protective layer. It was soft enough to be comfortable to move in, but still functional. Better than the corsets and leggings I'd fought in before.

I quickly dressed, feeling fabric mold to my skin, but not in a constricting way. I squatted and stretched my arms, testing how the leather moved with me. I looked in the mirror and between my black hair cascading down my shoulders and the black fabric covering nearly every inch of skin, I looked every bit the intimidating night enchanter.

I tried to make a breezy, indifferent expression—the 'I know I'm hot and intimidating' face—to complete the look, but it looked absolutely ridiculous. Uneasy smile it was.

I walked over to my dresser and spotted the arm cuff Ryker had given me. Without knowing exactly why, I threaded it onto my arm until it sat comfortably around my bicep. I braided my hair down my back to keep it out of my face and took one last look, letting my shadows swirl around me.

I ran into Rahni and Olyn on my way to the meeting room.

"Hello." I almost hoped they didn't hear, but Olyn nodded in acknowledgement.

"Ready?" Rahni's attention made me stand a little taller. Even if I was scared, I couldn't let her see it. I swore I saw a tongue flicker out from under her sleeve, but it was probably just a trick of the light.

"Let's do it," I said. At least I sounded confident. We walked through the double doors to Azden and Walcott already at the table, and I got deja-vu from when I had walked into the exact same sight, except with my hands tied. I flexed my fingers to remind myself they weren't anymore.

Azden looked up from the map he'd been pointing to and immediately caught my eyes. He was staring with such an intensity that I thought maybe I'd done something wrong, but the grin that spread across his face told me otherwise.

He looked every part the rebel leader. Leathers similar to mine hugged the curves of his muscles. He wasn't as built or intimidating as Olyn, but he was sculpted and it showed. His hair was still perfectly messed about his head, but his shoulders were tense and he looked prepared for battle.

Ready to go, Freckles? He was still looking down at the map, but I caught him glancing up at me with a sly look in his eye. My stomach started flipping for an entirely different reason, but I willed myself to focus.

Ready as I'll ever be.

"Alright, let's head out." Azden said it with an authority that made each one of us fall in line.

I followed a few steps behind and watched them walk in front of me, thanking the gods I was on their side. We were far from the exit Azden had taken me to before, so when we stopped randomly in the middle of the corridor, I almost smacked straight into the swords strapped to Olyn's back.

Azden reached for a sconce, pulling it slightly towards him like a lever. A section of the wall receded, revealing a dark stone staircase winding up. What was with these people and weird exits? Azden winked my way as if pleased with the surprise flickering on my face. I wiped it off as quickly as possible and looked away.

We walked up in silence, my hands braced on the wall next to me. The stairs were slick with condensation, and narrow enough that Olyn's heels hung off the edge as he climbed ahead of me. I looked back down to see the wall groan as it slid back into place, enclosing us in complete darkness. The only sounds were feet on stone, though notably not Rahni's, and shallow breathing.

As much anxiety as I'd felt, my heart was now speeding up for a new reason. Fresh air. Woods. Anything but dark, damp underground. I heard a key jingle, then light flooded the staircase. I lifted a hand to shade my eyes, peeking through once they adjusted. The large wooden door opened to a small room, but I couldn't see much with Olyn blocking me. When I finally reached the top, we were in a back storage room. Cleaning supplies and boxes filled the shelves around us. As soon as I cleared the door, Azden eased it closed and Olyn pushed one of the shelves in front. A backless shelf. It was not hidden at—

Light rippled around the wall until the door disappeared. Could I do things like that? Tricks with my shadows? I made a note to try later.

Walcott led the way, peeking his head out of the door before signaling us to follow. We walked through another room with fires blazing and swords lining the walls; a blacksmith's shop. Everyone seemed to know where to go, wordlessly weaving through the workbenches to a back door. Walcott looked first again before opening it to a dark alley. I walked out and took a deep breath, savoring the feeling of the cool night air on my skin.

Welcome to my city. Azden's voice interrupted my thoughts, and my eyes snapped open. I'd seen it from afar, but the city looked different inside. It was more densely packed than Artange, storefronts stacked atop one another, apartments stacked on top of those. I had a million questions, but Azden simply smiled at my confusion and slunk to the front.

He motioned with two fingers out to the street and everyone except for me nodded. They really should've prepared me better for this. It's not like spy hand-signaling was included in my education.

Walcott, Olyn and Rahni crossed the street, disappearing into the shadows. I went to follow, unsure of what I was supposed to do, before Azden's arm shot out to block me.

Not you.

You didn't really prepare me for this part, I thought at him. The prick shrugged as if he enjoyed watching me try and piece together the plan. He nodded back into the alley where a rusty ladder led to the roof.

You first, he said in my head. I squinted at him, which, like most things, amused him. I grabbed the first bar, and as I climbed I became increasingly aware of how the fighting leathers hugged my curves. I reached into Azden's thoughts—purely for mission reasons—and found that he noticed too.

I lifted myself over the low stone wall at the top, landing lightly on my feet as Rahni had trained me. Azden quickly followed, silent behind me. I wouldn't even know he was there if it weren't for his presence in my mind.

He moved in front, gesturing for me to follow, but I was frozen looking at the castle looming ahead. The white stone facade shone like a beacon in the rest of the grey city. No doubt it also helped protect against people sneaking around at night. I let out a sigh, shaking my head slightly as I grasped just how unprepared I was.

I followed Azden as he ran along the roofs and jumped across alleys. I hesitated at the first few, but he didn't slow down or check that I was following, so I swallowed my fear of splatting on the concrete below and threw myself across the gap. It got easier as I went, and I noticed how much stronger I'd gotten. I was barely breathing hard by the time we reached the castle walls.

Azden, ever the performer, jumped down to a balcony, pushed off and flipped before landing on the ground. He smiled back up at me, but there was no way he could make me out from down there. Even so, I shook my head as I looked over the edge, wondering how in the world I was going to get down.

Show-off, I thought at him, before spotting a ladder.

When I climbed down, I turned to see him just a few feet away wearing a massive smile. My face contorted, annoyed by how much he was enjoying this.

The castle wall towered before us, almost reaching into the clouds. I really should have asked for more details. Azden just turned to me with the same twisted excitement before taking off towards the wall. I looked up to the sky, praying the gods were watching over me before I ran to catch up with him, straight towards the heavily guarded castle.

As we ran along the wall, I called my shadows to wrap around us and hide us from any guards that might look down. Azden kept running, not slowing his pace at all. Did he think my shadows were that effective? I hoped they were, and continued running after him, careful to keep my footfall as quiet as possible, which didn't feel quiet enough in the silent night.

We ran along the castle wall, the slight incline feeling steeper with each block until we reached the edge of a forest. The city loomed below us, blending into the night with all the grey stone buildings and trees shadowing the streets. Azden started pulling rope out of his bag, coiling it on the ground between us until he found a hook.

"Oh, no," I said aloud, looking from the rope to the wall at least four times my height.

Oh, yes, he thought with an impish gleam in his eye.

He threw the rope, catching the stone at the top in the first toss. He pulled on it, testing the security before clipping a small metal device to my belt and looping the rope through it.

What are you thinking? There is no way I'm going first, I yelled in my mind because there was no way I'd keep it to a whisper if I said it out loud.

Well I can't go first. I'm a prince. He looked at me as if it was the most obvious thing in the world until he broke into a smile at my indignation. How could he joke at a time like this?

You'll be fine, he said, though it did little to stop me imagining myself falling to my death. For the second time this night. He hooked himself on below me, then demonstrated how to pull the rope through. I took a deep breath and looked up where the hook was secured twenty feet above me.

This was a pretty inefficient way to kill me, I thought at him before walking my feet up the wall and tugging at the rope.

It was easier than I thought, but my arms still strained as I pulled myself up the wall. True to his word, as I pulled the rope through the metal it caught, not allowing me to fall. I focused on breathing and pulling the rope, and soon I was at the top.

Even worse than being the first to climb, now I was on the top of the castle wall. Alone. I spotted a guard a ways down, and instinctively wrapped my shadows around me, crouching low against the stone. Luckily, Azden swung over the wall a matter of seconds later. How he did it so quickly, I would never know.

Without skipping a beat, he grabbed the hook and secured it on the inside of the opposite wall. He then showed how to feed the rope through the metal piece to descend. Right after, he pretty much jumped, only touching the wall twice before landing on the ground.

It was then that I realized I'd made a deal with a madman.

I squeezed my eyes shut before leaning back over the wall, walking down slowly. Either a minute or an hour later, I couldn't tell, I stepped onto solid ground again. I never thought I was scared of heights, but tonight was making me reconsider.

Azden unhooked the rope and it tumbled down in a pile before us. He shoved it back into his pack, and we took off once again towards a grove of trees at the edge. Adrenaline pumped through me, and my magic pumped through my veins, begging to be let loose. I leaked my shadows out, letting them hide us in a thin veil. We stopped running once we reached tree cover, instead darting between trees in short sprints. Eventually we made it close enough to see into the windows of a large, lit room. The entire castle was covered in windows, though most rooms were dark, except a study with a few leather armchairs and books lining the walls. Azden pulled me down behind a bush, yanking me so hard that I almost fell. I glared at him before turning back to the scene unfolding before us.

Ruzu sat in one chair, swirling a dark amber liquor in his glass. Next to him was a man that was almost comically large for his chair. I squinted, wishing I could see better, but too scared to move any closer. Ominous shadows danced on their features, their faces solely illuminated by a hearth and a few candles in the room.

Ruzu was all sharp angles. He was tall and slender, almost looking like a thing of nightmares. The light bounced off of his hands which were layered with rings on every finger. He wore a three-piece suit that was tailored to his body and didn't seem to wrinkle despite his relaxed posture. Altogether I couldn't see his eyes from this distance, I could sense power coming from him.

It's all coming together. Going exactly as planned. As I tuned into his thoughts, I heard his low timbre reverberate through my head. Every thought felt wicked and I had a sudden feeling that I needed to stop listening.

I tried to shake it off and focused my attention on the man next to him instead. The voice that came through was familiar, but I couldn't quite place it.

Thank the gods I don't have to travel back tonight.

I looked at Azden, but he was studying the interaction even more intently than I was. He barely noticed me next to him, lost in the world of thoughts.

The guest got up and turned to the window for a brief moment. It was then that I recognized him: Turrek. Tenebris' army commander. What was he doing here? Were they negotiating a peace treaty? Did he make a deal to get Calix? I tapped Azden, breaking his concentration so that he could hear me.

That's Tenebris' army commander, I thought, with a mix of shock and confusion.

I know.

What's he doing here?

Your guess is as good as mine.

I looked back at the library to see the room had gone dark. I looked at the wall, scanning all the windows until a room lit up on the second floor, illuminating Ruzu's silhouette. Azden and I crawled over to get a better vantage point, watching him shuffle around his room and ready himself for bed.

I listened to his thoughts, but they were mostly boring reflections on events of the day. He obsessed over what people thought, always coming to the conclusion that they adored him. I mentally gagged, but forced myself to keep listening in case he came back to the meeting we'd just witnessed. The closest thing to useful was musings on his own political genius.

Turrek's room must have been in another wing because no other window lit on this wall. I listened to Ruzu's thoughts until he drifted to sleep, and by the time his main train of thought quieted I was ready to scream. I looked at Azden to silently communicate how dull that had been, but his jaw was clenched. While I had been bored to tears, listening to Ruzu had only inflamed Azden's anger. I could see light almost seeping out of him, his magic growing restless with his ire. I rested my hand on his, hoping to bring him back to the moment, reminding him that light was the least helpful thing to have during a nighttime spy mission. He bristled at the touch, eyes snapping to mine. The gold had overtaken his entire iris, swirling and pulsing.

We should go, I thought at him, but I wasn't sure he heard. He kept looking past me, lost in his own rage.

"Azden," I whispered, tugging at his sleeve, "It's time to go." He shook his head slightly, refocusing his eyes on me. He nodded once and started to crawl back to the woods. We stayed low as we circled the building, moving deeper and deeper into the castle grounds.

Here. He stopped outside a section of the wall with no windows. *The dungeon is down there.* I looked down where he gestured at a seemingly innocuous section of wall.

I sat, preparing myself to reach. I was already tired both physically and mentally, but this was the most important part of the night. I concentrated on the stars dotting my mind, each a person's consciousness. I tried to go as fast as possible, tuning in for only a word or two at a time to hear their voice. Some were low and gruff, others scratchy and tired. More than one made me jump as I heard it, the promise of death dripping from their thoughts. After a few minutes and several dozen voices, my energy started to wane. I looked at Azden, but he was still focused. I closed my eyes once again, thinking of Azden and hoping some divine intervention would tell me which one Calix was.

I flipped through heads faster than I ever had before, the voices muddling my mind.

Prince

I stopped suddenly, caught on the word. I listened closer, learning that the voice belonged to Calix's guard. My heart stopped.

Between one breath and the next, my head filled with the sweet baritone of my brother.

No one's coming for me, he thought, and tears welled at the fear and pain in his voice. Although I risked giving us away,

I couldn't help but respond.

I'm coming for you Calix. Stay strong. I love you.

And now I'm going crazy. I suppose it was only a matter of time, he thought. My heart broke. I wanted to cry out, but I couldn't. I settled for silent tears as I listened to his voice. I wanted to burst in right then and there, forget the guards and plan and just whisk him away. He didn't deserve this.

I felt the rough pad of Azden's thumb brush a tear from my cheek. He grazed it down to my chin, angling my head to his. I broke my concentration on Calix's thoughts and looked at Azden, silent tears continuing to fall.

"They have him." My voice was small, and I felt small. Why couldn't I do anything? At least he was alive, I told myself, though it seemed a small consolation when he was suffering and I couldn't do anything about it.

Azden nodded, bringing another arm around my shoulders and pulling me into his chest. As much as I wanted to, I didn't sob. I just let my silent tears fall down onto his shirt, soaking into the leather on his chest.

He'll be okay, Azden thought, but I could tell it was more for me than anything. My mind felt blank. I couldn't even form a thought to respond to him, and it didn't matter because my magic was so depleted that I wouldn't be able to send it if I'd wanted to.

"Let's go," I said, wiping the last tears away and strengthening my resolve.

The trip back up the wall was easier. My muscles were sore, but I had a new numbness that dampened the rest of the journey. I thought I'd be happy to find that Calix was alive, but hearing the fear and pain in his thoughts sent me into a spiral of emotion I couldn't escape. Now I just felt numb. I landed at the top, barely checking around me.

"Hey, you," a voice shouted from further down the wall. The world crashed into me as I snapped back into myself. Azden still dangled below.

Come on, Azden. Hopefully he'd listen.

The voice was a few hundred feet away, but fast approaching. We had to get out. Azden jumped up, frantically switching the hook to the other side before clipping us both in. The impact shocked my knees as I slammed onto the ground, but Azden barely used the rope before landing and rolling to lose some of the momentum. He tumbled back up to his feet, tugging the hook down just as the guard peeked her head over the edge.

She didn't waste a moment, running to the door that exited right where we were headed. I looked the other way, but the ground behind us dropped off into a cliff peppered with trees. I helped Azden bunch the rope back into his bag and took off, hoping there was a chance we could beat her.

Azden was faster than me, and even he hadn't made it to the door when the guard barreled out sword first.

Fuck, Azden and I thought in unison.

Please don't make me hurt you, she thought, and I saw her hands tremble.

It was just enough to make me hesitate, and she slashed, catching my cheek. I spun away, feeling the blood dribble down to my chin. Azden dashed forward, disarming her in seconds. He then pinned her, holding her easily as she struggled to free her arms. I reached up to my cheek, feeling the cut that stretched along the side of my face.

Wait, I told Azden.

He looked at me for a second before nodding, keeping his hold but not delivering the killing blow. I walked up, looking into eyes I recognized. It was the girl I had kicked to the ground the night they took Calix.

I reached a few fingers to her neck, pressing the spot Rahni showed me until her head lolled forward.

"Alright, let's go." Azden whispered, his magic likely just as tired as mine. I reached down, grabbing her arms. She was heavier than she looked.

"Help me carry her." He stared at me as if I'd just suggested we jump off the cliff behind us.

"Are you fucking crazy?"

"Do you trust me?" He stood frozen, watching me struggle to hoist her over my shoulders. After a moment he shook his head in disbelief and walked forward to grab her other arm.

Even though I'd been getting stronger, carrying a person several miles back to the blacksmith shop was *exhausting*. I wrapped my shadows around us, hiding us from the few stragglers in the city streets, but even the shadows seemed lethargic. They lacked the normal mischievous temperament I'd come to love.

It took us more than twice as long as our trip out, but we made it to the shop. We pushed the bookcase back, opened the door and eased the guard down the stairs. I slung her over my back, my legs quivering on the last few steps. Azden rejoined at my side, bearing some of the weight.

"Who's going to move the bookshelf back?" I asked, looking back up the staircase as the wall slid back into place.

"Don't worry about it," he said, grunting as he shifted the guard's arm up over his shoulders. I could tell he wasn't happy with me, but I couldn't just leave her there. She needed to get out. I felt it.

We started carrying her towards the cells, but I stopped. "We can't put her in there."

"Why not?" He asked, trying to nudge me forward.

"We just kidnapped her. She's not going to want to talk to us if she wakes up on a cold concrete floor." The fatigue may have caught up to me, making my words seem a little more bitter than intended.

"So what do you suggest we do, *Princess?*"

"Let's just put her in one of the bedrooms. It's not like she's done anything wrong."

"We're just going to put one of Ruzu's guards into a bedroom? Are we going to serve her a three course meal while we're at it?" My irritation was simmering now, threatening to devolve into something nasty if I didn't control it.

"I know her," I said, trying to placate the situation. Azden frowned, confusion now lining his irritation. "She was there when they attacked Artange, and she's the reason I made it out alive. I think she could help us." He looked at me, thinking through what I'd said.

"Fine. We'll put her in the bedroom up on the right." Azden split off to grab handcuffs from the dungeons and I limped-dragged her into the room, propping her up on the bed. She looked so still. I panicked for a second, but after a moment saw her chest rise with a shallow breath. Azden came in, cuffing her arm to the bed rail and instructing Hemm to wait outside and alert us when she awoke.

Then he stormed out, leaving me to follow. Despite their fatigue, my shadows came out with an offer to disappear, but I called them back in. I would not back down.

I followed him to his office where he slammed the door behind him. I paused with my hand on the doorknob, reconsidering whether it was a good idea to talk when we were both exhausted.

The door flew open, and I almost tumbled in with it, crashing right into Azden.

"Just hear me out," I said, tilting my head to look up at him. He stepped to the side, letting me in but certainly not warmly. "I heard her thoughts when I first saw her and again tonight. She was scared. She didn't want to be there."

Azden stood with his arms crossed, looking down at me with a blank expression. I never thought I'd miss those irritating smirks.

"Just because she's not a cold-blooded killer doesn't mean she'll risk her life for us."

"That's true, but I felt it. I think she'll agree with us. She doesn't like how things are."

Azden looked at me with a cold fury that made me flinch. He breathed heavily, as if trying to collect his composure before he spoke again.

"No one *likes* how things are here. That doesn't mean they're willing to fight for it." He was seething; years of pent up frustration were coming to a head with this argument, and I could see what he thought of me: I was a naive princess. I knew nothing about his world. He was wrong about me.

I couldn't blame him. As much as my own anger wanted to react, say something hurtful just to spite him, I didn't.

"We need someone on the inside. If we can get her to work with us—"

"Even if she works with us, what if she's caught? What if she double crosses us? Estyn, I don't think you understand that there are infinitely many ways this could bite us in the ass."

"I get that, but if you'll just listen—"

"Estyn, I have been listening, but it's been a long night, and now, even though I knew it was a bad idea, we're stuck with her and are going to have to figure it out. Let's just talk about it in the morning." He ran his hand through his hair, pulling out a few strands with the rough gesture.

"Fine." He was clearly not in a place to discuss tonight. I looked at him for a moment, but he refused to look me in the eye.

"I trust you don't need help finding your room?" *Ass.* I turned and left, hoping he heard my thought loud and clear. I slammed the door behind me, my tenuous grip on my composure finally failing.

CHAPTER

16

My muscles ached with every movement, but I managed to force myself out of bed. My cheek throbbed and I felt the tender skin around the scab that had formed. At least it wasn't deep enough to need a healer.

I needed to see the guard before anyone else, mostly because I needed to see whether I was right. I dressed quickly, eying my clothes crumpled in the corner from the previous night.

Hemm stood outside her door, eyes drooping. He stood straighter when he noticed me approach with two tea mugs and a plate of scones balanced on my arm.

"Has she been up yet?"

"I heard some noise inside, but I haven't gone in."

"Okay, I'll just be a minute." I reached for the handle, but Hemm blocked me.

"I'm afraid I'll have to ask Azden first."

"He said I should be the one to see her this morning." I stared at Hemm, trying to read whether he believed me or not. He was conflicted, but let it slide. He also thought I looked as much of a wreck as I felt.

He lowered his arm cautiously, and I slipped inside.

A single candle burned on the dresser, causing shadows to dance across the figure crouched on the bed. She paused, staring as if I'd caught her mid-escape, but I noted the cuffs safely secured. I tested a few steps forward to see her reaction. She shrunk against the headboard.

"Good morning," I said, trying to sound as friendly as possible. She just stared at me, trying to read my thoughts as I read hers—not that she knew I could. Her eyes flicked down to my cheek, looking almost remorseful.

"Are you hungry?" I asked, and she didn't reply but her eyes drifted down to the scones. She was conflicted; hungry but wary.

"They were baked fresh this morning. The blueberry are my favorite, but I brought a few different flavors." I walked over and set them on the bedside table. I was close enough for her to kick me, but she wouldn't. She just stared, observing me as if my actions would answer all the questions brewing in her mind.

"What's your name?" I asked. She continued staring, not even shifting as if she wanted to answer. I stared for a few moments, sipping my tea patiently. I walked back to the armchair near the bed, shifted it to face her, and settled in for a long morning.

"I'm Estyn," I offered. Her eyes flickered slightly in acknowledgment, but she didn't know who I was beyond that. "I wish we met under more favorable circumstances, but I needed to talk to you. I think you could help us."

"Why would I want to help you?" Her voice was quiet, matching her meek posture, but it was more curious than bitter.

"We want the same thing," I said. She didn't respond, but raised a brow in question. "A better future." She scoffed, reaching for a scone. At the very least, she relaxed slightly and eased back into the pillows.

"So you want to use me." She sounded sadly resigned.

"No, I want to work together."

"Same thing." She nibbled on the edge of her scone.

"Do you like serving King Ruzu?" I asked.

"It is an honor." Bullshit. Mouths lie, but thoughts couldn't.

"What do you think of the King?"

"Is this a trap?" she asked, but her thoughts had already betrayed her opinion of him.

"What if I told you there was another option?"

"I'd say you were crazy, had a death wish, or both." Even though she doubted me, I sensed a twinkle of hope hidden under years of disappointment.

"You don't have to settle. There's always another way," I said with such conviction, I almost convinced myself. She shook her head, still disbelieving. "I'll talk to my team about the cuffs, but I hope you'll understand why we have to be cautious for now."

She was so disheartened she didn't even bother asking to be let go. I worried that she might agree with me, but not have the passion to back it up. Which is precisely what Azden had warned against.

"I'll be back soon." I started walking back to the door, but was stopped by a soft voice before I opened the door.

"Ketra." I spun around, making sure I heard correctly.

"It's nice to meet you, Ketra." I smiled, both at her introduction and at the small hope I heard in her thoughts. She was letting herself imagine that I could be right.

I eased the door closed behind me, still smiling as I turned to see an anxious Hemm and a furious Azden. I glared at Hemm.

"Don't look at him. This is on you." Azden seethed, turning and expecting me to follow. I gulped the last sip of my tea and followed after him, gripping on the mug handle for strength. I peeked into his head, trying to gauge just how mad he was, just to hear *pretty fucking mad*. So he was listening to my thoughts too. This whole not being the only telepath thing was a pain in the ass.

He threw open the doors to the meeting room, and I winced as they slammed into the walls. Rahni, Olyn and Walcott were already sitting, scowling at me as I walked in. I looked at Walcott for sympathy, but he just looked down and shook his head. This was not going to be good.

"What the fuck were you thinking?" Azden growled, his quiet anger almost worse than yelling. My stomach tied in knots, responding with guilt instead of anger. How was he even good at being angry?

Stop distracting yourself by thinking about how *I'm being mad at you instead of fucking* why *I'm mad.*

Get out of my head.

Clearly you can't be trusted. Although he had every reason to think that, it still felt like a punch to the gut. I had fooled myself into thinking we had developed a rapport; maybe even a friendship. This was just the reminder I needed that I was a means to an end, not a part of their group.

"We need her." I crossed my arms, digging in to defend myself.

"*We* need to avoid liabilities." He left it vague, but his pointed stare told me it wasn't just Ketra he was referring to.

"One night of reconnaissance isn't enough to plan an assassination. We need an inside man."

"If you thought that, you should have said something before fucking kidnapping a guard."

"You didn't stop me." The tension in the room was reaching a boiling point and it was painted on the others' faces. I didn't dare look away from Azden. It was childish, but it felt like whoever looked away first would be the one to defer. I wasn't caving.

The lights flickered then pulsed, almost blinding me. My veins ignited with magic inflamed by my emotions. I knew I should've controlled my anger, but I didn't want to. It was stoking my shadows, compelling them to chaos. So be it.

Azden's eyes were swallowed by gold. Even though he was better trained, his temper was also gaining control of his magic.

"Guys," Walcott said, attempting to pacify the situation, but the magic pulsing in my ears made him sound distant.

"She wants to help," I said.

"Is that what you learned over your morning chat? That she would just *love* to go back and feed us information on Ruzu so we can go murder him? Huh? Is that how it went?"

"I didn't give anything away. I'm not an idiot."

"Could've fooled me."

"You're acting like a child."

"And you're acting like a naive little princess."

"Stop." Rahni's voice cut through our bickering, and we both turned to look at her. When my eyes broke from Azden's I saw the effects of our fight. Shadows and light rays tumbled around the room, turning over the furniture in their wake. The room looked like tornado had blown through it.

"You're both acting like children. Estyn—that was ridiculously stupid, and it's not how we work. But it's done, so Azden you're going to have to fucking deal with it. Estyn's right about one thing: we need information, and if we can convince her to work with us, then that's the best way to get it." I opened my mouth to speak, but she held a finger up to stop me, "Don't get me wrong—Azden was right to say that you're naive. A million things could've and could still go wrong, and if you ever try something like that again—" she leaned in, enunciating every word, "you will regret it." The chair was somehow silent even as she slid it against the stone. As she left, her footfall was light as ever, but it was clearly her version of storming out.

Everyone was silent, but it did nothing to soothe tempers. I looked at Walcott for guidance again, and although he was still mad, he nodded towards the door. I took a deep breath, the sound making Azden clench his jaw, and then walked out.

The halls that had been impossibly long now felt suffocating. I needed fresh air, but I couldn't leave, so I just wandered. I heard Azden come up behind me and braced myself for another verbal lashing. It was immature, but I didn't stop walking, forcing him to half-jog to catch up with me.

He grabbed my arm just below my cuff, and I spun around to find him just a few inches away. If I thought the tension was too much with a table between us, it was unbearable now. He looked at my face, eyes darting around as if picking between insults. I refused to be the one to break the silence, so I pressed my lips together and waited.

Just as I was about to turn back around and walk away, he

pulled me closer, wrapped a hand around the base of my neck, and leaned forward until a flinch would've brought our lips together.

And then, because I'm a hotheaded idiot who makes poor choices, I closed the distance between us.

The kiss channeled all the energy he couldn't put into words, our lips tangling as magnetically as our magic had. I wanted to sink into the feeling, memorize how it felt to have his hands on me and for our need for one another to overrule any rational thought.

But ignoring rational thoughts didn't preclude others from slipping through the cracks, and as I felt a shadow tug at my ankle, the word *liability* echoed in my mind like a bad dream.

Azden thought I was a liability.

I pulled away and slapped him. After my hand connected with his cheek in a satisfying smack, he reached up to touch the tender area. A grin pulled at the corners of his mouth, dimples indenting the spot I'd just hit. Why the fuck was he smiling?

I decided he was the most infuriating person I'd ever met, then spun around and stormed off. As much as I tried to resist it—and I was trying pretty damn hard—as I felt Azden watch me walk away, I couldn't stop my own lips from curling into a smile.

My toes peeked above the bathwater, pointing and flexing as I tried to focus on anything but my thoughts. I told Ketra I would see her again, but I doubt they'd let me.

I should wait for the team to talk to her. If I went alone, Azden would be even angrier, though I couldn't see how that was possible. Maybe he deserved it. Who was he to think he could kiss me?

I wanted to be mad at him for it, but I was really mad at myself. No matter that I was furious with him, no matter that it was completely unexpected, my lips still tingled with his absence. Not that I'd ever tell him that. I made a mental note to never think about it around him. Like that would work.

I dunked my head under the water, holding myself under until my lungs burned and I had formed a plan.

I leaned around the corner, stealing a glance at Hemm where he stood posted outside Ketra's door. I had no idea if this was going to work, but I had to try. I closed my eyes, synchronizing the pulse of the magic in my veins with my breathing. I flickered the lights down the hall on the end opposite from me. Hemm turned, peering into the darkness. *Here goes nothing.*

I connected to Hemm's mind and screamed, hoping it would sound like it came from the other end. I peeked around again to see him running into the darkness, my knight in shining armor. I spared no time darting to Ketra's door and sliding inside.

She was sitting in the same position I'd left her in, but the plate of scones was now empty.

"Hello, Ketra," I said, slightly out of breath. She didn't respond, but nodded slightly, which was an upgrade from earlier. I walked over and set down the sandwich I'd lifted from the kitchen onto her plate. "It's on this special bread that Walcott invented—he double fires it to get a perfect crust. I hope you like it."

"Thank you." Her voice was still quiet, but she was warming to me. I wish I had more time to get to know her, but I didn't have that luxury.

"Okay, I'm going to get to the point. King Ruzu is keeping

my brother in his dungeons, and I need to get him out. He's too good for this world, and I'll stop at nothing to get him back. You'd like him—everyone does. I partnered with some people to overthrow the King in exchange for their help rescuing him. I know you hate the King; that much was apparent when we spoke earlier. We need someone on the inside, and I think you could do it. You wouldn't have to fight, just pass us information. What do you think?" She pondered my offer, trying to find the caveats.

"Now that you've told me this, are you going to kill me if I refuse?"

"No. I'd let you go."

"What if I report this back to the King?"

"You could, but I don't think you will." Her thoughts confirmed as much.

"You don't know me."

"That's true, but I'm willing to take that chance."

"Where's the rest of your team?" I winced slightly at the term.

"They need more convincing, but I'm willing to do it if you want to help." I held my breath, waiting for her response. It wouldn't fix everything with the others, but it would be a huge help for the mission, which was why I was here anyway.

She weighed her options, trying on each possibility and evaluating them as objectively as she could. Part of me bristled at the invasion of privacy. Did Azden feel the same? He probably explained it away, saying the ends justified the means. I wasn't sure I believed that.

"Okay," she said. I jumped, having gotten used to her wavering thoughts. "I'll do it." She sounded surer the second time. Even though she had taken a while to think about it, I knew that was what her instincts were telling her.

"Okay, fantastic. I'll go get the others so they can come talk to you and unlock your cuffs." She nodded, almost smiling. It was the most positive emotion I'd seen her express since being here; though given that we kidnapped her, that wasn't saying much. I beamed at her, wanting to show just how excited I was that we'd be working together.

"Rahni," I called, out of breath after jogging to catch up to her. She spun on her heels to face me, her usual mask of indifference twisted into displeasure. I never would have imagined Rahni being the person I turned to, but she had been the most open to working with Ketra. Not to mention I wasn't eager to see Azden anytime soon, and I couldn't find Walcott or Olyn anywhere. "She agreed to work with us." To my surprise, Rahni didn't balk at the fact that I'd seen Ketra again.

"People will say anything to be freed."

"I told her I'd free her either way." Rahni raised an eyebrow, both at my lack of tact and apparent lack of forethought, but her concern was assuaged nonetheless.

"I'll see for myself." She started towards Ketra's room, walking quicker than usual, which I had thought impossible. We made quite the pair; Rahni's graceful gait next to the erratic shuffling that I was desperately trying to conceal as fast walking.

She passed Hemm without so much as acknowledging his protests, bursting into the room in a much more abrupt way than I would have. I was hoping I could warn Ketra, or at least ease the two into an introduction, but Rahni dove straight in.

"You're willing to help us murder the King?" To my amazement, Ketra didn't shrink in Rahni's presence. She sat up and strengthened her resolve in response.

"Yes." There was no hesitation. It was as if I had seen a subdued version of Ketra, a mere shadow of the young woman before me.

"And you know the risks?" Rahni asked.

"Yes."

"Including the risk of me personally delivering a slow and painful death if you double cross us?" Even though the threat wasn't directed at me, Rahni's conviction was unnerving.

"Yes." Ketra barely flinched.

"Okay." Rahni turned and left, directing Hemm to free Ketra on her way out. I paused, unsure of whether to follow Rahni or stay with Ketra, but ultimately decided to regroup with Rahni.

"So?" I asked, eager to know her thoughts, or rather which ones she would choose to share.

"It'll work. You shouldn't have gone to her without us, and they will be mad, but I'll help convince them." I couldn't help but feel unstoppable with Rahni on my side. She was a force to be reckoned with, and I was glad to not be on the receiving end of her scrutiny for once.

"Thank you. For everything." Even though she didn't like me, she had worked with me and made me a better fighter, and now she was helping me with the team. If I didn't know any better, I would've thought she had gotten a soft spot for me.

Luckily, I did know better.

"No need to thank me. I haven't done anything that wasn't for my own benefit." Rahni walked off, presumably to talk to the others, though with her I could never be sure.

Ketra poked her head outside the door, examining the hallway. Her eyes opened wide, drinking in the environment, and I couldn't help but wonder if that was what I looked like when I first got here.

"Do you want a tour?" I asked, interrupting her inspection.

"That would be great, thank you." She risked a step outside her room, half expecting Hemm to detain her, but he just observed, still as a statue.

"Are you hungry?" I asked her. It was nearing dinner time and I had forgotten to eat lunch, which never put me in a good mood.

"I could eat." She wasn't quite as timid as before, but not as defiantly sure as she was with Rahni. I suspected she was getting closer to her normal self, albeit a version with a healthy dose of vigilance.

Ketra marveled at the stone hallways as we walked, trying to deduce where we could be. She had many guesses, some of them closer than others. I suppressed a smile, careful to make no indication that I could hear what she thought.

The dining room was quieter than usual since we were arriving at an off time. A few people ate alone, scattered among the tables.

"Sit over there and I'll go grab us some food." I said, gesturing to a table in one of the far corners. No one would pass unless they had reason to, which they shouldn't. I was trying to give her the welcome experience I wish I'd gotten, letting her soak in the room in silence and ground herself in this strange environment.

The kitchen was calm save for the sounds of dishes clinking in the sink. Walcott stood over the washbasin scrubbing at the grime on a large pot. He was so invested that he barely looked up when the door opened, and I was sure he didn't see that it was me. I grabbed two plates and started scooping some of the remaining food onto them, hoping that I could finish before Walcott looked up.

Whereas I felt something akin to righteous indignation with the others, when I saw Walcott all I felt was shame.

Despite my best efforts, however, he finished scrubbing before I left. I watched in slow motion as his face melted into unease when he recognized me, and my shadows started to materialize in response, begging to hide me.

"I'm sorry," I said, my voice cracking despite my best efforts. I wanted to be mad; rage was easier to cling to than whatever it was I was feeling now.

"I just wish you would've talked to me." The subdued pain in his voice was ten times worse than Azden's anger.

"I wanted to, I just didn't have time. I was only trying to help."

"I know. I don't blame you." Relief washed over me, but it was temporary. I yearned for his forgiveness as if it would solve everything.

"Are we good?" I wanted to go back to before, to our companionable silence and his comforting presence. He nodded slightly, warily, and although it wasn't what I'd hoped for, I clung to it.

"Meet in your lab tonight?" I knew it was a stretch even as I asked, but I was desperate for some sense of normalcy.

"Sure." He squeezed the sponge slightly, water dripping onto the stone floor before he reached back into the sink to scrub the rest of the dishes.

Although my chest still felt tight, I knew trust took time to rebuild, and I was willing to do it. I'd grown quite attached to Walcott in just the few weeks we'd spent together. *Maybe he'll come with Calix and me,* I thought. I tried to remind myself that I was a means to an end to these people, that I was simply a weapon for them to hone and wield, but my heart didn't listen.

I emerged back into the dining hall to find Ketra surrounded by a group of five people. A strange protective instinct washed over me and I rushed over to find them leaning over, hiding her face from view. My mind instantly jumped to the worst conclusions, imagining her cowering against the wall as they berated her for serving the King. I set the food down on an adjacent table and shouldered my way in, just to find Ketra's face lighting up in laughter. Lillya's friend sat in my chair, and they seemed to be the center of attention as they narrated a story about Azden and Olyn.

"And this has been going on for years—neither one will concede, so the token keeps getting passed back and forth."

"Token?" I asked, my curiosity thoroughly piqued.

"I was just telling the new girl here about Azden, Olyn, and" he paused, as if omitting a name, "sometimes Rahni's ongoing game of capture the flag. They've been scheming and stealing this same token for years—no matter what's going on, one of them is always protecting it. Rahni even got it one year, though she usually thinks herself above it. To be fair, it can get pretty childish so I don't blame her." He chuckled warmly, leaning back with a hand over his stomach. I suddenly remembered the time Olyn had run into me when I'd first gotten here, his hand clutched around something as he panicked about Azden being near.

"One time Olyn literally swallowed it to keep Azden away, but Azden just bided his time. I'm telling you, they'll stop at *nothing* to win." A girl said, her face lighting up in amusement.

"One time Azden gave it to me, thinking they wouldn't expect it, but it took less than a day for uh, the other to track it to my room and steal it back." Another man I didn't recognize smiled widely as he told the memory. He was clearly proud to have been included. I couldn't resist smiling; their energy was contagious. Even Ketra was relaxed, hanging on to every word.

"And they're still doing this?" I asked, surprised I hadn't heard of it yet.

"As far as we know. The last I heard Azden stole it right before you came," Lillya's friend speculated.

I started to send Azden a thought, ready to tease him relentlessly, but caught myself. I wasn't sure we were even on speaking terms. Actually, I wasn't sure about anything between us right now. Reality crashed over me, ending my brief respite.

The others felt my mood shift and made themselves scarce. I grabbed our plates, setting them before Ketra as she eyed me curiously.

"Is it Azden? Was he one of the ones who didn't want to bring me on?" She was clever, that's for sure. I narrowed my eyes at her, not even looking as I stabbed a piece of meat with my fork.

"Maybe." My voice was hostile enough to close the subject, but Ketra was not deterred.

"He's the leader here, right? How come you got to overrule him?" I took a deep breath, trying to collect my thoughts without outright shutting her down. She was probably concerned about her own wellbeing here, as anyone would be. I cooled off for a second, shoving all my feelings down to be dealt with later. Or not.

"He's the leader, but we work as a team. Everyone's opinion is important." At least it *should* be. I didn't miss the hypocrisy in my words given that I ignored everyone else when it came to her, but I couldn't just leave her to suffer.

"Even though you've only been here a few weeks?" Her

question was neutral, but I couldn't help but wince. I wanted to tell her that yes, it didn't matter and my opinion was important, but even I didn't believe that.

"It's more about the value in the ideas rather than who they came from. We're all working towards a common goal, so whatever helps us get there is what we're going to do." She nodded, finally satisfied. I pushed my plate away, no longer hungry. "We'll meet tomorrow with everyone to discuss the details, but for tonight do you need anything? I had Hemm grab you toiletries."

"I think I'm good."

"Alright then, let's go put our plates back and then I'll walk you back to your room." I stood, stacking our plates.

She seemed to have relaxed a bit already, worlds different than the skittish girl I'd first met. I hoped she liked it here, but more than that, I hoped I was right about her.

CHAPTER

17

After Ketra was settled, I started walking back to my room but took a few wrong turns. Or rather, they were wrong if I meant to go to my room, but I was being pulled in another direction. Before I knew it I was in front of Azden's office, staring at the door. *He knows I'm here, so I should just go in. Unless he doesn't want me to, which is why he hasn't said anything—*

Just come in already, he thought to me, and I rolled my eyes before turning the handle and walking in.

He was disheveled per usual, but it was more of a wild chaos than controlled mess. Bloodshot eyes looked up at me, filled with an emotion I couldn't place. It wasn't angry like before, but it wasn't pleased either.

"Hello," I said, mostly to break the uncomfortable silence.

"Hi," he returned, just as eager to delay the impending conversation.

"Rahni talked to you?"

"Yes," he said. I nodded, frustration brewing at his unhelpful response.

"And?"

"And we're working with Ketra." He wasn't bitter like I expected. Even though I should have been happy to hear he wasn't mad, my heart still sank. I was dying for him to address me, us, to say it was okay and we could be friends again. If we ever were in the first place.

We are friends. Shit. Of course he'd been listening.

"Fine. There's no use dancing around it when you seem to feel like you have an open invitation to my mind. Can we go back to before?" He paused, so I listened to his thoughts for a change. The asshole was waiting, leaving me hanging on purpose, and he was *enjoying* it. He smiled at my discomfort, watching me shift on my feet.

"Never mind. Forget I said anything. Let's just finish this, and we'll never have to see each other again," I said, saccharine and ending about two octaves higher than it started. The smile wiped from his face, briefly dipping into a frown before forcing a neutral expression.

"Is that what you want?" His question was innocuous, but it felt loaded. Now it was my turn to revel in the pregnant silence, stringing him along as I sorted through my thoughts.

What did I want? The only thing I knew was that I needed to get Calix, and that I hated myself for spending time on anything else. These other people, the drama and emotions surrounding them, it was all a distraction from what I should be singularly focused on.

"What do *you* want?" I countered, hoping it would help me sort through my own thoughts.

"I asked you first." He wore a mischievous smile, and

again I felt like wiping it right off his face.

"Aren't you still mad at me?" I asked.

"I still think it was stupid, but there's no use in staying mad. Plus, I *suppose* you might have been right that she'll be useful."

I cupped my ear facetiously. "What was that? I was what?" He scowled at me, refusing to comply. "I was… right? Hm… maybe I will stick around if you keep being this smart."

"I'll never admit I said that, so don't go around repeating it." Azden shook his head, but he broke into a grin.

"Who? Me? I would never." My smile now spread across my face as wide as it could go. It felt like a weight had been lifted off my shoulders. I hadn't realized how oppressive the tension between us was until we slid back into our easy banter. We both smiled like hooligans, basking in the other's amusement. Then, like minds are wont to do, my brain resurfaced the memory of our kiss in the hall. I tried to hide it, but my cheeks flushed with the phantom of his hands on my body, pulling me close. To make it worse, his eyes fluttered half-closed, confirming he'd heard it all.

"Stop it," I said, pursing my lips.

"Stop what?" he teased.

"You know what. Get out of my head."

"Oh, but it's such a fun place to be." He tilted his head, his thumb playing with his bottom lip, invariably drawing my attention to it.

"You're doing that on purpose."

"Doing what?" *Why did he always have to be so irritating?*

"I don't think irritating is the word you're looking for, Freckles." He plopped his chin into his hand, leaning to the side in his chair and watching me as if I were the most fascinating thing in the room.

"You're right, I think I was looking for arrogant, provoking and unbearable. Better?" He chuckled dryly, the low timbre of his voice catching my breath.

"Keep denying it if you'd like, but you'll just waste both of our time."

"Oh, and presumptuous. I forgot that one." He stood, walking around the desk and leaning back against it, his arm muscles accentuated as he gripped the edge. I almost stepped back, but I had to hold my ground. His head tilted down slightly so that he was looking at me from under his lashes, and they were so long—how was that fair? Not to mention they curled perfectly above his stunning eyes that begged me to trust him.

Your eyes are stunning as well.

I said stop that.

You could do it to me too.

I won't.

Afraid of what you'll find? He raised a brow, which only ignited my anger. My magic called to me, begging to be let loose.

I think anyone would be scared to look inside your brain. He laughed out loud, throwing his head back. *Fine*, I thought, giving in to my curiosity.

Thank the gods she isn't mad at me anymore; I much prefer her fake frustration as she tries to convince herself it's irritation and not attraction. Was she being honest when she said she never wanted to see me again after this? I know I shouldn't care; I expected that. I just don't know how I could go back to a life without her smile in it. Man, I'd give anything to kiss her right now. But I shouldn't. It was some kiss, though. Even she thought so.

"And this is precisely why you shouldn't be snooping around my head all the time!" I said, huffing out in frustration and poking a finger into his chest. I tried to pull away, but his hand shot up to cover mine. I tugged at it, but not with my full strength.

"Fine. I'll stop. I'm sorry." His lips turned down into an exaggerated pout, but he sounded genuine. What was his angle? Why was he doing this? I waited, listening for a quip in response, but none came. Maybe he really had stopped listening. I reached toward him in my mind and found him firmly planted in his own.

"Why?" I asked, acutely aware of how my hand felt on his chest, rising and falling with his breath. His heart pulsed under my palm, beating unusually fast. I waited for an inane question in response, but it never came. Instead he turned serious, studying my face as if he'd find the answer there. I relaxed, drinking in his expressions as he did mine. My lips parted slightly as I sucked in a breath, finding my chest constricted under his undivided attention. He opened his mouth, about to speak, but I freaked out and yanked my hand away, pressing it against my leg and stepping back.

"So you and Olyn are in some sort of extended game of capture the flag?" I asked, trying to retreat firmly back into friendship camp. My arm pulsed and the cuff suddenly felt unbearably tight, like it was cutting off my circulation. Azden looked crestfallen, but he bounced back fast.

"I guess you could call it that. If Olyn sent you, you better tell him he's not getting back."

"You have it?"

"I have it most of the time," he said with a self-satisfied smile. I shook my head reflexively, lightly admonishing his arrogance to cover my amusement.

"What is it anyway?" I asked, and Azden narrowed his eyes in suspicion. "I promise Olyn did not send me," I teased, tilting my head down in innocence.

"It's a ring," he said, reflexively twirling the one on his hand, "a gold ring with black onyx set in the center. Now that I've told you this, if you see the others with anything that fits the description, you must tell me immediately." His face was set with such determination I couldn't help but laugh. I remembered all the times I'd seen him anxiously twirl a ring around his finger and wondered if Olyn ever kept it for more than a day. Probably not, knowing Azden.

"You're ridiculous." Even as I said it, we both knew it had heavy undertones of something else my subconscious was begging me to say. "Well, I should be going. We have an early meeting tomorrow."

"So soon? It's barely a quarter past ten."

"Already? When did that happen?" I asked, shocked that so much time had passed. Had I really been here that long? It had only felt like a few minutes. Though time with Azden usually felt like that.

"Probably an hour after a quarter past nine," he teased, and I hit him lightly on his shoulder in response, but he caught my wrist just in time, pulling me closer. I held my breath, my heart beating impossibly fast as the tension between us grew, even more intense than it had been at the height of our anger. I scanned his eyes frantically, looking for doubt, something I could use as an excuse to pull away, but all I saw was unbridled desire. He looked at me like I was a goddess, and I felt unequivocally unworthy.

"Azden." I breathed, barely getting any sound out at all.

"Estyn," he whispered, his voice low and suggestive.

"I—I…" I wanted to say so many things. My heart begged me to stop thinking, to give in to his beguiling charm and lose myself in him, to let myself bask in his attention and feel worthy for once. But I didn't feel worthy, and I would never forgive myself for focusing on myself while Calix was suffering. I couldn't. So no matter how much I wanted to, I said "I can't."

He let go of my wrist and the dejection on his face made me want to take it all back. If only he was still reading my thoughts, he'd know how much I hated this. It was better he didn't know, better he didn't grasp onto a sliver of hope. Maybe in a different place and time we would have worked, but not here and now.

I bit my lip, wanting to look away from his melancholy expression, but wasn't strong enough to do it. Azden was the master at bright sides; he could always bounce back, and he would. It was just taking longer than usual. At least that's what I told myself.

"We should probably get some sleep," he said.

"Yeah," I muttered, a tear threatening to spill as I turned to the door.

I'm sorry. I thought at him as I walked away, down the hall, away from the first man who ever made me feel strong, capable and undeniably wanted.

Me too. He thought, the sadness more poignant in his head. It was my undoing. I finally let tears fall down my cheeks as I walked down the endless corridor.

Shit. I thought, sniffling in the most unbecoming way as I broke into a jog towards Walcott's lab. I wasn't too late, at least I hoped not, but either way it was not ideal when Walcott and I were still on uncertain terms.

Luckily when I arrived Walcott was still hunched over his workbench, tinkering with his newest explosive. I had tried to clean myself up on the way, but rubbing my snot on my sleeve and wiping my eyes did nothing to hide the fact I had been sobbing minutes earlier.

"Estyn? What's wrong?" he asked, pulling off his goggles when he heard me come in. I swallowed, trying to find the strength to answer, but as soon as I opened my mouth I started crying again. He walked over and wrapped me in a warm embrace, stroking my hair as I sobbed into his shoulder. He smelled of chemicals and smoke, but it was somehow comforting.

"I'm sorry," I whimpered, the words barely intelligible.

"Sorry for what?" He asked.

"I'm ruining your shirt." I started crying harder, now upset that I was forcing Walcott to comfort me when he was probably still mad. "Are you still mad at me?" I asked when I collected myself enough to pull away and look at him.

"Oh Estyn," he said softly, leaning back to look me in my silver-lined eyes, "I was never mad at you. I was just sad you didn't feel like I'd trust you enough to do what you thought was right." When he finished, I only started crying harder. Here was the unconditional acceptance and trust I'd always yearned for, and I was already fucking it up.

"Can I ask—is this about Azden?" he asked.

"What? No? Why would you think that?" I searched frantically around the room for no reason other than to not have to look at him. Every time I looked into his eyes I seemed to melt all over again, and if my lie was unconvincing now, it would be completely transparent if I met his gaze.

"You can tell me, you know. I won't judge you." There he went again, being supportive and kind and all sorts of things that I didn't deserve. I hated that I was acting like a blubbering baby and even more that Walcott wasn't looking at me like I was crazy. I was wasting his night by standing here, failing to pull myself together. I wanted to tell him about Azden and what happened tonight, but even more I didn't want to speak it into existence. Maybe if I ignored it, all the complications would go away and everything would return to normal. It was a nice thought.

I cried until I didn't have any tears left and I felt like an empty shell of myself. "I'm sorry," I repeated, this time slightly more coherent.

"Again, no need to apologize. I'm here for you." He was so earnest I would break into another bout of tears if I had any left.

"I don't even know why I'm crying so much. It's so embarrassing," I said as I wiped my raw nose yet again, further irritating it.

"You probably know, you just don't want to confront it." He saw my confusion and quickly amended, "There's nothing wrong with that. Sometimes we just need time to process things. Even if it's happening in the background." He smiled at me, seeing the hope in my eyes. I was going to be okay.

"There's *another* secret exit? What else is this place hiding?" I asked Azden as he pulled on another nondescript sconce, this time near the library. A section of wall slid away, revealing an iron staircase winding up into the darkness. From what I could gather, we were closer to the blacksmith shop than the cave, but knowing this place we could be anywhere in Myllanor.

"You'll find out soon enough," he said, smiling over his shoulder as he dipped into the darkness.

The only thing he told me was to bring a cloak, which I had secured tightly around my neck. I knew we would be training, but what? Thoughts? Shadows? Some other surprise he had up his sleeve?

I took the steps in twos, barely breaking a sweat. I was the strongest I'd ever been, both physically and mentally. My mind was quiet and calm. It was a far cry from the ever-present noise I used to hear, unable to fully plant myself in any single mind. I winced as light poured into the stairwell from the cracked door at the top. I lifted a hand to shield my eyes, only lowering it once I reached the top step. We were in… a bedroom?

"I didn't sign up for this kind of training," I said, widening my eyes as I teased him. I expected a clever retort, but he was silently stalking around the room, running a finger over the dust-covered pictures lining the walls.

"Azden?" I tried, but he didn't seem to hear me. I closed the door behind us and walked over to him to see a little blond boy tucked between two older siblings and their parents. Even if I didn't see the crowns atop their heads, I'd recognize those gold ringed eyes anywhere. The only person who looked out of place was a serious child with a darker complexion, a few years older than Azden with a protective arm slung around Azden's shoulders. Out of place wasn't quite the right phrase—he was definitely part of the family, tucked between the king and queen with his own crown balanced perfectly on his head. Who was he, and where was he now?

Where are we? I asked, slipping into his mind to reach him. My breath caught at the sad nostalgia in his thoughts as he remembered the portrait being taken. He shook his head, suddenly returning to the present moment and locking those thoughts away.

"Welcome to my house," he said with a half-hearted smile.

I followed him into the hall where more doors opened to the kitchen and a study. Every wall was lined with family portraits and art, some more serious than others. It was decorated comfortably, as if they never intended to host, which made the layer of dust coating the walls, railings, furniture that much more unnerving. It was as if everything had been frozen in time.

"This was your family home?" I asked, still unable to reconcile the humble furnishings with what I knew royalty to be.

"It was our private quarters. We kept it a secret," he said, voice still far away as he opened a door to the front sitting room. Rainbow light poured into the room through stained glass windows wrapping around an inset bench. I couldn't help but imagine myself curled up with a book and cup of spiced chocolate, watching the light shift over the room as the sun set.

"So the base," I reasoned aloud, "was your family's?"

"Yes. It was for worst-case scenarios, in case we needed to go into hiding," he said, again wandering into another room. "They never made it," he murmured, wandering aimlessly around as if this was the first time he'd been here in years.

"Azden," I said, "Why did you bring me here?" I grabbed his elbow, stopping him where he stood by the sink, looking out to the overgrown garden in the back. As if that one touch brought him back to reality, he shook his head and his hazy gaze snapped to attention.

"I needed to show you why this is so important," he said, back to being the calculated rebel leader, "And I needed to remind myself." *And I didn't want to come here alone,* he thought, which felt like a hand squeezing my heart. Why me? He had friends that felt such fierce loyalty, that were practically family, who would be here in a second if he asked. So why me?

"We need to slip out back," he said, no trace of lingering sadness from the ghost I'd just seen walk these halls.

"Az," I said, reaching for his arm with a comforting touch. He leaned away, averting his gaze and keeping his face blank. "I'm sorry about your family," I said. I couldn't imagine what he'd gone through.

"We're practicing on crowds today. I want you to learn how to pinpoint a mind from farther away, and with more distraction," he said, brushing over my words as if I hadn't said anything. I pulled my hand back. If he didn't want to talk, then so be it. Just business. *That's how it should be*, I thought, but no matter how many shoulds I told myself, I still wanted more.

CHAPTER

18

"Most importantly, we need to know about the military. Where they are, how loyal they are, and any potential weaknesses. We don't want any unnecessary casualties, but if people are in our way, we'll do what we have to do," Azden told Ketra, as confident as any prince would be. We were all sitting around the circular table in the meeting room, discussing strategies for her infiltration.

I'd made sure she and I got there early so we could claim our seats and not be relegated to the other end of the table, even though it may have bothered Rahni. Maybe particularly because it bothered Rahni.

"Ideally, we'd figure out a way to remove the guards from the equation entirely. Which is why we need more information, to even see if that would be possible, and if so, how." Walcott, ever the pacifist, attempted to soothe Ketra's nerves but was undercut by Rahni a second later.

"I mean yes, ideally they would be out of the way, but if they're loyal to Ruzu I wouldn't mind siccing my snakes on them." She smiled like a sadist which did absolutely nothing to comfort Ketra. At least Ketra was doing a good job of hiding her anxiety. We'd been throwing strategy and orders at her all morning, and she'd been sitting tall like a trooper. I had no reason for it, but my chest warmed with pride. I'd like to think I had a small part in her feeling welcome and trusting us enough to work with us.

"Okay, so I'll leave today and report back in a week?" Ketra asked, sounding objective despite the fear in her thoughts.

"Yes. And if you need anything, leave a note by the far entrance to the wall. We'll check it periodically throughout the week," Azden said.

"And if I'm captured and can't send word?"

"We'll have other ways of finding out. Don't worry too much about that, it's not worth wasting energy dwelling on what-ifs," Rahni answered.

"How do you plan for alternative scenarios then?" Ketra asked.

"Planning is different from worrying. I consider, plan, and move on," Rahni said as if it were the most obvious thing in the world.

"Easier said than done," I scoffed. Everyone's attention snapped to where I lounged in my chair, posture terrible after the hours of sinking further and further down in my seat. "You'll be great, though. Nothing makes you more confident than proving to yourself you can do it, and to do that you just have to start," I added, though I was distracted by Azden looking at me with resigned admiration. I hated how subdued he got whenever he looked at me now. I just wanted to hear his nonchalant banter, the way he smiled easily and readily at everything and everyone. Not this flickering sadness that he was trying to hide by diving into his work.

On the bright side, my words of encouragement seemed to resonate with Ketra.

"Alright, let's do this," she said, standing up with her hands braced on the table.

For someone without magic, Ketra was surprisingly undaunted in the presence of five incredibly powerful enchanters. Even though she didn't know the details of Azden's or my magic, I know I wouldn't have been that confident.

As grim as it was, it was best she didn't know. She wouldn't willingly give up information, but they had ways to draw it out. I knew that well enough from my family. If they found out I was a night enchanter, we'd be doomed. There would be a bounty large enough to tempt even some of our own.

Despite the dark twist my thoughts had taken, I offered Ketra an encouraging smile. She was strong and smart. She'd be fine.

"Let's go," I said, standing with her and walking her to the exit. I chewed the inside of my lip, apparently more nervous than she was. We followed Azden and Rahni and were flanked by Walcott and Olyn. The magic pulsing in the hall was almost suffocating, each of our powers fighting to be let loose and establish dominance.

Ketra jumped towards me, nearly pushing me into the wall as a snake slithered past. Rahni looked back over her shoulder, lips quirked in a knowing smirk as she called to her pet. As Ketra jerked away, brushing her shirt down and regaining her composure, I knew Rahni's message had the intended effect.

"We're here." Azden said, stopping in front of the sconce-lever. "Rahni will lead you back to the wall, and then you're on your own from there." Ketra nodded, stoic and unruffled.

The wall slid back and she didn't so much as widen her eyes at it. She simply started up the stairs, only looking back once to catch my gaze. I gave her a smile, offering her silent prayers but doubting she'd need them. Rahni and her snake slithered after Ketra, which would be an ominous sight if I didn't know they were going to protect her.

We all watched until they disappeared up into the darkness, the wall sliding back into place behind them.

"So what now?" I asked, breaking the silence.

"We train, we plan, and we prepare." Azden said, refusing to make eye contact.

"Can I help with the strategy?" I asked, and Olyn's eyes cut over to me, examining. I didn't want to go into the assassination with the same level of confusion I had last time. And I could be helpful. I had ideas. I was about to plead my case when Azden responded.

"Sure. But right now we need to keep training your magic." He said it like it was a chore, and if anyone else could I bet he'd get them to do it in his stead. Unfortunately Day and Night enchanters were rather hard to come by, so he was stuck with me.

"Alright. Let's go," I said, just as terse as he had been. I had a feeling this was going to be uncomfortable for both of us. Walcott and Olyn shifted uneasily, almost slinking back into the shadows to get as far from us as they could.

Azden and I started off towards the training ring, shouldering one another until we walked side by side, both tense and coiled like snakes ready to strike.

Training was quiet, but we both relaxed as we eased into

our normal routine. My magic was getting easier to channel. I could call to my shadows in a second, bending them to my will and strengthening them as I practiced hiding myself, lifting and moving things and forming a shield.

I was now attempting to have them wield a sword, but was failing miserably. They could hold it, but moving and striking felt harder than trying to grip it with my foot. Azden was awed by my progress, though he tried to suppress it. Despite my best efforts, he still looked at me with adoration. I had tried to explain it away as other things, but I couldn't deny it anymore.

We avoided telepathy work, as I'm sure neither of us was emotionally equipped to deal with what we might find. I only reached out a few times to hear his thoughts, and they all broke my focus instantly.

Azden suggested we spar, pit my shadows against his light. Even though I was tired and my magic nearly depleted, I agreed. I wielded the sword clumsily. Simply holding it took almost all of my remaining strength, but Azden swung his sword deftly, disarming my shadow in a matter of seconds. I formed a crude gesture with my shadow, sticking my tongue out at Azden to complete the picture and he broke into open laughter, nearly doubling over. I hadn't realized how much I missed that sound.

I couldn't help but notice how handsome he was. Azden was always classically beautiful, but I always found him most attractive in moments like these. How he could be so upbeat all the time when he'd experienced such pain, I'd never know, but it was magnetic. His dimples never failed to make me smile; unless they were accompanied by one of his teasing smirks, that is, in which case I could usually resist the urge. I hadn't realized he'd stopped laughing until I saw him staring at me, noticing me openly admiring him. *Shit.* This was not the way to convince him we were better off as friends.

To break the silence, I reached into the last dregs of my magic to compel my shadows to grab the sword from Azden's light.

"Ha," I said, but the effect was lessened when the sword crashed to the ground and my shadow slithered back to me, my magic overexerted.

"Good job," he said, his eyes still twinkling with mischief and something I decided was friendly affection.

"Thank you," I said, bowing with a flourish. He laughed again, and the sound was like music to my ears. How could I ever risk losing that to something as fleeting as romance?

"Hold still," he said, closing the gap between us in a few quick steps. Overwhelmed by his woodsy scent that mixed with the fresh pheromones from our exercise, I was barely able to put a sentence together. He gently pushed away a lock of hair that had stuck to my face with sweat.

"Much better," he said, smiling down at me. Here we were, once again in unfamiliar territory. Without our classic banter to distance myself, his presence flooded my senses. It took all my strength to rip away, convincing myself space would dispel the warm feeling brewing in my core.

"Meeting with the rest of the team before dinner?" I asked, my breath regrettably ragged.

"Yes," he said, retreating back into his nonchalant persona. He tucked his hands in his pockets, shifting his weight to one side. The earnest Azden was now tucked safely behind quick wit and indifference. "See you there." He strode out into the hall, leaving me breathless in the middle of the ring, trying to figure out what had just happened.

"Where is she?" Olyn asked impatiently, glancing back to the door every few seconds.

"You know Rahni," Azden said, leaning back and looking at the ring he twirled around his middle finger, another nervous tic I had come to recognize. I resisted the urge to reach out a hand and cover his, offering silent comfort. It wasn't my place, and I shouldn't be feeling that anyways.

The double doors swung open, Rahni striding in with a triumphant smile as she surveyed the table. "You weren't waiting long, I hope?"

"Let's get started," Azden interrupted before the bickering could begin. He stood, walking over to a chalkboard behind him. "We have already figured out our route in, the day and time, and where Calix is. We have a rough idea of what we're going to do with the guards, but hopefully we'll find out more when Ketra reports back." Walcott raised his hand, interrupting Azden's plotting. "Yes?" Azden asked.

"So we're getting Calix first and then going for Ruzu?" Walcott clarified.

"We can't risk spending that much time there. You and Rahni will set the distraction and go for Calix and Olyn, Estyn and I will take care of Ruzu," Azden answered in his assured leader tone of voice.

"No," I said, grinding my teeth.

"That was the agreement, Estyn. We need you for Ruzu."

"I'll help you get in, but I need to get Calix myself. How else can I ensure you've kept your promise?" Azden stared at me, pondering what I said and recalculating his plans.

"It doesn't make sense. We need to prioritize killing Ruzu."

"No. I'm getting Calix." Azden stared at me, but I was unflinching under his gaze. I would not compromise on this front.

"Fine. We will get Calix, but the second he's safe, we'll go for Ruzu." Walcott pursed his lips, clearly not satisfied with the change of plans, but he didn't object.

"Deal," I said, not wanting to continue the discussion and risk not being assigned to Calix's rescue at all.

"Moving on, Estyn's getting strong enough that she should be able to shadow us all as we enter, but I'd still prefer to have guards distracted. The last thing we need is to be swarmed once we're inside."

"Maybe we organize a rebellion in the city?" Olyn offered, but Azden shook his head.

"Ruzu wouldn't send troops for that," Azden said.

"What *would* he send troops for?" I asked. Everyone was silent for a moment, the floor suddenly the most interesting thing in the room. "Does he care about *anything*?" I implored, acutely aware of how difficult this mission was becoming.

"He cares about his power. And money I suppose, like most Kings," Walcott answered.

"Okay. So we attack one of those and we're golden," I said.

"Easier said than done," Rahni cut in dryly. I glared at her, but expounded upon my idea.

"His vaults are probably inside the castle, so that wouldn't work. That means we need to threaten his power. Hm. We could cause an uprising within the troops. Or make him think there was one?" I thought aloud, brainstorming to fill the silence.

"That actually might work. We'd need information on the movements of the troops, but Ketra can get that," Olyn added, almost excited by the idea. I was a little surprised, given that he wasn't my biggest fan, but I was thankful for the support nonetheless.

Azden worried his bottom lip, thinking through all the variables as he always seemed to do. If I peeked into his head I'd likely get a headache from all the simultaneous trains of thought. He could be arrogant, but even I had to admit it wasn't entirely unfounded.

"Yes, this might just work," Azden said quietly, everyone's attention turned to him. He looked directly at me, a smile spreading on his previously serious features. I smiled in kind, heart glowing with his approval. The rest of the room seemed to melt away until it was just Azden and me, sharing a conspiratorial look. Everything would be okay, as long as I had him.

"Alright, can we get a drink now? I'm positively parched from all this scheming," Rahni said, cutting through the moment. I looked back at the table, my smile refusing to fade.

"Yes, I think that's more than well deserved," Azden agreed, finally tearing his eyes away from mine. "Let's show Estyn Better Days."

My face twisted in concerned confusion. "Better Days?" I asked.

"It's the best bar in the city," Walcott said.

"And one of the only ones discreet enough to be safe," Olyn added.

"Oh. That sounds great." I felt oddly nervous. I had gotten used to being down here, safe from the world.

It'll be fun, Azden thought to me, somehow sensing my unease.

I looked at him and shoved my anxiety deep down.

We all adjourned to our rooms to freshen up and I had the

crushing realization that I had nothing to wear. To be fair, it was probably the least of my problems, but it *felt* devastating. I considered going to Rahni's room, but she didn't seem like the sharing type. At least not with me.

I didn't know where Lillya's room was, but I wandered until I located her in my head and could track her to a door in a hall of bedrooms. I knocked twice, light so as to not disturb her. I shifted on my feet, second-guessing the entire thing. I was just about to leave when the door opened to reveal Lillya blocking a half-dressed Sylryn behind her.

"Oh, hello Estyn. What's up?" She stood with the door cracked, and I instantly regretted coming, especially since I was obviously interrupting.

"It's nothing, never mind. I'll see you tomorrow," I said, starting to walk away.

"No, come on in. Just give me a second." She closed the door and I heard shuffling inside as they became decent. She reopened the door wider this time, gesturing for me to come inside.

"I don't have much time, but I didn't know where else to go, so I thought I'd ask," I stammered, the words spilling out. She simply lifted an eyebrow. "We're going out in the city, and I have nothing to wear."

"Well you should have started with that!" Lillya flung open her closet doors that contained a chaos of garments inside. Clothes spilled onto the floor and Sylryn dutifully picked them up, folding them as Lillya picked out more and flung them this way and that.

"This is perfect," she said, holding up a long black dress. It had a cinched bodice, ruched fabric down the abdomen, and two slits at the front that extended far past decent. Sheer sleeves billowed out from the sides, the most modest part of the entire ensemble. "Try it on!" She insisted, pushing it into my arms and guiding me to the bathroom. I came out tugging at the slits as if I could seal them with my hands.

"It's perfect!" She squealed, clapping her hands together. "Okay now go make Azden drool." She put a hand on my back, not leaving any time to second guess myself as she pushed me back into the hall. Before I could protest, she thrust a pair of black pumps into my hands and closed the door behind me.

I bit my bottom lip, looking down to the cleavage and skin that the dress highlighted. It *was* beautiful, and I didn't have any other options now.

Everyone was already gathered by the townhouse exit when I arrived. Rahni wore a short red dress and heels that I'd barely last a few feet in, let alone all night, but she looked completely at ease. She shot a look at Azden, presumably talking to him in her mind, then looked back at me with a distrustful glare. Apparently I wasn't supposed to know about this exit.

The men all looked rather dapper, Azden especially. His trousers were well tailored, and I couldn't help but admire how they hugged his muscles. As if on cue, he looked at me at the exact wrong moment. His mouth parted as he looked me up and down slowly, drinking in every inch of my dress. I took more than a little pleasure in the fact he had to blink a few times to regain his composure. I heard everyone chatting, but it seemed to fade into the background as Azden walked to me, meeting me a few feet away from the rest of the group.

"You look beautiful," he said, staring into my eyes with that same devotion that scared me every time.

"Thank you. And you look rather dashing," I said, though

I regretted giving him another reason to justify his inflated ego.

"I do, don't I?" He smiled as he looked down at himself and I dropped one hand from where it had been clutching my skirt so I could hit him lightly on the arm.

"You're shameless," I said, pursing my lips which only seemed to draw his attention to them.

"Are we going to wait around all night or are we going out?" Olyn called to us.

Azden didn't break my gaze. He just stared into my eyes as he called back "We're coming." Then, more privately, he whispered to me "You ready?" I nodded up at him, and he took my arm in his. I forgot all about worrying about what I looked like, letting my skirt swish around my legs as I walked and basking in the warmth of Azden's proximity. I inhaled slightly, sighing at the familiar woodsy scent.

"Did you just… smell me?" he asked, but his tone was more teasing than disturbed.

"What? No." I tried to remove my hand but he held it tight to his arm, trapping me. He chuckled bashfully and shook his head, looking at his shoes. I couldn't help but smile again.

Azden let go of my arm as we walked into the dark stairwell and I felt the absence more than I cared to admit. We followed the others into the bedroom, but the mood was different than when I'd been there before. Olyn whispered to Rahni, eliciting a muffled chuckle that surprised me. I glanced at Azden, who raised his brows in a look that felt far too familiar. I wanted to wrap my hand in his, the instinct so strong I had to pin my arms to my sides. *Stop it,* I thought, reminding myself that although tonight we would relax, I couldn't let my guard down too much.

I couldn't wait to get outside to the fresh air. Once we were out on the street, I inhaled deeply, savoring the crisp evening breeze in my lungs.

Rahni walked with purpose, weaving us down side streets until we stopped outside a small red door. I stifled a chuckle as I tried to imagine Azden and Olyn contorting themselves to fit through, two big tough guys raving about a tiny little bar.

"Ready?" Walcott grinned like a child, his excitement contagious.

"As I'll ever be," I said with an uneasy smile, nudging him with my shoulder. We followed Rahni through a narrow hall, following the distant pulse of music until we turned towards a massive (or possibly normal sized, it was difficult to tell after the child sized entrance), ornately carved door that seemed to be the source of the muffled music I'd heard. Rahni rapped on the door three times.

A small metal sheet slid away, revealing the bright orange eyes of a Summer enchanter.

"Password?" A low voice rumbled.

"Open the door before I make you." Rahni said, but her usually threatening tone was laced with teasing familiarity.

"It's always great to see you, Rahni," the man guarding the door said as he undid a copious amount of locks. As soon as the door opened a crack, Rahni slid her fingers in and swung it open. She sauntered past the man at the door, swinging her hips more than usual and offering him a sensual wink as she made a beeline for the bar. He barely looked at us, his eyes glued to her backside as she sashayed away.

Better Days had an air of overwhelming depravity as people indulged in vices of all kinds. The dance floor was full of people swaying and grinding to music played from balconies of musicians encircling the room. The bar where

Rahni sat, surrounded by a swarm of men and women alike, was covered in ivy that climbed up to the ceiling at least three stories high. Ivy dripped from the ceiling securing lanterns that shed light of various colors all over the room. The flames burned red and purple, likely a neat trick by the Summer enchanters.

The bartenders were all Summer and Winter enchanters and magic pulsed from the bar as they mixed all kinds of exotic drinks. Tables lined a small alcove, all low-lit booths with red leather cushions. Some people played card games, others devoured food that had my stomach grumbling.

I felt eyes follow me to the bar. More specifically, I felt eyes grazing up my body, taking in every inch of my dress that suddenly felt more than appropriate, and I looked over to find a table of men admiring me. They were certainly attractive; some were enchanters, but even the ones without magic were remarkably beautiful.

Walcott put a hand on my elbow, guiding me to the bar. Even though I hadn't had a sip of alcohol yet, I was already feeling looser and more inclined to make questionable decisions. I glanced back at the table of men to find Azden looking between us with a protective gleam in his eyes. He clenched his fist at his side but otherwise kept his space.

"She'll have a Red Volley." I heard Walcott say to the bartender, gesturing to me.

"Anything for the lady," he said with eyes promising all sorts of sins. My face heated under his stare, but I found myself returning his smile. His muscles tensed under his tight black shirt as he shook my drink, pouring it into a twisted crystal glass and finishing by lighting the top with red fire. I slid onto a barstool and crossed my legs, the slit sliding open to reveal my leg all the way to my upper thigh. I tilted my head, focused on the bartender as he slid my drink over.

"Careful of the heat." He winked, hand lingering on the stem as my fingers brushed over his to take it.

"I'll keep that in mind," I replied, my voice more reminiscent of Rahni's than my own. I felt Azden's eyes boring holes into the back of my head as he watched the interaction from a few feet behind. Was I interested in the bartender? No. Was I desperate to prove to Azden and myself that my feelings for him were inconsequential? Absolutely.

I looked to my left, but Walcott had seemed to disappear into the masses. The music was loud, but it was quiet enough at the bar to have a conversation.

Azden walked up, taking Walcott's seat. "Enjoying Better Days so far?" he asked, his voice low and gravely.

"Why yes, I am," I said with a suggestive smile back to the table of men that were still stealing glances my way. Gold flared in his eyes.

"You're trying a Red Volley?" he asked, drawing my attention back to him.

"I suppose so." I swirled the drink in my glass, raising it to my lips to take a slow, tantalizing sip. Azden watched every second, practically drooling.

Lust, that's all this is. For both of us. I told myself, explaining away the tension gathering low in my stomach. I ran my tongue over my bottom lip to catch the stray drops that had gathered there and Azden watched as if I was the most interesting thing in the room.

"Would you like to dance?" A mans' voice interrupted the exchange, and I welcomed the distraction. Azden's gaze was becoming hard to handle.

"I'd love to." I smiled at him, eyes fluttering half-open.

Azden's magic raged against him, begging to be let loose, but he just sat silently. I took a large swig, polishing off my drink, before taking the man's hand and letting him lead me to the dance floor.

Why? I heard Azden ask in my thoughts as I disappeared into the crowd, but I didn't have an answer for him.

The crowd was deliciously alive, my senses overwhelmed with the bodies moving all around me and the music blasting in my ears. I let myself be carried by the beat, swaying my hips in time. The man who had asked me to dance stood behind me, shuffling with the music, my anchor in the sea of people. I felt the cocktail's sweet effect on my senses, letting my mind focus on sensations rather than thoughts.

I wanted to stop thinking, to be outside of my own mind for just a moment and focus on the present, but the only thing I saw was Azden's light, clear and bright and ever-present. No matter where he was, my mind always belonged to him.

I pulled away, the high of being desired worn off and the one drink not nearly enough to dull the guilt setting deep in my stomach. I looked from face to face, trying to find Azden, but I was too short and the floor was too packed. I didn't even know what I'd do when I found him; all I knew was that I wanted to see him. For a second my mind caught on a passing thought like an old sweater snagging: Ryker.

I shouldn't be doing any of this, I thought, but I found myself lacking the need for should at the present moment. This bar felt like a different world, like nothing I did in here counted.

I thought about reaching out to Azden's mind, but what would I say? I didn't even know why I was looking for him, let alone what I'd do when I found him. I needed another drink.

I shouldered my way out of the crowd, my dance partner barely noticing my absence. I walked up to the bar, and despite being on the other end, the same bartender came to serve me.

"Another Red Volley?" he asked, bracing his arms on the counter. He was a man that clearly knew how he looked, and more specifically, the effect he had on women.

"Surprise me," I said, partly because I was feeling adventurous, but mostly because I was wholly inexperienced in this department. I looked back to the tables and crowds, scanning the room for Azden's face. I just needed to see him, then I could get on with my night. At least that's what I told myself.

The bartender slid me a dark green drink that matched the ambiance perfectly. I took a sip and flavors burst on my tongue, none of which I could recognize.

"Good?" he asked, still lingering by me despite the crowd of patrons trying to order.

"It's perfect," I said, giving him another smile to distract myself.

"You know, my shift—" He was cut short by Walcott grabbing my arm, turning me to him.

"Come over here," Walcott said, pulling me away. I turned to mouth sorry to the bartender, but he was already talking to the next girl.

Walcott led me to one of the booths where Olyn and Rahni sat closer than usual. I glanced under the table to find his hand resting protectively on her knee. I still had no clue about the nature of their relationship—was it a brotherly, protective type move? A friends with benefits situation? By the way Rahni flirted with anything with a pulse in here, if they were romantically involved, I hoped it wasn't supposed to be monogamous.

"Enjoying the music, Princess?" Rahni drawled, words slurring together slightly. It would sound natural for anyone else, but she usually spoke with such sharp enunciation that any softness was noticeable.

"It's lovely," I said, sliding into the booth next to Walcott. "Where's Azden?" I tried to sound indifferent, but Walcott wasn't convinced.

"Last I saw he was walking off with a tall brunette," Olyn answered, completely oblivious to whatever Walcott thought he'd picked up on. My chest tightened, feeling like I'd just gotten the wind knocked out of me. It was a completely unwarranted reaction, given that I had just been doing the same myself. I cursed the jealousy that pulled at my emotions.

"Good for him," I said, sipping my drink to avoid eye contact. I found myself once again scanning faces in the crowd, hoping to find him, hoping he was alone.

I could just send a thought. It would be so easy. Would he come? Would he even respond? He'd been keeping out of my head since I asked, but was that really what I wanted?

I finished off my drink, setting the cup down a little too forcefully.

"I'll be back," I said to the group who had gone on chatting while I was lost in thought. I stood up, debating whether to chase after him or find my own distraction.

I weaved through the crowd, searching face after face with no luck. Then there it was—that white-blond hair shining above the rest. I started to push my way towards him, but when he turned around it wasn't Azden at all.

What was I doing?

Where are you? I thought at Azden, more than irritated.

What does it matter to you? He thought back immediately, which he wouldn't do if he was preoccupied. At least I hoped not.

It doesn't, I thought, though it was a tinge too forceful to be believable. He didn't say anything for a few minutes and my pulse raced, scared he was back to whatever woman Olyn had seen him leave with.

I could track him. It would be difficult with so many people, but I'd find him. If I did I'd have to finally admit that I wanted to see him. No, I couldn't do that. Why was I even thinking of barging in on him and another woman? It wasn't my place.

I pushed my way back out of the crowd to the open area at the front by the bar. The bartender from earlier shot me a wink and I tried to return a smile, but it didn't come easily. I looked back to the table where the others sat, laughing with their heads back. I didn't belong there. Or here. Just a few more weeks and we'd never see each other again, and they'd go on as if they'd never even met me.

I slumped into a dark booth in the corner, leaning my head into my hands. My thoughts were so muddled I felt like I was walking through knee-deep mud just trying to identify what I was feeling.

"I think you'll like this one." The bartender had walked out with another drink, this one a simple dark amber. "Looks like you need it." Instead of staying to flirt, he just walked back to his post behind the bar. I was thankful, since I wasn't sure I was able to talk. I turned to the glass, running my finger through the condensation and watching it soak the napkin. My mind cleared as I focused on the dripping water coating my fingertip, swirling it around the rim.

"You look like shit." I looked up to see Azden, alone,

standing in front of me.

"What are you doing here?" I asked.

"If I recall correctly, *you* were the one asking where *I* was." He smiled, shoving me over as he slid into the booth next to me. I was acutely aware of how his thigh felt pressed up against mine. I kept staring down at my glass as my mouth momentarily forgot how to form words.

"What's wrong, Freckles? You know you can talk to me." His voice was soft, and he nudged me slightly, encouraging me to share. I wanted to, but how could I share when I didn't even know what was wrong? A single tear slipped down my cheek as I tried to piece together thoughts, all the while sitting silently.

"Is it the bar? Are you not having fun?" He looked at me with such selfless concern that I really started to cry. "Oh, Estyn." He murmured into my hair, wrapping me in his arms. I leaned into his chest, trying to keep my crying quiet, though there was no way I'd be heard over the music. I thanked the gods I'd found the darkest booth.

"I'm so sorry," I sobbed into his chest, barely intelligible.

"You have nothing to be sorry for." He ran his hand through my hair, placing a comforting kiss on the top of my head. I had just found a semblance of composure, but the act was so sweet I started crying all over again.

"No, I do—you're stuck here when you should be out with that hot brunette." He started smiling at me again, gently tilting my head up with his hand.

"Is that jealousy I hear?" he asked, amused despite the fact I was snotting all over his tunic.

"No," I protested, "No I swear, it's just you should be having a good night and instead you're here taking care of me." His gaze softened, but his grip on my chin forced me to keep looking at him.

"Let's get something straight. There is nowhere else I'd rather be right now." I gulped, then sniffled again, seeing nothing but complete candor in his face.

"Why?" I asked, just as he had earlier.

"You know why," he said, stroking his thumb over my jaw as he gazed at me reverently. I sat up a little, still leaning into him, our mouths now mere inches apart. My lips were still salty, and I bit the bottom one as my body tensed in anticipation. Azden moved his hand from my jaw to rest on my thigh, subtle but claiming. His eyes burned gold, and my magic stood at attention just from being so close to his. I wrapped the booth in my shadows, fully shielding us from the rest of the world.

Then, without thinking, I leaned in, closing the gap between us. The first kiss was hesitant, light. I pulled back to look him in the eyes as he searched mine. Apparently he found whatever he was looking for because the next moment he wrapped his other arm around my waist and pulled me even closer as our mouths collided. The kiss was all demand as his tongue parted my lips, tangling with my own.

My body pressed into his, my skin sensitive to every place we touched. I reached a hand up to cup the back of his neck and held it as if I could pull him even closer. My magic hummed with pleasure along with the rest of me. He lightly squeezed my thigh, and I let out a slight moan in response. He smiled, lips still pressed to mine, and I did what I'd been fantasizing about ever since I first saw him. I turned, kissing each dimple, making him smile even wider before pulling his mouth back to mine again.

After a period of time that simultaneously felt like a minute and hours, we pulled apart for air, both breathless. He pressed his forehead to mine, and I relished the contact.

"We should go," I said with difficulty.

"Probably," he said. His hand wrapped around the bottom of my thigh through the slit in my dress and he lifted me into his lap in one swift motion. I gasped but broke into laughter, tilting my head back, leaning against his arm braced at my back. I wrapped both hands around his neck, fingers absentmindedly stroking up and down.

"You're ridiculous." I laughed, gazing into his eyes. I could get lost in them if I let myself.

"I think you mean I'm dashingly handsome, hilarious, brilliant,..." I kissed him in the middle of his list, and he didn't object. I couldn't help but notice that he was an *excellent* kisser. I added it to my own mental list that I'd been keeping about him.

"Okay, okay, we should go." He leaned forward as I pulled away, making it all that much harder to stop. "Azden," I said, face serious but eyes bright.

"Estyn." He mimicked my serious face, running his hand up and down my exposed leg through the slit.

"It's late. We need to get back to the base." One of us needed to be responsible. I let my shadows dissipate around us and the rest of the scene came into view. I looked over to see the others had left their table. I glanced around, but couldn't see them in any of the groups around us.

"I think they left," Azden said, as if reading my thoughts.

"All the more reason we should get going," I said, though I made no move to get up. I wanted to memorize this feeling; how it felt to be settled into his warm, strong body. I felt safe. When I was halfway standing, he tugged me back down and I fell into his arms.

"One more," he said. I pressed my lips together, trying to

feign irritation, but failed miserably. My lips insisted on curling into a smile, and then, without my permission, they pressed themselves to his again.

CHAPTER

19

When we emerged back to the night my ears took a moment to adjust to the silence. I still heard a lingering ringing, but it wasn't incapacitating. Azden wrapped an arm around my waist as we strolled back home.

Base. Back to the base, I mentally corrected myself.

After a minute, both Azden and I were glancing back to see three soldiers following us. *Let's circle the block,* I thought at Azden, and he nodded in confirmation.

After the fourth turn, they were still trailing us. I tuned into their thoughts but didn't recognize any of the voices.

She's on to us, one of them thought. I glanced back again to find them a hundred feet closer, and gaining. I squinted at their arms, seeing the familiar red shape that I'd grown up with: Tenebris' emblem. What were they doing in the heart of Alynthia? How'd they get here?

Let's split up and meet back at base. I thought at Azden.

I don't know… he thought, but I had to convince him.

We can't risk them finding you.

His eyes searched mine frantically, trying to find a way to convince me otherwise, but we were out of time. They were closing in, and the window for Azden's escape was nearly gone. He sent me one last desperate look before turning and running down a side street.

As soon as Azden was gone, I turned to them as if I hadn't been running away.

"Hello," I said. They walked up with the same intensity, stopping mere feet from me. I resisted the urge to flinch, reminding myself they had my best interests at heart.

"Princess," one in the back said, more ominous than friendly. He stepped out front, followed by two jaguars, and my heart stopped. Lord Ramos. I stepped back an inch, my instincts telling me to run. "We're here to take you home." His tone felt damning.

"Did you get Calix?" I asked, though I didn't have high hopes. Their silence was answer enough. "Then I can't go back yet," I said, turning to make my escape.

"We can't let you," he said, showing no remorse, ever the dutiful soldiers Tenebris trained them to be. A shadowed figure moved in my peripheral vision, and I glanced up to see Rahni on the roof, watching the scene unfold. She disappeared as soon as I noticed her, thankfully before any soldiers spotted her.

"You can't make me do anything," I said, years of blind obedience culminating in this moment. I thought they'd react, try to force my hand, but my entire focus narrowed as the middle one pulled a sweater from behind him.

Not just any sweater—Calliope's sweater.

"We have your friend," one of them said with a sadistic

smile. My shadows pounded against my skin, demanding to go to them, but I couldn't, not yet.

I breathed in and prepared to flee their capture, but a sword swung by my side, catching me by surprise. I lifted my hand to feel blood pooling under my ribs. Luckily it was shallow; I had jumped away on instinct, just not in time. "What the hell?" I yelled, trying to put as much distance between us as I could.

"I don't think my mother and the King will be very happy about this," I said, wiggling my blood-soaked hands in front of them. They didn't find it funny.

I tried to clear the pain from my mind, pulsing my magic in my veins. I saw two of them exchange a glance, and I peeked into their mind for a moment to hear the mental exchange.

Remember, dead or alive, Lord Ramos thought, expressing it to the others with a quick facial expression. My surprise left me vulnerable for a moment and ice shards flew past me, grazing my arm. My magic dulled the pain, but I cursed that I had let my guard down. They were circling me now, the jaguars closing in with each passing second. I didn't want to show my magic; I didn't know whether they were aware of my abilities, but if they weren't, I couldn't risk them reporting back.

I was running out of options. A summer enchanter had created a ring of fire around us, closing off any chance of escape, and the last one held ice daggers long enough to pierce through me.

"Come on, Princess. Just come with us," Lord Ramos coaxed. If there was any chance of me going peacefully before, it was gone now. I whipped my head around, switching from soldier to soldier, trying to track them all but failing miserably. They had me and they knew it. Why did they send three enchanters for me? My magic purred, telling me that they must know. There's no other reason they'd waste so many high-ranking soldiers on a simple rescue mission. Even if I was the Princess. My magic beat against my skin, begging to be let loose.

Okay, I thought, which was permission enough for magic to erupt around me. It acted upon my fear, my shadows seizing each soldier. I held them by their throats, raising them slightly in the air, until the ring of fire dimmed to ash and the vines fell limp. Their eyes opened wide as they stared not at me but past me, blinded by the complete darkness wrapped around them. I clenched my fists, letting fear and anger take over my conscious thought. The shadows kept squeezing as I did, my nails digging into my palms and drawing blood. I barely felt it, a shadow of the pain shooting through my side. I let the darkness consume me too, my magic compelled to act not by thought but by emotion.

My muscles shook, bringing me back to reality as my legs collapsed. My knees crashed into the pavement, my arms not even aware enough to break my fall.

I blinked, shaking the shadows from my eyes as they dissipated around me. I heard three more thuds similar to my own as my shadows recoiled.

The night was silent besides the soft thump of paws on pavement as the jaguars ran. I clenched my eyes, hoping, willing to hear another noise. I reached my magic tentatively to Lord Ramos, feeling for a thought. Silence.

I opened my eyes to see all three collapsed at awkward angles.

I doubled over, vomiting all over the stones in front of me. I braced both hands on the ground, retching over and over until my stomach was empty. I looked back up, hopelessly wishing they'd be gone. Their lifeless eyes stared back at me, whispering *how could you*. Bile rose in my throat.

I needed to get back to the base, but what was I going to say? This wouldn't be it. They'd keep coming; especially now that I'd killed their soldiers. *Our* soldiers.

I could tell Azden. He'd know what to do, but would he help me? I wasn't integral to the mission; there was every possibility they'd simply cut me out, leaving me to save Calix on my own. Or worse, they might just kill me. I knew too much already.

He might do the calculations and realize I was a net negative to the mission now that I was being hunted by my own kingdom. He might break the deal and leave me with no way to get Calix, let alone a way to save Calliope. I wish I could tell him about Calliope, about how much I missed her and the visceral pain I felt when I saw her sweater.

Her sweater—where was it? I looked around, but the stones were covered in ash. I crawled towards the lingering embers, digging through them until my nails were caked in soot. Nothing.

Maybe Azden would understand. Maybe he would help me find her once this was all done.

Maybe isn't good enough. I touched my side, feeling the blood already drying. How long had I been sitting here?

It was too close. I was too close.

I stumbled back to the base, having long since sobered up, but lacking the energy to walk straight.

I made it inside, vision blurring at the edges. Somehow I found my way to the supplies closet, knocking over a few bottles of cleaning solution as I leaned on the shelves. I looked down, but I feared if I bent over I wouldn't make it back up. The shelf felt as if it was nailed to the ground as I tried to push it aside, eventually creating a slit just big enough for me to slide into the stairwell. I descended, almost slipping down every few, only saved by my arms bracing against the wall. I finally landed on solid ground, pulling the lever to open to the hallway. As light filtered in, I spotted someone slumped against the wall across from me. Azden was curled up with his hands in his hair, jerking up to look at me as the wall slid away.

"Estyn," he said, crossing the space between us in just a few strides. He wrapped me into his arms and I collapsed against him, the last of my strength long since gone. "Are you bleeding?" he asked, looking at the shallow scrapes on my arm.

Just you wait, I thought as he guided me into the hallway. His face furrowed in shock and concern as he took in my side, which was no longer bleeding but clearly still painful.

"We need to get you a healer," he said, frantically searching me for other wounds.

"No." I closed my eyes, unable to focus on anything but staying upright. I leaned on him, and even though I couldn't see him, I felt his worry through the way he gently brushed my hair off my neck and then lifted me into his arms. "Please don't tell anyone." I kept my eyes closed, tempted to drift off, but knew I should stay awake.

"Okay," he whispered, pressing a featherlight kiss to my forehead as he walked. I closed my eyes and lost myself in the swaying sensation with each step, pressing my cheek to his impossibly soft yet strong chest.

Before I knew it we were back in my room, then in the bathroom. He set me in the tub, then stood up, sliding his arms out from under me. I grabbed his forearm, finally opening my eyes.

"Don't go," I croaked, my voice only a hoarse whisper.

"I'll only be gone a minute," he said before turning and walking out. I closed my eyes again, focusing on each breath. Just as I started drifting off, I heard the door open again and forced my eyes open to see Azden walk in with a box of medical supplies and a few towels. He started by wetting a cloth and brushing it over my forehead and neck, the cold a welcome change from my skin that felt like it was on fire.

He rinsed it and came back, working his way to my cuts. He dabbed lightly, but I still winced as the fabric came into contact with my wounds.

"This is going to hurt, but we need to clean your wounds," he said, pouring a liquid onto a new cloth. I nodded, or at least I thought I did. I bit my lip at the intense stinging as he worked to carefully clean them. When he was done, he wrapped a cloth around my arm, then paused.

"I'm going to have to remove your dress to reach that one." He said with gentle consideration.

"Okay," I whispered, attempting to help him lift the fabric above my head. I watched him wrap the cloth around my abdomen, carefully moving it to cover the wound and tying it in place. He bent down next to the tub to grab my sleeping clothes that he'd brought in, and I lifted my arms to thread them through the sleeves.

I leaned my head against the rim of the tub, savoring the cold porcelain against my cheek.

"Alright, I have to get you to bed now. Is that okay?" he asked, running his hand comfortingly through my hair. I nodded slightly, not willing to move my head until I had to. I felt like a rag doll as he wrapped me up in his arms, carrying me to the bed. He had already pushed the blankets back and

I curled up on my non-injured side before he pulled them up, tucking me in. In my half-conscious state, I reached for him, brushing my fingers against his arm.

"Please stay with me," I whispered. He paused, and I knew he couldn't say no. He climbed in next to me, not touching me, just offering a comforting presence. I scooted closer, resting my head on his chest and timing my breaths to his until I succumbed to the sleep that had been pulling at my senses.

I woke up to find my leg sprawled across Azden's thighs and his arm wrapped around my shoulders protectively. I smiled, but it only lasted the few seconds before I remembered the events from the previous night.

I murdered not one, not two, but three people. *My* people.

My people who threatened Calliope.

I tried to disentangle myself without waking him, but it was impossible. He yawned, stretching out his arm under my head, the muscles flexing with the movement. I moved faster, scrambling away, which reminded me of the gash in my side. I lifted the wrapping slightly, finding it already healed more than last night. How had I not healed this quickly before?

"How are you feeling?" Azden asked, propping himself up on his elbows. I noticed he was still wearing his clothes from last night. How was *he* feeling?

"Fine," I lied.

"Can we talk about what happened then?" he asked, both the concerned friend and inquisitive leader. This was it. I needed to decide whether to tell the truth; that my king was hunting me, putting us all in danger, complicating the mission, threatening my best friend, risking my ability to save Calix, or find an excuse.

Azden likely knew that they would try to get me back. Maybe even that they were actively finding me, but I doubt he knew how close they were. If I told him the truth, there would be questions, questions I didn't want to think about and didn't have answers to.

The less I thought about it, the easier it was to fool myself into believing Calliope was okay.

"It was a few guys from the bar—they jumped me." His eyes flared in anger and his hands curled into fists, but other than that he tried to look unaffected.

"Who?" he asked, incensed, but not at me. His anger was blinding him, which I selfishly thanked the gods for.

"It was just a scrape. I'm fine," I insisted. He sat up, silently seething, but kept to his promise to not enter my mind. "Please don't tell anyone."

He searched my eyes, but I held firm.

"Okay," he agreed.

"Thank you." I put a comforting hand on his arm, hoping he'd understand just how thankful I was. From the dark circles under his eyes I could tell he hadn't slept much, and his worry was more than apparent. He cared about me. I wanted to run, to stop it from going any further, but my heart screamed for me to lean into it.

But I couldn't.

"So Rahni and I are meeting Ketra tonight?" I asked, pulling my hand away and folding it into my lap. He swung out of bed, pacing back and forth as if he could walk off all his emotions.

"Yes, and remember to ask about all the details—anything could help," he said, sliding into the rebel leader persona.

"Will do. See you at lunch?" I was trying to put as much distance between us as possible, and it was working. He looked momentarily hurt before recovering, nodding, and walking out of my room. A stray shadow tugged at my sleeve, begging me to follow, but I brushed it off.

"Good afternoon, Estyn." Rahni purred from her perch outside my room.

"Shit, you scared me." I couldn't shake the memory of her on top of the roof, watching me with the soldiers. Did she know who they were? Was she going to bring it up?

"Lunch?" she asked, starting to walk towards the dining room as if she assumed that was my intention anyway. It was, but I was suddenly wary of her unusual kindness. Not that Rahni was particularly *mean*, but she definitely wasn't the type to go out of her way to be nice. *She must want something.*

"Sure," I said, playing along. We walked side by side, at my pace rather than hers. As small as it was, that was the most disconcerting part of this entire interaction. I stole a few glances her way, but she wasn't looking at me.

"Did you enjoy Better Days?" she asked, making small talk. Small talk—with Rahni.

"I can see why you all like it so much," I replied, trying to find her angle. I listened to her thoughts, but per usual they were carefully curated and focused on the here and now. They weren't as perky as she was acting, but it didn't seem to be a front. Or at least she wasn't actively thinking about it.

"Yes, it is quite the place." She smiled, but it looked out of place. It was a casual smile, and oddly enough, it was for me. Was she finally warming to me? I relaxed a little, wondering if this was how she acted with all her friends.

We walked the rest of the way in silence, but I didn't feel the caution and hesitance radiating from her that I normally did. It was pleasant.

Olyn was slumped on the table, arms wrapped around his head. Walcott clutched a coffee in front of him, zoning out staring at the wall. Azden was at the head of the table per usual, talking, but we were too far to make it out.

"Rough night?" Rahni asked as we walked up. Olyn groaned in response but made no move to sit up. We slid into our normal seats, Azden's eyes trailing me as I leaned back in my chair. There was no mistaking the longing in his eyes.

"You were saying?" I asked, trying to draw the conversation back to before we interrupted.

"I was just telling Walcott and Olyn that we need to move soon. Maybe even as soon as next week."

"Next week?" I asked, first shocked and then excited. "That soon?"

"Is that a problem?" Rahni asked with a smile. It was sweet but seemed intentionally so. I shook it off, turning back to Azden.

"That's great. Once we hear what Ketra has found, we should be ready to finalize the plans, right?"

"Yes. It'll all be over soon. You'll get Calix." It sounded like he added the last part just to judge my reaction, to see if anything had changed during my time here. It had, but I had no energy to be anything but excited. Calix would be okay. I'd be okay; we'd be together. I smiled at Azden hopefully and he softened under my attention.

"Alright, you two better perk up. We have our own work to do while they're in the city," Azden said. Walcott rolled his eyes and Olyn finally looked up, just long enough to see

Azden's reaction as Olyn flashed him a vulgar gesture. Azden just raised an eyebrow, sipped his coffee, and chuckled to himself.

"Wait up," I called to Walcott as he walked away from the dining hall. I had been itching to get away after he left, uncomfortable under Rahni's heightened attention and Azden's overprotective concern. He turned around, smiling once he recognized me.

"What are you up to?" I asked, willing to tag along to anything to distract myself.

"I was just about to go for a quick workout. Try to sweat out the rest of last night."

"Can I come?" I asked, even though I doubted I had the energy for a workout.

"Absolutely," he said with a warm smile. We walked down the corridors until we came upon the familiar training ring. We weren't alone; there were others working out, some sparring, some weight training, others stretching. I hadn't ever seen the room so busy. Did they purposefully clear out when I trained before?

Walcott led me over to a section of the mats that were fairly secluded, which I was thankful for. I had been training with Rahni, which meant I was fitter than I used to be, but also acutely aware of just how out of shape I was. Everyone here seemed to be in peak form, trained to be ready at any time. I had spent the majority of my life weak and complacent, my only competence coming from Ryker's help.

Where was he? Was he okay? I had been thinking of him less and less, but I still wore the cuff he bought me. Maybe he would get Calliope and meet Calix and me once this was all over. We could start over. Walcott could even come with us.

I looked over to where Walcott was carrying four free weights over. Even though he was fairly slender, he was deceptively strong. He wouldn't come; this was his family. Whatever he felt for Calix and me, it likely paled in comparison to the loyalty he felt for the people here.

What if I stayed?

"What do you think is going to happen once this is all over?" I asked him as he set down the weights next to the mat. He picked up the heavier ones and I followed suit, grabbing the small ones he brought for me. We started curling them, and a dull pain shot through my side as my abs tensed.

"I don't know. What do you want to happen?" he asked thoughtfully. He dropped his weights after the first set, and my arms, which already felt like jelly, hung limp at my side. I reached for the cuff habitually, hoping it would give me some sense of clarity.

"Do you think I should go back?" I countered.

"I think that's for you to decide," he said, always the neutral listener. I tried to read him, but my attention was occupied by my arm muscles which were currently complaining about our second set. I probably shouldn't have, but I peeked into his thoughts. He didn't want me to go back, but he wanted it to be my choice. When he thought of my homeland, it wasn't just contempt or general disregard—he was afraid. And no matter how much I'd tried to deny it for the past weeks, I could see why.

"Remember to breathe through the exercise. If you hold your breath, your muscles can't get the oxygen they need to work. Here, watch me." He emphasized breathing in on the descent and exhaling as he lifted. He was right; it became far easier once I started breathing. I'd have to remember that.

"What if I didn't want to go back?" I asked after we finished the set, rubbing my arms. Walcott paused, deep in thought, before handing me a towel.

"Then we'd figure it out," he said as if it was that simple. I appreciated it, but he didn't know how complicated it was. The King was hunting me, so staying put them in danger. Saving Calix was one thing, but asking them to risk themselves to protect me was another entirely. Especially when I wouldn't be protecting myself, running straight back to the kingdom hunting me to save Calliope. Knowing that didn't make me want to stay any less.

I flopped on the mat, my arms sprawling out from me like limp noodles.

"We'll have to work on that." Walcott said with a dry chuckle. "Since you're already on the mat, let's try some sit-ups." He kneeled and held my feet down as I silently panicked. I couldn't say no, but the last thing I wanted to do was aggravate my wound. Too late now. I crossed my arms over my chest, pulling myself up to my knees and wincing with every effort. "Come on Es, there's no way it's that painful," he teased, and I shot him a glare promising all sorts of pain. Walcott smiled, ordering five more. The next time rose to see him, Rahni was standing over his shoulder staring down at me. I reached my arms behind me to help me stand up. My instincts urged that it was not a good idea to be on the ground and vulnerable before her.

"Looks like a good workout," she said with the same false cheeriness from before. Her voice didn't match her stance, which was guarded and intimidating as ever. It was an unsettling combination.

"It is—want to join?" Walcott asked.

"I'd love to," she said, flashing me a smile. I smiled back, but it was a poor attempt at disguising my unease. "What's next?" she asked Walcott, and he, who didn't seem as perturbed by Rahni as I was, guided us into the next core exercise.

I didn't speak again for the rest of the workout besides the few times questions were asked of me. I mostly let Rahni and Walcott chat, losing myself in my own thoughts. Was Rahni trying to foster some form of goodwill between us before our mission tonight? If I was being honest, I preferred her normal, slightly-aloof demeanor to whatever this was. Maybe it had something to do with her seeing me last night, though I didn't know what that could be. My thoughts kept flashing back to moments from then. I smelt the blood, felt the heat of the fire surrounding me, the cold of the breeze and silence of the night when it was over. I played their words over in my head: alive or dead, dead or alive, alive or dead. They must know, but how could they if I hadn't known myself? Had they always known?

If they'd always known, then… *no,* I thought. *My family wouldn't have knowingly harmed me.* Even as I denied it, doubts crept in. The conversation I overheard with my father, asking about my medication. My memory twisted his voice into a wicked, conniving tone rather than the concern I'd assumed—or rather hoped—it was. Even now, moving through Walcott's workout, I didn't feel the ever-present weakness and fatigue I'd grown accustomed to. I hadn't ever considered it was intentional.

Why had I been taking it in the first place? All I knew was that mother told me I was sick, that it was helping me. I'd taken it all my life, but I couldn't seem to remember why.

"Estyn," Rahni's voice cut through my thoughts. "Let's go grab some tea." She and Walcott were standing, wiping their foreheads with towels that Walcott had brought, while I was still sitting on the mat. She offered a hand to help me stand, and I took it. Maybe I was overthinking it, maybe she was just being nice. Last night had made me paranoid, but there was no need to be. Not here.

"I'd love that," I said, and she smiled, which without my compulsive need to examine her every motive seemed genuinely pleased. Though I was drenched in sweat, the workout had helped me work through my thoughts, leaving me with a clearer mind than before. Everything would be okay.

<h1 style="text-align:center">CHAPTER</h1>

<h1 style="text-align:center">20</h1>

Rahni and I spent the rest of the day together. She kept suggesting new things, and to avoid being alone with my thoughts, I went along with them. The only time I had to myself were the brief moments I spent washing and dressing in preparation for the night. I still felt weak from last night, but I figured adrenaline would carry me once we got into the city. It was strangely reminiscent of how weak I used to feel, and my stomach clenched at the thought. I couldn't go back to being that vulnerable.

I exited my room to find Rahni once again waiting outside, but this time I welcomed it. One of her snakes wrapped around her arm, prepared to strike at any time. She smiled at me and the snake hissed in greeting. I could get used to being her friend.

"Ready?" she asked.

"Let's do it," I responded, sheathing my dagger in my

boot. It seemed silly now that I had better control over my magic; what was a dagger to suffocating shadows? Still, it was comforting to have at my disposal. We arrived at the stairs to find the others waiting for us.

"Have everything you need?" Azden asked, looking at us from a respectable distance away. I felt his magic licking at my toes, begging him to come closer. If I was being honest, my shadows would do the same if they weren't so tired.

"Yes," Rahni answered, offering a perfunctory nod before ducking into the stairwell.

You good? Azden asked in my mind, and I could tell he didn't just mean about this mission.

I think so. I said, and despite the uncertainty ahead, I was telling the truth. I glanced at Walcott and his encouraging smile reminded me of what he said earlier. I wasn't alone; we'd figure it out.

Please be safe, Azden thought, and the depth of emotion in the thought communicated just what he felt for me.

I will, I promised, and I would. Though I wasn't particularly afraid of death anymore, I refused to go down until Calix was okay. Azden smiled in response and my heart fluttered at the appearance of both dimples. There was no denying the effect he had on me. I begrudgingly pulled my gaze away, looking at Walcott one last time. He winked at me, giving me the confidence I needed to leave.

"My gods, what took you so long?" Rahni asked as I emerged into the familiar supply closet. I glanced at the shelf where I had knocked the supplies to the ground, but all had been returned to normal. I thought I glimpsed a smudge of blood on the wood, but I was likely imagining things. My side seemed to sting in response.

"Stop whining, it wasn't that long." I smiled at her and she rolled her eyes, pushing the shelf back into place.

The night sky was shrouded in clouds, blocking the stars that I always found so comforting. We moved silently through the night, relying on nimble feet since I needed to conserve my energy in case I had to use my magic later. Before I knew it we were upon the castle wall once again, near the same place we had first met Ketra. We crouched in an alley that had a good view of the door, waiting until it opened.

Almost an hour passed, and I was growing bored. Was Rahni as bored as I was? I reached out tentatively to see what she was thinking, but it was muffled.

Let's just get this over with. She thought, but I couldn't be sure—it sounded distant and garbled, my magic straining with the small effort. I hadn't realized just how much I had exhausted my magic.

The door cracked open and I leaned forward, trying to make out the figure that emerged. The guard looked both ways before easing the door shut and scampering over to us. As she neared, I recognized Ketra's eyes from above the mask she wore.

"Did anyone see you?" Rahni whispered, her snake raising its head to attention.

"No," Ketra said, lowering her mask once she was safely obscured by the darkness.

"Good," Rahni said, leaning back against the wall. "So what did you find?"

"The King is sending a legion of his best troops to the border to intercept a group of Tenebris soldiers. The army is dwindling, so he's even sending some of the castle guards with them. They leave in two days." Rahni nodded, and Ketra took that as encouragement to continue. "They're posting more of us on the wall, which leaves most of the rooms inside unguarded. King Ruzu is still keeping his personal guards, but other than that the castle will be fairly empty. I also found and copied a floor plan," she handed a parchment to Rahni who squinted at the scribbles, "sorry for the mess—I didn't have very much time."

"Good job," Rahni said, studying the maps of guard locations. I, for one, thought that Ketra had gone above and beyond what we asked her to do. My heart warmed with pride, both excited that we'd have a better plan and that my instincts were right.

"*Great* job." I corrected, wanting her to know just how helpful she had been.

"Keep doing your rotations, and we'll be in contact tomorrow," Rahni said, dismissing her. Ketra pulled her mask back up and checked the top of the wall before running back to the door. Before I knew it, she was back on top as if she'd never left.

"We should check out the far end before we head back—make sure nothing has changed," Rahni said, not waiting for my answer before taking off towards the section of wall that Azden and I had previously scaled.

I ran after her, struggling to keep up. She ducked behind a tree, hidden from the guards and facing me. The waves lapped at the cliffs below, the ocean warning of the impending storm. As soon as I caught up, Rahni darted to the next tree. It was all I could do to focus on not losing her. When she finally stopped, letting me catch my breath, I looked around to see the wall had disappeared into the distance and we were mere feet away from the cliff's edge. I dared a glance down, but fog covered the water, making it impossible to tell how high up we were.

When I looked back to Rahni, I found animals encircling us—no, encircling me. Her snake had slithered in front of her, head cocked back and ready to strike.

"What are you doing?" I asked, trying to find a reasonable explanation but coming up short.

"What have you told them?" Rahni asked, and when I looked at her confused, she added "Don't play dumb with me. I saw you the other night." I started to piece it together, but I still didn't fully understand.

"You think I'm... working with Tenebris?"

"What have you told them?" she demanded, the animals prowling closer.

"I'm not working with them. They were trying to kill me!" I protested, backing away from the animals only to precariously teeter on the cliff's edge.

"Come on, Estyn. Do you really expect me to believe that?" Her eyes flared as she controlled the animals, inching them closer.

"I don't know what to tell you—it's the truth. Look, they hurt me," I said as I desperately grabbed at my shirt, pulling it up to show the bandages wrapped around my abdomen. "I killed them." My breathing was ragged, especially as I admitted the last part. She pushed the animals forward, undeterred. "Look, I don't want to hurt you—" I stammered. She smiled at that, a sadistic and knowing grin that had me pulling at my magic.

"Don't worry, you won't. You won't hurt anyone ever again." I attempted to call my shadows out, to have them form a protective barrier. Maybe even reach out and hear her thoughts if I had the energy, but I didn't. For either.

"What did you do?" I asked, suddenly far more afraid. All I had was a dagger against the swarming army of hungry animals that were pressing me closer and closer to the edge.

"Only the same thing they've done to you for years. Arrowwood." She said it as if that explained everything, but it only spawned a hundred new questions. "It prevents you from accessing your magic." I looked at my hands frantically as if I could see my helplessness in them.

"Either way, you're too dangerous. I won't risk it," she said, and I stepped back once more to feel rocks slip from under my foot, shattering against the cliffside as they fell into the fog.

"Please," I pleaded, my voice breaking. "I have to save Calix." I was at the brink of tears, ashamed that I'd failed him. I was out of time; the animals were only a few inches away, and I had to choose between falling to my death or being ripped apart.

"I'm sorry Estyn, but I have to do this." I barely heard the last part over the pounding in my ears as her snake finally struck, finding its mark on my leg and sending me reeling over the edge.

I couldn't tell up from down; the fog surrounded me and I lost my sense of time and place during the endless fall.

Please let Calix be okay without me. Tell him I loved him, and that I tried. I tried. I prayed to the gods, tears streaming out as I fell backward.

The phantom of a face appeared in the fog, but I likely imagined it through the tears clouding my vision.

Estyn, it seemed to say. The face belonged to a woman more beautiful than any I'd ever seen. The fog seemed to swirl around her, playing as my shadows did. If only I had my shadows now.

Don't give up hope just yet. Her voice wrapped around my thoughts in an omnipotent blanket of warmth and comfort.

I reached out a hand to the face, but it was too far. Before I could think of anything else, my back slammed into hard stone below me—*no, not stone*, I realized—water. I sunk farther and farther down, my muscles useless, struggle futile. The woman said not to give up, but what other options did I have?

I prayed.

I prayed to the gods I'd sworn had forgotten me. I prayed that Calix would be okay. Most of all, even though I desperately wished I had larger, altruistic prayers, I prayed that death wouldn't hurt.

I was out of time.

I breathed, the water clogging my lungs as I coughed, only to find more water pouring in.

My shadows twirled around me, languid as they moved through the water, trying and failing to protect me from the inevitable.

CHAPTER

21

I awoke to nothingness. It looked like the fog, but I could stand—though when I looked at the ground, it looked much the same. I took a few steps forward, testing the boundaries, but there didn't seem to be any. I looked behind, to see where I had come from, and the face from the fog was now corporeal, attached to a body draped in long, black fabric.

Am I dead? I thought at her.

Almost. She thought back with a sad smile, tilting her head to the side as she observed me. I had the feeling she could read much more than my thoughts; she knew every inch of me. She was running through my veins, pulsing through my heart and lungs and everything that made me *me*.

Who are you? I asked.

You know who I am, she said as shadows all too similar to mine pooled at her feet. Though I had no reason to, I did.

We don't have very much time. Estyn, you have a purpose in this world that you have not yet fulfilled, that you must, she said, her voice full of an urgency that shook the air around us.

What are you talking about? I asked, but she was already disappearing into the distance. I walked forward, reaching out as if to stop her, but she was already impossibly far. *Please, I don't know what this means,* I pleaded.

Just follow the light. All will make sense in time, she said, her voice trailing off as the fog swallowed her into its depths.

CHAPTER

22

My eyes snapped open to see the same cloudy sky I had died beneath, coughing up water that seemed to fill every part of me. Wet sand crunched beneath my hand as I turned over, coughing and coughing as water sputtered out of my lungs.

I drew a haggard breath, my lungs and throat burning, finally able to acknowledge my other senses. My leg stung where Rahni's serpent had sunk its fangs in, but that pain was acute and bearable compared to the overall throb caused by my impact on the water. All my bones should have shattered; I felt like they had. I ran a hand gingerly over my legs, but they felt normal.

I looked back at the ocean, half expecting the woman to follow me onto the beach, but all I saw were the angry waves crashing on shore. I drew my legs in, wrapping them in my arms. What did she want with me? And what purpose was she talking about? What could I do for the world? I was just me, and it was all I could do to simply stay alive.

Alive.

I was alive.

Tears fell down my face even though I'd expelled all the water in my body. I rocked, watching the waves come down on themselves. Why did Nyx save me? It felt too generous an act for someone who was determined to save her brother and disappear.

But that's not all I wanted anymore, was it?

I'd tried to convince myself I wanted a quiet life, but I was wrong. I wanted to help. Alynthia or Tenebris, maybe both, maybe more.

But first, Calix. I felt my magic slowly coming back, the arrowwood making its way through my system. I couldn't go back to Azden, and I couldn't go back to Tenebris, but once I found Calix he'd know what to do. We'd figure it out together.

I forced myself to my feet, my muscles protesting as I tried to walk the woods edging the cove. I needed to find somewhere to rest.

I spotted a small cave set into the stone and walked towards it. It seemed to get farther every step I took, but I was determined. I would wake up stronger tomorrow.

When I was just a few hundred feet away, the bottom fell out of the clouds and I was caught in a torrential downpour. No matter. I was already soaked anyway.

I reached the mouth of the cave, the inside damp and humid from the raging storm. I barely made it a few steps inside before curling against the wall and drifting into a deep, endless slumber.

Sunlight warmed my face, a stark contrast to the cold stone pressed against my skin. I opened one eye to see a seagull sitting at the mouth of the cave. It cocked its head, watching me but not moving any closer. I scrambled to a sitting position, remembering that I needed to get moving.

"Shoo," I said, gesturing for the bird to leave. It didn't flinch, staying planted between me and the exit. "Fine. Stay as long as you'd like," I said dryly, dismally aware that I was taking to a bird.

I tried to recall the castle plans from the brief moments Ketra had shown them to us. I knew enough about the guard rotations and layout that I just might be able to pull it off. I called to my shadows. The arrowwood had worked its way through my system, my thoughts clear and shadows strong. They swirled around me, blanketing me in their comforting presence. I smiled as one poked my arm in an almost loving gesture. I hadn't realized how much I grew to rely on them until yesterday, not just for protection but as part of my identity.

The seagull squawked at the magic humming in the air, flying away from the cave. I smiled. Soon others would do the same.

My shadows followed me out of the cave and to the tree line. They curled around me protectively as I climbed, high enough to see the surrounding area. As I reached the top, I spotted the walls of Myllanor in the distance, the castle sitting atop its hill on the edge. It looked to be about two days away on foot. Not impossible. I shimmied down, comforted by my shadows pressing into my back. I wasn't sure if they could catch me if I fell, but they were able to steady me on my descent.

The only problem with walking all day was that I didn't have anything to occupy my thoughts. My worst fears decided to rear their heads, posed as innocuous what-ifs.

What if Rahni was right—what if I was too dangerous? What if Azden was behind her attempt? What if Ryker was behind Tenebris' attempt? I spiraled, wondering if I could really trust them. Calix was the only one I was sure about. Which was precisely why I needed to get to him as soon as possible.

Was it foolish to go to him by myself? Likely so. It didn't matter, I needed to. I wasn't sure who I was anymore, but I would always be Calix's protective older sister.

I hiked through the woods, the slight incline to the city straining my calves. Fog gathered along the forest floor, obscuring the underbrush. Thorns cut at my legs, tearing into my pants. I barely noticed, singularly determined to keep walking.

A branch snapped to my left, causing me to stop in place as if any movement would draw the creature nearer. I paused, searching the fog for a silhouette, finding a hazy outline of a man. My internal alarms rang, and I darted behind a tree, wrapping my shadows around myself. I peeked around the trunk, trying to see if he had come any closer. Was he alone? What was someone doing all the way out here?

I closed my eyes, finding his mind and easily slipping in.

It can't be, she can't be, she isn't dead. He said she isn't dead.

I'd recognize that voice anywhere. The nerves on my arm became acutely aware of how the cuff felt wrapped around my bicep.

I searched, but he seemed to be alone. Why would Ryker be alone? I wanted to run to him, for him to wrap me in his arms and tell me it would all be okay and that we'd go get Calix together, but my instincts had been wrong more often than not recently. He neared the tree I was pressed against, seeming to wander aimlessly.

Even if it was stupid, I needed to see him, but I'd do it the smart way.

Ryker, I thought to him.

Estyn? He thought, surprised. I would expect nothing less since I disappeared weeks ago.

What are you doing out here? I asked.

Looking for you, he responded.

I peeled off the tree, readying to go to him. I could escape if I needed to, I told myself.

"You came for me," I said to his face, which looked drained. Bags lined his eyes, and his usual carefully cropped hair was mussed about his head. His face lit up when he saw me, the relief apparent in his eyes. I felt instant guilt, remembering how we left things and what I had done in the past months. He had been tirelessly searching for me while I shamelessly flirted with a boy who may or may not have ordered me killed.

"Of course," he said, rushing to wrap me in a bear hug. I leaned into his embrace, reveling in the warmth. "I'll always come for you." He pressed a gentle kiss on the top of my head. I closed my eyes, and the ever-present night sky in my mind started lighting up on the edges. We weren't alone.

I pushed away, putting a safe distance between us.

"You're not alone," I said, more accusatory than questioning. His silence was confirmation enough. "You're working with them? Do you know they're trying to kill me?" He didn't move, not surprised in the least.

"Estyn, let me explain—" he started, but I was too hurt to

hear his excuses.

"Do you have no shame? Using my trust in you to try and take me back?" Tears brimmed my eyes and shadows swirled around me in response to my heightened emotions.

"That's not it, but I don't have time to explain—please just trust me."

"Trust *you?*" I asked, incredulous. I had wasted too much time indulging my need to lash out at him, and his soldiers were upon us.

"Is she coming willingly?" they asked Ryker. I looked from them to him, trying to read his eyes, showing him the plainly written hurt in mine. He turned to them, giving me a chance to escape. I started running, feet pounding as fast as they could, taking me far away from the scene. I closed my eyes briefly to see how close they were, but they hadn't moved. In fact, I counted two less lights than before. I stopped, turning to check if Ryker was okay despite my better judgement.

He was more than okay. He was splattered in blood, two of his men fallen by his own hand. The last two held swords to him, confused but questioning. I debated running, sure to escape now, but I couldn't leave him. As crazy as it was, I still cared. I ran back towards them, sending my shadows out in front of me. They were disarmed seconds, leaving them vulnerable to Ryker, who struck instantly.

"What the fuck?" I yelled, both at Ryker and the entire scenario. He calmly wiped his blade on one of their shirts before sheathing it by his side.

"They'd stop us," he said, calmly wiping a drop of blood from his cheek. I nearly gagged.

"Stop us from what?" I asked, debating whether I should continue questioning him or just run. This wasn't the dutiful soldier I knew Ryker to be. Who *was* he?

"Getting Calix." And just like that, my world righted again. I wasn't alone anymore. I had hope. I hadn't realized how much I'd been dying to hear that until the words came out of his mouth, leaving me wondering if I had imagined the entire thing. "Estyn?" he asked, reaching to put a hand on my arm. I jerked away at the contact, feeling the lingering stickiness on one of his fingers. No matter how much I needed a friend, I couldn't ignore the gore surrounding us.

"So you just killed your men?"

"I had to," he said, gripping my arm and leading me towards Myllanor. I took a few steps before stopping, my muscles clenching under his grasp. "We have to go. We have much ground to cover before the sun sets."

He was right. The sun hung low in the sky and as much as I dreaded returning to the city, I didn't want to spend more time in the forest than I needed to. Besides, I was so, so tired. My body hurt and my mind hurt and my heart hurt and I would've given up by now if I could've, but I had to go on. I wished I was strong enough to do this by myself, but I wasn't. I wasn't very strong at all.

But trust Ryker? It seemed too good to be true. Right when I was out of options, he came out of nowhere, offering to help. Was I a fool for wanting to believe him?

Think, Estyn, I told myself. My options were either to take a chance on Ryker or attempt to save Calix by myself. I thought through the realities of getting Calix on my own. If Tenebris soldiers didn't capture me before I got there, I'd still be going into a heavily fortified castle with no supplies, no weapons, and no backup.

"We can talk on the way, but we have to go." He started walking again, but this time I followed. We fell into an easy rhythm of old friends, but he was covered in blood and I looked like I had been dragged through a watermill.

I had so many questions, but I was so tired. We didn't talk again until the sun set.

"We need to make camp," Ryker said, starting to collect logs for a fire. I gathered kindling, stacking a small mound of sticks for him in an effort to be useful. A chill fell over the forest as the sun set, and I shivered, suddenly aware of how thin my clothes were.

I crouched near the fire, warming my hands over the flames. I looked over to where Ryker was clearing the forest floor, presumably for us to sleep on. When he looked up at me, shadows danced on his face, making his cheekbones look even more prominent.

"What were you doing out here?" I asked, finally breaking the silence.

"Looking for you," he replied, which spawned more questions than it answered.

"How'd you know I was in Alynthia?"

"We got word," he said, again vague.

"You're going to lose your position," I said because, through all of this, the most unbelievable part was Ryker giving up all he'd worked so hard for. Isn't that what I'd resented before? That he'd chosen his career over me? I should be happy that he was here now, choosing me, but something didn't sit right.

"You're worth it," he said, eyes lit with the reflection of the flames. Just like that, I was back to the girl I'd been, my stomach fluttering with his attention. All of my questions melted away, not seeming nearly as important as him being here. I walked over to where he crouched on our makeshift bed, sitting beside him.

"Why did you stay with me in Braiwyth?" I asked the last

lingering question. He could've taken me back at any time. It would've been safer. By all his training and morals, he *should've* taken me back. He paused for a moment, pondering. I worried I overstepped my bounds, that maybe he wouldn't answer, but after a while he finally spoke.

"Because I wanted something for myself. If I didn't say anything, then it could still be our little bubble and you could be my breath of fresh air. I could forget that there are more important things at stake, at least for a little bit." Ryker looked ashamed, and I knew he hated feeling selfish. I reached out and placed my hand on his forearm, moving my thumb in comforting circles.

"Can we go back into the bubble for tonight?" I asked, equally desperate for a breath of fresh air before we went back to reality.

"I don't know…" he said, looking as serious as ever. I kneeled next to where he sat on the ground, tilting his chin up with a finger, forcing him to look me in the eyes.

"Let's just be Ryker and Estyn. Like before." I smiled and his eyes softened in response.

"Just for tonight," he said.

"Tonight," I agreed. He reached an arm around my back, pulling me to him. This was entirely selfish. Soon he'd learn about Azden and my treason and it would all be over, but I wasn't ready to let go just yet. All this time I'd been flirting with the enemy while Ryker was out looking for me, caring about me, being everything I'd ever need.

I knew everything would change once he found out, but I wanted to be held one last night. We laid down on the ground, his arm wrapped around my waist and my back flush to his. I nestled into him for both his body heat and the comfort he gave me. I laid my hand over his, tracing circles around his knuckles and twisting the ring wrapped around his middle finger until my eyes fluttered shut, lulled by the crackling fire and Ryker's steady breathing.

Ryker was already up and scattering the ashes by the time I woke. My back ached from sleeping on the ground for the second night in a row, but the rest of my muscles were already feeling better now that I had access to my magic again. I helped him scatter brush over the remnants of our makeshift camp, working in silence. The night was over, and we would have to return to the reality of our situation.

The forest seemed to get denser as we approached the city, nature's own guard against the outside. Gnarled roots twisted across the forest floor, tripping me on more than one occasion. We talked about vague outlines of a plan, but Ryker said we'd discuss more once we got closer. I didn't mind; I wanted peace and quiet, at least for a little bit. I could put off thinking through just how futile our efforts would be.

We walked until the ground rose, the beach to our right splintering into a cliffside. I kept my head down, watching the small creatures and plants on the forest floor to pass the time.

As the sun started to descend, the sky brushed with vibrant pinks and purples, I recognized the trees. The ghost of a memory played at my senses, Azden's voice floating through my mind as if he was here. If we were in that grove, that meant...

I looked to my left to spot the cave entrance in the distance. I looked up, but Ryker kept walking ahead, unaware of the panic rising in my chest. *Keep calm, just walk a little faster.* If Rahni came out and realized I was still here...*no.* I couldn't fixate on the what-ifs.

They had no reason to know we were passing. Just a few more minutes and we'd be gone, and I'd never have to think of them again.

As I looked up, I smacked into Ryker's back.

"Ryker, we have to keep going," I said, trying to keep my voice neutral. As I said it, I realized why he had stopped.

We weren't alone.

I counted three more people in my mind, all closing in. All people I'd come to recognize.

"We have to get out of here," I whispered into his back with a sense of urgency I hoped would push him, but he didn't move.

I backed away from Ryker, who turned around slowly.

"I'm sorry," he said, but I didn't understand. Why was he sorry? I looked from him to the trees where I'd seen the three people in my mind, then back to him. And then I looked to his middle finger, to that same ring I'd mindlessly touched last night. That same ring that Azden had described in painstaking detail.

"What—" I said, still in disbelief. He was *working* with them? No, no, no. Not my Ryker. It couldn't be. He loved Tenebris more than anyone I knew, more than anyone could love a Kingdom. He reported to my father for gods' sake.

They were coming at me from all sides. My only option was the cliff, and there was no way I was going there. I had to fight.

I felt my magic course through my veins, felt myself give in to its darkest desires. I let go of the control I held over my shadows, letting them swirl around me, creating a boundary.

"Estyn, if you'll just let me explain," Ryker said, but I ignored him. He wasn't my target.

He tried to approach, but I shot a shadow at him, knocking him against the nearest tree and binding his wrist to the bark.

"Estyn!" He shouted, clawing at the force he couldn't grasp. I tightened its grip, ignoring Ryker's shouts of pain.

This was my chance. I stalked toward the middle light in my mind, tracking her just as Azden had taught me, pursuing her just as she herself taught me.

Estyn, please, we just want to talk. Azden's voice broke through my mind.

It's too late for that, I thought before shoving him out.

My shadows ripped through the thicket in front of me, revealing Rahni in all her glory.

"Estyn," she said, cold, calm, collected and entirely infuriating. I didn't give her another chance to speak before shooting a shadow towards her, so fast she didn't have time to intercept it. Her snakes hissed, slithering towards me in defense.

I smiled, but it held no joy, only twisted satisfaction. Maybe this was the purpose Nyx spoke of. Just before my shadow hit, a beam of light knocked it off course, slamming it into a tree.

"Stop this," Azden commanded, coming into view beside her.

"You knew," I accused, shameful recognition washing over my face. I'd thought he cared for me, but I was just a pawn in his plan for vengeance and power.

"I didn't," he said, quieter than before, almost regretful.

Too late, I thought at him, and before he could react, I shot a shadow at his foot, yanking his ankle out from under him.

"I can explain," Rahni said, finally flustered. Good.

"Explain why you tried to kill me? You really think I'd want to hear that?" I shouted, my shadows billowing out even farther. My magic felt so potent, so pure, begging me to give in to every dark thought I had. *Let us at her*, they seemed to beg, bent on revenge. Even if I thought I'd been a better person, after all I'd been through…

I obliged them.

Rahni avoided the first few, dodging my clumsy attacks. Light shot at my shadows, intercepting some, but never targeted at me. Fool's move.

I shot a shadow at Azden, hitting him square in the shoulder and knocking him to the ground once again. My senses narrowed, my field of vision closing in on just the woman before me. The woman who'd tried to kill me days before. The woman who I'd thought was my friend.

"Calix would forgive her," Ryker shouted.. That was the wrong thing to say.

"Calix isn't here."

Sweat beaded on Rahni's brow as she evaded each attack, losing to more and more of them. Each brush of shadow on her skin left a bruise in its wake. I wanted to feel satisfaction, to draw it out and hurt her as she hurt me, but I felt empty. All I knew was the anger and the magic channeling it.

I only had the briefest warning of the arrow whistling through the air before it struck my arm, just below my shoulder. My shadows recoiled from Rahni, gathering around me protectively, feeling weaker with each second. I reached to grab the shaft, feeling it jut out from my bicep, just above my arm cuff.

So much for protection, I scoffed, trying to lighten my mood through the delirious pain. I dropped to my knees, clutching my arm. Should I pull out the arrow? I remembered something about arrowheads being dangerous to remove, but I couldn't remember much.

"Hold still," Walcott said, suddenly above me, pouring something into my mouth and holding my jaw until I swallowed. I called for a shadow to push him away, but my magic felt foggy.

Arrowroot, I remembered. That's what this feeling was. I didn't have the energy to fight back as Azden braced a cool hand against my arm and pulled the arrow out in one swift motion. I cried out, my scream echoing in the forest. Walcott walked into my line of vision, bow in tow.

"I'm sorry," he said, but he kept his distance. Azden ripped part of his shirt, wrapping it around my arm to staunch the bleeding. I should fight him, push him away. *After he wraps it,* I told myself.

Just as gently as he'd tended to my wound, he offered a hand, helping me stand. I ignored it, standing on my own and backing away from him.

"Please come inside. We need to talk, and it's not safe out here," Azden said as if I was a spooked animal. I looked from him to Walcott to Ryker, who was rubbing his wrist, still standing near the tree I'd pinned him to moments before.

I could run, but then what? My wound would likely get infected. I'd be in the same spot I was before, unable to save Calix and with no home to return to. I could listen to them, wait until I healed, and then leave.

I glanced at Rahni, who was favoring one leg, the other blooming with a large bruise from a blow to the ankle. Despite me just bombarding her, when she looked at me, she looked remorseful.

No number of apologies or rational thoughts could overpower the sheer fear and hatred I felt for her. So despite knowing better, I turned the other way and ran straight towards the cliff's edge.

CHAPTER

23

This is it. I couldn't do anything besides sink to my feet, ten feet from the edge, frozen in fear and overwhelmed with my own thoughts. What a funny turn of events it would be for my own mind to take me down in the end.

Don't be so dramatic, I heard Azden say in my mind. I hadn't heard him follow, but I'd become reliant on seeing him in my mind, tracking people without looking. Now that they had drugged me, yet again, I couldn't do that.

He walked up and sat on the brush beside me without a word. I felt him watching, knew his head was turned toward me, but I stared forward. Not at the edge; no, I couldn't manage that. I just stared at the horizon, watching the waves disappear into the sky.

"I thought you died," he said, so quiet it was almost to himself. I didn't respond, hoping he'd get the message and leave, but he continued, undeterred. "I felt it. The light I always see, it… it went out. I felt like I couldn't breathe, like I was choking on air."

"At least it wasn't water," I scoffed with a dry, humorless laugh. I finally glanced at him and wanted to scream at the pity in his eyes. He didn't deserve to look at me like that.

"I didn't know," he said, reaching out a hand as if to touch me before thinking better of it. I drew my legs in close, trying to make myself as small as possible. "When the light came back, I would've torn the world apart to find you. I tried tracking you, but it was like you were blocking me out."

I wish I could now, I thought, so spiteful I hoped my thought reached him whether he was in my mind or not.

"So Ryker works for you?" I asked, finally breaking the silence. No use dwelling on his feelings when the betrayal was still raw.

"Not exactly. He should probably be the one to explain," Azden said. *Great.*

"Still keeping things from me, are you?" I asked with a saccharine smile.

"I never kept things from you, Es," he said, and as much as I wanted to say something just to hurt him, his words rang true. Even when I was a spoiled princess, he took me in, trusted me, trained me and believed in me.

I supposed he could be telling the truth. Maybe Rahni really did plan it herself.

But either way, he still trusted her and she had tried to *kill* me. I didn't know how I could ever face her again after that, let alone hear her out like he wanted me to.

"Can I at least look at that?" Azden asked, nodding at my arm. The pain had fallen into a dull throbbing, but the sensation was ten times more acute without my magic. I was almost thankful. At least it took my mind off the betrayal.

I didn't say anything, but he took my glance towards him as permission to reach forward and pull back my sleeve. I bit my bottom lip, trying to focus on the pain, the pain Walcott had caused. The pain my *friend* had caused.

Whether or not they had known, they didn't even try to talk to me, drugging me like some animal, *shooting* me— except, even through the fog of my righteous indignation, I remembered that they did try to talk to me. I was the one trying to kill Rahni; they just wanted a chance to explain.

Besides which, it wasn't like I could get Calix like this, and especially not on my own. I could always leave after getting my arm treated.

"You should be fine once your magic returns, but we need some healing herbs to ward off infection," Azden said.

"Fine," I said, propping myself up on my good arm to stand. Azden stared at me like I was crazy, but he had full access to my thoughts. I wasn't that unpredictable.

"Do you need any help?" he asked, frantic as he stood, reaching out his arms as if I couldn't walk on my own.

"I was shot in the arm, not my legs. I can still walk," I snapped, ignoring his outstretched hand and marching toward the cave, not bothering to check whether he followed.

The meeting room looked remarkably unchanged for how different I felt. I was unchained, sitting in my usual chair, surrounded by the usual people and Ryker.

Ryker, sitting in the empty seat between Rahni and Azden, looking more at home than I'd ever seen him. There was obvious tension between him and Azden, but their conspiratorial looks said they were more than acquaintances.

Just how deep did Ryker's betrayal go?

The descent into the base had felt like a concession, and one I was not ready to give. I did not forgive Ryker, I sure as hell didn't forgive Rahni, and I didn't see myself doing so. My arm throbbed, but I hid it as best I could.

"I owe you an explanation," Rahni said, the first words since we'd entered. I didn't say anything, just glowered until she continued.

"On the night we went to Better Days, Olyn, Walcott and I had left early, but I decided to enjoy the fresh air and take a walk. I was coming around to the front when I saw Azden and Estyn leave together, looking rather comfortable." I glanced over at Ryker who visibly tensed. "I didn't want to disturb them, so I circled the block before heading back. I was roof hopping when I found Estyn, without Azden, talking to a group of Tenebris soldiers.

"I ran back to base and found Azden waiting in the hall for Estyn—" she turned to Azden, "I tried to tell you, but you wouldn't listen. I saw you were far too deep, that you were letting your feelings get in the way of the mission. So I made the decision to take care of it myself.

"The next day, I monitored Estyn, staying by her side. She acted suspicious, especially after she'd seen me on the roof the night before. So when we went out to meet Ketra, I," she paused for a moment, pursing her lips as she looked down at the table and tried to pick how to phrase it, "used the opportunity. It was for you all—she's more dangerous than even you realize, Azden." Everyone was silent, looking to me for confirmation.

"Do you want to tell them what 'the opportunity' was?" I said bitterly, though less bitter than one ought to be when talking to their murderer.

"I pushed her off a cliff." Her words were clipped. Everyone's heads spun to look at me, and I shrunk under their stares. They were all thinking varying versions of *how are you alive* and *how are you sitting here now*. I didn't know the answer to either, so I looked anywhere but at them.

"I was acting on the information I had, but if I was incorrect, I am sorry." She looked at me earnestly, and now her thoughts were truly apologetic. It softened me, but only enough to say the next words without wavering.

"As I said, I'm not working with them now, and never have been. They're trying to kidnap me and kill me if they can't. That night you saw the brief moments before they started to attack, and I killed them in defense. You're right— I am dangerous, but not to you."

As much as I hated her and wanted her to suffer for what she did to me, part of me agreed with her. I already saw what I could do if I let my emotions get the best of me, and if Tenebris got ahold of me, well, they had ways of forcing me to do their will.

That won't happen. I glanced up to find Azden looking at me with concern, but also confidence in me.

Get out of my head. I shot at him.

"I'm sorry," she said, and she meant it. Everyone looked at me again, as if it were my decision. I didn't know. On the one hand, she was a good person acting on the information she had at the time. On the other hand, she had tried to kill me. I deserved to have some revenge, didn't I?

"I never told you how I met the group," she said. Everyone looked at her in shock. I just stared at her, unaware as to how this could matter now. It sounded more like a get-to-know-you rather than a why-I-killed-you type of thing.

"No, you didn't," I said with an exaggerated bite to my

words.

Hear her out. Azden said in my mind, and I pushed him out.

"I'm from Tenebris," she started, which, while interesting, was not swaying me. "I was born in the castle, but not in the castle you know." *Well, there's only one castle in Tenebris, so your story isn't adding up.* "Below the castle, there's a network of tunnels and cages that house young women. Did you ever wonder how your 'mother' only had enchanter children? Or how many 'orphans' the castle had as staff?" *Calliope*, I thought instantly, wondering where this was going. "Well, the King has a harem down there that he uses to breed enchanters. I was taken when I was fourteen. I was breedable, they said." Her eyes filled with tears, but her face stayed stony as she continued. "After four years of being locked down there, fucked whenever it was 'that time of the season' or 'just because,' I—" her voice broke and tears pooled in her eyes, threatening her composure. "I bore a child. A little girl," she smiled at the memory, but it was fleeting. "She was born a day after the Winter solstice. She was beautiful, healthy, but she wasn't an enchanter. When they took her away, I almost lost it.

"They took all the women who gave birth that day to a separate room. We were barely given time to clean up before we were chained to the wall, one by one, and whipped for our failure." Silent tears streamed down her face, but she looked more determined than ever.

"I snapped. My magic consumed me, took over with only one goal in mind. I didn't fear death, I just feared dying without meeting my little girl.

"I killed them. All the guards. I made it up into the castle, and ran into the hall with no plan other than to kill my way out. That's when I ran into Ryker. I almost killed him too, but he knocked me out and brought me to Azden."

My eyes were wide in disbelief, guilty for all my snarky thoughts. Did that really happen? It made sense. There was no reason for my mother to be lucky enough to have three enchanter children. I thought we were just charitable, taking in the orphans. I should have realized after seeing all the homeless children in Artange that something was off.

But if she was telling the truth, then the woman who raised me was not my mother, and my brothers weren't really—

No. Blood or not, Calix was my brother.

Despite my moral compass urging me not to, I poked into her mind to see if she was lying.

She wasn't. The pain caused by recalling the story was overpowering, and I almost doubled over from the sensation. I pulled back immediately, but it left the room spinning. I couldn't even imagine the horror of what she went through.

"I know my actions are unforgivable. I just hope that you see where I'm coming from." A single tear fell down her cheek. If I were her, feeling her pain, I would be sobbing until my throat was raw.

I looked around to the other faces, which were twisted in concern, but lined with pride for her vulnerability. This was her family. That much was clear.

I turned back to her, and she stared at me as if awaiting a verdict for her crimes. What do you even say to that? Did she expect me to forgive her?

"The deal is still on if you want it to be," Azden said, and my attention cut to him. He sat unnaturally still, the stillest I'd ever seen him. He was always moving, fidgeting, but as he awaited my decision he sat as if frozen in time.

Ryker looked at me, as if trying to communicate with his eyes. Maybe he wanted me to read his thoughts. I suppose if he knew Azden he'd be used to that. I didn't want to hear what he had to say. It didn't matter how he came to work with them, how long, anything. I didn't care.

Walcott was the only one refusing to meet my gaze. He looked at the ceiling as if he'd rather be anywhere else.

"Fine," I whispered, barely audible, even in the heavy silence. Even if my response was reluctant at best, Azden lit up with hope. Ryker's usually expressionless face twitched with the slightest movement of his brows, a much more subdued version of Azden's. I resented them for it.

Walcott finally looked over, catching my eyes for a brief moment before averting his gaze. He was the only one who saw the truth behind my answer. Azden and Ryker heard what they wanted to, but Walcott saw the lingering resentment I held. I was back, but not in the way he wanted me to be. It was not the same. It would *never* be the same.

I'd avoided looking at Rahni until now. I didn't want to see her, to contend with the pain she caused. When I did, my stomach dropped as if I was falling again. In a way, it was helpful. It helped me focus; I was getting distracted, but now I knew only one thing was important: saving Calix. Everyone watched me, waiting as if I'd say something else, but I was done. I needed a real bed. A bath. New clothes. My chair skidded across the stone, making the most unpleasant sound as it cut through the silence, as I stood up and walked out. Azden peeked his head out the door, debated following me, but decided against it.

I was glad. I didn't need any more distractions.

I heard Ryker's thoughts before I heard the knock. He was nervous, trying to plan what to say. If he only knew I wouldn't care either way.

I'd hoped the bath would leave me feeling refreshed, but no matter how much I scrubbed, I still smelled saltwater on every inch of my skin. Even now, with a fresh change of clothes and a heavy spritz of lavender oil, all I smelled was salt.

"Estyn?" Ryker called through the door, and I realized I'd ignored his knocking. I cracked the door open, just wide enough to peek out. "Can we talk?"

I debated telling him the truth, that I saw no point and didn't really care why or how or about any of the excuses he had for me, but he wouldn't stop until I heard what he had to say. So I stepped back, opening the door in silent invitation.

Ryker rushed in, pacing in front of my bed, more nervous than I'd ever seen him. "I'm leaving tomorrow."

"Good," I said, unable to sound as unaffected as I'd wanted to.

"I need to explain," he said, finally meeting my gaze before I looked away. I tried to find the perfect insult, to deal just as much hurt as he caused, but my mind drew a blank.

"Azden and I were childhood friends." If they were childhood friends, then that meant… What was Ryker? To be childhood friends with a prince? "Our mothers were best friends." He paused for another moment, gathering the courage to continue. "But when I was ten, my family was killed by Tenebris enchanters. Azden's family took me in and raised me as their own."

Brothers. They weren't just acquaintances, unlikely allies. They were brothers.

How was he able to ingratiate himself in my kingdom after all that had happened to him? If I were him, I would either burn the place to the ground or collapse in grief.

And yet, he was able to not just work his way up the ranks of our army, but befriend me. More than befriend me. My gut twisted, looking at the face that was so familiar and foreign at the same time. This was the man who always had my back, who always offered a shoulder to cry on.

"When Ruzu took over, Azden and I were thrust into hiding. Everyone presumed we were dead, but really we were down here, gathering our forces. I was still young enough that I could go to Tenebris and join the army, so that's what I did." He refused to meet my gaze, entranced by the patterns in the rug. It suddenly made sense. His mysterious meetings, why he needed to climb the ranks so quickly. He didn't just prioritize Tenebris over me; he never cared about me in the first place.

"So it was all a lie?" I hated how broken my voice sounded. I didn't realize how much Ryker had felt like home until it was all taken away. He searched my eyes, which were threatening tears.

"No, Estyn. It wasn't all a lie." He paused his pacing, looking at me in the way that used to turn my stomach inside out. The way that still did. *Stop it,* I chided myself. This was a man who had been deceiving me for our entire friendship, our entire relationship. He was working with the people who tried to kill me.

"Why'd you pretend to care for me? You didn't have to do that." I whispered, almost to myself.

"That wasn't part of the plan," he said, voice low and gravelly.

"Do they know?" I asked. I don't know why; it wouldn't make a difference either way.

"No," he said, almost so quiet that I couldn't hear it over

the crackling of the fire in the hearth. His eyes drifted to my arm, catching on the cuff that still sat below the bandages. I didn't know why I'd put it back on after rewrapping my wound. It suddenly felt too tight.

"Don't go," he said with a lethal calm, still staring at my arm.

"What?"

"I'll make sure they get Calix. It's not worth it." He sounded fiercely protective, but I knew that couldn't be it. Was this the source of the tension I'd felt between him and Azden?

"I'm more than capable."

"It's not worth the risk." Why was he doing this? A small part of me believed it was because he cared, but I couldn't afford to be that naive anymore.

His mind was swimming with anxious thoughts and plans, but it quickly circled back to me.

Azden can't just use her, he thought, and my heart fluttered in response. He did care. *What if she's caught? What if she goes back? She's too dangerous.*

So that was it. I wasn't the same helpless girl he knew. *I am dangerous.*

"Well that's not your call to make," I said, opening the door for him. His eyes pleaded with me, but they didn't work like they used to. He started to walk out, pausing in front of me.

"Just think about it, Estyn. I don't want to see you hurt." With that he turned, making to leave, but I caught his wrist before he could. When he looked back at me his eyes had the same glimmer of hope I'd seen before.

I turned over his palm, thrust the cuff into it and said "I can take care of myself," before slamming the door in his face.

"We move in two days." Azden was at the front of the meeting room, pointing at the castle maps that Ketra had gotten us. All the details had been nailed down while I was away, and now was the perfect time to strike.

Both Azden and Walcott had come and knocked on my door the previous night, but I didn't have the energy to talk to either. I skipped dinner despite the pains in my stomach, the thought of enduring a meal with everyone worse than the hunger. At least I felt more human once I got cleaned up. It took almost an hour to work through all the tangles in my matted curls, but it was meditative, as if clearing the knots cleared the residual anger and hurt too.

Then this morning I had grabbed breakfast to go and headed straight back to my room from the kitchen. I'd heard Walcott's laugh rise above the rest in the dining room, and it hurt to know that I probably would never feel welcome again in the same way.

I was glad Rahni told me her story, but it only confirmed that our friendship was an impossibility. I represented the years of pain she endured.

"Estyn?" Azden asked, worry lining his eyes.

"What?" I had zoned out and missed what he'd said.

"I was asking if you were still okay with your role," he questioned gently.

"Yes," I said, my voice hard. Business. That's all this was. Get Calix and get out. He nodded, a little shaken by my brash response, but continued on. I paid attention as much as I had to, but my thoughts were elsewhere.

Before I knew it, everyone was packing up, gathering

papers and belongings, walking back into the hall. *I should leave*, I thought, but my legs disagreed. I stared at an imperfection in the wood tabletop, body not entirely feeling my own. I stared until I heard the door slam shut, only then snapping up from my fog.

Azden and Walcott were talking about me. They stood by the door, but they were glancing over every few seconds, probably arguing over who would approach me. Eventually Walcott relented, deferring to the rebel leader slash prince. I scoffed in my head.

Walcott slipped out, leaving Azden and me alone. I didn't want to talk to him. I had trusted him; he trusted Rahni. I knew it would just take a few quips and disarming smirks before I was right back in his arms, and that was something I couldn't afford. Not when I was this close to rescuing Calix.

I hadn't moved in quite some time, not so much as twitching a finger. I just sat and stared at the table. I realized Azden had come and taken the seat next to me. He didn't poke in my thoughts, he didn't try to talk to me. He just sat. I didn't have the energy or desire to see what he was thinking. It didn't matter anyways.

I didn't know how much time had passed with us sitting in silence when I saw a thread of his light peek into my line of vision. He twirled it to the spot I was staring, making it dance like a worm, gyrating on the table. My face stayed detached, but when he started beatboxing, I couldn't help but smile. I broke my concentration on the table and looked over at him, where he was making a fool of himself trying to cheer me up. He was smiling, but it didn't reach his eyes. They were lined with concern for me, willing to do anything to make me feel better.

I swallowed, tears threatening my composure. Azden

directed the light to me, nudging my arm in comfort. I looked at my feet, a tear spilling onto my lap.

"I'm sorry," he whispered, a wisp of light brushing the tears from my cheek. I pulled away, eyes still glistening as I tried to look serious.

"For which part?"

"For everything. For not knowing, for not being able to stop it, for not protecting you. I am so sorry, Estyn." I sat up, pausing in his gaze for a moment before standing.

"You don't need to be sorry. You don't owe me anything," I said as I wiped a tear from the corner of my eye and gathered the papers strewn before me. His brows knit in confusion.

"I do, though," he said, although there was more written on his face.

"It's fine. We just need to get through this, and then we won't have to talk to each other ever again." I intended to sound blasé, but my words were soaked in hurt.

"Is that what you want?" He sounded distant, almost despondent.

"Isn't that what you want?"

"No." He answered immediately and confidently, so confident I wasn't sure what to do with myself.

"I don't belong here," I said, and that much I was sure of.

"You can belong anywhere you want to."

"You all have this implicit trust, and that's something I could never be a part of."

"I trust you." He didn't hesitate.

"But I don't trust *you*." My voice broke. As much as I wanted to, as much as I wish I could, I didn't know if I could ever trust him. He stood, crossing to me in a few steps. I stared at the floor, refusing to let him see the tears that were pricking at my eyes once again.

He didn't tilt my chin for me to look up at him. No—Azden, the rebel leader, the Prince of Alynthia, knelt before me.

"I will work every day to earn your trust, Estyn Lamoret." I looked up at him through my lashes, where his face was still close to mine despite me fully standing. "If you want to leave when we're done, I will respect your decision, but don't think for a second that that's what I want. I want you." I was speechless. I tried to process his words, but my mind was blocking them, my guard not letting me believe him.

We needed to get away from this topic, and fast. I scanned his face frantically, hoping there was a sense of doubt I could latch onto, but I came up short. He believed everything he said.

"Azden, I—"

"It's okay. I don't expect anything. I just wanted you to know." My gaze followed him as he rose gracefully to once again tower over me. In that moment, despite all that had happened, as I stared into his beautiful blue eyes and watched the light dance within them, I let myself hope.

CHAPTER

24

I slid out into the hall, spotted a crowd gathering outside the dining room, and turned the other way, walking until I hit the training room. Shafts of moonlight shone into the ring, and it would have been beautiful if it wasn't marred with memories of what might have been.

I grabbed a few throwing knives, tucked them into my belt and found an additional dagger to wrap to my thigh. I would be given weapons tomorrow, but I needed to be safe tonight.

My afternoon was spent weighing the pros and cons of waiting to save Calix. It was worth any personal risk to have better odds rescuing him, but that didn't mean I would let my guard down. Physically or emotionally.

"Help!" A voice screamed from down the hall, and I heard the doors to the infirmary crashing open. Chaos ensued as people flooded out from the dining hall, trying to get a better view of what was going on. I wrapped myself in shadows, melting into the crowd seamlessly.

It was Calliope, limp in Ryker's arms.

No—not Calliope. Ketra.

There was so much blood. I traced the trail back to the entrance, and then again to where it disappeared into the medical room. I pushed my way through the crowd, trying to see over their heads. Eventually I made my way out of the throng, almost pushed into the gurney with a half-conscious Ketra. No one paid me any attention, clamoring for medicine and explanations. Our single Spring enchanter stood over her, healing what she could, but the wounds ran deep. Ryker reached out a hand as if to stop me, but I ducked and knelt beside Ketra. He didn't bother me again. Ketra's eyes fluttered open, latching directly onto me.

"Estyn," she croaked, but it was barely audible.

"Shh," I coaxed, taking her hand in mine. "Don't be scared." Tears fell to her pillow, thankful for my presence. It was the least I could do—this was all my fault. I felt her pain through my mind, calling me to soothe it. Despite my own instincts telling me not to, I peeked into her mind, her pain flooding my senses. I breathed in, squeezing her hand harder.

It's going to be okay. I said in her mind, and her eyes widened, but only a crack. The left was nearly swelled shut.

Am I going crazy? She thought, and I responded instantly.

No, I am here. I said in her mind. *Can you tell me what happened?* I asked, not wanting to push her too much, but equally needing to know who I could punish for her pain.

They found me. She swallowed deeply as if she was talking out loud. *I was poking around King Ruzu's office, and one of his generals walked in on me. I panicked, trying to run, but he caught me before I could escape. He said he was going to make an example out of me.*

I rubbed my thumb over the back of her hand, carefully avoiding her swollen knuckles.

I fought, but they took me to the dungeons. Her eyes turned cloudy as if she was back there. *I met him. Your brother, I think? He's—alive.* She was careful with her word choice, not giving me any false hope. I had long dreamt about the state Calix would be in, but I didn't harbor any unrealistic expectations.

Thank you, I told her, hoping she felt how much it meant to me.

They tried to get information, but I wouldn't talk. I didn't talk. I cried as she did, seeing the proof of what it had cost her.

I did find something, though. In Ruzu's office. They're in peace negotiations with Tenebris—Ruzu is going to let them station troops here, finally give Alynthia over as long as he keeps control. Prince Bastian will be here tomorrow to finalize the treaty. I saw the fear in her eyes. This time it wasn't for herself, but for the future of her kingdom. They had suffered enough; they didn't need to be subjected to yet another foreign ruler. My eyes flared with my anger, the light flickering. Everyone looked up to me, where I had been silently sitting at Ketra's bedside.

"Sorry," I told them, and they all returned to the task at hand.

Are you sure? I asked her, but I already knew the answer. I had to find Azden. *Are you going to be okay if I step away for a moment?* She nodded almost imperceptibly, trying to be strong through the pain.

"I'll be back soon, I promise," I whispered, giving her a hand a quick squeeze before pushing my way back into the hall.

I reached out, looking for Azden among the crowd of consciousnesses in my head. I finally found him in his office across the complex. He must not have heard all the commotion.

I ran all the way there, wanting to return to Ketra as soon as possible. The door was closed, but I didn't bother with formalities.

"Estyn," he said, looking up as I barged in.

"It's Tenebris. Ruzu is about to strike a deal, signing away Alynthia to secure his spot as ruler. They meet tomorrow to finalize the plans." He looked as frantic as I felt, leafing through his papers quicker than he could possibly digest the information. "We need to move tonight," I said, cutting through the chaos inside his head. He stopped moving, staring blankly at me.

"Yes, we do." His words were grave; despite all our planning, we were still going in unprepared.

I rushed back to the medical room as soon as I finished alerting Azden, but it wasn't soon enough.

Ketra was unconscious by the time I got there. She was still breathing, albeit irregularly. I took her hand back in mine, planting myself by her bedside.

I closed my eyes, finding her light in my mind. It was dimmer, as they usually were when someone was not in conscious thought. I spoke to her, though I wasn't sure it went through.

Everything is going to be okay. I promise, I said, though I knew the dangers of promising what I couldn't control.

I brushed the hair back from her temple, feeling her forehead burn as my hand grazed it.

"Is she going to be okay?" I asked no one in particular. Several people avoided my gaze, not wanting to be the one to deliver bad news.

"We're going to try our best," the Spring enchanter said, though she was visibly drained after using her magic for so long. There was no way she could continue until Ketra was healed; at this point she was doing damage control.

I stole one last look at Ketra's fluttering eyelids before leaving. I wouldn't see her again.

The hall had cleared at Azden's command. The air was ripe with tension, people hurrying to prepare for tonight. It would only be a few of us going, as to not draw too much attention, but everyone had a role. Even with the short notice, the base was running like a well-oiled machine. I had to admire Azden's ability to lead—it was clear he was the rightful leader of Alynthia, by birth or otherwise.

I felt like I was walking in slow motion, carefully observing everyone scramble. I was secretly grateful that the mission was expedited; I wasn't sure how much longer I could pretend everything was okay.

I was already dressed, already armed. There was not much left for me to do but wait. I wandered to the library, each turn heartbreakingly familiar.

As I brought my hand to the door, I stopped, hearing two voices inside. I'd been so lost in myself I hadn't seen their lights, two lights I knew far too well.

"Do you have to go?" Azden asked Ryker, far more insecure than I'd ever heard him, though it may just have been because his voice was muffled through the door.

"You know I do. You're going to be fine. You're Azden fucking Duramoux," Ryker said, with such fondness my scowl softened. He sounded like the strong, caring older brother that I'd always wanted Bastian to be. They were silent for a few moments and I jumped, convinced Azden had noticed me lurking, but then Azden spoke again, so soft I almost missed it.

"I miss you," Azden said, and even without peeking into his mind I felt his melancholy. This was his only remaining family, and he sent Ryker off time after time no matter how hard it was because of the long game, the bigger cause. Because he loved his kingdom more than anything.

And Ryker went, again and again, because he was strong and brave and loved Azden.

I sunk against the wall, knowing I shouldn't eavesdrop, but too conflicted to move. Then the doorknob turned and I melted into the wall, my shadows covering me against the stone.

Azden emerged, but he didn't spare a second glance my way before rushing down the hall. As much as I hoped he didn't notice me, I knew he always did. He let me listen.

I released my shadows, waiting for Ryker to come out, but he didn't. I peeked my head into the open doorway to find him balanced on the edge of a chair, head dropped between his shoulders.

"Ryker?" I asked cautiously, not entirely sure why. I was glad he was leaving, that I'd likely never see him again. Happy.

He stood up abruptly, shaken that I'd caught him in a moment of vulnerability. "Estyn," he said, voice just as calm and level as always. So composed, that if I wasn't looking so hard, I may have missed the light reflecting off of the damp trail falling from the corner of his eye.

I tried to find the right words, the perfect goodbye to encompass all my thoughts, but I didn't know what I felt, let alone what I would say. He stepped forward, reaching to his back pocket for a crumpled envelope. He wrung it in his hands, wrinkling the paper further before extending it towards me.

"I know you don't want to talk to me, but please just take this," he said, and I took it. "Be well, Estyn." He waited a moment, sinking me under his heavy gaze as if memorizing my face before walking out the door.

I stood among the books, unable to tear my eyes from the distinctly round, cuff-sized imprint in the envelope with my name hastily scrawled across the front.

The door creaked open and I spun around to see Rahni's head poke in, tucking the envelope into my pocket.

"Oh, I'm sorry," she said, far more squeamish than I'd ever seen her.

"It's fine," I snapped.

"I just needed to grab something." She walked in, keeping a healthy distance between us, before turning to the shelf and pocketing something I couldn't see. She was almost out the door when she paused, turning to me.

"Are you okay?" she asked, face calm and collected, but eyes deep with regret.

"What does it matter to you?" I asked, too stressed to fake any cordiality.

"For what it's worth, I am really sorry. I know I made a mistake. Please know I'm on your team." Her voice was quiet, and I knew she'd been contemplating this for a long time. Whether she meant it or not, we were *not* on the same team.

I turned back to the book I was staring at, or rather staring past, subtly dismissing her. I didn't look up again until I was sure the door had closed.

After the library, I wandered to Azden's office. He was elsewhere preparing for tonight, leaving the room empty. It felt dark and gloomy without his presence. My heart ached, even though I begged it to stop, picturing all the times I'd been in here with him. I felt a whisper of his warmth on my skin from when we'd been close enough for me to smell his intoxicating scent.

I ran a hand over the books on his desk, a mess per usual. Five minutes. I would give myself five minutes to ponder what if, what could have been. I sunk into his leather chair, propping my feet up on his desk. Would I have done this more often? Probably. I'd come in here as often as possible, and he'd walk in to find me, act as if he was mad. I'd smile and laugh, the natural laughter that only he could draw from me. Then he'd walk over and whisper sweet nothings in my ear, the kind that were both naughty and endearing, enough so that I'd pretend to admonish him, all the while laughing inside.

That's a nice image. Azden said in my head moments before he came inside.

"You said you'd stop that."

"I was worried. I couldn't find you anywhere."

"You're supposed to be busy. Don't you have a rebellion to lead?" I teased.

"I always have time for you."

"You missed the part where I said it could never happen," I said.

"But of course. We'll be in a much bigger office. One with those fancy windows I hear everyone raving about." He smiled, his dimples begging me to forget all the reasons, the *good* reasons, that I couldn't just sink into his arms.

"Azden." I was serious, but his smile only dimmed a little. "I'm not coming back." I didn't know why I said it; I hadn't even told Walcott. It would be so much easier if he didn't know. I wouldn't have to sit through him convincing me to stay. I wouldn't have to see the hurt in his eyes when he wondered if it was him, if he wasn't enough. *You're more than enough. That's why I have to leave.* I thought, praying he wasn't inside my head. It would only make this harder.

I swung my legs off the table, sitting up straight in the chair as Azden cautiously walked a few steps toward me.

"Where are you going to go?" he asked, which, of all things, was not what I was expecting.

"Calix and I will stay in Braiwyth until we find something more permanent."

"You'll always be running," he said, suddenly the calculating, rational leader. His brows furrowed and he crossed his arms, not begging me to stay for him, but rather tempting me with logic.

"We'll find a good hiding spot."

"After everything you've learned, you're okay to just run away?" He looked almost horrified, and his condescension flared my anger.

"I'm not running away. They have my friend," I snapped.

"Your friend…?" *Shit,* I thought. Now I'd have to tell him about Calliope, and he'd laugh at me for thinking I could save her when I'd seen what Tenebris could do. Either he read the concern on my face or in my mind, but either way he said, "we'll get her together," without a second thought.

"I can't ask you to do that. You don't even know her," I said, backing up a step in sheer disbelief.

"You care about her," he said with a shrug. How could he be so cavalier? This wasn't going to be easy. Why would he do this?

Because I care about you, stupid. Plus I'm going after Tenebris anyways. It's on the way, he thought, and for once I didn't even feign being mad at him for listening to my thoughts.

"Is this another bargain? So I'll help you take down my family?" I asked, trying to find some rational explanation.

"No," he said slowly, far more serious than usual. "I'll help you either way. But I hope you help us. I hope you see the pain and suffering and want to help, want to use your gifts for the greater cause because after all they've done to your people you can't just walk away."

I just stood there, unable to form a response. I wanted to yell at him, to blame him for preaching about morals and get off his high horse, but he was right. I *wanted* him to be right. He said it as if it was a given, as if it was the natural progression of events to challenge a kingdom that could easily obliterate him, but it wasn't that easy. I didn't know if I could do it.

"You can't beat them." I wouldn't put his people through that, not after everything they'd suffered through already.

"And why not?" he asked. I searched his eyes, wondering if he was really that naive or just that stubborn.

"They'll kill you."

"Estyn, even if we ignore all the atrocities they've committed, they've personally hurt most of the people I love," he looked pointedly at me, "and I won't stand for it. I won't let them keep doing that to others."

"You're crazy. Or stupid. Likely both." I shook my head, wondering how long it would be until he ended up dead trying to save everyone.

"Probably. You'll have to try harder than that to change my mind." He smirked again, enjoying goading me just as much as if we weren't about to risk our lives in mere hours. "I need your help. You can't just leave," he said. I knew he didn't just want me to stay for my help; in fact, by the look on his face I bet it was barely a top reason at all. "Calix will be safe," he added, trying to find my hesitations and assuage them. My breath hitched, his read on me accurate as always.

"No one trusts me." As I said it, I realized the reasons that I had so carefully developed were slipping through my fingers. Why did Azden always have that effect? Just when I thought I had everything figured out, he came and turned the world upside down.

"Now you know that's not true. You've charmed almost every person here, and you more than proved your loyalty to the one person who was unsure." He walked around the desk, matching the metaphorical ground he'd gained. "I know staying is the harder choice. I know we have a lot to figure out. I'm telling you that I am here for you, and whatever you choose, I will support you, but if you leave," he had to stop, swallow and regain his composure as he stumbled over his words, "there won't be a single day I don't wake up thinking of you. Worrying if you're okay. Wondering if you're happy. Cursing the fact that I couldn't be the one to give that to you." He leaned over the chair, and I realized he'd closed the gap between us. "I'll give you the whole damn world if you give me the chance, Estyn. Please. Just give me a chance."

His smell washed over my senses, soothing my anxiety, blanketing me in a sense of what I could only describe as home. Our faces were only inches apart. I looked up at him through my lashes, and I saw the emotion swirling in his eyes.

"Okay," I whispered, finally letting myself believe in the vision he'd painted for me.

"Okay?" he asked as if it was too good to be true.

"I'll stay. If we live through tonight." I smiled a little, his joy contagious. Azden broke into a full grin, not deterred in the least when I mentioned the impending danger. In one fell swoop he had lifted me up into his arms, and I wrapped my arms around his neck and legs around his waist. I ran a hand through his hair. It was impossibly soft.

"I've wanted to do that for so long." I laughed and he leaned into my hand, somehow smiling wider.

"You can do that anytime you want, Freckles." He chuckled, and the sound was music to my ears. I leaned in, closing the distance between us.

The kiss was unlike anything I'd ever experienced. It said far more than we ever could, our minds tangling just as our lips did. I let go of my magic, let it swirl around us as I gave into him with my whole heart. I lost track of which thoughts were mine and which were his, barely able to think past the feel of his body pressed against mine, his teeth nipping at my lip. I smiled against his lips, and he did the same in return.

I squeezed tighter, not wanting to leave our bubble. When he set me down, reality would set in, and we would have to go. We were spending borrowed time, but there was nothing I'd rather be doing. I took a deep breath, feeling like I could finally get enough air for the first time in a while.

Azden kissed me once more, this time as if it was our last and he was determined to drink in as much of me as possible, before setting me down on my feet, which now felt both more and less stable than before. I tried to catch my breath, steeling myself for the rest of the night.

He took my hand, our fingers lacing together like they belonged there. He stroked his thumb down the side of my palm, reminding me I was not alone.

"Ready?" he asked, watching me as I watched the door.

"Ready as I'll ever be," I answered, far more nervous than I had been before. It was so much easier to run into danger when I had less to lose.

CHAPTER

25

I glanced into Ketra's room as we walked to the exit. She was sleeping peacefully, and might have looked normal if it wasn't for the bandages wrapping her head. I vowed to avenge her, outrage powering each step forward. The others were ready, waiting for me at the door.

"Took you long enough," Rahni said, then immediately recoiled. Walcott scowled at her before turning to me with a sympathetic smile.

"Everyone ready?" Azden asked, readjusting the dagger strapped to his leg. Together we made quite the impression. All dressed in black fighting leathers head to toe, weapons strapped wherever they could be. Two snakes wrapped around Rahni's shoulders, creating a harness protecting her chest. Olyn had a skin of water to manipulate, not outwardly intimidating but deceptively deadly. Walcott had a pouch of flint along with a strip of incendiary chemicals strapped to his chest. The comfort he felt wrapped in explosives spoke to his own lethality.

Azden was by far the most unassuming, only equipped with a few blades. It was unnerving. The only indication of his power was the gold flickering in his eyes, light reflecting off of walls that could be traced to no source. Any fear I felt was assuaged knowing he would be by my side.

Then there was me. I wondered if I looked as out of place as I felt. I wore the same clothes, the fabric impossibly black as darkness clung to me, melting me into the shadows.

In my hands, I twirled the cuff between my fingers, the last words from Ryker's letter playing on repeat in my mind. The entire message had been short and sweet, true to Ryker, but the last words held such striking honesty I had to reread it several times to make sure I had it right.

I wasn't supposed to love you.

He'd never said he loved me. He couldn't love me.

I was still so mad at him, but it melted with each passing minute. The lingering anger was more for him not being here for me to fight with, to talk about it. Why did he get the last word?

I wouldn't stay behind like he asked me to. I couldn't. So I did the only thing I could think of; I looked at the cuff, slipped it on my arm, and rushed into the stairwell.

We ran along the roofs, jumping across alleys like they were only inches wide. I basked in the wind against my face, blowing the few curls that had escaped my braids away out of my eyes.

Azden gestured discreetly to Rahni and Walcott who then split off, heading for the west end of the castle. We slipped down to the street, Azden rolling to a stand and looking at me as if waiting for applause.

Show-off, I thought at him, running ahead with Olyn. We made it to the shorter section of the wall and Olyn started unloading the ropes. I was the first to go up, scaling the wall in a few seconds, giving Azden a run for his money.

I was looking down to see Azden's reaction when a leg swept me off my feet. I kicked back up, just barely in time to miss the sword crashing down where my head had been. I hadn't even seen the guard. I knew the wall was going to be heavily fortified, but I couldn't have expected this. It looked as if they had guards every few feet. A few others were running toward us, which I just barely acknowledged before pulling out my dagger and deflecting his next strike.

I wanted to yell down to Azden and Olyn to stop. I couldn't risk them being cut down before they reached the top, tumbling to the rocks below in certain death, but my attention was occupied dodging the guard's advances, trying to save my own skin.

I reached my shadows out, pulling his feet out from under him and slitting his throat as he fell. The other guards swung, but I was ready. My shadows twisted their wrists until their swords clattered to the floor, and while they tried to find their footing in the swarm of shadowed clouds, I was upon them. It was mere seconds before they joined their comrade on the ground.

Olyn crested the wall, staring at me in admiration.

"Guess the training paid off," was all he said before he picked over their weapons, weighing a sword in his hand before discarding it.

Azden joined us a few seconds after, a twisted smile spreading at the carnage. "Good job, Freckles," he praised, and my stomach turned over. *Focus,* I told myself, refusing to look at their bodies. A few guards further down had noticed us, running over to see the commotion. We couldn't risk them reporting us, stopping our mission before we got anywhere.

Luckily, Azden took charge, throwing daggers at each chest from an impossible distance as Olyn threw bodies over the wall. I tried to help, struggling to lift even one guard, his lifeless form unwieldy as I tipped him over the edge. I grimaced at the thud as he landed on the rocks below. Azden had run to the guards and was back in moments, wiping the blood on his pants before sheathing his knives once again.

I tried to stop myself, but I pictured a tally running in my mind. Seven. So far.

These are the people who have imprisoned Calix and tortured Ketra, I reminded myself, latching onto my anger. Shadows swirled around us, blocking us from further detection as we descended into the perfectly manicured grounds.

I wondered if Rahni and Walcott were having as much trouble as we were. I doubted it. They had probably already disposed of several of the King's guards, picking through them like sitting ducks.

The grounds were not nearly as unguarded as Ketra was led to believe. Had they recalled some of the soldiers because of the peace treaty? The castle was unnervingly quiet, the only noises coming from caws of crows balancing on spires and low growls of larger animals pacing the perimeter.

We ran into another guard, Olyn taking care of him from behind, catching his body before it crashed to the ground. He dragged the guard into the bush, roughly covering it with brush before continuing toward the castle. My counter continued ticking, and four guards later we reached the back door. I wrapped us in shadows as Olyn directed some water into the lock, freezing the handle off the door.

Azden called a small ball of light to illuminate the hall. I was reminded that this was *his* home as he confidently walked to one of the many doors, revealing a stairwell that descended into the depths of the earth. Azden extinguished his light, plunging us back in darkness as we started down to the dungeon. I scanned for thoughts and placed four guards at the entrance.

I didn't dare reach into Calix's mind. I needed to stay focused, detached, and I knew even one second of his pain would be too much to handle, if he was even conscious.

You take the left two, I'll get the right, Azden directed. *Give us cover.*

We stopped at the bottom of the stairs, and I reached my shadows beneath the door, blanketing the room in darkness.

"What the hell?" One of the guards asked before we burst in, silencing them before they could reach their weapons. I took off to the left, passing rows and rows of cells. Hands reached through the bars, begging me for help, asking if I was going to save them. I barely heard them over my blood pumping in my ears. I scanned each face, none of them belonging to Calix.

I let my anguish drive me, closer to him, closer to freedom. I assumed Olyn and Azden were behind me, but I didn't bother to check. I was close; so close.

The back wall came before Calix did. I spun around, double checking all the cells, but none of the faces belonged to Calix. I closed my eyes, scanning all the minds in the dungeon, none of them his.

I ran back to Azden and Olyn, senses dulling to everything besides what was directly in front of me.

"He's not here," I said gravely.

"Are you sure?" Olyn asked, looking around at the cells as

if he'd find proof.

"Yes. But he's still in the castle; I can feel it." I couldn't. I didn't know if he was, but I needed him to be. He had to be. They both looked sympathetic, but we were running out of time and we all knew it. There wasn't time to search the entire complex *and* get to Ruzu before he was whisked away by guards. We didn't even know if Calix was here, or, gods forbid, if he was still alive.

"Estyn," Azden cautioned, but he was interrupted by steps pounding down the stairs.

We have to be smart about this, he said in my head as I wrapped us in shadows, pressed against the wall.

I'm not leaving without him.

You don't even know if he's here.

I have to try.

After—after Ruzu, we will have control of the castle and be able to search every inch of it. Azden was calm, collected, calculating. I tried to mirror him, but my words were all emotion.

What if he hid Calix somewhere else? He won't be able to tell us if he's dead.

We'll find out, but we need to go. Now. He used a tone that left no room for argument. I wanted to convince him otherwise, but even I knew my reasons were not well-founded.

Two guards came through the door, but instead of acting, Azden froze. He knew them.

I didn't. I channeled all of the anger and frustration that had been simmering precariously below the surface, killing them in a matter of seconds. I ran up the stairs without looking back.

We emerged to find the corridor full of guards running towards the west wing. At least Rahni and Walcott were doing their job. I cloaked us in shadows as we edged towards the King's personal chambers.

I stopped suddenly, Azden crashing into my back and whispering a string of curses. Luckily it was too muffled for the passing guards to hear. That guard was familiar—too familiar. I tried to remember where I knew him from, but I was just trying to find an answer more palatable than the truth.

He was a member of Bastian's personal guard. Maybe he was reassigned, maybe he was sent ahead of time to scope the place and prepare it. Maybe, I reasoned, because the alternatives were unthinkable and it was too late to back out now. For better or worse, we needed to carry out the rest of the plan.

For all our scheming, Bastian was one variable I had failed to consider.

The corridor turned, and the guards here were not rushing. They were heavily armed and on high alert. The King's personal guard.

I couldn't help but note that for all the commotion, his rooms were sparsely guarded. I glanced back at Azden, unsure, but his eyes were glazed. This was his parents' room.

You go left, I go right? I asked, hoping to cut through whatever memory he was reliving. He blinked back into focus, offering a small nod. I looked back to Olyn who was posted by the turn. He nodded once, and I lifted the shadows.

The guards registered us too late to be of much use. They fumbled to unsheathe their swords as they were seized by wisps of shadow and light, intangible but impossibly strong.

I closed my eyes as their blood sprayed across my front, collapsing against the floor in quick succession.

Azden opened the door before I could.

There was no opportunity for stealth, not with Azden's rage. We stormed in to find King Ruzu sprawled on a settee, surrounded by women in varying degrees of undress lounging on rugs as if nothing was amiss. His insouciant demeanor stoked my anger, and before I knew it a dagger flew from my hand and embedded itself into the wall by his head. His slight flinch was the only sign that he even registered his near brush with death.

The servant girl scrambled away, more concerned with her life than propriety. The rest of his party sat up languidly. I could feel Azden's anger emanating from his body, his skin wrapped in a halo of light, his magic unruly with unchecked emotion. It seemed to blind him, and he failed to notice the lack of guards, Ruzu's unfocused eyes, and the overall sense that something was truly and terribly *off*.

"It's you," King Ruzu said simply, finally sitting up to greet us. His words were slurred, and he spilled a bit of wine on the rug below as he gestured widely.

Something is wrong. I thought to Azden, but he was lost in vengeance.

"It's over, Ruzu," Azden gritted out, the room's lights pulsing with his words.

"You're alive," he said, clearly disoriented. I knew he was an arrogant, cruel King, but I never thought him to be this careless. He was supposed to be a powerful enchanter, but I saw no attempt at using his magic.

"Where's Calix?" I asked, finally earning his attention. His brows knit in confusion, then recognition.

"And you have the lost princess," his words were still slurred as he turned to me. "You're in high demand, you know," he said with a sinister smile. He took a long swig of his wine, not noticing as it spilled over his chin.

"Where is he?" I demanded again, this time more forcefully.

"I returned him," he said, waving me off as if Calix's safety was immaterial. I exhaled, glad to know he was alive, even if he was now imprisoned by a different type of captor. "You two are boring me," he determined, turning to one of the women draped over his leg. "Guards, please escort them out."

Azden knocked the guards off their feet before they had the chance to take a step. I secured them with my shadows, pinning them to the walls. They relented easily, not so much as struggling after a moment. My shadows pressed their necks as Rahni had shown me, and they all fell unconscious.

Fear finally flashed across Ruzu's face as he watched my magic unfold.

"It's you," he said, scampering off the settee and backing towards the door. Even though Azden was closing in, the light in his hands promising a long and painful death, Ruzu looked at me. Cowered before me. "So that's why they kept you away."

"What?" I asked, but before he could answer Azden whipped his light to Ruzu's throat, lifting him off the ground. His companions scrambled to their feet, fleeing to other rooms as Ruzu gasped for air. Ruzu grasped at the cords he felt tightening on his neck, but they slipped through his fingers.

"Was it worth it?" Azden demanded. "Was it worth killing all of them?" The light tightened around Ruzu's throat, and the hands that had been clawing at it fell limp to his sides.

Just before Ruzu shut his eyes, Azden's light recoiled and Ruzu fell to the tile with an unnerving crunch. Azden stormed forward, towering over Ruzu's crumpled form. He crouched beside Ruzu, who was coughing, desperately gasping for air.

"You're nothing but a coward. A selfish, loathsome man who had no right to rule." Azden grabbed Ruzu's chin, yanking his face towards him. "You are a disgrace to the crown and all of Alynthia." He slammed Ruzu's face back to the tile.

I didn't recognize Azden. Lost was the irreverent but kind-hearted man I knew, leaving only the vengeful depths of his anger. He kicked Ruzu, who made no effort to get up.

I knew I should feel some form of regret for Ruzu's suffering. That's what a good person would do. But looking into his face, all I could think about was Calix.

This was the man who kidnapped Calix. He threw Calix in his dungeons, made him suffer. I wanted him to know what suffering was. I wanted Azden to do his worst.

"Please, I'll do anything," Ruzu wheezed, clutching his stomach. He looked so helpless. How was this a man who'd taken over an entire Kingdom? Why wasn't he using his magic?

Azden answered by twisting Ruzu's arm around his back at an unnatural angle. I looked to the door as Ruzu cried out in pain, sure someone would have heard by now. Olyn and I were here to block the guards, but there was no way Olyn could hold off that many. Especially with all the noise Ruzu made.

There had to be guards descending now. Rahni and Walcott's diversion could not have been this effective.

Azden didn't look away from Ruzu, relishing in his suffering. I backed up as Azden closed in, looking around at the lack of guards. I realized with a grim finality that I wasn't mistaken before. It had been one of Bastian's guards.

We need to get out of here, I thought to Azden, but he was lost in his need for revenge.

"This is for my family," Azden said, unsheathing his dagger and raising it above Ruzu's chest.

If Bastian's guards were here, then…

Ruzu said he'd given Calix back. When was that?

"No!" I shouted as Azden plunged the blade down. My shadow shot out to stop him, but it was a moment too late.

The thud of Ruzu's head dropping to the tile echoed ominously.

No guards descended.

It was just Azden, me, and the recently deceased King of Alynthia.

The one person with answers lay dead before us. Azden stood unnaturally still, staring at Ruzu's bleeding form before him.

"Azden, we need to go," I said, pulling his arm, but he stood still, watching Ruzu with a blank face.

"Azden," I pressed again, walking into his line of sight and reaching up to turn his face towards me. "Something is wrong."

He finally looked down at me, seeming to come back to reality slowly, then all at once.

"He's dead," was all Azden said, not acknowledging my sense of urgency. "It's over."

"Yes, but I'm telling you, something's not right. Did you notice how few guards there were? No one tried to stop us. Not even Ruzu. He didn't even try to use his magic." I worked through my half-baked theory as I went, but it was the only explanation. We weren't the only ones who wanted Ruzu dead. Which meant we weren't the only ones going for the throne.

"We have to go," Azden said, finally on the same page.

The hall was empty. No guards, no Olyn. My heart sunk.

"What do we do now?" I asked Azden, hoping he'd know better than me. He looked at the spot where Olyn had been for a few moments, saying nothing as a plan started to form.

"We find Olyn," he said. Turns out, it was no better than my plan because it was my plan. And I didn't have high hopes for it.

We covered ground meticulously, Azden checking each room carefully and me following blindly. I couldn't shake the feeling that we were being followed, that danger was at our heels. I tried to ignore it and move quickly.

We both searched with our minds as well as our eyes, but I only found guards and other castle staff. None of them seemed to know that their king was dead.

We were searching a small parlor when I heard it.

I blinked, not sure I was right.

My mind recoiled at the sinister laugh that echoed through the halls. I reached out, easily finding a familiar mind, one I'd hoped to never enter.

Bastian.

And he had Walcott. He was questioning him now, delighting in his torture. I'd forgotten just how depraved he was. Now that I was trained enough to listen to his thoughts, I had even less confidence in his humanity. He was every bit the violent ruler he was raised to be.

"Azden," I whispered.

"Yes?" he asked, hand on the doorknob he was about to open.

"He has Walcott."

"Who?" Azden didn't know Bastian; he couldn't pick him out of the crowd of other minds. He didn't know how afraid he should be.

"My brother," I breathed, losing hope by the second. "They're in the throne room."

"Calix? He found Walcott?" Azden's hope just heightened my despair.

"No. My other brother—Bastian." I didn't know how much Azden knew of Bastian; if he'd heard stories from Ryker or others. I know I hadn't told him anything.

Suddenly memories flashed behind my eyes. Bastian killing a classmate's pet for sport; Bastian teasing Calix; Bastian ignoring me, deeming me below his station unless forced to interact with me; Bastian, my brother, but not my family.

"Do you think he's here for Calix? Maybe he was the one sent to broker peace?" Azden asked, trying to reason out his presence. I had the same ideas, but hearing Bastian's thoughts I knew it could not be the case.

He was here for the one thing he'd always wanted: power.

"I think Bastian drugged Ruzu," I said, distant, feeling like I had almost all the pieces but still wasn't able to put them together.

"Why would he do that if they were about to strike an alliance?" Azden asked.

I shook my head, and I knew why because I knew Bastian.

"He would never settle for an alliance. He wants Alynthia for himself," I said darkly, and the words finally sunk in. Azden backed up from the door, realizing that Tenebris was no longer just an obstacle; they were the opponent.

Screams wailed from the throne room, pushing us to action.

"Well he's not going to get it," Azden said, which, while passionate, was not a plan.

"We can't just march in there," I said, shutting the door as he opened it a crack.

"What do you suggest we do? Stand by while Walcott suffers? Wait until his guards seize us? Just let him claim the throne? You know I can't let that happen." His eyes were blazing, screaming for action.

"We could wait for backup? Find Rahni and Olyn?" I asked, grasping for an idea that had a higher chance of success than charging him.

"We don't have time," he lamented, looking into my eyes with the same sense of dread I felt earlier. It was not a good idea, but it was our only option.

"Okay," I said, finally lowering my hand from where I'd been holding the door shut. "But promise me something," I said, stepping closer to him. "If it gets too dangerous—if you know we can't win, we'll leave. We'll try again later. I can't have you dying." My voice broke, betraying all the fear I'd been tamping down.

He refused to meet my eyes, staring at the floor instead.

"You know I can't do that," he whispered before opening the door and slipping out into the hall. I choked down a tear as I followed him out, heading directly for the throne room.

CHAPTER

26

Soldiers were posted at every door, more than could possibly be necessary. It was as if he'd brought an entire battalion for a *peace negotiation*. Which wasn't a peace negotiation at all, I reminded myself.

I cloaked Azden and myself in shadows. We wouldn't be able to fight them all, but we could slip past. By the time they noticed the door open we'd already be inside.

The throne room was lined with more guards, many of them enchanters, lined up shoulder to shoulder around the perimeter. There was no way we could take them all.

Bastian lounged on the throne as if he was already crowned king. Wolves slumbered around the dais, seemingly relaxed but with ears perked at attention. He had the pompous, self-indulgent demeanor. All that was missing was the crown.

Walcott hunched in front of him, bloodied and broken, yet

unyielding.

Olyn was held next to him, bleeding from his nose but otherwise unharmed. They must have caught him.

I wanted to rush to them, but I held Azden and myself against the back wall. Since we didn't have much else on our side, we needed good timing.

"Where are they?" Bastian asked, lazily twirling a ring around his finger.

"I don't know who you're talking about." Walcott answered, spitting blood onto the floor next to him. Bastian nodded to the soldier standing nearest, who then turned and kicked Walcott in the gut. Walcott doubled over again, clutching his stomach.

I couldn't just stand here and watch this. I knew Azden couldn't either. So I released my shadows, walking straight towards Bastian.

He looked surprised, and despite the dire circumstances, I delighted in seeing him ruffled. Especially when underestimating me.

"Sister." He didn't move from his relaxed posture, as if we weren't a threat worth acknowledging. "And who might you be?" he asked Azden.

"What are you doing here?" I demanded, though it was rhetorical, of course. I just wanted answers, and maybe an opening.

"Why, I'm simply taking advantage of an opportunity. The leadership here was weak." Azden's hand clenched in a fist. We couldn't fight him; not here, not surrounded by his guards and facing a pack of wolves ready to attack at his command. I couldn't help but think what an utterly useless, hopeless plan this was. "You know, everyone has been looking high and low for you. What a relief it will be when you return home safe and sound." He slid the ring up and down his finger, almost distracting me from his menacing grin. Almost.

"I'm not going back," I said with as much authority as I could muster. I didn't want him to know how helpless I felt.

"So you're going to continue traipsing around with these delinquents?" He gestured to Walcott, who still hadn't risen, Olyn, who was shoved onto his knees, and Azden who was fuming by my side. "They won't be free for much longer, I'm afraid, so that's not really an option." Light poured from under Azden, his tenuous restraint finally broken.

Bastian looked at Azden with wide eyes, shifting to the edge of his seat and calling his wolves to attention. "So it *is* you."

How did he know who Azden was? Why was he not surprised that Azden was alive? I blazed past it, not wanting to give away all our secrets just yet. "Just go home. You'll be King of Tenebris soon—isn't that enough?" I hope I sounded more assured than I felt.

"Impressive that you're trying to threaten me given the position you're in. Looks like you finally found a voice after all. I, for one, didn't think you would." He turned to the soldiers at his side as if sharing in a personal joke, but they stared forward stoically.

I couldn't help the shadows from pouring out beneath me, magic flowing with my anger.

"Ah. I see you found your magic too," he said thoughtfully, calculating. Always calculating.

I wanted to lash out, to strangle him on the spot, but either the guards or wolves would stop me before I got what I really wanted. "You know, I wasn't sure if you would come," he said to Azden, who had been uncharacteristically quiet. Both of us perked up, unsure where this was going.

"When I left the breadcrumbs for the spy of yours, I was afraid she wouldn't make it back. Especially after she was caught by the late King Ruzu's guards." I barely resisted dropping my mouth wide open. This was a trap? I knew Bastian was manipulative, but scheming on this scale seemed out of his reach.

"I'm glad you did, though. It would have been terribly unfortunate to start a new reign with you sowing discord amongst my people."

"They're not your people," Azden bit out, which only made Bastian smile wider.

"Well they aren't yours either, lost Prince," Bastian said. I wondered at how Azden wasn't giving in, finally advancing and giving Bastian what he deserved. That's exactly what Bastian wanted.

I glanced back to the doors, which were now closed behind us. No one was coming.

What happened? I thought at Walcott as Azden and Bastian exchanged more tense repartee.

I heard Calix and went to find him. Even his thoughts were haggard, as if he was barely holding on.

Just a little longer, I thought at him, more for my sake than his. *I'm going to get you out of here.* He laughed dryly, making everyone turn their attention on his body that was still slumped on the tile.

"Is something funny, boy?" Bastian drawled. Oh, how I wish I could stab him right now. "No matter. Seize them." He flicked his wrist and the windows shattered as murders of crows swarmed the room. I threw an instinctive bubble of shadow around Azden and me as glass rained down. The doors burst open behind, cougars and a whole host of other animals prowling in from the hall. Had they been there the entire time?

Azden and I shared a brief look, both of us understanding what we needed to do. We pushed through the crows diving toward us, going in the direction we remembered Walcott and Olyn to be. I heard Bastian squeal in delight over the thunderous caws and shot an aimless shadow in his direction.

There were too many, we moved too slow. I couldn't see more than a few feet in front of me as we pushed forward. My only hope was the two lights in my mind, Walcott, and Olyn, getting closer and closer.

Azden shot beams of light, hitting bird after bird out of the sky before they hit our makeshift shield. I tried to help, but it took most of my energy to maintain our cover and track Walcott and Olyn.

The guards detaining Olyn didn't see us as we descended and we disposed of them quickly. I enveloped Walcott and Olyn in our bubble, my head pulsing with the effort.

"Come out come out wherever you are," Bastian called, a shrill, menacing sound that pierced through the chaos.

"What do we do?" Olyn asked, spitting blood to the side as he turned to Azden for direction. Walcott made an effort to look up, but he was so beyond fighting shape I worried he wouldn't be able to escape, let alone help.

For the first time since I met him, Azden had no plan. I knew how we looked. I strained keeping the shadows around us, especially as animals continued to pound and claw their way towards us, breaking past Azden's defenses. No matter how powerful Azden and I were, it was impossible to take on this many animals and enchanters at once. Bastian had a meager defense compared to what we had in Tenebris, but he must have at least ten enchanters with him. There was no way we could beat them all.

My muscles strained keeping the shield around us. I couldn't do it much longer.

As Azden opened his mouth to speak, a wolf broke through the herd, leaping straight towards us. There was no way I'd hold it off.

I closed my eyes, bracing for the impact, but it never came. I heard a thump as the wolf fell to the ground, its head rolling away from its body.

A lithe figure clad in black dropped from the rafters in front of us: Rahni. I never thought I'd be this happy to see her.

All the animals around us started swerving at her command, and I finally dropped the shield.

We stood back-to-back, Walcott between us, fighting off an endless stream of guards.

Azden shot light, picking off unwitting enchanters one by one. Every time a larger animal neared, Rahni turned it on its neighbors. Olyn took care of the crows, shooting ice into the sky with deadly aim.

Even Walcott managed to pick bombs off his vest, throwing them towards the dais and igniting them with the little energy he had left.

Bastian's enchanters shot shards of ice and flames at us, commanded animals to swarm our feet and grew thorny vines around our legs, relentless even as Azden picked them off.

Rahni's snakes slithered among their legs, biting them with fast-acting venom. My shadows lashed out, swallowing enchanters and dimming their advances, suffocating or strangling them.

We were close. The air was no longer clogged with flapping wings, and the floor cleared as we picked off Bastian's makeshift army.

I'm going in, I thought at Azden and then Rahni, and they effortlessly closed my spot around Walcott as I pushed towards the dais. I cut down soldier after soldier, thorns ripping at my legs with each step forward. My shadows almost moved of their own accord, knowing which enchanters were the strongest, which to suffocate first. I gave into the magic, letting it take over and exact boundless destruction on my path to Bastian.

Two of his wolves charged me, but I leashed them with coils of shadow, then slashed them with daggers. Blood sprayed my face and I got a twisted sense of satisfaction, knowing how long Bastian took to train them.

Bastian stood in front of the throne, sweating with exhaustion, only protected by two lingering wolves by his feet. Animals faltered as he broke his concentration to look at me.

"Just stop, Bastian. You're not going to win this." He saw the carnage behind me, his carefully laid-out plan failing before his eyes. "I don't want to hurt you."

Even if he was a conniving, hateful person, he was still my brother, and I was tired of the killing.

"Never," Bastian said, eyes crazed with violence as he commanded his last two wolves to attack.

My shadows shot out on instinct, but with Bastian's magic the wolves were stronger than I'd expected. I put all my strength behind it, but even after draining myself, it wasn't enough.

I closed my eyes, ready to be tackled under their weight, but light flashed before my eyes. Azden's rays tangled with my shadows and the wolves dropped to the steps, shot down under the combined power of our magic. We didn't stop and the twirled beam fired at Bastian and knocked him to the floor. All around me animals fell, collapsing without Bastian's magic to drive them.

I saw the lingering lights wink out in my mind as the others picked off Bastian's forces.

"Give up, Bastian," I said, walking up the stairs as I kept him pinned under my shadows. Azden came toward us, his light still tangled in mine.

"Enough." General Turrek's voice bellowed out over the furor, and the room stilled. My shadows faltered in shock, giving Bastian the chance to escape. He rolled away, standing up behind Turrek, the most terrifying sight I could've imagined.

He held a knife to Calix's throat.

If I thought I was furious before, it was *nothing* compared to now.

"Let him go," I demanded, my shadows reaching towards him reflexively.

"No. Call off your friends or I'll kill him." Calix was barely able to resist, his body frail after weeks of imprisonment. Through all the years of teasing, all the contentious encounters, I never believed Bastian capable of this.

I glanced back just once to see my friends tired and broken, encircled by enchanters and ravenous animals back under Bastian's command. Their eyes held fierce determination, but their strength was waning. Walcott tried to go to Calix, but stumbled back to his knees, struggling to stay conscious.

My mind raced, trying to find a way out. Any way out. I wanted to scream, my magic wanted me to let go, to let it descend into chaos and kill everyone there.

We weren't going to beat Bastian. We never were. This was not Azden's chance to save Alynthia. I knew that before we came in, and I more than knew that now.

There was no hope for our original dream, the original plan. There was only damage control.

Take care of Calix. I thought at Azden, then shut off the connection before he could argue.

"Let go of Calix, let them all go, and I'll go with you," I said, hoping it would be enough. Hoping my value as a weapon was enough.

"No," Azden shouted, lurching forward. Guards closed in, making him think better of rushing to me. "Estyn, don't do this," he pleaded, not caring that everyone could hear.

"Intriguing offer," Bastian said, adjusting his collar and reveling in the tension of the moment. He scratched his chin, considering. "You'll behave yourself?"

I nodded solemnly.

You have to leave. As soon as he lets go of Calix, take him and get out, I told each of my friends, leaving their minds before they could protest.

"Then it's a deal."

Turrek released Calix, shoving him forward onto the steps. As soon as he was free, I used the last of my energy to plunge the room into darkness.

Sound exploded around me, orders echoing across the room as Bastian tried to wrangle my friends. I didn't listen, focusing all my energy on their escape. I watched Azden's light dim in my mind, getting farther as he left the room, feeling weaker without his support but thankful he listened. Just before they stumbled out into the hall, he whispered *I love you*, and I closed my eyes, refusing to let myself feel anything in fear that I'd crumple.

Let go, I heard a familiar voice say in my head, wrapping around my senses and tugging me back into my own mind.

I can't, I told Nyx, even though I was painfully aware that I should heed her warnings.

Your magic will drain you. You must let go.

Her last words drifted into the background, the thrumming pulse of the shadows around me drowning out all noise. I fell to my knees but didn't relent, singularly focused on each light of my friends as they scattered.

Azden and Calix were in the hall now, fending off Bastian's enchanters standing in their way, Walcott and Olyn were stumbling toward the side door, and Rahni—where was Rahni?

Light flickered in the room as panic set in. What if she was lying this entire time? Was I wrong to trust her again?

No matter what I did, how much I tried and trained, I was still that naive little princess.

My skin was on fire. At first I thought Bastian's Summer enchanters must've reached me, but as I looked down I was still untouched. It was the magic, draining me from the inside out.

I should've listened to Nyx. She was a goddess and I was me, but no matter how mortal I was I would use every bit of magic I had to get Calix to safety.

So close. He and Azden were in the garden now. Let go, I could let go.

But I couldn't. The shadows swarmed me, taking everything I gave them and more. I barely heard Bastian's lingering wolf approach, scenting me through the chaos.

And as it lunged, jaws bared, I wanted to thank it.

Take me out now, stop the pain. Don't let him take me alive, I thought, holding on right up until it crashed into me.

I had fulfilled the purpose Nyx spoke of, I was ready to be done, but it wasn't over.

The wolf missed.

It landed just beside me, standing idle as if waiting for something. As much as I wanted to be strong and hold on, I fell back, the world falling even darker than my shadows could make it.

I felt an arm thread beneath my arms and swing me onto the beast, felt someone swing up behind me, and then I felt nothing at all.

CHAPTER

27

I thought the afterlife would look different.

Not that I thought I was hot shit or anything, but after Nyx talked to me—not just once, but twice—I thought she might be there. But no, it looked just like the rooms at the base, albeit a little bit bigger.

The walls were carved with vignettes of the gods, but they looked almost mortal-made. Beautiful, sure, but not that ethereal quality I expected.

I also thought I'd get to ditch my physical form, but with each passing second I became more aware of the throbbing pain in every inch of my body.

I rubbed my eyes, clearing the sleep and coming to the bittersweet conclusion that I was in fact not dead.

Estyn? Azden asked in my head, seeming to be just to my left, and I turned my head to find him kneeling beside me. His hair was a mess, dark purple bags hung below his eyes that looked beyond worried. Had Bastian gotten him too?

No, Azden was outside, he had Calix, there was no way Bastian got him.

Then… was I in our base? Had I made it out?

"Whe—" I started to ask, but my throat was so dry it came out as barely a croak.

Where are we? I asked him.

Home, he said, and I could've cried.

How?

Rahni went back for you, he replied after a moment, still cautious when he said her name. Rahni, who had deemed me too dangerous to keep around, who Tenebris had imprisoned and tortured and raped risked getting captured by them again for me?

She got control of one of Bastian's wolves, he went on to explain, *and carried you on its back. You were unconscious when she found you. The darkness was unrelenting, coating your skin and even the castle. She said you burned her when she touched your skin. We didn't know if or when—*

Is Calix okay? I asked, because as much as I cared about my life, I cared about his more.

Yes. Do you want me to take you to him? Azden said, unaffected by my brazen interruption. I nodded and tried to sit up, still feeling warm but not burning anymore. As I rose, I looked straight into the mirror hung opposite the bed to meet eyes that were not mine.

Azden backed up as I swung out of bed and walked closer, ignoring the cold stone beneath my bare feet.

There was no grey, no shadows swirling. My iris was almost as black as my pupil.

I rubbed them and looked again, but it was the same. The shadows had taken over.

"Are you okay?" Azden asked, walking up behind me and putting a hand on my shoulder. I spun around to meet his gaze and if he was surprised, he didn't show it. All I saw was unadulterated relief.

You're alive, he thought with such relief I wondered how long I'd been unconscious for. A few hours?

A week, he replied. A week? I was out for a week while Calix was down here alone, adjusting to his new environment and…

He has Walcott. He's fine, Azden said, soothing my quickly derailing thoughts. I took a deep breath. He was fine and we were going to see him. It was over. He was fine.

"How long were you waiting here?" I finally asked, clearing my throat more than once to get the words out.

"Well, you know, everyone visited for a bit, and—"

"How long?" I asked.

"The whole time," he said softly. The prince of Alynthia, who had yet another imposter on his throne, who had just lost a war his family had waged for years, had waited by my bedside for a *week*. I stepped forward until I had to tilt my head back to look into his eyes. He looked down at me with such a mix of wild emotions, the light dancing around in his eyes in response to my proximity.

My pain dulled just being near him. *So this is what it's like to be someone Azden Duramoux cares about,* I thought. It was overwhelming.

"I'm sorry we didn't succeed," I said, because I knew how much it meant to him to get his kingdom back and finally give his people the ruler they deserved. He shrugged and looked up at the ceiling, stuffing his hands into his pockets.

"Everyone's okay. Calix is safe. We succeeded in the ways we needed to," he said, and his voice reached into the depths of my mind that still worried, soothing them and coaxing them into the light.

I rose to my tiptoes, wrapped my arms around his neck, and pressed a tentative kiss to his lips.

And as if that unlocked something in him, he grabbed my thighs, hoisted me up until I wrapped my legs around him and kissed me like he thought he never would again.

But he would; we'd have many more opportunities. There was still work to do, but things were different now. We had time.

I let myself fall into the heady feeling of his affection, the taste of his mouth and the feeling of his hair running through my fingers, the warmth of his body, and the demand of his tongue as it pressed my lips open.

I wanted to melt in his arms, to stay there forever, but more than that I needed to see Calix. So I pulled back slightly to see Azden's hair more mussed than before and his eyes unfocused as I said "let's go."

He set me down—albeit slowly, savoring every moment of my body sliding down his—and we left to find my brother.

I heard the laughter long before we saw them. I thought I imagined hearing Calix's joyous voice amongst the rest, but when we arrived at the door to Walcott's lab, I knew it was real.

Rahni and Olyn sat in the chairs by the tables, both holding mugs of steaming liquid; spiced chocolate, by the smell of it. Had Calix asked for that or did Walcott make it for him because he knew that would make Calix feel at home?

Then, a little to their left, Ketra sat cross-legged on top of a table. She held her mug with one hand, the other still constricted in a sling. The swelling was far better than the last time I'd seen her. She was almost recognizable now, her face framed by a bandage wrapped around her head. I wondered if they'd had to shave all her hair to tend to her headwounds.

Anger swelled at Bastian, for torturing her, using her, all to manipulate me. Shadows pooled at my feet, responding to my sudden shift in emotion, but a cool hand on my back brought me back. I smiled, focusing on the relief instead of the resentment, and then turned to the table beside her.

Walcott huddled over a pile of amorphous mug-shaped blobs, and Calix leaned on the table beside him. Before Calix noticed me in the doorway, he pressed a kiss to Walcott's cheek and Walcott lit up. It was so casual, so domestic, something I thought Calix would never get again.

Calix looked remarkably well for having been imprisoned for weeks. Still far too thin for my liking and paler than he should've been, but he looked surprisingly positive. Despite all the pain, he managed to laugh and smile.

He finally looked up and saw me, and when I saw the endless love in his expression, I felt like a hero. His smile always did that to me; I was suddenly his big sister who could do no wrong, who could answer all his questions and would always be there for him.

"Estyn!" He exclaimed, running around the table and only managing to knock over one notebook before wrapping me in a tight embrace. I put my arms around him, still in disbelief that he was really here, really okay.

And even though everyone was there watching us, I started to cry. Not cute little tears, but gut-wrenching sobs that made Calix squeeze tighter. I felt his tears on my shoulder as he rested his head.

"You're really here," I said between sniffles.

"And we have spiced chocolate!" He pulled away and wiped at his eyes. Without missing a beat, he rushed around the table to grab me a strange-looking mug. I didn't want to see it, and if I didn't know him so well I wouldn't have, but underneath his excitement was a heartbreaking hollowness. He was clutching to small pockets of happiness like one moment without them would drag him under. "Walcott engineered these mugs that keep it warm until you're done." His voice was so warm and proud and completely enamored that I had to laugh a little.

"Thank you, Walcott," I said, turning to my friend who watched me apprehensively from behind his workbench. He still had bruising around one eye and crutches balanced beside him, but also looked well considering the state I'd seen him in last.

Once I collected myself, I realized how quiet everyone was. It was like they'd seen a ghost.

"I'm not dead, guys," I said with a wobbly chuckle, walking further into the room. Azden followed, just behind me.

"I don't think you could die if you tried," Rahni said in a dry voice that seemed like she was cracking a joke. Everyone fell silent, looking between her and me in shock.

I stared at her for a moment, dumbstruck, until I couldn't keep it in anymore. Hysteric laughs wrenched through me, stealing my breath as I clutched my stomach. For a moment everyone just watched, gauging my reaction, until Walcott slowly joined in, and then Calix, and the rest. It *was* pretty funny.

"I hate to break up the party, but we have work to do," Azden said from where he stood, leaning against an empty table. After all that had happened, he still managed to say it with a smile and twinkle in his eye. He was a fugitive, still lost in his own kingdom, but despite the worst, I knew he'd find a way to have fun.

And no matter the danger ahead, the almost guaranteed pain and loss, I was excited for our next adventure too.

EPILOGUE

ONE WEEK LATER

The crowd swelled and anxiety bloomed in my chest like an old friend. I felt the shadows purr, begging to force personal space, but a cool hand brushing my wrist tamped down the instinct.

It was a different city, a different people, but it felt all too familiar. Azden and I wove through the streets, careful to stay hidden even as we neared the dais. I kept my eyes on the ground, only lifting my gaze when a poster fluttered in my peripheral vision.

Shit.

My face stared back, almost unrecognizable in the calm, royal portrait. I pulled the hood of my cloak closer.

If I'd thought my father was crazy for the number of enchanters he surrounded himself with, then Bastian ought to be committed. Enchanters and predatory animals nearly twice their size encircled him, snarling at the children that dared to step closer.

A hush fell over the crowd as Bastian rose, holding his hands out in an ostentatious gesture undoubtedly intended to command respect. If I wasn't smashed between people, I would've spit on the ground.

353

Again, Azden pressed a hand to the small of my back, sensing my growing ire. *Right. Calm.*

"My dear people of Alynthia," Bastian started, his voice artificially kind, "it is with great pleasure that after decades of fighting, I usher you into an era of peace."

Bastian paused, but the crowd remained silent. I heard a lone cough somewhere behind us. After a moment one of the wolves growled and the Alynthians nearby started clapping, spreading the reaction throughout the crowd until Bastian's scowl melted back into smug pleasure.

"However, there is still a threat to your peace. Many of you have heard of the rebels who bombed your soldiers, killing hundreds of innocent people," he said, and whispers scattered through the crowd. I poked into a few minds, finding them still distrustful but falling further into his trap by the second.

"Although we have rid you of the tyrant that plagued your lands, these traitors continue to walk among you." Gasps rang out and a middle-aged woman beside us clutched a hand to her chest, her thoughts running rampant with worry, just like Bastian wanted. "I know I have a long way to go to earn your trust, but there is something I must ask of you—" he paused and I wondered where he was going with this. Inside, his mind was just as calculating as always, but his face twisted with a rare display of emotion. He brushed a tear from the corner of his eye and seemed to center himself before lying like the devil.

"They kidnapped my sister, and I need your help finding and bringing them to justice."

No. No, no no, this can't be happening. I flipped from mind to mind, hoping everyone saw the deceit as I did, but each person was more sympathetic than the last.

I turned to Azden, hoping for some comfort, but his characteristic nonchalance was shaken. *We need to get out of here,* I thought at him, and he nodded almost imperceptibly before light flickered in front of my face. I had already cloaked it in shadow, but that might not be enough anymore. People were turning around, looking at those beside them, questioning their fellow Alynthians instead of the imposter on the throne.

We needed to slip out before the crowd settled again, but I couldn't help but look back to see Bastian's devilish smile one more time.

It was a mistake.

Calliope, dressed in clothes finer than I'd ever seen on her, stood beside him. "Please bring my Estyn home," she said, unrecognizable as she stood above the crowd, poised and dignified as any noble. I couldn't tear my eyes away, watching in slow motion as she intertwined her fingers with Bastian's and leaned into his arm, clutching it with her remaining hand.

For once, my mind was silent.

I froze, watching the horror unfurl until Azden yanked my arm back. A knife swung dangerously close to my shoulder as a fight broke out beside us. I tuned out Bastian's voice as he called out an astronomical reward for my safe return, my focus narrowed on his thumb subtly stroking my best friend's finger.

I slipped from Azden's grasp, trying to find Calliope's mind before he pulled me away for good. The second her comforting voice rang out in my head, I knew something was wrong.

I only heard one phrase before I let myself be led from the chaos.

I had fought. I had killed. I had been betrayed and almost

died.

And yet one phrase, one damned phrase was all it took to shake my world.

My king.

ACKNOWLEDGMENTS

I cannot explain how excited I am that you, dear reader, read even one of my words, let alone an entire book of them. Thank you so much for coming on this journey with me!

I feel incredibly lucky to have so many people I owe thanks to, and I'm not sure I could ever do them justice, but here it goes (in no particular order).

Thank you to my brother Win who heard the initial seed of this story and helped me flesh it out into a whole world with its own politics and magic system. Thank you for always reading my early pages and believing in me.

Thank you to my mom, who is a fantastic beta reader and has read this book 5+ times now in all its iterations. I would not be who I am today without you and your love of literature. Thank you to my dad who always emphasizes empathy and precise word choice and makes sure I am never hungry for even a second.

Thank you to all my beta readers, for reading it multiple times in some cases and giving me the hope that a stranger might like my work. Thank you to my critique partners who helped rework entire sections of the plot.

Thank you to my house-mates Lillian, Soha, Winnie, Yanela, and Anthony for listening to my rants during the years of drafting and editing and feeding me when I retreated into my writer cave. I love you all endlessly.

Thank you to Emily and Ashley who make me believe I can do anything.

Thank you to my community on Tiktok, who has provided the best support along this entire journey. I appreciate each and every one of you.

Thank you, Jennifer, for your diligent proof-reading.

Thank you to my author friends who helped me believe I could actually do this whole publishing shindig.

And finally, thank you to DJ for being my best friend and favorite person. Not a day goes by where I don't feel lucky to have found you in this lifetime.

ABBY GEIGERMAN is a tea-loving hopeless romantic who likes to write about badass women, unique magic systems, and found families. She grew up in Raleigh, NC (and will rave about it to anyone who listens), graduated from Rice University, and currently resides in Austin, TX where she works as a Product Manager on a machine learning team. She always loves connecting and hearing new book recommendations, especially on BookTok @abbygeigerman.

ageigerman.com